GLASS CENTURY

GLASS CENTURY

A NOVEL

Ross Barkan

Tough Poets Press
Arlington, Massachusetts

ISBN 979-8-218-53680-0

Tough Poets Press
Arlington, Massachusetts 02476
U.S.A.

www.toughpoets.com

"Steel, glass, tile, concrete will be the materials of the skyscrapers. Crammed on the narrow island the millionwindowed buildings will jut glittering, pyramid on pyramid like the white cloudhead above a thunderstorm."

—John Dos Passos, *Manhattan Transfer*

For V.K.O.

I

Vena Amoris

1

Here was Mona Glass.

Down the hallway and out of the dark, she was running because she always ran, her legs wired with muscle, her elbows firing with polished violence. Even though this was the night before what was supposed to be the most important day, she was wearing frayed Pumas, the same that glided across tennis courts and gym floors, one lace licking the beige carpeting. She ran because she could, because she was still twenty-four, and if she was going to be late, she couldn't blame the speed she was gathering. Flustered waitstaff looked on, a man with a miniature mustache and a woman in dark red, their eyes pulled from the Rudolph Lodge script against the wall to the woman dashing past them, her head shooting forward, deer-like. A cart of thick plates and dining forks trembled. Washrags tumbled down. There were gasps but they were lost to her, soft against her crashing footsteps. Suddenly she was suspended in the air—a stumble sent her outward—but she caught herself on the edge of the carpet, her calves flexing in the denim she had decided, at the last moment, to wear. Right, left, right, she had a notion of where she needed to go—one more swerve and she'd be in the ballroom.

Her breath was hot on her lips.

"Don't worry, it's just us," Liv said, smiling up at her.

"And we haven't even ordered," Al said.

It was true. She had left her room with the belief, rooted in nothing, that her friends would not be there to eat with her—that they would, upon her lateness, vanish into the autumn air.

"I want to go home," Mona said.

"What did you say?"

"I want to go home."

"You aren't serious."

"I just can't."

"Of course you can. Think of your parents."

"Fuck them."

"Mona."

"No, really. Fuck them."

"Look, I can't stand my old man either and my mom is loopy but c'mon, you know they'll be happy and then you can go on with everything."

"I'm tired."

"Then get a good night's rest. Look, the whole thing will take what, a half hour? You say the vows, Hank Lefkowitz blesses you or whatever the rabbi does, and you're done. Go eat dinner with mom and pop and we'll be on the courts Monday."

"I don't know."

"It'll get him off your case."

"That was the idea."

"Saul's great idea."

They ordered, Mona unthinkingly pointing to a menu item. Chicken. In the time before it came, she tried to push them toward any other topic, even Nixon. Liv and Al cooperated, as much as they could.

The waiter bringing them their entrees, she realized, was the same man with the mustache she had startled before. Al smiled, as if he knew, and headed to the bathroom.

Mona began to chew on the chicken leg she had broken off, the skin too tender, a slight tangy aftertaste leaving her uneasy. The Rudolph Lodge was a place Liv had looked up in a guidebook, a quasi-rural hideaway built sometime in the '40s and smelling, to Mona at least, like burnt potato and pipe tobacco. It was her father's smell, even if her father wasn't here, instead staying with her mother at an inn only a short walk from the farmland where she'd be married to Saul tomorrow. They would spend the night before their daughter's wedding where they could see, from their window, the lush field where she would be betrothed to Saul, a nice older man. They thought it a little strange that Saul himself, past thirty, had not yet found a partner before Mona but at least Mona was not that old, she could still bear them grandchildren at a feasible and, more importantly, *reasonable* age. It was crucial not to be alone. Her younger brother, Vic, was a mere twenty-two and could afford a few more years of remaining unattached before Manny and Esther would begin to prod, asking when and where he was going to meet a nice young lady and suggest, gently at first, he could start attending the single's mixers at Temple Shalom. Vic had his own room at the inn, one door down from Manny and Esther.

Her older sister Melinda, gleefully married to Dr. Harold (never Harry) Hyman, was staying with her husband at another, more expensive cottage somewhere down Route 9.

"Do you think they'll care it's a small crowd?" Mona asked. "Do you think they'll suspect anything?"

"Your mom and dad? Nah. Listen, they're just thrilled this is happening. You've been seeing Saul for, what, five years?"

"No one from Saul's side will be there. Won't it be obvious?"

"His friends are coming, right?"

"He's got the gang from his office coming. They're all around his age though or younger. It'd be good to get one or two people over, I don't know, forty, just for plausibility. Someone who looks like a cousin you never talk to except for gatherings like these."

"It's a small affair. *Intimate.* Modern."

"I told them it was modern. At first, they really resisted Saul paying."

"Oh sure. But they let him, right?"

"Yeah."

"Just like my parents. Good old Long Island Jews, descended from the Lower East Side Jews. *No, no, no, no, we insist* and then the check is there and after forty seconds or so of waving his hands my dad puts the roll of cash away, subtly, gingerly. It's an art, Mona, to not pay for things. It's not so easy to master."

"They kicked in a little."

"For the food?"

"For the food."

"C'mon, let's order a bottle of wine. It's your last night of, um, freedom. And where the hell is Al?"

The waitress, a young, thin woman with hair almost down to her waist, drifted over, nodding like a small bird as Liv told her they wanted a bottle of white wine, the *house* brand, whatever that was. The waitress, who may have been twenty at most, inched away when Liv stopped talking. Moments later, Al was standing in her place, back from the bathroom. He exhaled and sat down, his chair rattling.

"How are we, girls?"

"That took long."

"I want to look good, Liv."

"You constipated?"

"Ha. Ha."

"Eat your asparagus."

"Okay, mother."

"Doesn't Mona's chicken smell good?"

They both turned to her, their eyes bugging on cue. Mona felt like she was trapped in a sitcom. Usually, Al and Liv were refreshing company, locked in vaudevillian exchanges for Mona's amusement, as well as their own. Liv, in her castigations of Al, would play the masculine brawler, while Al, when he felt like it, was the femme, or occasionally the schoolmarm, harping on Liv's alleged lack of style.

"Wine would take the edge off," Al said.

"I'm okay."

"Seriously, here," and he poured her a glass.

"I'm not—I'm not, no substances on the night of my, uh, wedding."

"You know it's not *real*, right? This whole thing? Hank Lefkowitz dropped out of yeshiva when he was like sixteen. I feel like you're forgetting," Liv said.

"I'm not forgetting anything. I wish Saul was here."

"He's with his friends, remember? That's how it works."

"Right, *works*."

"Hey cheer up," Al said. "Maybe after this, when we get back, I'll go swat some tennis balls with you."

"I'd rather crochet with my mother."

"I'm that bad?"

"Absolutely."

Mona took a sip.

"All they talk about is marriage. Every time I go down to see them. And they ask about you. Lately, it's gotten worse. You know he had that heart issue recently, right? Nothing severe. Doctor just said to take it easy with the salts, try not to get so worked up over everything. Try to tell Manny *not* to get worked up. Once he got accidentally stiffed for change at Woolworth's and ended up berating the clerk for running an *anti-Semitic* establishment, as if the Gestapo had infiltrated goddamn Woolworth's. Now he's on to marriage—every time, and then my mother, normally the quiet one, you know, is on it too, both of them sitting in their kitchen smoking away. Melinda will be pregnant soon, probably, so that'll distract them for a month . . . God, where was I? The heart, right, my father also thinks he doesn't have *much time*. He's fifty-five! *Mona, I want to be a grandfather before I am cold in the ground. My heart isn't what it used to be and I can't just go down to the store to get the spare parts.* On and on and on and on . . ."

When Mona told Liv the plan she and Saul eventually cooked up, Liv squealed with delight. Al thought it was funny too, especially how she was going to marry someone who was already married with two children, living in a house in Nassau County. They both relished absurdities. It would be another adventure, especially since Saul was fronting the costs. It was Liv who suggested Hank Lefkowitz to play rabbi. He would be explained, to Mona's parents, as an "up-and-comer" with an ordination from the Harvard Divinity School, just twenty-five but already making "profound contributions" to the world of Conservative Judaism. Hank was their only friend who knew any Hebrew, thanks to the few years he spent at a yeshiva, and his black tortoise-shell glasses created the impression of great scholarly depth, though he primarily spent his time getting high in the upper deck at Shea Stadium and may have read one or two books, cover-to-cover, in his life. Hank agreed to do it for $100, $50 paid in advance, the other $50 paid out if he didn't fuck it up.

"They'll think we're married and leave you alone," Saul had said. "What could go wrong?"

This was true. Her parents, cloistered in Flatbush, never traveled further than Lower Manhattan. Whenever they saw Saul, which was once a month at the most, he could remember to slip on the ring. Mona would have to become a ring person too, at least for the time being. She hated jewelry, necklaces and rings and earrings, and would often wonder why boys didn't have to strangle or mutilate their bodies with sparkling metals for the enjoyment of other people.

"There you go," Al said. "Take a drink."

Mona was drinking from her glass. She was done and wanted another after all. Liv and Al had drained much of the bottle. Liv, who always managed to be flush with cash, waved the waitress over for another. Once the second bottle came, Al refilled Mona's glass.

A current rippled through her skull.

"We'll drink one more bottle and then go to bed."

"Liv, you're nutso."

"Nutso? Who says that?" Al asked.

"I do," Mona said.

"It's like something I used to hear in the Catskills as a kid, from one of those beach ball-shaped comedians."

"Al is afraid to say *Jewish* because he's *Italian* and doesn't want to start a race war the night before your wedding," Liv said.

"My parents watched the comedians. I was always at summer camp, playing and playing. Baseball, softball, kickball, tennis," Mona said.

"Jews and Italians have always gotten along just fine," Al said, swallowing another gulp of wine, his cheeks reddening. "My Uncle Carlo says I'll probably fuck up his books because I'm *not* Jewish."

"The Italians I met in Levittown were always fat and greasy but they had money," Liv said. "Where Al came from, they were poor and greasy."

"Oh Livie, if this weren't the night before dear Mona's wedding, on the memory of my grandmama Carmela from the sweet land of Sicily, I would throw this white wine all over your pretty Jewish face."

"I'm gonna go to bed," Mona said.

"It's not even 10 p.m.!"

"I'm okay. Really. The wine, everything, dinner—the chicken was good. Thank you, Liv. Let's just get some rest."

"She really *does* think she's getting married," Al mock-whispered to Liv, his lips pursed like he was blowing an invisible flute.

"I'll see you all in the morning. Sweet dreams."

When Mona's head touched the tight, starchy bed sheets of her dark little room, she was asleep before she could remember why she had drunk so much white wine in the first place.

You need a wedding dress, of course.

Mona's head throbbed with daylight, the words looping through her, in Saul's voice and then her mother's, repeating until she stood in front of the bathroom mirror with bloodshot eyes too wide.

Her wristwatch, left on the nightstand, told her it was almost 7:30. Too early for Al, early enough for Liv. Her parents were already at breakfast, most likely, slurping coffee and nibbling at their runny eggs. She didn't want to eat anything. Only drink water, lots of it, her sudden thirst like a hammer in her stomach. She ran the faucet, cupping her hands to drink. Between gulps, she splashed her face until all of last night came back to her.

And the dress.

Since it was all Saul's idea, he provided the dress. It had been his sister's, he said, and they were roughly the same size. She lived in Washington now but had left the dress behind at his parent's house in Glen Oaks. She won't miss it at all, Saul said. She'll never know it's gone.

The dress was locked in a black trunk at her bedside. It would be time, soon, to put it on.

When Saul had suggested the marriage over the summer, it only occurred to Mona, a day or so later, she would actually have to wear a full-blown wedding dress, transforming into a walking sheet cake. The only wedding she had ever attended was her sister's, to Dr. Harold (not Harry) Hyman, and it was very clear from the outset Melinda not only relished shedding the surname Glass for Hyman but longed always to be a walking sheet cake. All her life, Melinda had worn oodles of make-up and elaborate dresses, preparing for the day a man with more money than her would sweep her off her feet. It was a culmination, Mona remembered thinking, of Melinda's hard work. She wanted nothing more than that day, dancing beneath a skylight with a Columbia-trained cardiologist, her girlfriends pondering just how much her dress really cost.

Mona, in her own garish dress picked out by her mother, nursed a glass of soda and begged for nightfall.

It was one thing to play pretend for Esther and Manny, who had earned this ruse through their ceaseless nagging. Was it cruel to deceive Melinda, such an ardent believer in the transcendent power of holy matrimony, too? Mona recalled the story of her birth: Melinda, then almost eight, wanting very badly to remain the only child, sobbing when she heard another girl would join the family. She believed she was going to be replaced.

"Think of how much easier things will be for you," Saul had said just the other day. "You'll be a married woman. Your parents won't give me the stink eye when I drop by."

"My father has seemed much happier of late. He curses less at inanimate objects."

"All that joy for such an outdated convention. But people like institutions."

"It keeps them in line."

"Like religion kept the peasants in line."

"It kept you in line, after all."

Mona knew she couldn't press much further. In their years together, or whatever it was she could call this linking of her life to Saul's, the topic of his own, very-legal-under-New York-State-law marriage to Felicia would not be broached unless Saul mentioned it first. He had the right of first move. It had always been this way, since he was teaching her American government seminar at City, and the years after, when he got the job for Rockefeller. Saul could give her so much and so little.

A part of him always in shadow.

The trunk's ancient clasps would not open. Mona pressed and pulled, her head swimming, her rage building. She wanted to take the trunk and throw it through the window. All this for what? For two parents who could not understand the modern world—that this was not 1920, that a woman could exist and not be defined by whether she had formalized a partnership with a man. It made it just a bit easier that Manny and Esther, who each never made it beyond high school, were slightly in awe of Saul, a lawyer and government official. He knows up from down, sideways from noways, her father would say approvingly. Saul was not a traveling salesman, like Manny, and he was not one of the grease monkeys in the auto body shops Manny was sure were always trying to purposefully break and then repair his Ford. He was a "college boy" and that meant he was haloed.

Mona put a sneaker on her right foot and began kicking at the trunk. Fucking shit, fucking shit, she said. It felt good to curse loudly. She didn't hear the low knock on her door, the jangling of the handle, or the faintness of Liv's voice from beyond the threshold. Sweat stung Mona's eyes. The trunk groaned with each thud of her sneaker. Her right foot swung all the way back and cracked open the trunk.

All of it for a dumbly folded dress.

On the fifth knock, Mona opened the door.

"What's that banging?" Liv asked.

"I was trying to get the dress from the trunk."

"My Mona, I figured you would need help."

"I feel like shit."

"Let me help you get ready. This will be my twelfth wedding. I've been in more wedding parties than weddings you've even attended."

Mona eyed the dress like she would a raccoon carcass left in her wake. Wearing it had always been theoretical, a lark, an image that now joined the reality of the flowing fabric over her skin, the ivory-white gown swallowing her whole. And a veil! At the City Hall Community Task Force, where she worked, she still wore a skirt and light eye make-up to work, but otherwise she preferred tennis shorts or denim, clothing that cost little and allowed her to forget it existed at all. She could collapse to the carpet, thinking about three hours from now when she would have to be a bride in white, trying not to trip on the train of fabric trailing down her back.

"Let me help you. I will make you a bride for Saul in no time."

"Fine. It's all just, well—"

"Strange?"

"Well, yes. I'm never going to get married. I know that. Never."

"Never?"

"Liv, I know a lot of people want to, dream of it. My sister, even you, and that's okay. I'm just not doing that."

"I don't blame you. Times are changing. My mother was married at twenty-one. We're older than that now. I haven't found anyone to settle down with. I don't want to rush."

"I'm not *settling*, though."

"You're twenty-four."

"So? I know what I want."

"What you want may change."

"I'm not like other people. It won't change."

"Saul is old, yes, but there may be others, well, a man you *want* to marry . . ."

"I'd only marry Saul!"

Mona was surprised at the sound of her own voice rising, the sharpness of it in the otherwise bare room. Liv had placed her hand on Mona's shoulder.

"Then maybe you will someday."

"But I don't want to. That's my point. It's him or no one and I'm not getting married so no one."

"It is all a little, I don't know, *fucked*, with him having a wife."

"Imagine if my parents knew."

"Oh, I can. They'd drive out in their station wagon to Long Island and light his house on fire."

"And then come for me."

"The yelling."

"The *kvetching*."

"The *how could our daughter do this to us?* How could she betray us? Like this? With a man with a wife and a fake wedding!"

"Something like that. Melinda would pile on too. She'd love to."

"Melinda would disown you."

"Dr. Harold Hyman would disown me."

"*You aren't my sister-in-law.*"

Hearing Liv laugh, Mona thought about how nice it would be

if the trip had ended right now, on this morning, the trunk busted open and the dress unworn, two friends in a hotel room mocking this strange world they had inherited.

2

Saul Plotz backed his 1972 bolt blue Camaro out of the driveway of the motel, dutifully looking both ways. The roadway was empty of everything and everyone except the foliage, the leaves a whirl of ashy orange, drawing his roving eye. When he first had the leisure to do so, he had traveled to the Hudson Valley each autumn to take in the changing of the leaves. Felicia would insist on coming. He always assented, whether he wanted her there or not.

"The boys know where to go?" Saul asked Sonny Cannon, who was riding shotgun to the farm.

"They know. All five of them. Some crowd."

"Well, I do appreciate it."

"It's no big deal. And I won't turn down a free meal. They won't either."

"Still, it's good you could do this."

"She means a lot to you."

"She does."

The tux was cut too tight at the arms and the crotch and Saul kept flinching in the driver's seat to give his body air. He readjusted his tie in the mirror and drove faster, onward to the wedding. He'd do anything for a cigarette but he wasn't going to stink up his suit in front of Mona's parents. After, at dinner, oh, he'd bust into his Parliaments and feel that beautiful rush. Then next week, when he was in the city, he could grab lunch with Mona and they could laugh about what they had done. He was already thinking about a red sauce joint on Chambers he could take her on her lunch break on Wednesday. Rocky had him in Midtown that day and he could shoot straight down for a long, easy lunch, rigatoni and some white bread.

First, this. Why the hell had he gotten the tux cut so tight?

"This is a pretty, pretty car," Sonny said.

"I didn't want a muscle car, to be honest, but my jalopy had broken down and I figured why not treat myself?"

"You sure did."

"Felicia says it makes me look young."

"Cars will do that."

"God, I can't wait for a cigarette and dinner."

"You want one? My old Chesterfields."

"I'm not going to smoke until after the ceremony."

"You want nice breath when you kiss Mona."

"Something like that."

After he had mentioned the possibility of the wedding to Mona on that beach day, he immediately understood he had made at least one grievous logistical error: no family members of his could actually attend. They knew him as a happily married father of two, husband to Felicia, resident of the village of Roslyn, all-American taxpayer. They could not come to watch him pretend to marry the woman he had been sleeping with, off and on, for five years. They had already come to watch him marry Felicia a decade ago. In the comic books, they would call this a continuity error, and Saul could not simply erase the memories of the Plotz clan to convince them to drive to Rhinebeck for the benefit of Mona's parents, Esther and Manny, who very much wanted to see their young daughter marry.

Saul, who often felt compelled to tinker with solutions to problems both imagined and real, conceived of an answer to his dilemma just a day later: trusted friends and friends-of-friends. Some would have to pose as family. All needed to be sufficiently removed from a social circle that could border upon the kind of people who spoke to middle-aged Jewish parents on a not infrequent basis. When Esther and Manny inevitably asked about where Saul's parents were, he could plausibly say they were dead. He was thirty-four. Manny believed he was on his deathbed at fifty-five. So his own parents, fitfully alive, would have to be temporarily banished from the Earth.

Who to bring? He immediately thought of Sonny. Though he didn't personally enjoy classifying friends as best or second best, it was Sonny who had emerged, through attrition and genuine affinity, to take the crown. Most of his college friends had fallen away, his law school buddies as equally busy as he was and unable to formulate proper relationships that didn't involve some exchange of money. Both Saul and Sonny were in the employ of Rocky, Sonny in the sanctified inner ring, Saul on the outer rim, shunning Albany as much as he possibly could. Sonny lived in the city but was up there every week, piling miles on his state-issued Chevy, puffing on cigars and listening to his Beatles and Beach Boys tapes. Saul, as the Queens borough director, was paid less but granted a wider latitude, and he and Sonny would always manage a few days a week on the phone, and at least one lunch, to swap Rocky tales.

Sonny was loyal, to Rocky and to Saul. He kept secrets. It was the WASP in him, Saul often thought, his ability to expertly tuck away whatever needed to be tucked away. Sonny could come to the wedding. When Saul told him to tell no one else in the office, he knew Sonny wouldn't. It was the old boy honor. A network devoid of *yentas*. They could all hold their drinks.

He watched Sonny finger a leather pouch on his lap. Sometimes, Sonny liked to smoke a pipe.

"If you're not gonna smoke, I'm gonna smoke. I'll smoke for both of us."

"My uncle smokes a pipe."

"All the fucking intellectuals do it, Saul. Haven't you seen a jacket cover of a book?"

"I like the smell."

"Women like it. You'd be surprised. They get a whiff and can't get away. I'm trying to bring it back."

"Twenty years ago, you'd be cutting edge."

"Now you're cutting edge. A real live bigamist. I never thought I'd get to meet one. I almost want your autograph. Rocky would love it."

"It'd be a scandal."

"But he'd love two or three wives."

"If he hadn't gotten that divorce, you'd be in the West Wing already."

"Probably. But the big guy is horny. What are you gonna do?"

Saul drove on, his heartbeat beginning to increase. He was surprised to find himself sweating, though it was crisp outside and he had brought an overcoat just in case of cold rain. His head felt light, his hands slick on the wheel. All of the sensations associated with nervousness without the literal rationale—it didn't count, after all. Nothing would change. Could he be afraid that he would somehow be found out? Over the years with Mona there were close calls, but Felicia never suspected a thing, couldn't really because she left Roslyn so infrequently. She quit the stenographer gig in the city years ago to raise Tad and Lenore, dividing her time between the house and her friends in the civic association. There was no probability of Felicia venturing, on her own, to Rhinebeck, to this roadway with Sonny, to this farm. No one at the wedding beyond Sonny knew her well enough to even engage her in casual conversation. And Sonny only spoke to Felicia on Saul's turf, at a couple's dinner once every few months whenever Sonny's schedule made enough sense for it to happen. Sonny hadn't even told his own wife.

It wasn't that, then. He wasn't afraid for himself. Perhaps, subconsciously, he feared for Mona's sake, for her own parents somehow seeing through the ruse. But how? Perhaps if Hank Leftkowitz fucked up. He always could. He was a Mona friend from college, a flake going nowhere who happened to have a working knowledge of

Hebrew. He didn't like Hank much.

Hank was the loose thread here, Saul thought. He didn't want Mona to be embarrassed. Wherever he went, he always found time to worry about Mona, though she wasn't the type to worry about herself. She was so *direct*, so hard-charging, an arrow aimed at the future. She betrayed so little. He had never seen her cry. He had never heard Mona call herself a feminist—he supported the cause, if he found the adherents shrill and overly confrontational—but she was, in all senses, the ideal of what the movement called for, a woman living life on her own terms. That he was sure of. And he couldn't deal with seeing Mona undercut by her parents, belittled by them, made to feel inadequate for failing to marry *him*, as if it were her fault, somehow. Felicia had just showed up first! It was a temporal problem he could not fix. He could see how her parents had ganged up on her since Melinda, who was a real bitch to tell the truth, married the doctor, blessed Harold Hyman, and was inducted at last into the sainthood of spouses married to Ivy League-trained cardiologists. Without a doctor in the picture, their next best hope was Saul, a nice older Jewish man who worked for the *governor*. He could see how he served as an embodiment of power to them, a person to be admired and even slightly feared. They decided this was the person Mona should marry because they had *met* him—Mona rarely brought men around—and he was Jewish and he earned a comfortable living at an occupation that Esther could brag about at the laundromat.

Saul wasn't about to deny Mona. He wanted to, however he could with his limited power, make her life easier.

That explained him driving, with Sonny, to the Deer Hollow Estates, where he was set to be married to Mona Glass at 12:30 p.m. with Hank Lefkowitz officiating. Afterwards, the small wedding party would depart for a large luncheon at the nearby Sebastian Grille, rated highly by the guidebook he had consulted. Most of it on his dime, which was fine. It made it easier to think of it as a vacation for Mona and himself, in the company of her parents, cousins, and a select number of friends.

Raindrops began to hit the windshield. He wondered what Mona would look like in a dress.

They were only a few minutes away. Sonny was toying with his own tie. He ran the windshield wipers and listened to the sound of rubber grinding on glass, his thoughts quieting, his heart slowing. It was okay. They'd be in and out. He was glad Mona had suggested they pay for a tent.

Saul caught sight of the sign and swerved. The parking lot was unpaved, an expanse of gravel. Sonny whistled and took a puff from his pipe.

"Here we are, looking good," Sonny said. "I've always liked the rustic."

"This will work."

The drops fell steadily. He could see the grass softening, the mud rising, the farmland's gradual sink. He walked along a stone path, his dress shoes clicking softly in the rain. All they had to do was make it look real and how hard was that?

He loved her, after all.

3

Mona didn't expect the door to creak open when it did. Liv was still sitting with her, checking her own make-up in a small pocket mirror. Gray light fell through a moon-shaped window. They had been sitting in silence, the small, wood-paneled backroom hissing with rainfall.

Saul stood over them, his overcoat dripping with rain.

"Hi," he said.

Usually, he led with a joke. Saul always had jokes. His voice was softer now, his eyes dipping low and away from her. It was the dress. She knew it. It was wrong. The walking sheet cake. She was inhabiting another body, taking on a new reality that she had to square with what she used to be, the collision too much to bear. It was all supposed to be funny, get married, har har, but she hadn't considered the weight of the dress, the rise of the fabric, the sheen in the light. She wanted to be married in a windbreaker and shorts, her tennis racket clenched in her right hand. She wanted Hank to do the schtick and be gone. But it wouldn't be like that. Her parents were already in the tent, with Cousins Morty and Eugenia and Freda and Julius and Rosa, along with the gelatinous Aunt Sarah. Uncle Lester, Manny's dreadnought brother, was there as well. And more would come, additional cousins and their spouses, small children, the offspring of other Glasses and Lipskys, her mother's family. It was the same assemblage she had witnessed at Melinda's wedding, the same winding small-talk, the breath smelling like Jarlsberg, the coughing into handkerchiefs and the lipstick applied in two or three sopping layers.

"It's good to see you," was all Mona could say to him.

Liv stood up.

"I can leave you guys alone for now," she said. "That's what they do at weddings."

"Christian ones, mostly," Saul said. "I mean, Jews do that too but it's not, I guess, required."

"You know I am a Jewess myself, Saul. Unlike Mona here, I was even bat mitzvahed."

"My bar mitzvah was traumatic."

"Vic got the runs at his," Mona said, smiling slightly. "At the synagogue. He was in the bathroom for twenty, thirty minutes. He ate some bad fish. It smelled, well—it smelled like fish turned to shit."

"On that lovely note, I will leave you two lovebirds. Put on a good show!"

When Liv had gone, they moved closer on the cold wooden bench, their knees touching.

"Weird, isn't it?"

"Well, you've been through this before."

"God, it was a decade ago, eleven years . . ."

"Did you enjoy it?"

"Did I enjoy it? That's a question. It was a lot more lavish than this, which made it, well, kind of terrible. Felicia's family comes from money, you know. They're German Jewish stock, almost not Jewish at all. I'm from a bunch of Russian anarchists who didn't want to fight in whatever war the czar was waging and fled here sometime before 1900. The Plotzes have a proud tradition of dodging military service. Anyway, so, we did it at this big temple, Shelter Rock. Out on the Island. God knows what it cost, her mother and father front everything, I was fresh out of law school and had hardly anything to my name, the cash I'd socked away from being a camp counselor."

"Did she look nice?"

"Felicia?"

"Yes."

"She did."

"I don't think I look nice."

He took her hand in his.

"You look beautiful, Mona."

"Let's just get this over with."

"Your parents are going to have to walk you down the aisle. To the *chuppah*."

"You know, I had to sell them on a farm wedding."

"They wanted it in the city? In a temple?"

"Manny and Esther complain about going further than the supermarket. But you know, the fact that this is happening—it's enough to keep them quiet. I think they thought I was a lesbian."

"So this is their moment of great relief. A man! She likes men!"

"They probably think Liv is a lesbian too because she hasn't married anyone. They fell in love at sixteen, allegedly. Met on a street corner in Yorkville. Could you fall in love at sixteen, Saul?"

"In love? I was in love with Duke Snider."

"Boys are stupid at that age and there was no boy for me, in high school, to love. They were popping pimples, jerking off in the bathroom, trying and failing to get haircuts like Paul McCartney. You can't love boys."

"Only men then."

"Even most men are slobs. Let's be honest. But try telling that to Esther. She couldn't comprehend a girl who wanted to play sports past the age of ten and not get married. I was a Martian to her—a Martian that came from her womb."

"That must have been rough."

"I've told you about it."

"A little, I mean . . . we talk about a lot of things, I feel like, except each other. Or we do but not so much. We're always talking *about* things. Sports, politics, weather, sex . . ."

Mona took a small breath. "Weddings and funerals blur together for me, it's the same suits, the rituals, the money—two industries just, I don't know, completely *tied* to each other. This is what I think about."

"Existential Mona."

Saul leaned in to kiss her on the lips. Mona, her eyelids closing, accepted him. The tobacco didn't smell as sharp on his breath as it usually did.

"I love you."

"I love you, too."

Mona considered how they had grown so used to saying this word to each other, a word she had reserved only for her parents on rare occasions, once or twice for Vic, perhaps never for Melinda. It was a word that was foreign to her, a lump of clay on her tongue, until she saw Professor Saul Plotz lecturing on American government at City College. It turned out to be one of only two classes Saul would ever teach, caught between jobs and hunting for extra income before Rockefeller would hire him. She didn't know that he would permanently insert himself into her life and begin to alter it, but she understood there was a difference here, of aura or wavelength, the way her body was pulled to his even when he was standing still. She could hardly remember his lectures, only the movement of his hands and the swimming of his lips, how his skin, the color of sand at the lip of the surf on a great white beach, caught sunlight from the bracketed windows. Each day he wore a starched dress shirt with a stark red or blue tie and tan slacks, his sleeves rolled up to his elbows, the dark hair on his forearms curling gently. Once fall came, he arrived in a slim corduroy jacket. On the blackboard, sea-green, he methodically scrawled factoids with a thick piece of chalk, click clack click, the rhythm of her heart. He called on students without asking them to volunteer, his left index finger shooting wherever he desired, every first and last name committed to memory by the second class. She remembered when he first said her name out loud, the way his mouth circled around the *o* and his tongue pressed gently against his bottom teeth, the release on *a*, the lightness of his breath. She hated her last name, so blunt and Jewish, but from him it became something like a talisman, to be hunted for and cherished when it charged through the air, his gift. *Mona Glass.* Present, she cried, too loudly, her hand flailing skyward.

He was, absolutely, the first person to make her love hearing her own name. She could sit next to him and listen to the way his lips bent vowels to her ear.

"We should probably go out there soon," he said. "They expect a show."

"I'm a little nervous."

"Me too. But hey, come Monday we will be talking about all this at lunch, laughing about it, another day in the books. That's all. Think about all the peace you're buying yourself. A married woman for Manny and Esther."

"A married woman. That's right. And you'll be a married man."

"I certainly will."

"You can wear the ring your wife gave you around my parents now. No need to stick it in your pocket."

He turned away from her, his eyes on the raindrops striking the window.

"I can."

"I think I hear the crowd building in that tent. They must wonder why we're in the tent, and not at a temple in Flatbush. I'm going to blame you."

"Feel free. I can't wait for an earful at Sebastian's."

There was a knock on the door. Saul stood up to nudge it open. Liv peeked in.

"They're getting ready. Hank's here, the chuppah, the whole she-bang. Saul you come out now. I'll get your parents, Mona, they'll walk you down to Saul. You gotta get veiled too, the Bedeken they call it. You know the deal right?"

"Just put the veil on me now."

"You'll help her out, Saul. Our girl here is an honorary goy. No sense of her people."

Her people were all in a tent, beneath the rain, waiting for her. She took a heavy breath.

She would have to go to them now.

4

Hank Lefkowitz didn't have to speak Hebrew. He couldn't, not in any Talmudic sense, but more and more Jewish weddings of the modern vintage were conducted in English anyway. When Mona saw him, he offered his lantern smile.

As her mother and father interlocked her arms to walk her down the mauve carpeting, she could feel the soggy earth beneath the tent, how her heels, which she hardly wore, pressed deeper into the hidden mud. They were both looking at her, their faces now hardened masks of approval. She felt the turn of heads, the cousins upon cousins and friends of friends, an army of rouge and lipstick. This, she considered, was a historic day for them, one they would recall for years to come. *Do you remember Mona Glass's wedding, the one in the tent?* She was preparing already to forget, to wipe her memory clean once Monday hit and she was back on the train, hustling to work. Hank was running a finger under his nose to wipe away mucus. There was Saul next to him, grinning, knowing what was about to be done, the last performance that she would give for her parents. This was the culmination of one life.

"You look beautiful," her mother whispered to her.

"We are so proud," her father said.

Through her veil, the world took on an uncanny quality, of being there and not, a gulf between what was supposed to exist and what actually was, all of it lost in the pale gauze of the fabric. She was a girl in a dress. She had never arrayed herself in such a way, marching forward into the light as the doll made into flesh. Her stomach hurt, though she hadn't eaten anything. The wine hangover clung to her.

Hank was making a speech. Or trying to. She drifted away. He was talking about the union of two people, man and woman, how this was as the Torah willed, whatever that meant. He was sneezing savagely.

They were standing now under the chuppah, the four-posted canopy structure made of prayer shawls, her parents at her side, Saul with no one. She had never met Saul's parents and it came to her, with a grim finality she didn't anticipate, that she never would, that the circumstances could never permit it. These two old Jewish parents, similar to her own, would only know of Felicia as Saul's love and the mother of her children, just as her parents would consider Saul her lifelong partner in the eyes of God.

Hank, recovered, pushed his glasses back up the bridge of his nose. Through a nasal whine, he apologized again.

"These two will form a union and we will celebrate the joining of their lives," Hank said, apropos of no Talmudic riddle. "May Hashem bless them always."

Hashem was God. Despite not attending Hebrew school—only Vic went, as the boy—Mona had scraped together the relevant terms needed for an education in the faith, the way God must be named and nicknamed and obliquely referenced, how her parents and cousins could not just write out the word "God" on a sheet of paper but needed to slash the "o" and hyphenate it so "God" became "G-d," a show of reverence that only made her think it was a curse word, something to never be uttered in polite company.

"Let us now take our vows."

Yes, this is what people do when they marry, she thought. Say vows to each other. She had none prepared. Due to her limited wedding experience and the fact she had spent most of Melinda's wedding desperately willing time to pass, so focused on the single task of advancing seconds along that she could hardly recall relevant details about that day—were she quizzed by detectives she wasn't sure she could prove she was really there—she had brought precious little prior awareness of a seminal institution of contemporary civilization to this very moment. And Saul was talking, his lips moving, and she would have to listen.

"I, Saul, take you, Mona, to be my beloved wife, to cherish for all my days . . ." He was holding a ring in his hand and sliding it onto her finger, a gold ring she hadn't seen before, perhaps another hand-me-down from an aunt or cousin. It shimmered as it met her flesh, cold to the touch. She wanted to know who it belonged to and when she could slide it off her finger and return it. But no, she could not simply *return* it, not as long as she hoped to see her parents again. She would always have to remember to wear it in their presence. That was a new burden, the price of admission to a marriage to quell their hunger.

"I, Saul, give you this ring as a sign of our covenant with each other. With my body, mind, and spirit, I will honor you, cherish you, and stay with you all my days."

Now Mona had to speak. She stared down at her hand and then back up, to the caked face of her mother and the dark jowls of her father and the family jammed onto the white folding chairs, Al and Liv among them, Melinda sitting in the front row, her smile too wide. All Mona had to do was say something.

Exactly what she just heard.

"I, Mona, take you, Saul, to be my beloved husband, to cherish for all my days, to form, um, a covenant with you. I will cherish you, honor you, stay with you forever."

Good enough.

Hank, again with his fucking finger near his nose, slid a piece of glass under white cloth. She knew this part. This was what separated Jews from every other people on the planet, their sanctioning of smashed glass.

"Saul, please step on the glass," Hank muttered.

"I'd like to as well," Mona said quietly.

"Well okay then. Both step on it. You're married!"

Together, their feet fell on the covered glass, blasting it to pieces. There was applause, enough to ease Mona's heartbeat, and she found she was laughing, nearly giddy, Saul meeting her eyes and giggling with her. It was done, they were here, Hank had performed as a man of Hashem, they could soon go home. She took Saul's hands and kissed him, hard, and she could feel his desire, how his tongue was stealthily trying to find her own, as if they could neck and then fuck right here in front of everyone at the wedding. Her eyes closed.

They considered her a married woman now. If enough believed her to be that way, maybe she really was. Reality was perception. Manny and Esther would now tell friends and strangers alike about their two married daughters. Look at what she gave them.

"See, that wasn't so bad," Saul whispered in her ear.

5

That night, they stayed in Saul's hotel, an inn down the road from where Mona and her friends had slept the night before. Mona was thankful for the quiet, to be able to change out of her dress and spend a night just with him. They walked across the parking lot, hand-in-hand. He held the door for her.

"Mr. Plotz?"

It was the old woman at the front desk, one hand on a crossword puzzle.

"Yes?"

"A call came in for you today. From a Ms. Leila Drinkwater. She said to call her back as soon as possible."

"Did she stipulate a time?"

"Day or night is fine, she said. As soon as she was available. She didn't leave a number."

"That's alright."

Mona turned to him.

"That's just my new secretary down at the Queens office. Started a month or two ago. Probably something for work. She panics. I'll call tomorrow."

"Are you sure?"

"I'm sure."

"You told her you were here?"

"In case they needed to find me for some Rocky shit. Don't

worry, I told them Sonny and I were taking an overnight trip with some buddies to play golf and visit another buddy."

"You don't play golf."

"But Sonny does."

Saul's room had a photograph of a lake, the peeling walls painted a light blue, like a spoiling robin's egg. She sat on the edge of his bed as she began to undress. The dress fell away like excess skin. She wanted to plunge it into darkness and never see it again. She didn't regret deceiving her parents—they had what they wanted, she had what she wanted, an even trade—but the wearing of the dress was, if not a bridge too far, a gesture toward another kind of existence she wasn't ready for and never, maybe, would be. How did so many women so willingly subsume themselves in such ways? At least men could wear suits no different than what they normally picked out for a day of business. Saul always wore suits. Even in a tuxedo, he didn't have to feel the extraordinariness of the day like she did, how transmogrified she was in the mirror, a woman being veiled in white, floating to the altar. He was shirtless now, his light muscle and swath of dark chest hair shown to her, and she wanted to fall into his arms and forget all of it, to go to sleep and wake up on Monday or Tuesday, the weekend flushed away.

He lay back on the bed and put his hands behind his head. He yawned, his chest rising and falling.

"That was fun, wasn't it?"

"I hated wearing the dress."

She was naked now, she realized. He began sliding his underwear off.

"I liked seeing you in it."

"It was strange."

"Weddings are really strange anyway. All the medieval rituals. They were sprung from a time when we were all dead at thirty-five and the only way to guarantee any kind of legacy was to get someone impregnated by sixteen and hope for the best. And all of it sanctioned by the church or the rabbi or whoever."

"I'm glad we can just be us again."

"I'm glad too."

Mona settled next to Saul, curling into the crook of his arm, the light on the nightstand cast on his cheek. This was one of the few times she could recall ever being naked in a place that wasn't her own apartment. Her small one-bedroom on Ocean Parkway was a safe haven for him, far away from anyone, his wife included, who may know who he was and question why he was visiting the apartment of a much younger woman. She could think of this as a vacation, one with an elaborate dinner and costume performances, and on Monday she could resume her life anew. Though she had traveled a fair amount in college and after, even backpacking across Europe against her parents' wishes, there was an aspect to leaving home that always unsettled her, the changing of spaces and the way people, robbed of context, could assume new identities and even purposes for being. Away from Brooklyn, in Rhinebeck, she was the young bride of a hard-charging government official. She was *his* woman, like Melinda clearly belonged to Dr. Harold Hyman. She didn't feel this way but this was how she was seen: by her parents, relatives, and even the hotel staff, who had the reservation under Mr. and Mrs. Saul Plotz. Who was she to contest this reality, particularly when they had numbers on their side? She could battle it with all the force of a protester outside City Hall—I am *not* a bride!—but she could feel the impotence of taking such a position, especially when it would either lead to disbelief or rage. *What is it we just witnessed then? Are you a liar, Mona Glass?*

"I'm a liar," she said out loud.

"What?"

"I am."

"Everyone's a liar. We all play pretend. But look—we did this for a good cause, the cause of getting a pretty big monkey, your parents, off your back. We did. You shouldn't feel bad."

"I *don't* feel bad. I just said I'm a liar."

"We're both beautiful liars," he said, reaching over to kiss her. She kissed him back, her hands pressing against his shoulders, her breasts falling into his chest. When they first had sex, he had always been the aggressor, the lead partner guiding her legs open, pressing into her like a good, horny boy. They knew each other enough, or he had been simply liberated enough, to let her take control, to impose her desire on him. He was still the most receptive lover she ever had, receptive in the sense of what the word really meant, reduced to its essence. He could follow a cue, read her body, keep pace and rhythm like a tennis player at the net volleying back each ball with precision and ease. He fucked without an ego—or less than what she was used to, certainly not like the other men she found in college and later at the bars in her neighborhood, men who were really just interested in masturbating with her body.

Mona would often wonder how he was with Felicia.

When she talked to Saul, time flaked away, no more than an accident of existence, unrelated to what really mattered: the two of them, together in conversation. She couldn't tire of his voice. And he wouldn't tire of hers. It was as good as the fucking. That's what had kept her with him so long, able to tolerate the unalterable facts of their union, how another reality—Felicia, his children—always loomed just offstage. His counter-life. If she thought about it hard enough, her stomach could sink two, three levels. She, Mona, was the one who represented the counter, the *other*, the hidden, ongoing phase that Felicia Plotz, dutiful housewife, could uncover one day only as a damnable transgression, two bodies slinking in the darkness. Felicia Plotz, entitled in every way to the ur-reality, the base from which all others flowed, the lawful wife of Saul and the mother of his children and the one who could summon him home when she needed, who appeared on all the mortgage documents and health insurance forms and bank statements that confirmed what existed and what did not in this machine civilization.

What did Mona want then? To usurp Felicia? To *be* her? To inherit the life Saul had first constructed with Felicia in the nullity of another decade?

No, no, no. No. And maybe.

6

Once Saul was dressed in the morning, he went to the payphone in the lobby to place a call to his secretary. It was Sunday, she'd be at home. Mona was still sleeping, looking cute as always. He had an idea to take a drive deep into the woods somewhere, just the two of them. Sonny and the boys would be heading back. They'd enjoyed themselves at dinner, tearing apart their steaks and loudly arguing about whether the Mets could get back to the World Series next year. It was November, the month of speculation, and Sonny was sure the Mets had missed their window.

Saul listened for the ringing. Leila wouldn't let it get past two. She was an eager girl, fresh out of Pace, and seemed to have a real interest in not just the job but the politics too. He could appreciate that. The best governments were those filled with young people who cared.

"Hello?" she asked sleepily.

"Rise and shine. It's Saul."

"Mr. Plotz! Yes, of course. I'll fill you in quickly because I know you're really busy—"

"Slow morning, Leila, don't sweat it. Tell me what's going on."

"Fred wants to meet Monday and I know it's last minute and you hate last minute meetings but he seemed adamant and serious about it, like it had to be Monday, he was insisting on it."

"Did he give a time?"

42

"He wants a morning meeting."

"Can he do late morning? God, he's such a prick."

"Should I tell him 11?"

"Tell him 11:30, let him rub up against lunch. Or, well, actually, we can stick with the 11, because I may have to spend the afternoon in the city. Have him come by the office at 11. Did he say what it was regarding?"

"He said it was about a development. He didn't specify."

"Rocky is on vacation so he got antsy. I'm the nearest thing. He's a pain in the ass. Let's do it then. Tell him we have one hour."

"One hour, got it."

"Thanks, Leila."

Saul didn't want to think about Monday yet. He knew, unlike most meetings, this wasn't one he could simply blow off. This was a person with a great deal of money who, like all people with a great deal of money, had cultivated an ego to match. Rocky was interested in keeping him happy so Saul would have to care about keeping him happy too. That was the downside of serving a principle, particularly one as megalithic as Nelson Rockefeller, the governor of America's most important state, as far as Saul was concerned, and a likely future occupant of the Oval Office. As independent as you may fancy yourself—suave, urbane, a shot-caller *par excellence*—you were always in service of another human being, one who had amassed more power than you could really imagine, the lives of millions reliant on his wisdom and instinct. In Queens, a county of two million, Saul was the emissary of the governor, a small embodiment of his colossal gravity. By proxy, he could enjoy the Rockefeller fortune, the deference it had purchased, the awe commingled with fear. But unlike some of Rocky's other hangers-on—and like Sonny, ultimately—he understood all his clout derived from a single source that, at any given moment, could be gone altogether. Rocky got sick of people. He could, one day, get sick of Saul. So Saul trod through the kingdom mindful of his mortality, and never, in his mind, overreaching—let the other Rocky men curse out subordinates, throw chairs against the wall, promise to cut the nuts off this or that man, vow to rain down holy hellfire if calls weren't returned fast enough. Sonny wasn't a yeller, and neither was he.

Sonny would survive.

When Saul got back to the room, Mona was awake.

He watched her fold and stuff the wedding dress into the trunk. She clearly didn't want to see it anymore. She had been so striking in it, veil and all. He had to admit he didn't expect it, the way she looked before him, how, despite everything, she seemed to be in full bloom, actively resisting what was plain for all to see: she was beautiful. He thought so, her parents thought so, even Sonny thought so. He knew he would never see her in a dress again, she was back to sweatshirts and dungarees and the occasional skirt. That would do.

"Can you help me close the clasps?" she asked.

He could and did. They hauled the trunk to the car, he paid the bill at the front desk, and they drove off to eat at a diner in town. Mona got scrambled eggs, he went for pancakes and poured on extra syrup. They were another couple on another Sunday. Recently, Sonny had played a dreamy song by an obscure rock and roll band that had disbanded a few years ago. The singer, who sounded a bit like Dylan, sang about Sunday morning with a tinkling piano in the background and he was moved by how closely the song could approximate the sensation of waking on a Sunday, the first hours passing like a dream. He tried to remember the name, something with the Underground, and he was amazed that Sonny, through his restless and idiosyncratic reading of music magazines, always managed to rustle up these bands. Sonny was the only WASP with a trust fund who read the *Village Voice*.

Saul swallowed his pancakes. He was always a fast eater. So was Mona. Neither of them lingered over food. If it was there, it would be consumed. Mona kept her figure through relentless exercise, tennis and bicycling and walking at a maddening pace, two to three steps ahead of whomever she was with, including Saul. It came naturally to her, the speed and drive, while Saul liked to take his time, meander, consider his steps. She chided him for walking slowly, for not keeping up, for being like an old man. Always with a sly grin. She couldn't survive in New Jersey or Long Island or any suburb, not where shoppers lingered over cans of soup and the automobiles puttered down empty streets into smooth, vacant driveways. There, she would have to drive or sit still. No one walked anywhere.

The drive back was easy, a glide down the Taconic State Parkway through Westchester and into the city. Mona fell asleep, her head dipping against the window. He lowered his window to feel the highway breeze. The radio played jazz standards. Felicia rarely slept in cars. She was always up and alert, staring straight ahead. He tried to compare her to Mona as little as he could. It was unfair to them both. Eras separated them. One operated with the knowledge of the other and one did not. He was lucky he could see Mona as much as he could. Working out of Queens gave him distance, both from his wife and the governor of New York. He could tell Felicia he was doing work for Rocky and see Mona instead. As far as Felicia knew, Rocky had him working a lot of evenings and weekends. That's how billionaire governors were, he'd explain apologetically, kissing her on the cheek.

He knew, as the years wore on, he cared less about disappointing her. In the beginning, the first year seeing and sleeping with Mona, he was wracked with enough guilt to be on the verge of confessing to his wife that he was a no-good husband, disloyal and unfaithful and maybe he would even cry in front of her for forgiveness. Felicia was a good woman who didn't deserve it. He could remember exactly when that was, the urge to cry. Early December, a hard chill in the air, the sky like cement. He and Mona were walking on the old grounds of the World's Fair, through Flushing Meadows Park. She had been a kid when the fair came and he was in his twenties, drunk on the promise of the future, flying cars and biodomes and rocket ships to Mars. He told this to her, what it had meant to be there, even if the fair itself proved to be a money-wasting disaster, an embarrassment for Moses, the former parks commissioner who ran the whole state before Rocky did. They walked, hand-in-hand, by the Unisphere and he leaned in to kiss her. He held her there and he was riveted then with the awareness that he had come to the base of the Unisphere, that stainless steel ode to Planet Earth, with Felicia too, during the day of the World's Fair. A man had taken a Polaroid of them holding hands. He still had it in Roslyn tucked in a bedroom drawer. He was kissing Mona in the same place he had stood with Felicia and he could now understand, in that membrane of time with his lips held to hers, that this kiss with Mona could mean so much more than any single hug or kiss or sexual encounter with Felicia and this would always be true. As he let go of Mona, looking up to the enormous steel globe above, he felt a drop in his stomach and throat, this notion of time tugging at him, his marriage to Felicia, a legal and formal present, frozen suddenly behind the glass of a past he no longer wished to revisit, not even to tap in and peek. He loved this kiss so much more and yet he was sorry for that too and he felt the onset of a panic, a powerful urge he couldn't name, to rush in his car and drive back to Long Island and tell Felicia all of it, from the first time he saw Mona in class to the sex after work to the deep kiss beneath the Unisphere where they once dreamed of a world in the clouds. *Felicia, honey, I met this girl, this woman, her name is Mona Glass and I am in love with her and I know I promised to be with you the rest of my life and we have two children together in this sturdy home but I love Mona Glass.*

He was going to do it! He was so close that day in Flushing Meadows. But he didn't. Perhaps, looking back, self-preservation had won out. A fear of confrontation. A divorce filing that would rob him of his assets. A hysterical promise to never let him see his own children again. In the years to come, he would run through all the scenarios of a possible confession to Felicia and none of them ended well for him, even if they could also mean, somehow, a lifetime at Mona's side, boyfriend and girlfriend or husband and wife or whatever liminal, lovely state they wanted to occupy. He could not bring himself to tell Felicia and leave her for good. He could not bring himself to rudely disrupt his own life.

You fucking coward, he told himself, driving through the Bronx, over a bridge, now swinging down the East Side of Manhattan. You piece of shit coward.

They had playacted for her parents. Did he want it to be more than acting? Could he confess this to himself? Better yet, tell Mona?

He found his right hand shaking her awake.

"Yeah, what?"

"Are you awake?"

"You just woke me."

"I wanted to see how you were."

"Sleeping. Now awake. What? Are we there?"

"No, we're not. I just wanted to ask you something."

"That's Saul's serious voice. Go ahead."

"What if we *did* get married?"

"What?"

"I don't know—what if it wasn't pretend, if we could really do it?"

"You'd be a bigamist."

"No, just you!"

"You have a wife."

"But I was thinking, I don't know . . ."

"A wife and two kids. A house."

"I know, but you know, modern times, people leave people, and . . ."

"I'm not marrying you, Saul. I love you but I'm not marrying anyone. I told you."

"I get it, independence, you're young but one day, you know, you get older and I'll be older."

"It doesn't make sense. You and I know that."

"What doesn't make sense one day can."

"*One day.* Okay. Not today."

"I just thought you looked so lovely in that dress, really."

"I told you I didn't like the fucking dress!"

The sharpness of her voice shook him. The car jerked out of the left lane and he came close to swiping a small van before yanking the car back to where he was, at a steady cruise near the Queensboro Bridge. She was not afraid to yell; he always knew this. His volcanic Mona. He looked over at her and saw she was lightly shaking, settling her head against the window. She didn't like the dress. He had to admit to himself that this was a weekend that was as much for him as her, even if he had sold it as a favor to help her deal with two overbearing old world parents, not so different than the ones he had. That was the implicit nature of the scheme—*I, Saul, with my money and status, am helping you.* But it was never quite that. He was helping himself too. He was seeing Mona how he had always wanted to see her, since the day he kissed her under the Unisphere and understood you could declare your love for one person and legally bind yourself to that same person while actually loving, deeply and incontrovertibly, another. This was obvious, any mediocre novel or movie had taught this lesson to him dozens of times, but it was another matter entirely to learn it unmediated, on a weekend in Rhinebeck, this truth. He wasn't going to stop loving Mona.

It wasn't as if he hadn't, in their five years, considered all of this. It was only now he was doing it in the context of his mistress wearing a wedding dress, standing at the altar. None of it was supposed to matter, not really, that was his pitch on the beach over the summer, the cigarette burning. He had offered with a tinge of irony, a winking detachment. He could only be so earnest that afternoon. And then they went and did it and he saw her like that, what she could be.

He kept driving. He wished she hadn't yelled.

"Should I take the tunnel or the bridge?"

She didn't answer.

When he pulled up in front of her tan brick apartment building, like so many others in this enormous and indifferent city, he reached over to kiss her goodbye. She offered her cheek. He popped the trunk and watched her take out her suitcase. He had the urge to smoke and did, lighting a Parliament right there, blowing a cloud out the window. He couldn't think of what to say.

"Let's do lunch this week?" he asked.

"I'll call you," she said.

7

Saul was in his office, his feet propped up on the desk and the *Post* in his face, when Leila knocked on the door. He put the paper down but left his feet up, exposing his argyle socks. Leila knew by now he liked to relax in the morning.

"Fred is here," she said. "He's also got someone with him."

"Shit. Fine."

He lit a cigarette. This would be the last one for a while.

Fred Christ Trump would bitch and moan if Saul kept smoking in his face.

Everywhere else he was Mr. Trump or simply Trump, but among the Rockefeller staffers and those who dealt with him intimately, he was Fred. He was to be endured, like winter in New York, too overwhelming and inevitable to question for long. At least Rocky was Rocky—playboy, slapper of backers, irredeemable horndog—and understood money alone wasn't going to get you through your days. You need *good* time, not simply time, and not *all* time equaled money. A fine cigar, a bottle of liquor, or a good fuck was not going to increase Rocky's net worth or build a thruway, but it all still mattered, added lushness to an existence. Fred, who hated to be called Fred and therefore was never called Fred to his face, believed in none of that. He had allegedly sired several children, though Saul could not understand how such a frigid son of a bitch channeled warm blood into his prick to make love to a live female. Fred had never laughed, at least as far as anyone in state government knew.

"Right this way, Mr. Trump," Leila said.

Fred arrived in a large black overcoat and an old-fashioned felt derby hat of the like Saul's father always wore. He nodded, saying nothing, and settled in one of the chairs in front of Saul's oaken desk, which bore his files, scattered newspaper, an Olivetti typewriter, and a fresh pack of Parliaments. He quickly swiped the cigarettes out of Fred's sight.

A kid followed Fred in. Well, not a kid exactly. He was somewhere in his early to mid-twenties, wearing a dark blue suit and a maroon tie that matched Fred's, though his, unlike Fred's, did not have small polka dots. The kid looked a little like a demented Robert Redford, blonde hair combed and gelled aggressively, a slight smirk cutting across his face. He was taller than Saul, over six feet, and bore a glancing resemblance to Fred, mostly in how his nose and chin punched outward, the bone assertive and alienating in a way that nevertheless could be construed as sufficiently masculine or even handsome. Robert Redford crossed with the Joker, Saul thought. The kid sat down hard, crossing his legs, his smile fading as Fred turned, lips shut tightly, to regard him.

"Mr. Plotz, this is my son Donny. Donny, why don't you *shake* Mr. Plotz's hand?"

The kid's rose-gold complexion drained. He offered a small hand and Saul shook, feeling the warmth and strength of his grip. He had never met any of Fred's kids before. Fred's family was never much of a consideration. At some point, one would have to take the reins of the real estate empire, but Fred was nowhere close to relinquishing control. He was, Saul guessed, close to seventy, his hairline long receded, grays shining through the brown coloring he still applied to fight time. If he spoke like an older gentleman, softly and icily with a yawning New York accent, none of it undercut his naked weight, what he carried as a builder. His apartments were everywhere, housing tens of thousands, his name slapped on as many developments as custom would bear. Saul had known of him since he first entered government, this morose, Germanic presence in bespoke three-piece suits lording over the outer boroughs, omnipotent once you entered a certain inner sanctum of deal-making. Fred always lurked.

Now there was a kid shaking Saul's hand. A new Fred. He was thankful Donny let go of his hand and settled back into his seat.

"Donald," the kid said, trying to smile.

"He likes Donald now," Fred said. "Kids grow up, right? You've got a couple yourself, if I recall."

"Two, yes."

"I've got five. Donny—*Donald* here, he is in the family business, as you might know. I recently promoted him to president. He is still learning, though. If you don't mind, Mr. Plotz, I invited him here to sit with us and note take. See how two men talk about the important matters." Fred turned back to his son. "You remembered your pad?"

"Yeah," the kid said. He reached into a small bag at his feet and pulled out a yellow legal pad. Fred dipped into his pocket and fished out a pen. Donald pinched it between his fingers like a dead fish.

"Good. What I am trying to teach Donald, Mr. Plotz, is that our trade is vitally important to the survival of the metropolis, but it's not all glitz and glamor. He wants to be a Manhattan builder. I can't begrudge him the bright lights, it's a lure, but we all start somewhere, and sometimes the fortune to be made is right under your nose. We're all Queens boys here."

"I grew up in Brooklyn, but close," Saul said.

"Very good. How are things overall? How is the Governor these days?"

"He should be back from vacation soon. A little family trip to refresh."

"Of course, politics is a rough business. Donny—" Fred peered over at his son, the gangling blonde who could not pass for the A-list, Saul decided, but could easily slot in with the B and C-list Hollywood actors stumbling on and off the lots. The kid had an off-kilter magnetism. He looked up at his father.

"Yes?"

"What are you doing?"

"Note-taking, like you said."

"Note-taking on *what*? We've only exchanged pleasantries."

"I'm just, you know, making a record."

"Make a record when it's worth making one. Lesson one." Fred peered at Saul. "You've learned that one, I'm sure, a long time ago."

"Maybe, yes . . ." Saul was not sure where all of this was going. Mona was probably getting lunch by now. If he weren't in here, stuck with this old fucker, he could be out with her, eating pasta or seafood and having an actual good time.

"I like that map over there."

Fred gestured to the side wall where Saul had pasted a large map of Queens County, all the streets, avenues, boulevards, and highways colored in. Saul had an affinity for maps, poring over routes and imagining himself an explorer of old, charting a course through the unknown. He liked to follow the red and blue arteries on map paper to see where they led, how they tangled.

"Oh yeah, I've had it a while. It's a reminder of just how important the job is, how big the borough, all that's at stake."

"Yes. Very much so. Queens alone has two million people. We would be one of the very biggest cities in America if we broke away. So many lives bound up in this place. Since I was a little boy, I've thought of that."

Against his father's advice, Donald was taking notes again. Or doodling. It was hard to tell.

"It's an enormous borough, indeed. The Governor keeps Queens near and dear to his heart. Especially since we've got so many Republicans," Saul said, forcing a chuckle.

"I apologize for coming on short notice."

Fred leaned back in his chair. He had the moustache, Saul thought, of one of those Prussian generals, dark with the lightest gray flecks peeking through in the corners. He cleared his throat.

"I'm concerned about next year."

"Next year?"

"The legislative session. The Governor has been very good to our business, I can't complain too much, but more will be needed. We have projects in the pipeline and many more we would like to start, if only conditions can improve."

Saul rested his elbows on his desk. "Conditions? Do you mean economic conditions?"

"Allow me to explain. We at the Trump Organization are not optimistic about the economic forecast. Building is slowing, the bond market is slackening. Cities, unfortunately, are not what they used to be. Crime is a tremendous drag on growth. I know the Governor is concerned about this, that he understands the lawlessness we see, the robbing and killing on our streets, cannot persist unabated. If the state of affairs continues as is, I know many developers who may walk away from the business altogether."

"We're still seeing many shovel-ready projects."

"*Legacy* projects, Mr. Plotz. I pray for the future of the city. If the builders migrate, the people like you and I who *do* things and want to put in the honest day's work, if the shiftless and the criminals are allowed to inherit what we've left here—I fear, truly, what's to come. Imagine maggots feeding on a carcass."

"That's vivid," Saul said.

"The city is full of criminals," Donald said, looking up from his pad.

"Governor Rockefeller can't control the urban crime rate alone. Maybe you should have this meeting with Mayor-elect Beame."

"My boy has a small point, in his crude way," Fred said.

"I can't go ten feet without some bum asking me for money. It's disgusting. There's garbage everywhere, on all the sidewalks, all the prime real estate. If you go out after 10 p.m., someone is going to put a gun in your face. All the wrong people have power now—the thugs, they have it," Donald said, seemingly gaining confidence as he spoke. It was like a football fan getting a chance to opine about the Giants offensive line during a mathematics seminar.

"The NYPD has its hands full, yes." Saul was still trying to see where Fred, with his blonde lug of a son, wanted to go with this. "These can be uncertain times."

"More cops on the beat for starters. But I know that isn't your job, Mr. Plotz. What I came here today to talk about is the context of what I am going to need next year. Business, as it's done, in my field—it can't continue as it's been. The center, as they used to say, cannot hold."

"And why can't it hold?"

"The Trump Organization will all but cease construction without a new tax abatement from the city and state. It's that simple. Construction is still hardly budging at all. I plan to travel up to Albany myself to meet with the Governor about this but I wanted to first make him aware, through you, that the men in my field feel very strongly about this. It is hard enough to do business here."

"The state and federal government has been generous to you, over the years, Mr. Trump—"

"I would not characterize it that way. But what I will say is that I fear the next generation of politicians and leaders will lose appreciation for all we do. Development undergirds the modern society."

"That's true. But we just created the 421a abatement two years ago. We cut your property taxes for developing the vacant land."

"It's a start, Mr. Plotz. What I am saying is, to steady this city against the decay, the rot, Governor Rockefeller is going to have to do far more. 421a is a finger in a dyke."

"Let's say I wanted to develop, I don't know, a hotel—what good will 421a do me?" Donald asked.

Saul could feel his heart begin to pound. "What hotel? Where?"

"Donny is floating a hypothetical, Mr. Plotz."

"Donald."

Fred placed a hand on his son's shoulder. His brittle smile was like a wood-carving, inert in the fine, queer flesh of his reddening face.

"Yes, how I forget. My son is a quick study and you will see, his mind can be very active, overactive even, but he makes a point. There are derelict properties across the boroughs, in Manhattan, that would need far more than a property tax cut, especially if these properties are not vacant. Individualized, longer-term abatements, with a guarantee to last decades—this is the future, Mr. Plotz. The tax burden placed upon our shoulders, in easy and fat times perhaps, would not be something for us to grumble about. But we live in extraordinary times."

"So you want a new abatement for next year. A new designation? I'll have a message sent to the Governor and you and he can work out the particulars."

"Quite frankly, any new project we break ground on, from here on out, should have a forty-year abatement or some similar range."

"That's many, many years."

"You object, Mr. Plotz?"

"Governor Rockefeller would have concerns."

Fred pursed his lips. His son continued to scribble on the yellow pad. Saul wondered if Donald was drawing cartoons.

"Permit me a moment to tell a story. I take it you have a little more time?"

"Always for you, Mr. Trump."

"You live on Long Island, correct? Nassau County?"

"I do."

Saul didn't like that Fred knew that. He was trying to remember how. There was a rumor the old man kept dossiers on all government officials he needed to interact with on a regular basis.

"I do not want to leave my beloved home. In Jamaica Estates, I raised my family in a Tudor-style home I designed myself. It was an oasis. The city can be a rough place, but never our neighborhood.

The greenery, the quiet, the good cheer. It showed what was possible if everyone worked hard and came from good stock. It was a society. And every year, just beyond our border, I could see the city changing. It was not what I grew up with."

"Nothing is as it seems when we were young."

"Ah, but you are still young, Mr. Plotz. Not even forty. Wait until you are my age and you have seen what I have seen. Wait until you learn to measure the present against the past. The past gains most resonance as it recedes. We see its flaws, as well as its strengths. Today, I fear, Jamaica Estates may be little more than a Fort Apache. The barbarians come to the gate."

"And who exactly do you mean, the barbarians? Who do you mean, Mr. Trump?"

Saul had to be careful. He could scald Fred with his righteous liberalism, his unstinting belief in the equality of man and the urgent need to further the cause of civil rights, but a pissed off Fred C. Trump would be on the phone with Rocky, Saul's name in the old man's mouth.

"You are an educated man. I do not need to spell it out for you. The law-breakers, those who'd rather terrorize hardworking New Yorkers than work themselves. There's an element here, sadly inherent to their make-up, to their the genetics. But I am not a scientist. What I am saying is that we may find ourselves more besieged in the future. Neighborhoods are changing. I have nothing personally against Negroes. There are a fine number of their lot. But it's a numbers game now. The more of them, the land value decreases, it costs more to build, the profits aren't put back into the community, into the workforce. I was talking of Jamaica Estates, my Fort Apache. My son here remembers what it was like when you could cross Hillside Avenue without fear for your life."

"I remember," Donald mumbled, still poking at the yellow legal pad.

"It's not sustainable," Fred continued. "Once my neighbors start to leave Jamaica Estates—many of them are selling, Mr. Plotz—it is all, tragically, downhill from there. They are the canary in the coal mine. If the hardworking taxpayer with a sturdy home, a two-car garage, and a well-manicured lawn can no longer live here, no longer *wants* to live here, you will not have a society."

"A new tax abatement then to stem the tide. I'll tell the Governor what we discussed. And I am sure he will be happy to meet with you too."

"An abatement that carries further, goes deeper, does the real work that needs to be done."

"We will discuss it."

"That's all I ask." Fred stood up, reaching for his hat. His son, still lost in his legal pad, put the pen down and turned his head. He yawned. "I really must be going now. I am going to take Donald here out on another construction site. He enjoys the action. The workers are fond of you, aren't they?"

"Yeah. The ones who aren't lazy," Donald said.

"It was good, as always, to see you, Mr. Trump," Saul said, his tongue sufficiently bitten.

"Likewise. Government is a business too. We are here to provide for people. I'm confident Governor Rockefeller will continue to do the right thing."

"He always does his best."

Saul shook Fred's hand and then his son's. For a moment, Donald held his hand and stared straight into him, as if he were hunting for the answer to an especially penetrating or violent question. Saul did not blink. The kid let go, his teeth flashing.

"I'll be seeing you," Fred said, the office door closing.

Once the two were safely gone, Saul sprinted to the bathroom. He poured water and soap on his hands and scrubbed and scrubbed, relishing the heat against his skin, how it flared red as the germs slowly dissolved away.

8

That afternoon, Mona sprinted from the subway, already sweating when she raced to her car parked around the block from her apartment building. She had a tennis date with Liv at Marine Park, on the tail end of Brooklyn, and was desperate to play. At work, it was all she thought about. She could feel her muscles tensing, the dread of another minute not passed—time, once an inexorable arrow, darkly held up—filling her lungs. Every moment built toward her two hours on the tennis court.

On the court, she wouldn't have to think about a wedding, her parents, or even Saul. Monday, she decided, would be solely for her, and maybe Tuesday too. The court was liberation. It always had been, since she first discovered the sport as a teenager and was told this was something athletically superior girls could play, unlike baseball or even touch football, the sports she had preferred growing up. The first time she held a racket, the pimply tennis instructor at summer camp telling her what the difference between a forehand and a backhand was, she knew she had unlocked some kind of key to adulthood, as significant, in many ways, as sex with a man, because tennis wouldn't be dependent on anyone else's wants or abilities. She was alone on the court, freed to crush the greenish, whitish ball as much as weather or court availability would permit, as long as someone could be summoned to stand on the other side of the net and take a beating.

And tennis partners, unlike other partners, required a lot less maintenance: the difference between babysitting a kid and raising a kid. What Mona discovered quickly was that her preternatural gifts on the court were not transferable to the classroom or the romantic arena—where she could be foiled by quadratic equations, the dullness of Shakespeare, or boys who either ignored her altogether or demanded she put her mouth on their revolting little cocks. Tennis was a game she understood on the level of blood, had been raised to play without even knowing what it was. Her forehand was flatter than what the instructor, an ex-high school player, preferred, but her stroke arrived with a frank and devastating power, the girls in her age group quickly chased from the net and confined to the baseline where they could impotently wave and miss at her furious shots. And woe be the girl who tried to play serve and volley against Mona: head-hunting soon became a favorite pastime. Her backhand, a one-hander with a slice she quickly taught herself, could be called a weakness, but she ran around it enough to make it not matter, the forehand punishing everyone who stood against her.

Naturally, Mona's serve was humbling too. As she began to play more at camp and later on the public park courts, she encountered girls who had been schooled in the game from early childhood, their footwork impeccable, their topspin crisp, their second serves dutifully sliced in after the firsts, without much pace, sailed wide. They could be dangerous because they were trained to not make mistakes, to keep the rallies going, to serve and then volley and plop drop shots like gentle kisses just over the net. Against each other, they were never rattled, committed to the principles drilled into them by their early coaches: the stutter steps and rhythmic breathing and visualizations of probable success. But Mona's serve could cancel it all out. It was the equivalent of a deus ex machina, arriving from nowhere, a violator of all preconceived narratives. At first, she couldn't always get it in. Unlike the other girls, she didn't bend her knees much and stood too upright, her ball toss not soaring enough, the approach of a so-called amateur. She never changed it. In the early matches, she persevered, missing first serves and trying to smack the seconds with almost equal power, living the life of a double-faulter, learning to break her opponent's serve with her liquid reaction time and forehanded aggression. Eventually, repetition allowed her to control the first serve, to keep it in the box, and soon she was racking up aces against the daughters of industry, poor things who had never met an angry Brooklyn Jew who needed to make up for a lot of lost time. She had never played on the tennis team in high school because one for girls did not exist. At expensive private schools and certain academies, girls could play, and play they did, holding their own against Mona until she decided it was a waste to beat herself with unreliable play—too many forehands sizzling beyond the baseline—and far more preferable to make others beat her, which they could rarely do.

Liv, when they met, was one of the best players she had ever encountered. Her father, who played for the tennis team at Brandeis, had given her lessons since she was six years-old, taking his toddling, blonde little girl to the clean, unmolested courts of Nassau County—no cracks in the cement, no open cans of beer poured in the double's alley—and showing her the advantage of the continental grip, how to lob an opponent at the net, how to *brush up* on the ball to make sure it bounces nice and high. Liv had played in tournaments as a teenager, never winning outright but always walking away with a medal of some kind and eventually a junior East Coast ranking. By the time she fled the suburbs for City College, her interest in the sport had waned and only picked up again when she met Mona and learned she had an unquenchable, almost savage thirst for the sport, beyond anything she ever knew.

At first, Liv would win. She had to. Liv's pride kept her from succumbing to her new friend on the court. Victories would come with friendly tips, how to bob on the balls of your feet when waiting for a shot, how to deaden a drop shot, why she should turn her body to the side to hit an overhead. They were only five months apart but Liv could feel like a mother on the court rearing a much more talented but unfocused daughter. Their early matches followed a predictable pattern: Mona's raw power knocking Liv on her heels before the unforced errors piled up, Liv rekindling her composure, and slowly but surely wearing Mona down. Mona once shattered a racket head over her knee.

But unlike other teens who could let a tumultuous relationship with a sport spoil their overall commitment to getting better at said sport, Mona had the champion gene for making rage useful. An athlete could take one of two roads: self-immolation or self-actualization. Tennis thrilled her too much to let it destroy her. She would rather tame it. Liv saw the improvements sometimes mid-game. The serves that screamed in, not out. The backhands that generated just enough spin and slice to compensate for their relative weakness. The forehands that were primal, entirely unreturnable when Mona could set her feet and clobber them down the line. The speed Mona began to acquire, her calves toughening with the months and then years spent hustling up and down the burning cement courts of the New York City Parks Department, was astounding too, her body willing itself to wherever the ball was going to be.

By the time Mona and Liv met for their Monday afternoon tennis date in Marine Park, Mona was winning all the time.

Did this bother Liv? At first, a little. It was only natural. Liv had won far more than she lost in her lifetime spent playing tennis. A loss to a friend was still a loss. If she didn't crave tennis as much as Mona did, she still took pride in her effort, the precision and guided aggression passed down from her father. Losing was a yucky feeling. Yet she had to concede, once Mona mastered herself and the forehands and serves began thudding between the lines, she was in the presence of an athlete who had arrived on this planet with that ineffable and inexhaustible quality, *talent*, that could simply not be taught. Had Mona started a little earlier, maybe found her way to a girls' program or an academy or had just been taught the game

by a tennis-playing father, she could have competed on the professional circuit. Liv liked to go watch the U.S. Open at Forest Hills, the
game played on grass, and the women there did not hit the ball much
harder than Mona did. They had simply been engineered at a much
earlier age to play.

Those years, Mona would never have back.

They came to Marine Park early enough to get a court. It was late
fall, almost winter, but the real players played through all seasons,
even shoveling snow off to get a game in if the sun was shining and
the temperature hovered above freezing. Mona was first, pulling into
the lot, wrenching her bag out of the backseat, two rackets and a
can of balls bouncing within as she flung it over her shoulder. She
secured a court in the corner, #5, and began stretching and waiting
for Liv. She watched idly as two men, somewhere in their thirties,
rallied to her left.

Liv came fifteen minutes later. They didn't talk about the weekend. While Mona preferred shorts and a sweatshirt, Liv still played in
white tennis skirts unless the weather turned too cold. Today, above
fifty with a strong sun, she could wear the skirt, a crowd-pleaser with
the men who always managed to hover. After a bad break-up last
year, she was militantly single, but that didn't mean she couldn't take
the time to flirt with the right target.

Mona found most men too boring to flirt with.

"Two out of three?" Mona asked. They were knocking balls
lightly back and forth, Liv just beyond the service line, Mona a little
further back.

"I don't have three sets in me today."

"Then just beat me in two."

"Easier said than done, Mona my dear."

"We have to play two."

"Maybe one?"

"Two sets. C'mon."

"You could play nine sets if you wanted to. It was a tiring day today, Bentley was all over me with nonsense paperwork." Liv was a secretary at an advertising firm in the city. Ward Bentley was her incompetent boss. "I also feel a little twinge in my knee."

"Emphasis on little. Play through it."

"We aren't all iron women."

"Give me two sets today and I won't bug you on Wednesday."

"Two sets, fine. Maybe I'll throw in a nice friendly rally after."

"Alright."

Liv spun her Wilson racket. If the W landed up, Mona served first. If upside down, Liv served. Mona watched it spin. The W was upside down and Liv took her position, a ball tucked in her pocket, the other in her left hand. As soon as the game began, Mona knew it was going to be over quickly, and that made her a little sad. Liv's serves were weak, flailing to Mona's forehand side, and she found herself putting the ball away crosscourt and down the line with routine precision, a union of accuracy and power she had only discovered in the last year. Liv only won a single point in the first game, two in the second, none in the third. When Mona served, all Liv could manage were defensive pokes. If Mona didn't ace her, she drove the ball straight at Liv so all she could do was crack the ball off the frame of her racket. If it happened to bounce over the net, Mona slammed it away.

It was 3-0, 4-0, 5-0. Mona had a habit of announcing the score but eventually stopped when she realized she was saying "love" far too much. It was "forty love" or "love forty" a staggering amount of the time. She was unused to this. Liv usually scraped for more. In the sixth game, Mona decided to work on her backhand, and this didn't spare Liv much either. Her one-hander had gained strength, cutting the ball on a sharp diagonal away from Liv's outstretched racket. She smacked it on the second bounce, far wide and onto the neighboring court.

"Set point," Mona said quietly.

The ball rolled down the middle of the next court as the two men were rallying. The taller of the two, tanned and deceptively muscular in a white V-neck sweater, smacked the ball from their game into the net and groaned loudly. He watched the ball from Mona's court continue to roll, past the service line to the double's alley, nearer to him. He bent down to pick the ball up, pinching it between his thumb and forefinger.

"Ladies," he said in a baritone. "Please keep the ball on your court."

"Sorry about that," Liv said.

The man bounced the ball back to Liv. "If you can't keep it on your court, you shouldn't be out here where others are trying to play."

"Relax," Mona said.

"I was perfectly relaxed until this cheap, deadened ball came bounding onto my court. In the future, be much more careful."

"Fuck you," Mona mumbled.

She won the first set 6-0. In the second, Liv battled as much as she could, finally holding serve as she strained to hit as many balls as she could to Mona's backhand. After Liv's first game victory, which gratified Mona because it meant she could play at least a seventh game in the set, she reared back to serve, driving the ball deep into the corner of the service box. It scraped the line, a perfect angle, and Liv raced to place her racket on the ball, survival on her mind. She was too far away. Instead of tapping the ball back toward the court, she stumbled and slapped it sideways, right toward where the two men, tennis sweater and his shorter friend, were in the midst of yet another rally. Mona watched Liv's face collapse. This time, her ball was rolling straight at the man's white sneakers. Just as he stepped back to hit a forehand, the ball bounced off his heel. The forehand connected, but the rally ended on the next shot when his opponent drove another forehand cross-court that the man in the sweater couldn't retrieve. Rather than pick up the ball his opponent had hit, he turned to Liv and Mona.

"Ladies! Again!"

The man walked over to their court, his fingers beginning to clench. They couldn't quite become fists but they were verging in that direction.

"If you can't keep the ball on your court, seriously, you should not be out here. It is deeply disrespectful."

"Look, I'm sorry, it was an accident—"

"You've ruined our game with your shoddy play. Why don't you go play in the back courts with the other girls? This is a men's side anyway."

"I wasn't aware of any gender designations," Mona said.

"These are *informal* arrangements that keep everyone's sanity. I am glad you feel liberated enough to play out here but if you can't do it adequately, you are going to spoil it for everyone with your lady playing."

"What do you mean, *lady* playing?"

"You know exactly what I mean. Now, I've wasted enough time here. I suggest you either learn to play tennis or go somewhere else. Preferably, learning elsewhere, so more errant balls don't end up on my sneakers and I don't nearly trip and fall and break my ankle.'

"Fuck you," Mona said, louder this time.

The man's eyes predictably narrowed. He had the face of a state trooper in a low-budget movie, solemn and sun-scorched, his dark sideburns subtle but visible enough. He began a slow walk in Mona's direction. She wondered if he had a sidearm on him.

"What did you say?"

"Mona, let's just go," Liv said to her, approaching the net.

"I said, *fuck you.*"

"The girl is angry I see. Tennis is a hard game. Maybe someday you'll learn it."

"I'll kick your ass right here."

Everyone turned toward Mona. The man in the white sweater began to smile.

"Oh really, Billie Jean King?"

"Best two out of three. Or three out of five if you want. I don't care. I'll beat you."

"Did you hear that?" The man spun around to call out to his opponent who, like Liv, seemed to want no part in whatever was going to happen. "She wants to play me. The lady who can't hit the ball straight wants to waste my time. I'll pass. Women's lib is cute. Go home, get your nails done, and work on that game of yours. Maybe someday I can give you a lesson."

"You're scared of me. I'll kick your ass and you know it."

"Foul language, girlie."

Mona approached him. She sniffed weakness in his bravado. "Let's play and after I beat you, I can shove this racket up your ass for good measure. Let's see if you can walk home straight on those tan little legs of yours."

"I'm not going to embarrass you. Besides, you've already embarrassed yourself."

"Let's just go," Liv said through gritted teeth.

"Hey Alec! Why don't you just play her? It'd be fun." It was the park attendant, Lonny, shuffling up to the center court. Both of Lonny's hands were jammed into his pockets.

"I am *not . . .*"

"Battle of the Sexes, part two. Avenge one for mankind! Eh?"

Mona began to smile.

"He's afraid, Lonny. Afraid of a girl."

"I'll cream you in two sets and then I'm getting a beer somewhere far away from here. This all such a waste of time."

"I'll be the line judge," Lonny said. "Got nothing better to do. Let's do this."

Mona walked to the side of the court where Alec's opponent had been. He sheepishly shuffled away. She wasn't quite sure what she had done, beyond guarantee herself more tennis. Before he began shouting at them, she had hardly noticed how he played. He was a man, which meant he probably hit harder, but other than that there was little else to go on. But she would use the rage as fuel, as she always did. That would have to be enough.

"Ladies serve first," Alec said.

Alec, she thought. What a stupid name.

"Gimme the fucking ball."

She watched him get set at the base line, his knees low, his ass out. She could tell he was a club player and had taken lessons, maybe read a book on tennis psychology. His grip on the racket was ideal. He shifted on his feet as she tossed the ball skyward, coming down as hard as she could, a sharp grunt cutting open the silence. She rarely made a noise like that. The ball smacked the middle of the net. Fault. Again, she would come just as hard, she decided, conceding nothing on the second serve. As the ball flew out, well out, Alec had his first point.

Her next serve hit the net again, popping back onto her side instead of rolling over for a let. She could slice in a second serve—the slice was a weakness, hit with only a mild spin—or come in for something flatter but with less speed, a get-me-over serve. But that would be giving him a gift and Alec wasn't getting any gifts from her. She reached up, her muscles burning in her back, and crushed the ball straight into the net. Now Alec had two points.

"Thirty love," he said, shaking his head and smiling.

Her hand began to shake. She couldn't double-fault three times in a row. She hadn't done it in years. Not since she first started out and the serve was an equal source of power and mystery. Turning to Liv, who was pressed up against the windscreen, she shook her head. "Take it easy, Mona," she said. "Nice and easy."

The next serve came in but it was nothing like her usual first serve. It was straighter, slower, down the middle of the court and she knew the mistake as soon as the ball left her strings. Club players don't miss serves like that. Alec's forehand was long and artful, an imitation of the technique employed by most of the pros on tour, the topspin sweeping her away. He had a crosscourt winner, a 0-40 lead, and one more fuck up would mean he had broken her serve.

The first serve wouldn't connect. She cursed under her breath. The ball was so far out it almost struck the baseline. The second was a wobbly slice, barely in, and Alec took it on the backhand, crushing a topspin one-hander down the line. Mona raced and caught it, keeping the ball in play long enough for Alec to direct a winner to the spot she had just run from. It was the end of the most brutal game Mona could remember.

Alec's serve, predictably, came much harder than Liv's. He leaned back further and uncoiled his body in one electric motion, slamming the ball down Mona's throat. The first serve caught the white line and Mona made enough contact to get it back over the net, using some of Alec's pace against him. He immediately rushed the net, catching the ball on the short hop and pushing her into the corner. Mona hated the lob, both trying to do it and when others tried to do it to her, but here she had to try. Sprinting around her backhand to spin a forehand, she knocked the ball high into the air but not very hard.

Alec, laughing, crushed the overhead winner.

"Fifteen love."

He won a quick two points, serving her deep and volleying winners past her. This was abominable. Leading 40-0, he smacked his first serve into the top of the net. The second spun wildly, bouncing to her left when it should've gone right, shooting up to her shoulder line. It wasn't a slice, no, it was that rare bird, the kick serve. She had no idea how to do it. Liv said you needed to whip your wrist in a certain way to create a brushing effect, to apply sidespin. Mona's backhand punched the ball impotently down the center of the court. She could see that fucker Alec's eyes lighting up, his tongue poking out, another winner coming.

Except he hit the ball too hard and low. Mona shuddered with joy when it struck the net. She had her first point.

Tennis gave you an hour, often more, to discern your opponent's weakness, to observe every conceivable shot in their arsenal and the way they reacted to your own. Beyond the court, in the cauldron of everyday life, you didn't get the same luxury of such studying leading to a binary outcome. What she hated about academics—the numeric and alphabetic rendering of judgment—she relished about athletics, how a score, without bias, *could* define you. She had the power to vault herself, almost all of the time, to the right side of the binary. She wasn't nervous here. Alec was expecting her to fold. The next serve came in hard and after a short rally, Mona missed her passing shot and Alec volleyed her into oblivion but she could see, in the sweat beading his forehead, a man used to getting his way who would not know what to do once the tide began to turn. The men in her office across the street from City Hall *always* got their way and so did men like her father, whose occasional self-effacement and unintentional Borscht Belt shtick couldn't mask the fundamentals of his relationship to his wife and who believed, as most men who trundled into and out of Mona's life with the exception of Saul and maybe Al, that one sex was made for talking and one sex was made for sitting and listening. Alec belonged to the same class, muscled in his sweater, strutting up two games to none, sure he could embarrass her in front of a gathering crowd.

Yes, she realized, just about all of Marine Park had clustered around the court. Lonny, a beer cracked open, had summoned them.

Mona would have to give them a show.

"I'll make my serves," she said out loud to no one.

Her first serve bounced in, just enough, and Alec drilled his forehand down the line as much as he could. Mona knocked the ball back with her backhand and she could see, the longer she kept the point going, the more uncomfortable Alec would become. He was trying to come to the net and she kept him moored at the baseline, using his power against him, generating the extra punch from her own legs. The longer the point went, the ball dancing back and forth over the net, the more she felt the building of the crowd, their anticipation and excitement ringing her. She wanted them closer. On the ninth shot of the rally, a forehand she stroked deep down the line to Alec's outstretched backhand, she exhaled loudly. He was there, but not there. His return didn't even land on the court.

There was physical fitness and mental fitness. Both were preached as essential for a successful life on the tennis court but one was much more easily mastered than the other. Anyone could run laps in the park to shed pounds and build stamina. Anyone could get a gym membership. Alec very likely had one. No time on the weight machines or in the lap pool, though, could teach a player how to stave off panic when the game plan, so meticulously conceived in the minutes before the match, no longer worked. Alec was used to either blowing players off the court or wielding his superior technique against them, serving and volleying like the elegant grass court player he probably wanted to be.

Alec didn't like the long rallies.

They went to deuce, she got the advantage, and won her first ad point. 2-1, now she had to break him, and she did, transforming herself into a backboard, bouncing back every shot he launched at her, deciding then and there she would control the pace by letting him set the pace and keeping the ball in play long enough for him to get sick and tired of yet another rally. At 2-2, he let out his first audible curse. At 3-2, her first outright lead of the day, Liv was yelping between points, even though tennis spectators were not supposed to make noise at all. Lonny was stuffing his pockets with dollar bills, taking bets. She recognized other regulars, Boris and Mickey and Carlotta and Harriet, leaning now against the fence, observing coolly what had unfolded before them.

Up 3-2, Mona decided it was time to break Alec for good. He was an inveterate serve and volleyer, a pale imitation of the players on the pro tour, and she was going to make him sorry for being one. He won the first point of the game because the serve was good enough to push Mona back for a weak return, leading to the put away volley, a favorite. But he faulted his next serve and spun in a weaker kick serve that gave Mona time to set her feet and power a forehand deep. Alec, already charging, volleyed across his body, stumbling slightly as he rushed the net.

There he was, in the center of it all, floating to the net, both hands clenched expectantly on the racket's faded white grip. The smirk was gone. Maybe, in that vanishing second, he knew it was coming. Mona's body swung sideways, her right arm firing back for the hardest, flattest forehand she would hit, a full step from her left leg, the right foot dragging along. The ball exploded from the middle of her racket. Mona had aimed for his heart, or somewhere nearby, and to her delight the ball was shooting to his head, first his racket firing up in self-defense and then the squeak of his sneakers on concrete as he began to duck, tripping backwards, the ball skimming the strings of his twisting racket before striking his collarbone.

The crowd, more than a dozen deep now, collectively gasped.

She watched Alec's lips, how they began to form the word "fuck" before melting back into each other, only a small sound escaping. He was going to shout out to her and then didn't. She stood still as he retreated from the net, swiping angrily at the ball and readying himself for the next serve.

It was 4-2, then 5-2.

He scraped together one more game, Mona's backhand slice nicking the net and falling backwards, but she was harassing him on every point, like a souped-up defensive lineman smashing the quarterback after every throw he uncorked. No point was easy. It was all glorious.

When she won the set, on a hard first serve that he returned meekly into the double's alley, she clenched her fist and let out a small scream. Liv clapped wildly. Lonny distributed dollar bills. Mona resented the break between sets, reluctantly slurping water from her bottle, eager to demolish Alec again. She watched him run a towel over his damp face. She was hardly sweating.

"You're doing it," Liv said.

Mona could only smile. "Of course I am."

And then Alec, after slapping two consecutive forehands well beyond the baseline, began to limp. First lightly, then exaggeratedly, clenching his thigh and grimacing.

"My hamstring," he said, loud enough for everyone to hear. "I've been playing through it and—and it's really acting up on me."

"Oh bullshit," Mona said.

On the third point, Mona returned a slower first serve into the net, an accident of hitting too downward on the ball. Alec continued to limp.

"I'm going to try to play through it."

"You better."

Mona easily knocked back the next serve, ending the point with a fierce overhead at the net. She had her first game of the new set. Alec's limp, or performance of it, kept increasing. He could hardly walk at all.

"I think I'm cramping."

"You said you had a hamstring."

"And a cramp."

"Fella, you gonna finish or not?" Lonny asked.

"If I can, you see, the hamstring is a serious matter and I'm under doctor's orders—"

"What doc?"

"Excuse me?"

"What doc? Whose orders?"

"If you *must* know, my personal physician, Dr. Fishman, he has an elegant little office on East 74th Street—"

"You don't gotta give me *War and Peace* here."

"You asked . . ."

"Hey," Mona said. "Are we playing or not? Are you quitting on me?"

"I am not quitting. Sometimes, there are more important things than one little game."

She turned to Lonny. "He's quitting because I'm kicking his ass."

"Looks that way," Lonny said.

"You both don't know what you're talking about. I am not risking my health here. Especially not on *these* courts."

Mona sincerely wanted to knock all of Alec's teeth down his throat.

"If you refuse to play, Mona wins. That's it," Lonny said.

"Then Mona *wins*," Alec sneered.

"Good game, asshole."

"Such refined people out here, with such good manners."

"Shake her hand," Lonny said.

Liv was now standing at Mona's side. "Do it."

Alec, shaking his head, offered his hand out. Mona took it, gripping as tightly as she could.

"Good game, Alec," she said.

"Good game."

Mona understood what she had done when just about everyone who had been down at the courts playing that afternoon surrounded her. They rubbed her shoulders, patted her back, whooped and congratulated her, Liv at the forefront. It was the greatest tennis they had ever seen at Marine Park. *A woman beating a man.* Just a few months ago, Billie Jean King had defeated Bobby Riggs, a former male pro, who had taunted and belittled her, but Riggs was past fifty, washed up, doomed from the start, everyone who really followed the game knew. It was a stunt. Riggs may have even thrown the match to pay off debts to the mob, that was the rumor. This was something else entirely. Alec was well-muscled, not even forty. She embarrassed him. In the spring, someone told her right there, the Parks Department was hosting a citywide singles tennis tournament. She could beat all the ladies.

"If they all have glass jaws like Alec, I will," Mona said.

It took a half hour, maybe more, for the players to disperse back to their courts, for the normal play to continue. Lonny took his usual post on the folding chair at the front gate. The sun was setting and Liv threw her arm around Mona's shoulder.

"Well, that was entertaining. What do you want to do?"

"Let's get a beer somewhere," Mona said.

Out of the corner of her eye, she saw Alec in the parking lot, dipping into his little black coupe to drive away. She laughed out loud.

9

Snowfall came early, burying the first week of December. On weekends, when they had a date at the Knickerbocker, Mona would play doubles with Liv and the members there, all older and slower than she was. Playing beneath a white bubble, on the dark red clay, frustrated her. The color reminded her of bloody stool. She hated how the ball bounced.

The night before the family dinner, Al wanted to get a beer. Liv wanted to go but had to get dinner with her father on Long Island. She suspected her father was looking to divorce her mother. This was more inevitable than sad, she said. Both would be better off alone.

Al said he'd meet her at eight over at Patsy's, a neighborhood dive where they had a couple of color TV's to show sports. On the phone, as he hung up, she had called him Alphonse, his proper name, as a little in-joke. He hated how Italian his name could be. Al Sr. wanted his son to play in the Major Leagues and there was a moment, she knew, when Al played the game very well, starring as a speedy center fielder at Lafayette High School. Al didn't like talking much about his time playing high school baseball. His father screamed and hit him when he struck out. He made Al take batting practice until his blisters bled. He loomed like a vicious sentinel over Al's ballplaying childhood, ready to yank him by the ear off the field for a perceived lack of hustle. Unlike Mona, Al had no joyous relationship to sports and had spent his adulthood avoiding athletic activity. No softball leagues. No tennis. He was wiry, sans much muscle, glad to be free of the punishing afternoons on interchangeable fields and lots, fear baked into every swing he took. He was lighter and freer now. Lately, he had told Mona and Liv he wanted to take up painting.

Shortly before Mona left work, she was called into the office and told what she expected all along but didn't quite believe: as of January 1st, they'd be all out of a job. The city was contracting. Layoffs were here. Mona had to reckon with the implications of not having a job. She still had a few weeks to look for one and she'd probably be due one or two more paychecks in January, given how the cycle ran. But she wasn't sure where to apply. What she wouldn't do was ask Saul.

In the meantime, there was the dinner to navigate. She couldn't forget to wear the ring. They would both have to reference time spent together that hadn't been spent together. Since the wedding, she hadn't seen Saul at all. After avoiding him for these weeks, she now very much wanted to see him. That couldn't be denied. She looked at herself in the mirror. Saul was the only man she wanted to be pretty for.

At 7:30, she rode the elevator down in her building. The bar was a twenty minute walk away, several avenues over. Even in the biting cold, she didn't mind the walk. Exercise was increasingly crucial to who she was, the peak power of her body a reflection of what she had to offer the world. The brain was hidden away, but the body was always on display. The memory of beating Alec on the tennis court still thrummed within her. At odd moments, with no one speaking to her or asking things of her, she could relive each point, the force of her strings on the ball and the wrenching of Alec's face, his anguished realization that he would not beat her. Others wrote books, painted pictures, or delivered lectures—she would produce beauty on the tennis court. This was its own calling. Beauty could be synonymous with domination. When the spring came, she would start with the tournaments. Men or women, it didn't matter. If she couldn't overpower them, her will would be enough, her unshakable faith in her game.

She turned a corner, losing her thoughts, when a man thrust a knife in her face.

"Give me everything you got."

It was a demand she almost took quite literally, when she first heard it from his mouth. *Everything?* My talent? My family? Saul? The man was wearing a black cloth mask with slits for eyes. He was her height, maybe a little taller, and his knees were slightly bent, almost as if he were getting ready to return a serve.

The knife was so close she could kiss it.

Shock and confusion melted into fear. She was getting mugged. She was going to be stabbed. She would lie on the ground, bleeding out, no one around to hear her cries. They were on a quiet side street away from the phalanx of apartment buildings that held the eyes of people who could see her and call the police. She didn't know where he had come from. He had slipped between gaps of awareness, to rob and kill her.

"Are you fucking serious? *Everything.*"

The knife blade could graze her chin. Her left hand, beginning to shake, reached for her wallet, buried in the small pocketbook slung around her right shoulder. Along with the ten dollars and change and the stray tokens she had in there was a Polaroid she took with Saul from a trip, years ago, to Flushing Meadows—they had stood under the Unisphere—and she wanted to ensure, somehow, this wasn't accidentally gripped, buried in the folds of her wallet. Her trembling fingers hunted for the cash. Random death—hadn't she always feared it? From a young age, asking her mother where the dead people went and getting no satisfactory answer. The idea that people could simply be *removed* from the Earth for no good reason was always the silent torture of her young life.

When she had her hand around the dollar bills, the man ripped the purse from her hands.

"Hey!" she cried out.

The tip of the blade touched the skin beneath her chin, releasing the first drop of blood. She staggered backward. Purse in hand, the man was inching away from her. Through his mask, through the imprint his lips had created, she could see he was smiling. An instinct came to lunge for her purse, to fight for its return. The man was running away, deeper into the darkness. Her voice had left her. She stood there, pointing weakly, her mouth beginning to move.

"I've been robbed!" she finally shouted.

No one answered back.

Al was flipping through a newspaper he had bought in a nearby bodega. Usually, he read the *News* or the *Post*, same as everybody else. He had never seen this newspaper before. It was a tabloid called the *Daily Raider*. A publisher's note on the second page said it had started just this year.

"Hey, you heard of this paper?" Al asked the bartender, a man he recognized from previous nights at Patsy's.

"I've been seeing it around. They got good photos in there. Very splashy. And they put in a lot of pretty ladies."

It was a paper with extra pop, Al could see that. Some of the stories—BRONX MAN OUTDRINKS HORSE—were downright surreal. A story in the "neighborhoods" section warned of "acid tests" in Brooklyn for the uninitiated, LSD so powerful and illegal it was driving young boys and girls to endless sex and then suicide. On the comics page, he was pretty certain one strip, though drawn in an abstract manner, depicted two dogs making love. Sports featured an anonymous column written by a woman who claimed to be the mistress of a major star on the New York Mets. Al kept on reading.

"You want anything else?" the bartender asked him. His beer mug was empty.

"Yeah, fill me up, another Budweiser."

Mona was running a few minutes late, which was unlike her.

As long as Al had known her, she compulsively kept to whatever schedule was laid out before her. There was a running joke with Liv that if you wanted to get Mona on-time, actually on-time and not punishingly early, just tell her the movie or the party or the tennis match was an hour later than it really was. Liv and Al both liked to be fashionably late. Mona could remind Al of his parents, who also had no fathomable ability to arrive late anywhere. Today, he was the early one. There had been a chunk of time between the end of work and the bar meet-up and here he was, breezing through this *Daily Raider*, sipping a beer. He had an itch to sketch the bartender, a balding, mottled man with a nose like a stuffed fig. He had forgotten his sketchpad. An oversight, he vowed, that he would never make again.

Where was Mona? He checked his watch. Fifteen minutes over. Another beer, half drank. He tapped his fingers on the wooden countertop, tilting his body back on the stool. A long time ago, in dull moments like these, he would practice his swing, an invisible bat gripped in his hands. Quick wrists, dad said.

As he turned back to his *Daily Raider*, Mona shoved open the double-doors to the bar. She passed through a cloud of cigarette smoke, blown by a couple of hardhats smoking cigars in the booth, and sat down on the stool next to his.

"Sorry I'm late."

The first thing he saw was her chin.

"Mona, you're bleeding."

"What?"

"Your chin. Don't you know? Do you need a bandage?"

"Let me see."

She coolly touched her chin, on the point where bright red blood had broken through. It was now on her fingertip.

"I should go wash up," she said.

"Did you fall?"

"No."

Mona sped off to the bathroom. In the women's room, which

was one toilet with a flaking door barely hanging on its hinges, she peered into the mirror. The mark was worse than she thought. It would heal, but it was undeniably there. It hadn't been a dream. The masked man, the knife, the disappearance of her purse. She could file a police report. But she knew it was pointless. Last year, Liv had been mugged on the subway. The transit police couldn't do anything. There was so much shit going on, what was one purse worth? One photograph with one lover? And now a scar. She dabbed it with wet paper towel, wiping away blood. Her heart, she realized, was still racing.

She could hear her mother's voice. *It wasn't like this when I was growing up. Neighbors used to leave their doors unlocked. People were nicer.* Could that have been true when her mother's adolescence coincided with the rise of Hitler? Stalin's purges? Mussolini's savage buffoonery? She hated that she would now have to explain what happened or at least concoct a cover. Al and Liv could have the truth. She would need another story for her parents, something about a tennis injury, if a person could cut their chin playing tennis. But Manny and Esther didn't know the sport from ping-pong, so that would work.

She dabbed her chin again.

"There you are," Al said, putting down his newspaper.

"What're you reading?"

"Something called the *Daily Raider.*"

"I haven't heard of it."

"It's apparently a new paper. A bit zany. I'm enjoying it. But tell me what happened. You seem, I don't know, quieter."

"I got mugged."

"Oh shit."

"So cover me on a beer and I'll pay you back."

"The guy took your purse?"

"Yeah."

"You should file a police report, Mona. Go down to the precinct."

"I'll go tonight."

"The longer you wait, the longer this guy goes running around—"

"Do you think it will matter? They can't do anything."

"Give them a description."

"A guy in a black mask. That narrows it down."

"I'll go with you. Let's go, beers can wait."

"I was looking forward to just sitting here, relaxing. They're cutting my job. But I guess I should go. I do want my purse back."

"It had all your money."

"There wasn't much, honestly. I don't carry a ton of cash. It'll be a pain in the ass to get a new driver's license. I had maybe five subway tokens in there. The purse was a piece of shit. It's why I buy cheap—for situations like these. But there was a picture I want. It's important."

"Family thing?"

"Kind of."

"Friend? Me? Liv?"

"Not quite."

They were standing now, walking out of Patsy's.

"Old flame?"

"No."

"Ah, *current*. I can guess. Our friend Saul."

"Yeah," she said quietly.

"Hubbie."

"Let's walk to the station."

Al rolled up the newspaper and started waving it around like a wand, for no reason at all. Her chin throbbed. When she got back home, she would rub the wound with alcohol. Already, she was imagining the sharp sting on her raw skin. The streets they walked were dark, bathed in the sort of shapeless shadow she had hardly ever considered, never menacing because it all held so little, only the ordinary absence of light. Now she could see where darkness festered, the men with knives who took things, the killers and rapists, those who wanted to negate life. She felt frail, her breath weak. Al, usually a step behind, was now ahead, hovering to wait for her. He tucked the newspaper in the pocket of his coat and smiled at her.

"I've never outwalked Mona Glass."

"It was a rough night. How far is the station?"

"A few blocks. Shit, I'm sorry, I'm just not used to seeing you this way. We'll get this creep."

"We won't. But let's get it over with."

The precinct house was a squat, brutalist building occupying most of the block, cop cars haphazardly parked on the sidewalk out front. She never quite trusted the police. While her friends—the boys—growing up always wanted to be cops or firefighters and later, with the Mercury crew, astronauts, she had no attachment to the people in dark uniforms who carried guns and nightsticks everywhere, deciding who rotted in jails and who got to walk free. No one in her family was a police officer. Any conversation that went on too long with one of them was asking for trouble. If you showed them a person, they could just as easily show you the crime. But she also wished one of them had been around to stop the mugging, to keep a knife blade from cutting at her skin.

Inside the station, beneath the chemical yellow of the heavy florescent bulbs, Mona told the sergeant the story. A heavy-lidded man with brown sideburns and a large mole on his right cheek, he jotted unreadable sentences into a small notebook. She told him the street where it happened. He nodded along as she tried to describe a man wearing a mask.

"How tall was he?" the sergeant asked.

"A little taller than me."

"Five eight? Nine? Ten? What?"

"Five, um, nine."

"Five nine. Okay. Black? Puerto Rican?"

"I don't know, he was wearing a mask."

"Yeah but you couldn't catch the skin color? That's important."

"No."

"Eye color?"

"Uh, it was hard to see, it was dark—brown, I think."

"Five nine, brown eyes. Type of knife?"

"Type?"

"Kitchen knife, butcher knife, bowie knife . . ."

"I guess something like a kitchen knife."

"And he nicked ya."

"Yeah."

"That's assault. I'll make a report. Lotta muggings out there. Were you keeping your purse close?"

"I wasn't swinging it around."

"Young ladies like you, I know you need to look good—my wife is like that—but you can't be uh, you know, out flaunting it and dropping your guard. It's tough out there."

"I wasn't flaunting anything. I was walking to a bar to grab a beer."

"Uhuh. Well this guy, this masked man, we'll put an APB out there. Have the patrolmen looking for masks. I gotta say, it describes a lot of people. It'd narrow a little if you had a race. A white man with a mask, less common you know. Was he white?"

"I don't know."

"Right, well. Let me get your number and we'll call you when we have something."

Mona wrote down her phone number on a piece of paper and passed it to the sergeant. She read his nameplate—Jacklin—and wondered what kind of woman would make a husband out of him. Al was again fiddling with the newspaper. A horsefly passed over the sergeant's nose. He hardly seemed to notice.

"Thanks," she said, and they left.

Al asked her, when they were out again in the street, what happened with her job.

"They didn't fire you, right?"

"Cutbacks. The whole city is shrinking, basically. The budget outlook is shit and that means they lay people off, young people like me. I'm really starting to process it. I'm not sure what I'm going to do. In a few weeks, I won't have a paycheck."

"Jesus. If there's an issue, you're always welcome to stay with me."

"I don't think it'll come to that. I've got some savings, enough for a couple of months, and I plan to find something. I'm gonna start looking."

"God, I hate going through classifieds. And you never know with them. I should see what classifieds this newspaper has."

Beneath a streetlight, he opened up the *Daily Raider* again. He shuffled through the pages, hunting for the job ads. From what Mona could tell, every listing depicted some cartoon or photograph of a scantily-clad woman.

"Uh, all the ads here are for escorts, apparently," Al said. "Erotic massages. Both for men seeking these things and also, well, businesses and agencies looking for people to give them. Oh, and here's one ad seeking a carpenter."

"I think we'll have to try another paper."

"Yeah, this thing is *weird*. Though it's hard to put down. They've got an interview coming next week with someone who said he was with Oswald on the grassy knoll. Right there."

"None of this is helping me get a job."

"You want to work the amusement park with me?"

"I don't have any accounting experience. I don't know how to cook books."

"I don't know anything either."

"Just a run of shit luck, you know? This job and now my purse."

"It'll get better. You'll bounce back. You're Mona, after all."

"*I'm Mona*. Sure. What does that mean?"

"You beat a man at tennis. I wish I was there for that."

"It's what I was thinking about when I was mugged."

"So there's a connection?"

"Either everything in life is connected, or nothing is."

They circled blocks, ignoring the cold as it pressed on them, the black wind sharpening. It was late and she wasn't ready to go to sleep. There was a comfort to Al's voice and what he could represent, a friend who never asked too much of you. You didn't have to perform for him. You would never struggle under his gaze. His intelligence buried itself amiably inside of him, allowing conversations to drift with ease, even if they had weight. He liked to paint. He used to hit baseballs. He grasped the alchemy of mental math. She understood why Liv had dated him. If he didn't exude sexual energy—Saul gave off heat, Al did not—he could still exist in the non-platonic hypothetical, his dark eyes flitting your way, alluring and careless.

"My brother Gino, he's nothing like me," Al said as they passed a pool hall, the neon signage casting a faded magenta shadow on them both.

"You don't mention him much."

"He's actually taking the cop test. He wants to be a police officer."

"I never would want to do that, but I guess people do. I don't want to be near a gun."

"Gino thinks anything that isn't drinking a beer, busting a skull, or, like, a ball sport is *faggot* shit. That's what he always says. *No faggot shit.* I am so thankful I don't live with him anymore. One time I made the mistake of showing him a painting. You know, I was messing around in my room a bit, just watercolors, trying to get down a face. For whatever reason, I decide to show it to him. He's in his room, leaning back in his kid's chair, drinking a beer. My dad always let us drink, by the way, maybe it's an Italian thing, so he's seventeen then, I'm nineteen—it's summer break, a Saturday. Honestly, I don't know why I brought it to him. His eyes get really narrow and he just stares, as if I am literally showing him my penis. *What the fuck is that?* It's a painting, Gino, I said. I am working on a painting.

Why would you do that? See, if a thing can't earn you a buck or get you laid, it's worthless to Gino. He's like my dad. Just like an animal sometimes."

"Melinda and I don't really get along much either. I don't understand her values."

"It's amazing people can be related, right? It makes me so mad remembering his face, like a little ram's. *Why would you do that?* Because there's more to life than fucking broads and the New York Jets, Gino! I think going in that cop station gave me Gino flashbacks."

"Well, it was your idea to go."

"You want the purse back. I feel bad that happened. I'm sure that picture with Saul is nice. How is he? Some wedding that was, glad it passed the parent test."

"We're doing family dinner tomorrow."

"With Saul?"

"Yeah. He's coming. I'm gonna have to wear the wedding band. God help me if my parents catch me on the street. I never wear it. The plan always is, only around them, only with Saul."

"Gino's engaged to his girl already. She's terrible. They both deserve each other."

"Another brassy Italian broad from Bensonhurst?"

"You know the type. The difference between us Italians and you Jews is we are loud but you guys at least have class. Jews would appreciate art, culture, the finer things."

"There are plenty of Italian artists and writers, filmmakers . . ."

"Yeah, none of them on Harway Avenue. I get sick of the place sometimes, is all."

"Maybe move to the city?"

"I should, right? Get a place in the Village. I've thought about it. It's a jump, Manhattan."

"The psychology of being *in* the city. It's one thing to visit. Another to sleep there."

They were standing in front of her building now. She was glad they hadn't stayed at Patsy's. Even the trip to the precinct, with the useless Sergeant Jacklin, was something new. And as much as she loved Liv, she saw the value in one-on-one time with Al.

"Let's get another beer next week," she said.

"That sounds like a plan."

Back upstairs, in the quiet of her apartment, she imagined the man with the mask holding a knife over her as she slept. He would stab at daybreak.

10

Saul was so close, almost to Ocean Parkway in Brooklyn, when the taillights in front of him began to all glow red. Traffic was stopped. The radio told him nothing. No updates from the Prospect Expressway. He could hear a man in a vague mid-Atlantic accent droning on about Nixon, his paranoia, his chances, his ability to win by losing, whatever that meant. Like any impotent flesh-and-blood creature stalled in the carapace of a several thousand pound machine, Saul slammed the horn. The sound did nothing. Other cars followed. The honking melded with the radio man's gray voice. He sat and seethed.

He had to pick up Mona and then swing around to the Italian place on Atlantic Avenue in Brooklyn Heights, Carpini's. Her parents had picked it. More than anything else, he didn't want to be late. Time with Mona could *not* be traded for time alone, in his fucking car. He needed to get there. If this van in front of him could just move, if the tractor trailer ahead of *him* could just get the hell out of the way, if he could mount heavy weaponry to his windshield and blow them all away . . . these kinds of thoughts burned through him, distant genocide on highways, as his car inched uphill, toward the far away traffic light. He could walk to Mona's faster.

The man with the Mid-Atlantic accent was warning of deflation, *worse than inflation, we must consider all possibilities, one can beget the other.* It made little sense. Saul changed the station.

He forgot to tell Mona on the phone to wear the wedding band.

He knew what her parents were like, that Manny and Esther would look for it immediately. Verification. They were of the early century, physicality begetting belief, and a marriage would not be a marriage without trinkets on fingers. He understood. He wore his ring every day. At some point, he had made the continuity error of wearing his actual wedding ring in front of Manny and Esther, years before his playacted marriage to Mona. They hadn't commented. It seemed enough that their daughter had found someone who loved her and also was in possession of a career, material advancement always in reach. This all worked because of who he was. When they shook his hand, they knew this same hand had touched the hand of the governor of New York and, more importantly than that, a Rockefeller, a genuine American king. There were so few of those.

The traffic cleared enough for his car to inch across the intersection and then swerve right to get to a side street. He was ten minutes later than when he said he would be—he very much hated being late anywhere—and, to his despair, he saw Mona standing outside her apartment building, scanning the street for his car. He honked his horn three times and waved through the shotgun side window, which he had rolled down breathlessly.

"Hop on in!"

"There you are."

"Traffic was shit."

"From Long Island?"

"Brooklyn, actually. Let's get over there. You ready for spaghetti and meatballs?"

"Linguini. Slather everything in cheese. For Manny and Esther, this is Jewish Christmas."

"I think they call that Chanukah."

"They prefer eating Italian food to celebrating Chanukah. Especially Carpini's."

"I've never actually been there."

"We went a lot when I was a kid. Me, Vic, Melinda. My father was in awe of the free bread rolls. The idea of getting his basket refilled an unlimited number of times—this was the American Dream. This is why his parents came from pogrom-blasted Europe. For the free bread at Carpini's. Sometimes they have a guy there who plays the piano."

"That sounds nice. A little live music."

"Barely. Usually, it's someone pushing a hundred. They really like those Civil War veterans."

"How are Manny and Esther?"

"Hungry."

"How else?"

"I haven't had time to see them much."

Saul squinted at her when they reached a red light.

"You got a cut on your chin there."

"I do."

She had to decide whether to tell him. Of course she would tell him.

"I got mugged."

"Jesus Christ. When?"

"Last night. I put in a police report, don't worry."

"God almighty, Brooklyn really, it's a place—"

"It's not the suburbs, I know. Wrong kind of people."

"No, I wasn't going to say that at all."

"What were you going to say?"

"Just that, you need to watch out. There are some bad people out there."

"The wrong kind."

"Absolutely not."

"We can't all lock ourselves out there beyond the city."

"If it were up to me—"

"What?"

"I wouldn't live there at all."

Mona hadn't exactly heard this from him before.

"You'd move back?"

"To Brooklyn? In a heartbeat. Even Queens. I've been on Long Island a decade now. That's where we are supposed to go—the so-called serious adults with money—but it's not where I'd like to die. No."

"Then where?"

"I'd live with you."

"You can't do that."

"Not now."

"Not this again."

"Mona."

"Every time we do *this*, get together, now with my parents—fuck Saul, I don't know. It's like we *are* married. But we aren't! It used to be so much easier between us, simpler."

"It still is."

"Maybe for you. You can swoop in and swoop out."

"I would love to swoop in a lot more. I can be around more, if that's it, I can get more time away."

"It's a lot more than that."

"Then what is it?"

"Let's talk about something else, okay." She was staring out the window. "I need a cigarette."

"You said it's 'a lot more' but I'd like to hear what you meant by that."

"You have this obsession with finishing off conversation threads."

"I want to know what you meant."

Saul tried to hold his smile.

"I meant, let's just try to enjoy dinner, enjoy each other, and not let the pressure, the tenseness, whatever it is between us, fuck it up."

"I don't think there's pressure."

"Maybe not."

He tapped his fingers on the steering wheel, the church steeples and rundown brownstones and dun-colored apartment blocks rushing by, the borough locked behind the chilled glass of his car window. On Long Island, with its identical tracts and soot-colored bands of highway, he could feel himself dissolving. Into what? Wending through the city now, he remembered how it teemed, the architecture and organisms so variegated, tugged forth from every conceivable corner of the human mind. In front of Mona, he had been ready to slander New York City. Why? He was sounding just like Felicia. Like every taxpayer gnawing on stale rolls at another Roslyn civic association meeting. He believed in this place after all, he had to, even from afar. Even if it gave him new reasons to anticipate its destruction. Mona was mugged. The fiscal picture, like the crime rate, was not good. The bond market was weak. The rich assholes, with their precious tax and investment dollars, were speculating elsewhere, trying to stake new frontiers in swamps and deserts, all these swelling citadels of resentment in Florida and Arizona and wherever the hell else people went to die in air-conditioning. He was a patriot of the city, now an expatriate, entombed in lily-white affluence.

He sped down Fourth Avenue and swung a left at Atlantic. Carpini's was down toward the water, near a decent used bookstore he knew, run by an old Russian man who barely spoke English. He was eighty at least, old enough to have remembered the czar. Maybe after dinner, he could stop in and browse books.

"There's a bookstore I want to show you," Saul said. "They've got a lot of first editions from the nineteenth century. I think the guy who ran it fought for the Bolsheviks."

"I'd go. My mom and dad will probably want us to go to their apartment after for tea or something, but I don't want to." She held up her left hand, the gold-colored ring slipped on. "How the hell do people do jewelry? Really?"

"What do you mean, 'do'?"

"Wear it? Even this ring, just having it on for a little bit, it just chokes my skin. Jewelry is absurd, I think."

"I don't love it."

"You're a man, though. It's so *easy*. No one expects you to wear a necklace, pierce your ears, put all these rings on your fingers, bear this shit on your skin. Men don't have to perform for anyone. Women are always performing. For you, mostly—for men, but for themselves too. It's a circular firing squad."

"I do just rotate between three or four suits, five or six ties."

"That's the society we've built: one gender, dressing like an action figure in interchangeable identical clothes and with the other, it's like solving a riddle every day. Blouses, skirts, twenty different perfumes, pearls, high heels. I can't do heels. Heels are murderous. They should be illegal."

"I wouldn't want to wear them."

"Tell Rocky to make them illegal, for men and women alike."

Mona saw her parents' station wagon parked right out in front of Carpini's. They had come early. Saul maneuvered into a space four cars down and put quarters in the meter. For him, this would be easy. He had been a husband for a decade. Playing one for them was merely an extension of that existence. She would have to summon another self, one that believed in the marital institution wholeheartedly and had decided to bind herself for life to one individual under New York State law. She would have to summon her *we file our taxes jointly* smile. Saul's double-life was tucked away, a burnished secret far enough from home. Her own would have to be performed for her parents *indefinitely* in the theater of her own life, which had no escape latch elsewhere, no second county to neatly mask it all. Saul could leave Long Island and come here. Her parents were fifteen minutes away. As long as she loved Saul and wanted to see him, it would mean, in some form, perpetuating the marriage lie for the benefit of two middle-aged people who could not stomach a daughter who did not want to live in the way others always had, who was rejecting not just the American dream, but the tradition that undergirded societies everywhere. Her double-life could never be in shadow; by definition, it could exist only without it. Her parents were right to think Saul a married man. He was. They would always have to think the same about her.

If they lived another thirty-odd years, it would be a ruse longer than three or four presidencies. And she'd still be married.

They entered Carpini's together, hand-in-hand.

Manny and Esther had a booth toward the back. A small candle flickered on the white tablecloth. They were talking loudly about a neighbor or relative who had a son who had failed the New York bar and was taking it again. A basket of bread rolls already lay between them, half-consumed, and it was up to Mona to clear her throat and break the thread to show they were here, the husband and wife.

"Mona!" her mother cried out, rising to hug her tight.

"It hasn't been that long . . ."

"There's our bride and our groom," her father said, also rising, his thick hand swallowing Saul's in a salesman's shake. He wore a dark blue tie and an oversized, olive-tinged corduroy jacket, his breath smelling like tobacco. Her mother, in make-up and bright lipstick, was in a dress, her weekend best. It was like the wedding all over again. She sat across from her mother, Saul landing across from her father, the ideal match-up. Manny liked engaging him man-to-man. He was too rotund and phlegmy, too old country, to intimidate, nothing like the WASPs of the boardrooms Saul had to face down every day. He could be won over rather easily, Manny Glass, impressed by the casual flash of a material good—a new watch, a brightly-painted car—or an especially choice anecdote, particularly anything having to do with a Rockefeller. Both of her parents could be placated and angered at the same clip. It was merely a matter of the situation, what was on the offer. Now that Mona was married, she sat under, briefly, a golden penumbra, fawned over like the daughter they always wanted her to be.

As her mother began to talk, asking about the drive over, urging the married couple to order the fried calamari *our treat*, Mona was again thirteen, her mother's manicured fingers digging into her chin. Why this came back now, in Carpini's, she could not be sure. That was the brain's mystery, the illogic of reminiscences, an almost drunken movement from one image to another. Playing rough touch football with Vic and a mixture of her friends and his. A squad that included her scrawnier, less athletic brother. Sometime in the late afternoon, while playing receiver, she caught a pass over the middle and shoved a boy, Felix Sensenberger, out of the way, delivering a hard stiff arm to his face. After the play was over Felix, still incensed, ran over to Mona and started yelling about the "cheap shot." If it was so *cheap*, Mona thought, why was his nose bleeding? Mona told him to stop whining. She turned. Felix yelped and slapped her right across the face. Mona bent over, stunned, feeling the harsh tingle riding her jawline. This time, her hand curled into a fist and she drove it straight into the side of Felix's wobbling face, dropping him to the damp Prospect Park grass. Now all the boys were around them in a ring, screaming for a fight. *You can't lose to a girl, Felix. You can't lose to a girl.* But he could and did. The punch had robbed his language. Bleeding fully, beautifully, he clenched both hands around his face, tears blotting his little chipped glass eyes. He limped away. She lined up on first down and caught another pass, guarded more timidly by a different boy. An hour later, the game done, her mother sat at the kitchen table, smoking a cigarette. Mona and Vic had dirtied their jeans with mud and grass stains. There was a small tear in Vic's white and red-striped t-shirt. When Vic passed, she said nothing, continuing to smoke her cigarette. She stopped Mona. There was a long pause as Vic trudged through the kitchen to pour a glass of orange juice. "Victor, please go to your room," she said. From her voice, he knew this was a command he couldn't shrug off. The glass struck the countertop, empty, and he hurried to his room, the door clicking shut. "Mona, what's on your face?" Mona genuinely had no idea what the question meant. She had not looked at her face in hours. Why would she? Prospect Park didn't have a mirror and she didn't care anyway. Her mother repeated the question. "What's on your face?" Finally, she put down the cigarette and picked up a hand mirror, flashing it like a sword. Mona saw she had redness around her cheek and the beginnings of a bruise, nothing strange after a game of football. "Oh, a kid just hit me. It's no big deal."

Her mother set the mirror down. The wooden backing rattled against the dining room table. "Not a big deal. Your face could have been ruined."

"But it wasn't. It was just, you know, Felix from down the block, he hit me as I went over for a catch—"

"You are no longer a girl. These games are going to end."

"No longer a girl?"

"You are becoming a *young woman*. I didn't raise a savage. These games aren't for you anymore."

"But I'm invited, I play."

"These boys are not going to want to play with you and they shouldn't. Women do not play games."

"Yes they do."

"Who? Tell me. Are there women on the Yankees? The New York Giants?"

"No, but, women play, there are sports . . ."

"I do not see, anywhere, a league for women. And there shouldn't be, quite frankly, because it would be a waste. You are wasting your time, Mona. These boys are going to ruin your face and a woman *needs* her face."

"My face is okay."

"You will stop talking back to me this *instant*, Mona Eunice Glass."

"I'm not talking back."

"You are. You aren't listening to me. Melinda listened. Why can't you? You are not going to play games in the park with boys. You are forbidden."

"But that's not fair."

That was when her mother, her eyes darkening, reached over and grabbed the flesh of her cheek, right where Felix had hit her an hour ago. The pain was immediate and intense, of a degree she never knew on the football field, where the blows lacked the same maturity or intent. Her mother held firm.

"Mona, you will *listen* to me. If I see another scratch on your face from a game you are not supposed to play, you will not be seeing the light of day. Do you understand?"

Her face crushed, the pain searing, Mona could only nod that afternoon. Her mother released her. It wasn't the last football game she played, but it would be the final time she played a game with such abandon before taking up tennis years later, safely beyond her mother's reach. Shortly after grabbing her cheek, her mother had turned on the radio to listen to her "stories" and Mona didn't know what to do except to keep sitting there, nursing her wound. Melinda, back from a shopping trip, shook her perfumed head.

"You should listen to Mother," Melinda said.

Mona was silent.

"No boy wants to date an animal."

And here she was, all these years later, with a man who *did* want to date her, even marry her, the sort of man who was inconceivable to a thirteen-year-old. Mona eyed her mother, older and softer now, rouged up and beaming. She couldn't grab flesh anymore. She believed she had won. The little barbarian daughter had gotten married.

What had happened to Felix Sensenberger? Last she heard, he had graduated from Brooklyn Law and was clerking somewhere. It was strange to think of all those runny-nosed little boys on the Prospect Park grass transforming into men with incomes, wives, and sexual proclivities. Felix would forever be thirteen in her head, smacking her across the face as she caught a lofted pass from Louie Braun over the middle, first down. Felix would forever be the last boy she technically decked. She was sure, wherever Felix and Louie were, they couldn't fathom Mona Glass eating fried calamari in Carpini's with Governor Rockefeller's Queens borough director. As she aged, her twenties beginning to flake away, she understood that childhood selves never vanished into adulthood the way she once imagined when peering up from the vantage of childhood. When she was eight or ten or even thirteen, she conceived of adulthood as the butterfly breaking from the chrysalis, the past shedding, dead and forgotten. The adults were enormous, distant creatures, and to achieve that distance meant to eradicate whatever came before. Now that she was of the age when her parents began having children, she knew this was untrue: childhood could never die. The memories were too thick, too rich, visceral in the way a kiss lingers on the lips or sun burns the back of your neck on the beach—if these sensations never left you, only replayed and strengthened with time. She could remember being thirteen better than where she was a week ago. The past, a ghostly exoskeleton, wrapped her and would not let go.

"Are you looking at any properties?" her father asked.

Mona was chewing a piece of calamari, looking at no one. She realized Saul and her parents had been engaged in a conversation and now they were trying to find a way to draw her in.

"Properties?"

"Not yet," Saul quickly answered. "But soon."

"Get on it. You two deserve to live together. Now, I have a friend who is a realtor, he's very good, if you want any help . . ."

"They don't want to talk to Bernie Green," her mother said, her fork penetrating one of the little fried tentacles.

"Why not? What's wrong with Bernie, Esther?"

"They should go with someone more *modern*."

"Bernie's been in the business thirty years! He knows it like the back of his hand! This is a sin?"

"They might want to go to Manhattan. Right, Saul? You were thinking that? Manny, what apartments can Bernie possibly show them in Manhattan?"

"He has a large inventory and he's very well-respected."

"I like my apartment," Mona said quietly.

"It's hardly a place to raise a child," her mother said.

"I don't know if I'm having children."

"*Yet*, Mona. You don't know the joys of it. I was blessed with you and your siblings. You will be blessed too."

"I said, I'm not interested—"

"How about the Mets?" Saul asked. "I, for one, think they'll be back in the Series next year."

"Not *interested* in children. What can that even mean?"

"It means what you think it means, mom."

"Not *interested* in the human race? In the natural order that has sustained us for thousands of years?"

"I like their pitching," her father said. "Matlack really came on. And Seaver, oh boy, best I seen since old Carl Hubbell, he was before your time."

"I wish I saw him pitch."

"That *screwball*."

"I am *too* interested in the human race," Mona said.

"I don't know what means. I know at least one of my daughters is having a baby next year."

"Melinda is pregnant? Since when?"

"She should be telling you soon."

"God almighty."

"That's great," Saul said, straining to reach a pitch that could convey equal excitement to Esther and nonchalance to Mona, and offend exactly no one.

"That's all she ever wanted to do," Mona said.

"What is wrong with raising a family with someone you love?"

"Nothing is wrong with anything. We are taking our time. That's it."

"What is everyone going to order?" Saul asked.

"I was going to get lasagna," her father said.

"That sounds great."

The waiter came and took their orders. She considered the length of time still left in the meal, an hour easily, and she wondered how prisoners of war managed the suffering and the monotony. Thank God, as time passed, Saul kept scooping up conversation threads, like a hungry point guard chasing loose balls. She knew he was doing it for her, so she had to talk less, and Saul was a subtle master of the conversational filibuster, summoning paragraphs of reasoning and anecdotes on every topic conceivable. She politely nodded, pleased to be ignored, when he expounded on the frailty of the current real estate market and how cities were nevertheless worth the price of investment. Never mind average apartment sales (how did he know this?) plunged for the third consecutive year. Real estate was the soundest investment you could make. Her mother mused about selling their apartment off Prospect Park and moving to Florida, Boca Raton or Del Ray Beach, she had friends going there, and Mona said a silent prayer to the God she barely believed in to make it so. Her father said he didn't like the heat or the mosquitoes.

"But you don't have the winters!" her mother almost shouted, the entrees arriving.

"I don't want to get a mosquito disease."

"You won't get a disease, Manny, if you wear a *spray*."

"I don't want to walk around getting sprayed every two minutes."

"Then you keep staying here with your winters and your crime. I'll be in Florida having a lemonade by the swimming pool."

"You go! Drink the mosquito-filled lemonade."

Her mother, reprising another role she played in Mona's youth, narrowed her eyes and stared at Mona's chin.

"What's that on your face? That a scratch?"

"What?"

"On your face. You have a scar, a cut."

"That? Who knows."

"It certainly wasn't a shaving accident," was her father's attempt at a joke. No one laughed.

"Something caused it."

"Nothing caused it, *mother.*"

"You never tell me anything. Your own mother. And so insolent."

"We're just worried about you," her father said.

"You just want to pry for no reason, to accomplish nothing, to drive me up a wall."

"Mona was ice-skating with me, actually," Saul said, casually putting down his fork, coiled with linguine. "She's a little embarrassed because, well, I'm usually the bad one—I can hardly stand on the things. And she's such a natural and was out there gliding on the ice, trying to show me a trick, one of those, what do you call it, axels, and I got a bit excited and *I* was stumbling and in her attempt to come after me, to help me, she fell. It was at the Prospect Park rink. It wasn't a big deal, right honey?"

"No, it wasn't," Mona said.

"Ice skating, eh? You really got interested in the sport," her father said.

"She used to skate as a little girl," her mother said.

"I liked football more."

"I recall."

"Mona is good at whatever she plays. You should see her on the tennis court."

"Swatting those balls back and forth. My knees couldn't take it," her father said.

"Your knees can't take what exactly?" her mother asked.

"There you go, with the comments."

"Manny, *you* make the comments. You sit there and make them."

"I'm just trying to enjoy a nice and quiet dinner!"

"God help me," Mona said to no one.

"The linguine here is to die for, Manny. But that lasagna sure looks good," Saul said.

"It's very fresh, is what it is. You can tell the sauce was made on the premises."

"It's like Italy."

"Have you been there, Saul?" her mother asked.

"I went to Rome in college. It's the eternal city, you know. You just feel the weight of history everywhere. Such a lovely place. If you go, you must stay in a hotel downtown. I was near the Spanish Steps. It was right around when they were gearing up for the Olympics, so it was a real hive of activity."

"I would love to go abroad. Manny hates to fly."

"I would fly with you, *dear*, that's not true."

"I remember when Mona here hitchhiked through Europe in college without telling us. She just leaves, Saul, can you believe that? I got two postcards that summer. She went without even telling us."

"I did tell you."

"The night before!"

"Well, one day, we can all do a big family vacation," Saul said.

"With your children," her mother replied.

"Yes, with our children," Saul said, smiling.

Mona caught his eye, knowing what he was thinking. There were two children and none of them were ever going on a vacation with Manny, Esther, and Mona. His smile, at least, seemed genuine enough. She couldn't begin to imagine what her parents would think if they knew the truth about Saul. They had so much admiration for him. This was a strength of their relationship, she had to concede, as much as she didn't want to perceive it in relation to her parents. It would be much harder if they weren't slightly in awe, if he didn't have the sort of job that was beyond their reach, in a place of real consequence. Her father had sold women's clothes, traveling to withering cities with single strip downtowns and no professional sports teams. Her mother stopped working when she married. They weren't in a position to challenge the reality Saul crafted for them, of a single man who had no children and married their daughter.

During dessert, a slice of cheesecake on her plate, Mona decided to light a cigarette. She deserved it. Her mother didn't like smoking at the dinner table. Though she was a chain smoker, puffing through a pack a day, she had always insisted on not smoking over food. But she couldn't chastise her daughter because Saul had used his silver lighter to light her Virginia Slims and therefore sanctioned the action. Her mother and father were temporarily tongue-tied.

"Have you picked where you're going to honeymoon?" her mother asked, Mona's smoke cloud dissipating not very far from her nostrils.

"Where were we thinking?" Saul turned toward Mona. "Well, perhaps Vermont."

"Vermont, eh?" her father grunted. "I once went up to Burlington to sell a whole line of garters. It was cold as you know what but you know, I did good business up there. Vermont."

"There must be some scenery there to see," her mother said.

"We're thinking of renting a little cabin. Right, Mona?"

"A cabin, yes."

Somehow, the dinner ended. Mona couldn't remember the check appearing but there it was. A tussle ensued between Saul and her father, who each insisted on paying. She knew Saul would end up paying because he had more money and her father wouldn't turn down a free meal. But he needed to save face, and this took longer than it should have. They each made physical contact with the check. They each, playfully, tugged at the ends. Her father feinted for the roll of cash in his pocket. Saul made the same move, but meant it.

Her mother hugged her goodbye.

"We can't wait until you find a new apartment. You'll want to have plenty of space," she said.

"Yes mom. Tell Melinda, when you see her, congrats on the baby."

"I will dear."

"Mona," her father said, sucking in his breath. She noticed a fleck of cheese between his teeth. "Take care."

"You too."

Saul hugged her father and they separated, finally, for their cars. Mona put out her cigarette, pulled another one from the pack, and Saul lit it for her.

"God almighty, that's over. Thank God."

"It wasn't so bad, was it? Your parents have a little funky charm to them."

"I just can't stand them. The questions. The judgment. There's so much we have to do for them."

"They're old-fashioned, Mona."

"Good lie, by the way. Ice-skating. I haven't skated since I was fifteen. I actually never liked it too much, but I was good."

They were sitting in the car, Saul starting the engine.

"You're good at everything."

"Not really. Tennis and smoking these Virginia Slims. Now, what the hell is this about Vermont?"

"Just an idea I had. A friend of mine lives up there."

"When would this be?"

"In the new year."

"Well, I won't have a job then, so maybe I will be free."

"Shit, right. All the cutbacks. That fucking hack becoming mayor."

"It's fine. It was time to go anyway. I'll land on my feet. Like a cat."

Saul remembered he wanted to show Mona the bookstore run by the Russian. But they were driving now, down Atlantic Avenue toward the water.

"Well, if you need me to look around."

"I'll be fine. I can sniff something out. I am worried though about what we really do about my parents. They expect us to move in together."

"That's true."

"And we literally can't."

"Maybe there's a way to make it *seem* like we live together."

"How?"

"You get a new apartment and you can say I live there too. It'll be a rental but say I bought it. I'll put a few of my things there. It'll be yours, but it can be like a new place."

"I'm getting sick of having to rearrange things for them. I'm half ready, after tonight, to tell the truth."

"They will be quite pissed, I imagine."

"My father could have a heart attack. I almost want to see the look on Melinda's face. That's so like her, though, having a baby and not telling me. You heard my mother?"

"I did."

"Melinda's dream is realized. Isn't that exciting, to know you've done all you set out to do? Have children? That's actually *it*. The be all end all. To reproduce and die."

"I know what you mean. Melinda wants to stay a housewife. You want much more."

"It's natural to want more, right?"

"Of course it is. That's why we're here."

Saul was taking a longer way back, winding along the industrial waterfront, circling toward the highway.

"Yeah, let's go to Vermont next year," Mona said, waving her cigarette out the window. "Something to do. Something different. I'll need a break from the city anyway."

"I'll look into lodges and cabins. I'll try skiing with you. I'm horrific."

"At least you were honest with my parents about one thing—you also can't ice skate."

Saul laughed and Mona did too. They found their fingers touching, then interlocking. He could not remember ever holding Felicia's hand and driving anywhere.

II

Vengeance

1

Mona was old enough to know new years didn't mean new people, new life. It was one cold month, December, rolling into another, January, the snow on her boots the same charred-looking slurry it was a month ago. On the final night they would be employed, the office went out to an Irish bar on Chambers Street. She drank enough to ride the train home drunk, her eyes blurring over newsprint of a *Daily Raider* that had been left on the seat next to her. In the train's corner seat, a homeless man ate a peanut butter and banana sandwich, his lips slopping over the soft, ugly bread. He smiled malevolently when it was gone.

In January, she hunted for jobs in earnest, surviving on savings. She calculated she could pay up to three month's rent before depleting it all entirely, which was more than Liv, who viewed money far more theoretically, could do, though Liv had the fallback of a guilty father always willing to wire her something. Mona would lie on the tracks and let the Sea Beach Express murder her before asking her father for money. Not that he would give any anyway, at least not without a lesson, a proverb, a dead-world anecdote.

Her strong desire not to ask for help would compete with the reality of a job market that quickly wanted to debase her. No one with any income to match her government job was hiring and the government jobs were vanishing by the day. Rumors of layoffs rapidly hardened into fact: thousand of people like herself, young and not particularly feckless, were thrashing about for salaries to fund lives one or two levels removed from bohemian squalor, with a pension thrown in for good measure. Resumes dropped off with secretaries at office buildings were equivalent to resumes dropped off in her toilet bowl, floating uselessly in the murk. No one called her back. At first, too worried to do anything other than trawl classified sections in every daily and weekly newspaper, she remained confined to her apartment, believing that she was building some sort of goodwill by limiting herself to the four sallow walls of her bedroom. She was being the good girl, not playing tennis, not seeing friends, not setting up dates with Saul. She was hunting for work. The second week of January, like black magic, conjured the third, and then the month was over.

She counted fifty-two resumes dropped off or mailed out. Two interviews, one at the Board of Education, the other for a social worker position with a nonprofit that paid $4,000 less than what she earned with the city. Both interviews were without obvious stumbles or gaffes, her performance rated as adequate to mildly exemplary in her own mind, each ending in such a way—a firm handshake and a smile—that could have connoted a job offer. But what she was finding out was that this year was going to be worse than the last and the following year could very well be even worse. The economy, that impenetrable, billion-eyed beast drooling the manna that fed and clothed all living things, was ailing. *Depression*, a word that haunted her parents, was whispered, as was its indolent cousin, *recession*, which Mona learned simply meant negative growth in consecutive quarters. Stagflation was a new one, stagnating wages conjoined to inflation, your capital withering in your pockets. She could feel herself stagflating in real-time, her bedroom constricting, the snowflakes beyond the windowpane disappearing against the glass like the dollars in her bank account. It was February.

Saul wanted to get dinner. Al got to her first, calling and saying he was bored, he wanted to watch her TV. His wasn't working. Mona suggested Liv should come. Al, who could grow fickle when you least expected it, drew a long breath and let the silence in the phone eat at her until she said she'd call Liv. They had a tennis date for Sunday at the Knickerbocker, under the bubble in the clouds of grim clay, and she didn't mind two consecutive days of Liv. As a child, Mona's dream of the 1970s never included stagflation or winter. It was warm, there were rocket launches, money materialized from the recesses of her bright and sunny soul. Maybe, by then, they would let women play professional baseball, and she could patrol center field for a rein-stituted Brooklyn Dodgers, the sin of Los Angeles locked in the cof-fin of history. It was true what they, the inventors of weary maxims, say: you don't appreciate what you have until its gone. Without a job for the first time in three years, she could feel herself receding from the machinery of civilization, less and less a person each day. The little socialist in her, nurtured by pink-friendly Saul, told her this was sick, to define a life itself against capitalism's numeric churn. This was true, she was still Mona Glass, with or without an employer to slide her a paycheck every two weeks. It was also true her values, whatever they were, could not feed and cloth her alone, and indig-nity was not going to be an acceptable payment to the cable, gas, or electric companies.

"Liv, come over," she said into the phone when her friend picked up.

"What's up?"

"Al is coming too. Let's make a day of it. Maybe we can go into the city."

"My cousin wanted to take me to a Broadway show but I'd rather not."

"She bought the tickets?"

"She's one of these box office people, popping up day-of, trying to sniff out a deal. I hate Broadway, especially the musicals. How do we suspend belief and watch plot-driven shows with people singing? We don't sing to each other in real life. We don't belt out showtunes while getting fucked by these men. Well, maybe Al does."

"You're killing me, Liv."

"Let me dump this cousin and I'll come by. Should I bring a bottle? It's one of those cold afternoons. Tell Al I say hi."

Arranging a day with her friends was not like getting a job, but it was an activity she could commit to for the next few hours. She cooked scrambled eggs and threw on a record, choosing *Revolver* over *Songs of Sinatra*, the music of her parents, soothing if unhip. Her childhood had been the Beatles, crackling from car radios and five and dime stores and stray record players in the afternoon light of a friend's apartment, the songs as familiar as lullabies, slowly losing their heat. She loved them but she knew them: John, Paul, George, and Ringo, saints painted on the walls, beyond the sober logic of flesh and blood. She was looking forward to Liv and Al in her apartment, in motion, the kinetic nature of a hangout on a Saturday at the beginning of another ice-flecked February. The snow had stopped. Lennon's cry was real through the kitchen.

Her buzzer rang out. Al was first.

The delay between when the buzzer rang and the person arrived at the door was always a bit strange to her and could send her imagination running. She conceived a scene: Al in the armpit of a lobby, checking himself in the mirror, heaving open the old door and entering the elevator, cat piss at his boots. Maybe Ingrid, the woman who owns the cat, gets in with him. Or Danny the super, the big Irishman, crowds in with his linebacker shoulders, a thin cigarette petering out in his lips. Al was coming. She finished the eggs, laid them out on the plate, and took a bite. She cooked out of necessity. She didn't like to cook. Melinda and her mother were the cooks, proud to assume the roles society gave to them, women in the kitchen, obsessing over the morsels to put in the man's body and later their own. She cooked to feed herself. Saul liked that, he once said, how defiantly against kitchen life Mona was, and she could sense that it was his wife, Felicia, who spent her time there baking cupcakes or banana bread or stuffed shells, taking measurements like a little scientist, tasting a dab of sauce with the soft pink of her index finger. Five years into whatever she had with Saul—a love affair, a soul-bond, a sham marriage—she began to understand, finally, the hold she had on him, in part, was predicated on how much she could defy Felicia's example, be the anti-image, rerouting expectations.

There was a knock on the door, Al's familiar two-part, and she opened it up. He stood there grinning, in his dark overcoat. She let him inside and he took off his boots. Something, a black case with a strap, was around his neck.

"Did you see the piss in the elevator?" she asked him.

"Only the dog shit."

"A big steaming pile?"

"Always. I always ride up with a pile."

"What's that around your neck?"

"A camera. I actually bought this without you. I wanted to show you."

Along with the camera came a copy of the *Daily Raider*, balled up under his arm. He handed her the newspaper.

"Turn to page four."

She turned to the fourth page, where black blocky letters announced a murder on Coney Island Avenue. Unlike typical photos in newspapers she saw, this was in full and brutal color, an image of a bloodied body sprawled on the sidewalk, hands splayed out like Christ's. The man's mouth was slightly open, as if ready to receive a few thirst-quenching raindrops.

"Look at the bottom of the photo."

"In the photo?"

"No, underneath. The caption."

Enoch Gelby, a local supermarket clerk, was found stabbed to death last night. Authorities believe it was a mugging gone wrong.

"Do I know an Enoch Gelby?"

"See who it's by, Mona. Jeezuz. Help me out here."

Photo by Al Falcone.

"That's you!"

"That's me, indeed. You're looking at the new photojournalist for the *Daily Raider*. It's a stringer job. That's what they call it. Freelance. But they pay well for photos like that. Then you get your name in the newspaper. My folks don't read the *Raider* but I'll make them just so my fat fuck father can see my name in there, all the time."

"I didn't even know you took photos. You always paint."

"Listen, I needed to hustle up something extra. The amusement park is struggling and they're actually looking to cut back. It's not long-term. I don't know how long they can keep me on, helping with the books. People don't have money like they used to, Mona. They aren't coming out to get their kicks on quarter bumper cars and a water slide with a mild sludge color. The thing is, what they have me on, they basically call the blood beat. Or, if you work overnight, the lobster trick."

"How long have you been doing this?"

"Only two weeks. I didn't want to tell you. I wanted to have a picture there and surprise you. I wanted to see the reaction on your face, Mona."

"Well, you have. I'm impressed."

"And you can do it too."

"What?"

"Listen, I know money has been tight. You haven't been working a few weeks. The thing is, while just about everywhere else is cutting back, shrinking, bleeding out, the *Raider* is *expanding*. It doesn't quite make sense but from what I gather, they're run by this eccentric British guy, he came into America with millions, maybe a billion, trying to make a splash. Edwin St. Felix. I never heard of him either. Some kind of British cosmetics heir. No one ever sees him. I just responded to an ad in the *Raider*. They don't care about experience. They just want young people who can hustle and have cars. We both have cars. You have that used Lincoln, right?"

Mona did. She drove it maybe once a week and spent the rest of the week trying to park it and dodge tickets.

"I do."

"Well, think about it. You need to buy your own camera. I know a secondhand shop down near where Radio Row used to be. You would like the beat. It's a real rush. You need a stomach for blood."

"I don't know if I have it."

"I bet you do."

She continued to stare at the photograph Al had taken, the man bleeding out on the cement, death in the middle of night. In the first moments Al had made the proposition, it sounded ludicrous, and so different from what she had been doing before. It surely paid far less than what she made working for City Hall. There wouldn't be the promise of a pension, healthcare, the paid vacation. But choices were evaporating. She had been unemployed just about a month. The constricting city, perhaps the fallen city, was not offering her anything more. By not working, she was proving herself to be extraneous to whatever constituted the body politic, the private and public occupations that kept the city from crumbling to ash or heaving itself into the sea or simply not turning the lights on at night. Enoch Gelby—who was he, really? An existence, perhaps, as rich as her own, or maybe more so, and now dead. And she would have to photograph many more to earn her dinner.

"Here's the thing," Al said, straddling a chair in the kitchen, his dark dungarees tight. She had to admit he looked a little attractive. "Murders have been going up every year. It's sick and terrible, but it means opportunities for stuff like this, especially if you turn the lobster trick—"

"Which is?"

"Working the overnight, I told you."

"You didn't tell me."

"I thought I did."

"Thought is an illusion. I can't prove you have thoughts. Produce words to create action. Your inner life means nothing."

"It is rich and fruitful. What I am trying to say is, they'll pay you a decent amount of money to take photos of dead people. You can also get paid per hour to work shifts. I actually have a police radio."

"I've never used one."

"You hear everything. *Shots fired, shots fired.* The mad scramble over life. I'll say this—it detaches you from life's value a bit, if you are prepared for that. It's what the news does. People become fodder for your story, your photograph, their intrinsic value devoured."

"And you like it."

"I like it. I think you will too. Come meet the editor with me."

"The editor?"

"Heed Ezekiel. That's his name. He's not British. I think he grew up on a remote island off the coast of Maine. He talks like he's from Brooklyn, though. Strangest thing. Come with me next week."

"I'll think about it," Mona said.

Al began to gnaw at one of his fingernails. He stopped when Mona shot him a look.

"How's old Saul? You ever going to shack up?"

"I tell him to stay put. I have my own life. I do like it. But sometimes I think it would be nice if he lived here."

"Your parents want you two to move in together."

"I tell them we're apartment hunting, looking for the right place to buy. *Saul insists on buying. He wants good value, a good investment.* I make him out to be such a good capitalist to mom and dad. Saul owns a house. I drove by it once. He didn't know. Can you believe it?"

"Mona Glass, in a lonely car on a quiet suburban street, the swallows in their trees . . ."

"It was four years ago. I don't even like talking about it. It's a minor embarrassment, like getting caught touching yourself. That's how I think of it. It was a Sunday night, I drove out there, the lights were on. It's a quaint two-story house, I can't describe the architecture, I'm bad at that, I lack the words. He has a large front lawn, bushes, flowers, a flattened cobblestone path leading to the door. A red door. The color of a firetruck. That I remember. I sat in the car. Fifteen minutes, twenty minutes, thirty minutes. Do you know how time slows when you are just waiting for it to pass? It's like time knows it's unwanted and sticks to you out of spite. I can't say I know what I wanted that night. Maybe a confrontation. *Here I am.* But what would that bring me? The frilly white curtains on the bay windows were drawn. Like I said, lights on. Dinner time. There were shapes behind those curtains but I couldn't say who belonged to who. I couldn't say much of anything. I was also a shadow, in a car, in a street."

"Did you go again?"

"No. Somehow, it was enough. I did what I had to do. It was to prove something to myself I can't explain."

"Saul, I don't know—"

"You don't like him. You never did. We were in the class together that he taught. We didn't know each other that well, then. I had become friends with Liv first. You were the wiry ex-boyfriend. I remember once you asked Saul about the causes of the Cold War."

"I did, yes."

"You were more of an internationalist then."

"What am I now?"

"A photographer for a strange newspaper. I've got enough socked away to pay another month of rent without working. Then I'm in trouble. I suppose I'll have to meet Heed Ezekiel, after all."

The phone rang. Mona sprang to the living room to pick it up.

"Mona dear, I'm coming over soon."

"Liv, where are you? Al is here."

"I'm calling from a pay phone a few subway stops out. I ditched my prior obligations. Tell Al I say hi. Do you have a bottle of wine?"

"I probably do."

"Well I'm bringing one. Have you been outside today? It's a cutthroat winter day. I use that term quite literally. It can wound."

"Get the *Daily Raider*. Al took a picture of a dead man there and he got paid."

"How wonderful. I want to hear all about it. I'll see you soon."

"Bye."

Revolver finished. Al had fished out a carton of orange juice and was drinking straight from it without asking. That was Al. She said nothing.

"*Revolver* is the best Beatles album," Al said with finality.

"I like it. I like *Sgt. Pepper* more, I think."

"You have it?"

"I don't, actually."

"I like to think about the Beatles when they stopped touring. They knew they couldn't play the songs from *Revolver* live with any authority. The old ways wouldn't work anymore. They were sick of performing, facing death threats, and, from an artistic standpoint, wasting their time on stage. I went to one of the Beatles shows on their last tour. I was just a kid but I knew it was bad, they were going through the motions, you can *feel* a band in a decline. They were wasting away. And then you get the bigger than Jesus controversy."

"I remember that. Even though he was a Jew, it still upset my dad. He called the Beatles arrogant little punks. If Jesus was a fraud, as my dad surely believes, still no one should claim to be bigger than history's greatest fraud. What an affront."

"Lennon thought rock and roll would outlast Christianity. I don't know if that's true anymore."

"Christianity has a two thousand year track record. Hard to argue."

They heard the buzzer a few minutes later.

"And that's Liv."

"I'll get out the wine glasses."

When Liv walked through the door, she rushed to Mona and hugged her. Liv was always a hugger, a cheek-kisser, someone who led with her body. She appeared goyish like her father, Irving Gottlieb, who did not resemble a Jew as much as his only daughter also did not. The one time Mona saw him, on a day trip to Liv's Nassau County childhood home, she was struck by how Aryan he appeared, his eyes light blue, his hair of the same color and thickness as grain. Liv did not like spending much time around him. What she inherited from him, as far as Mona could tell, was a confidence in body, an unapologetic comeliness. Liv wore a bright red designer winter coat, something Mona couldn't fathom trying on, let alone purchasing, and set down her purse on the small glass coffee table Mona kept in her living room. She also put down a wine bottle-shaped paper bag.

"Al was educating us about the Beatles," Mona said.

"A tumultuous period, when *Revolver* was released and they didn't want to tour anymore."

"I always liked the Beach Boys more," Liv said.

"Brian Wilson had a mental breakdown hearing *Sgt. Pepper*, it was that good," Al said.

"Well, I hope this wine is that good too."

"No wine is that good," Mona said. She turned toward the *Daily Raider*, now rolled up in the kitchen. "Liv, do you want to hear about what Al is up to?"

"Oh, I am sure Al will tell me."

"He will," Al said, smiling. "You're looking at a new photographer for the *Daily Raider*."

"But what about the painting? You aren't giving that up?"

"Hell no! But there's money in taking pictures. Until I get a gallery, get representation, until gay guys are buying my art, I need to snap photos of dead people."

"That's a weird newspaper. Interesting, but weird."

"Is it the sex advice columnist that gets you?"

"I read an article in there once about werewolves in Prospect Park. I have not seen a werewolf in Prospect Park."

"It's the speculation of werewolves, the mythos—it did not state it *definitely*."

"It's quite the operation."

"It's a good photo," Mona said, holding up the newspaper. "That's death, right there."

"I can't imagine what his last thought was. Was he already dead when you took the photo, Al?"

"Yeah."

"So they have you out on assignment, photographing dead bodies?"

"I go where they tell me. It's good cash. And you get extra if they use your photo. I get paid an hourly rate. Mona is going to do it too."

"I never firmly committed to it," Mona said.

"You're thinking about it?" Liv was popping the cork on the bottle of white wine.

"She's gonna need money, our out-of-work friend," Al said.

"I don't *need* money. Savings are covering me."

"But they won't always. And it'll be fun. I think you'll be a natural. You don't really have to know much about taking pictures, that's the truth. Just point and shoot. You get better at it, the more you do it. You just have to be in the right place at the right time."

"The right place at the right time," Liv said. "Easy enough, right?"

"Saul actually likes to say that a lot. *Life is luck and timing.* It's obvious, but true," Mona said, reaching for a glass to pour some wine. "You can be born at the right or wrong time. I am starting to believe that."

"And were we?" Liv asked.

"Born at the right or wrong time?"

"Yes."

"Right!" Al shouted. He was gliding in his socks, reaching for a glass of wine.

"I don't know," Mona said. "I think about this more and more. There is an argument for right, obviously. We aren't in medieval times, we aren't living in our own shit, we aren't walking around with age thirty life expectancies. I'm not a man, so I don't have to fight in Vietnam. In the future, they will probably draft women. My brother, Vic, was almost born at the wrong time. Do you know he was drafted at eighteen?"

"I had a trick knee, thank God," Al said.

"Trick brain," Liv replied.

"Har har."

"What happened with Vic? I don't even remember you mentioning it. That would've been what, four years ago?"

"Just about."

Mona wasn't sure why she was talking about Vic's draft story. Vic didn't like discussing it. He had never explicitly forbade her from telling it. That wasn't his way, to level demands and constrain conversations. He was an easy boy, he could fade into a scene, adapt to the currents of his time. He didn't have her skin-level intensity, the burning that would not abate, day or night. As far as she could tell, Vic harbored no grudges. He was starting a job at the post office and if she was told in thirty years from now, in the time of the flying cars and nuclear fallout, Vic was still there, ready to collect a pension, she wouldn't be surprised.

The day he found out his number was called was a day, like King's assassination, she'd rather forget.

"He had the trick knee too, I bet," Al said, winking.

"Not quite."

She considered what she should say next. It was odd to even be in this position, since she hadn't planned on it and there was no external pressure building toward the story of how Vic got out of Vietnam. It was a cold Saturday, the record had run out, and the wine was poured. Here they were. Vic's number had been called the summer before his freshman year at Brooklyn College. It was, she remembered, one of the only times she had seen her parents in the way other children probably perceived their own parents: guardians at a slight remove, imbued with a mysterious power unique to all those who had lived longer than yourself, an ability to summon reams of knowledge on alien topics—taxes, mortgages, car loans—that were, unlike Superman villains and baseball statistics, far beyond them. When the letter came, her father said, very firmly, Vic was not going to war. Vic was not going to die. She remembered him saying derogatory words, years earlier, about anti-war protesters, but her father had never been a strong proponent of the war. He had been too old for World War II, too young for World War I. It was her mother who said Vic should see a doctor, in Yonkers.

"Mona, you will ride with your brother there."

Dr. Dov Yurick, she remembered. She would later learn he was the doctor many teens in her childhood building would see. How he gained a reputation in Flatbush, Brooklyn was beyond her knowledge, just as her mother never revealed how Dr. Yurick was found in the first place. Her father gave them a blank envelope with cash, to be handed to the receptionist for the visit. The way her parents told them what to do made it seem like they had been waiting for this day to come, planning for it like they would a wedding. There was a dark efficiency to their language and movements, not a breath wasted. Vic would go to Dr. Yurick. By the time they boarded the subway to ride to Grand Central, where they would take the Metro-North to Yonkers and then walk, Vic had run out of tears, his face hard and quiet. It was on the subway, sunlight beating through the windows as they crossed the Manhattan Bridge, that Vic told her what their parents had told him to do.

"They said I have to tell Dr. Yurick I want to kill myself."

"What?"

"That's the way I don't go to war."

His hands were shaking lightly, his small fingers interlocked. He did not want to die. By saying such a thing out loud, he was afraid he could make it true. It was a command from Esther and Manny that could not be ignored.

"You're going to do it?"

"Yes."

Dr. Yurick's office was in an obscure brick building fifteen minutes from the train station, his name among many on a row of faded gold panels advertising the people and businesses hidden within. A buzzer let them in without a voice from the intercom. In the waiting room, *Life* and *Time* and *Look* magazines sprawled on a single table, frozen Americana in their slick pages. She couldn't look at them. Several walls had photographs of flowers. She stood with Vic as he told the receptionist, a woman not much older than herself, he had an appointment with Dr. Yurick for 3:00. The receptionist nodded and told him he could have a seat, the doctor would be with him soon. Vic passed the envelope across the table, flashing the cash. The receptionist smiled and told him he could pay at the end.

They waited until 3:30, when the receptionist called Vic's name. The *t* in Victor hissed through her teeth, as if she were reading from an important scroll, a lost page of the Talmud floated into Yonkers. *Victor Glass.* She never appreciated how a sharp name it was. Vic rose, smiled slightly at Mona and then the receptionist, and walked to the room where the doctor would be. She never saw Dr. Yurick. He would remain mythic in that way to her, a name on a panel in a room she would not go. Victor, when asked, said he was bald and well-tanned, streaks of gray hair above his ear. He looked like Freddie Ryker's uncle, a kid they knew from the pick-up football games, an uncle they had seen a few times with his large, ruddy hands clamped to Freddy's forearms, dragging him home. She did not like Freddie Ryker's uncle.

Vic would be gone for forty minutes. In the time of his absence, in a doctor's office in Yonkers that gave her photographs of flowers, American magazines, and a woman with steel-colored hair sitting across from her who kept sneezing, angrily, into a handkerchief, she was alone to consider the future. She could not read the magazines. She imagined the white walls and flower photographs were part of a twentieth century exhibit on how humanity lived, her body in the plastic-coated chair staged for the benefit of a future race that wanted to learn about doctor's offices in Yonkers. She had been embalmed, her blood drained and her body pumped with fluids and chemicals, her heart a shriveled teardrop in her chest. The lights above could never turn off. As long as the exhibit was necessary, her body would expand with the fluids. She would not rest.

At some point when she gazed into this future, Vic had told Dr. Yurick he wanted to kill himself. Her mother and father strongly implied, without saying it directly, Dr. Yurick expected all the eighteen year-old boys who came to him to say this. And he would take it as the truth and write a diagnosis accordingly. She never learned why Dr. Yurick did this. Was he against the war? Was he a good liberal? Or did he relish the act of deception for its own sake, the small power he held in telling the United States government something that was not quite true? A lie is an invention of reality. A lie can make a minor god. Dr. Yurick could have been this kind of man.

Vic returned, paler than he was before. He nodded to the receptionist. She smiled at him, taking the envelope. Vic didn't say anything to her. Mona was sitting and staring, letting the magazines go untouched. The sneezing woman had gone. Now there was a man in an outdated homburg hat smoking a cigarette, clouds floating around his face. She had brought cigarettes with her and decided to light one. Vic gestured for her to stand up and they left the doctor's office without saying a word.

"There will be a letter for the draft board," Vic said quietly when they were outside again, late afternoon sunlight smothering the flat, colorless buildings around them.

"That's good."

"I didn't like that man. But I'll live."

He meant it in all ways, as a flippant throwaway, *I'll live, I'll survive,* and in the literal sense of what the phrase could mean, a continuation of life in the city they would return to, the overgrown grass of Prospect Park, the clattering of trains, the smoke billowing out from manhole covers. Death would stay at a remove. Vic was now a survivor. Men his age were shipped to die in Vietnam every day. Mona could rage against the indignities of her gender, but she was quietly thankful the American war machine had deemed her sex too weak to die for it on distant lands that meant nothing to her. She was safe too. Vic didn't betray great relief. Perhaps he believed Dr. Yurick or his parents could fail and the letter would be torn up. But his expression didn't change much when he got confirmation, in another letter, he had been deemed 4-F. He only read the letter with his distant eyes, a shade of the lightest brown, and set it down on the dining room table. She didn't ask him to explain how he felt. That was a question their parents could ask, the architects of the life-saving scheme, or Melinda, who inherited the desire to demand answers out of others, their little cop. She never asked him why he didn't like Dr. Yurick.

"My parents sent Vic to a doctor and he told him he wanted to kill himself," Mona said to her two friends, regretting it already after the words left her mouth.

"Was it true?" Al asked.

"Of course fucking not," Liv said. "It's how he got 4-F, though. I would've done the same. I would've lied to every doctor in town. I don't blame Vic at all."

"I don't either, I mean, I just told you, my trick knee . . ."

"No one wanted you in the Army anyway, Al."

"They could've done something with me."

"Target practice."

There had been several boys in her graduating class who went straight to Vietnam. Eric Dansby, Sid Leichter, Charlie Amaro. Sid, she knew, had been killed in action. She didn't know what happened to the other two. She couldn't imagine the loneliness and horror of dying in a foreign country, in a place no more familiar than the surface of the moon. She had seen pictures and watched broadcasts and was no closer to understanding why we were there. The only natural law of the United States seemed to be war in perpetuity.

"Vic doesn't like to talk about it," Mona said. "Maybe I shouldn't either."

2

Stray newspaper tumbled across the avenues, smacking up against the steel teeth of a shuttered storefront. The bars and movie theaters, bathed in their spectral neon, shone curiously in the cold rain. A city bus, bright like a hospital waiting room, roared past, faces gray against the window. When the streetlights flickered to life, Mona and Al were two lonely figures below, pushing against the wind. It was almost five, the appointed hour, and if they reached the *Daily Raider* offices in six minutes, they'd be late. While most of the newspapers were ensconced in Midtown, the *Raider* had chosen a prewar building south of Canal Street. When she worked next to City Hall, she had never lingered there long after work was over. Usually she ducked into the subway and went home. There was nowhere to eat, few places to drink, and a heavy desolation that came with nightfall, with the disappearance of bodies.

Al had been to the office before, on his interview, but he was still confused, wending between the narrow streets, muttering.

"Pretty sure it's White Street," he said.

"*Pretty* sure?"

"Yeah. Okay. I recognize it."

He sped up and she followed. He could be quick when he wanted to be. It had been a week since the day they had all hung out in her apartment. The next day, she played tennis with Liv at the Knickerbocker, on the dreaded clay, and still won. At the Knickerbocker, there was an advertisement for a spring tennis tournament at Marine Park, women under thirty-five, and Liv immediately told Mona to sign up. She would too. It would be the first tournament they both played in. She also had dinner with Saul. They didn't discuss her parents, which was nice. He asked if she needed help with a job. She said no and changed the subject. In that moment, she decided Saul would only know about this if a photo of hers ended up in the newspaper.

They arrived at the building, a ten-story slab with small gargoyles carved into the edifice, a long flag pole hanging from the second story. Al said the *Raider* had the top three floors. He shoved open the glass double-doors and told the guard in the chair that they were here to go to the offices of the *Daily Raider.*

"We are here to see Heed Ezekiel," Al said proudly.

"I don't really give a fuck but enjoy. Seventh floor."

They slid into an elevator, which didn't rise for five disturbing seconds. It gurgled to life, heaving at each floor without stopping

"It always does that," Al said.

"How many times have you been here?"

"Once or twice."

On the seventh floor, they saw a receptionist in front of a wall with a bold red RAIDER logo painted on, her eyes on a typewriter, gum popping between her teeth. Mona saw, beyond her, a fog of cigarette smoke, and heard the rhythmic clacking of typewriter keys, the voices of hidden men growling at one another over the din. The receptionist did not look up. Al approached, leaning on her desk.

"Hi, uh, we have an appointment to see Heed Ezekiel. It's about a new photographer. I called the other day and a woman, uh, said—"

"That's *me.*"

"Yes, of course. You said to come in at this time to see him. Is he available?"

"Is he available."

"Yes."

"As in, to see you two."

Her painted fingernail, a bright red, aimed for each of their hearts.

"Yes, to see us."

"Lemme see. Okay. He's a very busy man, Mr. Ezekiel. Lemme see, lemme see."

The woman, who was at best Mona's age, walked in high-heels around the corner, disappearing behind a cubicle wall. Al dug out a cigarette and offered her one.

"I think Ezekiel likes to see people smoking."

"I'm not really in the mood, but fine."

She took one, a Pall Mall, and Al lit it for her. They waited in front of the empty desk until the receptionist returned, frowning.

"He'll see you. Go around the corner and straight to the back."

"Oh I know, I've been here before," Al said.

"Good for you."

She followed Al through the large, open room, with cigarette smoke haloing the cream-colored cubicles. There were men shouting into phones, others racing up and down cramped aisles with pieces of paper, the typewriters ringing out. Al approached a closed office door with a nameplate, H. Ezekiel, and knocked.

"What?"

"It's me, it's Al Falcone, I brought the other photographer . . ."

"Just get it over with."

"Excuse me?"

"Come in!"

They entered the office of Heed Ezekiel. Hundreds of newspapers, magazines, and loose papers piled on the desk, against the wall, and teetered from the carpet. They were yellowed and burned, thin dust rising from the surfaces, cigarette ash scattered on top. *Raider* front pages were framed against the wall, one screaming about a bloody six-car pile-up on the West Side Highway, another about a headless body discovered on the Coney Island sand. The man behind the desk was much smaller than she imagined, his miniature red necktie tight on a reddened neck that seemed on the verge of erupting from the cloth. He was mostly bald, aged at least fifty, and his arms were crossed over his wide, bubbled chest. A clock ticked loudly above his head. Empty potato chip bags rested at his feet.

"What's this?" Heed Ezekiel asked, sweat gathering on his upper lip.

"Mr. Ezekiel, hi, it's Al, remember, I took the photo of the Gelby murder on Coney Island Avenue and I had mentioned to you I knew another photographer, she's young and, well—she's right here. She'd like to start too. Right, Mona?"

"Mona," Heed Ezekiel said.

"Yes."

"A lady photographer, yes, we could use one of those. Who are you again?"

"Al Falcone, sir."

"I thought you were bringing me Serenity Moonlight, our new sexual advice columnist. This is not Serenity Moonlight. It appears I was misled."

"Sir, I'm sorry, I didn't know, I didn't mean—"

"She's a cunt, anyway. But a lady photographer. I like that. The *Post* and *News* are very cock-centric. You'll find we aren't so. Mona, what—what do they call you?"

"Call me?"

"A surname! What is this, Al Falcone, what have you brought me?"

"Mona Glass."

"Glass . . ." Heed Ezekiel closed his eyes. Al and Mona looked at each other, saying nothing. His eyes opened again. "Are you related to a Hymie Glass?"

"I don't think so."

"He served with me in the Pacific. The bastard still owes me fifty bucks. Lost a fucking poker game to me. Ever since then, I think of Glasses . . . no good, no good."

"I don't know what to say."

"Say? Can you shoot?"

"A gun?"

"Photographs! Photographs! Let me tell you, first, I don't understand young people. The hippies, the yippies, the baby booms, longhairs, the drugs, your trippy fucking novels. I don't understand any of it. But I've got orders here to be *relevant*. The *Raider* can't lose money forever, the Brits won't like that, so we do outreach to the young. Like this kid here, whatever his name is—Alvin, is that what it is?"

"Alphonse."

"Anymore Italian and I'd have to deport you. Hey, that's a joke—don't be such a stricken liberal. You out in Brooklyn, Glass?"

"Yes."

"We could use another runner out there. You got equipment?"

"I—I do."

She didn't. But she sensed this wasn't a place, despite it being a newspaper office, to tell the truth.

"And you got experience?"

"I do."

"Where?"

"A few places upstate, I did a tour, in, um, Poughkeepsie and Elmira."

Two towns she had heard of north of New York City.

"Fine. Listen, if you're any good, the photos get in the paper. If it's shit, we stop paying you, no skin off my asshole. That's that. You get paid the rate here Alphonse gets. No low-balling the ladies in this joint. We have a few lady reporters and let me tell you, they know how to dig in the bud for a scoop, really sniff it out. You should see these lady reporters. The women's lib people would love this place."

"I bet," Mona said.

"Yeah, so you'll get called or you go follow where the police radio says to go. Get one and follow the blood. This city is filled with blood.

It's a Medieval wasteland. But that means we can go tell the story. We aren't afraid of shit. You go turn a lobster trick and get me the stuff I can put on page one."

"The overnight shift."

"Yeah. What do you think it is? Didn't Alvin here teach you the lingo?"

"He did."

"You need to learn the lingo. It can be life or death. Words are all we have. Words are the separation point between humans and beasts. We are drowning in words but they are like water and we need them. There's an insanity to this city and that's what you'll find in the *Raider*, Maura, if you ever do get into the maw of it, if you come down here headfirst—"

"Mona, Mr. Ezekiel. My name is Mona."

"Assert yourself. Good. The words matter. Let me tell you and Alphonse something. There is nothing more insane than a city. Eight million people choose an ugly little spit of land to call home. Why? Why crowd here? Why fight, elbow-to-elbow, in these subterranean tunnels, why feel the cement hell press down upon you, the screaming babies, the dark-eyed mothers—why bother at all? The death in the afternoon, at nightfall, the rapes and murders and the strangulations, the *failed* murders—do you understand how absurd, unhinged from fate, that can be? You think I talk differently now, not like before. I have a doctorate and then I met the Brit and he installed me here. Now I make news. We reflect, we create. Think again on that murder. Have you seen a failed murder?"

"No," Mona answered. Al was the quiet one now. She would answer for them both.

"A person, left alive, drained of all life but the bloody nib, the flickering light, the pain so hellish that whatever consciousness remains buried inside begs for eternity. We had four of those just last week. An axe man. A shooter. An arsonist. Another shooter. What is it about cities that invite these sort of events? I used to live in the country. Have either of you ever done that?"

"No."

"In the country, death is private. It's concealed. The crime is of the mind. Think of general stores, hunting dogs, long walks in witch-craft woods. There is death but we experience it as rumor and then it comes up upon us, suddenly, in the night. Here, in the city, death screams at us on the downtown IRT. He beats his bloody goddamn paws against your skull. I am here! I am here!"

Mona decided to speak on what happened.

"I was mugged, recently," she said.

"Were you? And how did it feel?"

"Quite terrible."

"Yes, well, that's the sort of confrontation I need photographs of. Fill my newspaper. Anyway, that's it. Now get lost. We're at our deadline. I can't believe I'm even talking to you. I think the Chinese food I ate last night made me loopy."

They rode the elevator down in silence. Finally, Al began to laugh.

"Heed Ezekiel. Can that even be a real name?"

"Who cares as long as they pay us."

"You're all-in?"

"Show me how to use a camera. This will be my work until some-thing better comes along."

3

The lobster trick usually started something like this.

Mona would jump into her car, a clunky Lincoln, sometime after nightfall. It was still winter, frost climbing on her windows, the steering wheel like shaved glass in her bare hands. With Al, she had gone to an electronics store and purchased, with much of the money she had remaining, a police scanner. If they worked shifts on the same night, they would trade off who had the scanner and who didn't and if they were on separate nights, one of them wouldn't be deprived. In the first few weeks, Heed Ezekiel seemed to want them together, same night, same shift, 12 to 8 a.m. One could also be on from 12 to 8, the other 1 to 9. She liked to drive, Al riding with him, telling her what to expect.

"Nothing at first. There's always a lull."

She thought of it as underwater time. Deep down near the seabed, a lightless hour, the city drained of shape. *Lightweight*, a slur in the day, a declaration of weakness, meant something else to her now, as her mind turned over and dissected it now, 1 to 3 am, their bodies waiting on the underside of a world. The weight of light. This was derision, *light weighs nothing therefore you are nothing*, but when she drove through her deep streets in the only city she knew, the weight of light was everything. The starbursts of traffic lights on her windshield. The flash of the camera in Al's smooth hands. The streetlights like frozen one-eyed angels, leaning over them, cutting open dark.

When the scanner crackled, Mona accelerated.

"Shots fired! Shots fired!"

The scanner picked up the police and it told them where to go. It was like magic. A cop in a shootout with a perp. Flatbush Avenue or Cortelyou Road or East 15th or maybe all the way down to Stillwell Avenue, Coney Island, in toothless neon, waiting. She watched Al, how he worked, the way he positioned himself with the equipment. The real value, though, was acclimating herself to blood, moving closer to death while distancing herself, locking her fear and disgust in a temporary cage. She had to do the job. People were dying in front of her, almost every night. She was here for a picture. She was not here to deliver a benediction. She was not here to save lives. Witnessing death would have to become routine, like brushing her teeth or emptying her bowels. Al had done it. He was lithe, unthinking, the flash lighting up skin and teeth and hair, the blood pooling in sidewalk cracks.

She learned the basics. The rule of thirds. Leading lines. The golden ratio. Symmetry and asymmetry. Mostly, she allowed her eye to follow the action. In a few weeks, she was on her own, and the police scanner spoke to her. Saul actually called her up the day after her first photograph ran. It was a hit-and-run just after midnight, a van had plowed into a Puerto Rican delivery worker on a bike and sped off, and she was there curled over his lifeless body, collapsing the brutality of a life shortened into a saleable photograph for Heed Ezekiel. The only confirmation of her success was the photograph's appearance in the next edition of the newspaper. And there it was, page fifteen, her name in the smallest of agate. Mona Glass. She had, in her own way, arrived.

"That was a ghoulish picture. You did a good job," Saul said over the phone, just after she had eaten another dinner alone, a chicken leg and a side of salad.

"Thanks. I'm up all night for these."

"And you like it?"

"It's a life in motion. That's how I can describe it. Like and dislike aren't as important as the fact you feel, in these moments, unusually alive, even as you are moving closer to death. The camera is powerful."

"I can get you a job."

"I haven't asked you for one."

"I want to see you."

"I'd like to see you soon."

"Let's go on a trip."

"Where?"

"I don't know, Vermont?"

"Not now."

"Why?"

"I have too much to do now. I am finally finding a rhythm."

"A rhythm with the *Raider*. Why not just drive out here tonight?"

"Tonight?"

"Yes."

"You know why. You need a good excuse for your wife and family. I'd fuck you, Saul. I'll say that. Come here."

"You're being forward. I like that."

"You're too much of a pussycat sometimes. You still call from that phone booth near the train station? I think I hear its mournful cry."

"It's the 7:45, in from the city. Here come the men, the hollow men, the stuffed men, leaning together."

"I think I know that one."

"Modernism comes back to you at the strangest times. I want to come. What do I tell Felicia?"

"Rocky needs you in Albany."

"It isn't plausible."

"Office emergency."

"She knows it's closed."

"A friend is sick."

"Which one?"

"Make one. Don't make a real one. Someone frail, someone who goes to analysis, who thinks of killing himself. Not Sonny. He's nothing like that. But someone who lives in Manhattan."

"Someone who lives in Manhattan. I like how you think. This is a triple bank shot. Good fucking God I miss you."

Fifteen minutes later, her phone rang again. It was Al, somehow out of breath. Neither of them were turning a lobster trick tonight.

"We're going into the city tomorrow."

"What?"

"Heed wants to meet with all the photographers. I got a call from his secretary, of all people, who said to tell you. The Brit who runs the paper wants a picture of Vengeance badly. Really badly. The *Post* and *News* are finally writing about it. They don't have a photo. If they get one first, after we've been writing about it, they're gonna blow their lids. It will be bad. Someone needs a photo. Apparently, whoever gets it, there's some huge bounty. Big money. So let's get in there. I figure if one of us gets it, we split the dough. Not a bad haul. I think we can do it. We're the youngest ones. We can track this guy, figure it out."

"I like that idea."

"Yeah. Meeting is at 9 a.m. So sleep tight. I'll just meet you at the office."

She had been reading the Vengeance stories. He was a wanted man now. Not only would they be competing with the other newspapers but the police too, who weren't tolerating vigilante justice, even now. Even if all those who had their lips split open or jaws broken by Vengeance were, in fact, guilty of something. With her sleep schedule so flipped, she was wired the later it got, new energy crackling in her stomach and limbs. It was like getting ready for a tennis match. Twenty minutes later, as she flicked on the TV, her phone rang again.

"I'm going to come," Saul said.

"Goodie. I'm getting up early. But I'll be up for you."

It went like this. There were days she would hardly think of Saul at all. There were days when the lovely absurdity of what they had built together was laid bare for her, in its dream logic: a man with a wife and children who fucked her and pretended to marry her and convinced her closest family they were legally bound together, even if they still hadn't properly honeymooned. It all made such little sense as Liv or Al, if they weren't being agreeable, reminded her. Especially Al. But there were the other moments like these, when just his voice, an electric charge through a telephone, could stop her, and all she would want—the logic inside her, the brute chemicals too—was him. She never liked to think of herself as a girl wanting a man. That was painfully cinematic, trite, like her sister, who believed women had been placed on Earth to simply fuse their livelihoods with wonderful men and should be *thankful* for this arrangement. It hurt her, sometimes, to admit how excited she could be by the possibility of Saul's unexpected arrival. A dinner was a dinner; Saul loved *scheduling*, plotting, dreaming in logistics, contemplating the next Italian or Greek or Chinese restaurant just as they were leaving one, his life lived, always slightly, in the future tense. If Saul arrived when he wasn't supposed to or violated the order of their affairs, her heart could thud that much harder. If he abandoned his future tense, like he was now, pulling out of his somnolent driveway and heading west, for her little apartment, she could straighten herself on the couch in anticipation, leaning ever so slightly toward the doorway where he could somehow enter.

So much of existence here, in a room, time sliding away from her. The camera sat on the table, a stark declaration of what she was becoming. This camera would find Vengeance. In the moment, this was decided.

She could start with the graffiti. Vengeance had begun spray-painting his name in bright red. In random spurts, his tag had appeared on storefront gratings, subway platforms, fire escapes, the sidings of apartment buildings. What was less clear was if Vengeance was doing it. In the most recent story in the *Raider* about Vengeance, the police sources were debating, in real-time, if the graffiti was homage or from the man himself. She imagined both could be true.

Why was it always the men who wore masks? What did Vengeance do when he took it off? *Who* was he?

One would-be Prospect Park mugger, whom Vengeance cornered and punched in the throat, said the masked man lectured him on a war against crime. "We must stamp it out," the man recalled Vengeance telling him. "We must drive it down to zero. I will drive you down." It was all too comic book, wam, bam and pow, and Mona remembered why she never bothered with them as a kid, the sappily Manichean arcs, color too washed out. Superman had nothing to tell her about life on Earth, with the threat of nuclear war hanging over her. Batman had nothing to say about Brown vs. Board of Education, Black men and women getting hosed and beaten in the streets. The Flash could not outrun entropy. The boys in her elementary school obsessed over them, who was stronger, who could defeat who, do you remember when Superman raced the Flash? She was not interested in gods. Gods couldn't help her, they didn't answer phone calls, they didn't take out the trash, they wouldn't stop her mother from telling her that playing sports was for boys, not girls, and she had to grow up.

Now there was an imitator, a man somewhere in the cold alleys of this enormous city playacting the fantasy he too learned as a child. A man, maybe, who looked to another hero of the comic book age, Captain Marvel. She didn't like Captain Marvel much either and it was Superman who owned the imaginations of most of the boys by the time she was growing up. But the older boys, those crusted in their teens when she was floating through elementary school, worshipped the Captain above all others, reached to the sky, on lightning-fused summer nights, and hunted for the bolts that would turn them from boys into gods. That's all Captain Marvel did: he was a child, Billy Batson, a runny-nosed orphan boy who cried out shazam to the heavens and a lighting bolt came crashing down, transforming him into a superman. Flight, super-strength, super-speed, all of it.

Nauseating, really. Yet she could, in her own way, comprehend the longing. Saul had talked of Captain Marvel, once or twice. He was old enough to have been one of those boys. In the age of mass death, the one they now dwelled in, forever and ever—she learned about the atom bomb in elementary school, turned thirteen during the Cuban missile crisis—there was an appeal for the hero of such simplicity. He was not alien. He was not a psychologically-scarred billionaire. He did not achieve speed, by accident, like the Flash achieved speed.

She could see Vengeance, a man who could be her age, looking to the skies too. But a lighting bolt would not come, could not come. So he strode through the streets, with the mask and the bizarre fedora, seeking out crime he could crush, adding purpose to his unknowable life. She picked up her camera and aimed it for the living room window facing the back alley of her apartment building. The darkness hid what was beyond the glass. She still knew so little about photography. It was like tennis, with worlds still to be discovered, new techniques and strategies to be unearthed with time. She was sure she would be playing tennis for the rest of her life and it was possible this camera would be with her too, a necessary appendage. The money she earned was not the money of a municipal job, with a biweekly paycheck, taxes scooped out, sick and vacation days slowly gathering. It was sporadic, smaller, but more exciting. It was just enough to make rent. She wasn't saving anymore. This was mildly irksome, like a horsefly that kept nibbling at her flesh on the beach before flying away. She had liked the comfort of money in her bank account to buttress her against catastrophe.

Just after 11:30, she heard her buzzer. There was a warm surge in her chest she didn't expect. She let Saul in. She decided to fiddle with her camera until he walked through the door, which she propped open. Propping a door at this hour, in this kind of hallway, was an invitation for a robbery, but she felt powerful in this moment, as if she too could cry out shazam and kick the robber through the window. She was bent over the camera, checking the lens filter, when

Saul entered, in his topcoat and tie, dark blue with yellow stripes.

"You came."

"I used your excuse. I do know a guy who's in analysis. He's not a good friend, someone in Rocky's office. I said he was having an issue."

"You had to comfort him in Manhattan."

"It was so fucking implausible. I do feel the kids suffer when I leave them like that."

"Your wife will tell them the truth?"

"She doesn't know the truth."

"No, what you told her. You created a truth. The friend who needs help. She would say, 'daddy has a sick friend.'"

"I don't know. Probably not. She would say something for work. She doesn't like them knowing much, in general. She's discreet."

"But you don't want to talk about her."

"Not really."

"Undress me."

It was a hurried, almost furious sex, her favorite kind, a clash of bodies on the couch. They didn't even make it to the bed. He was inside her and his shirt wasn't fully unbuttoned, it would take too long, his dress pants and belt sloshing at his ankles, his tie ripped off. She wanted to be naked. She came quickly, too soon for him to release, and she let him keep fucking her, getting to where he needed to be. Sex could be like visiting a foreign country, a new language inhabited, old identities lost.

She didn't recognize him and she didn't recognize herself. They held each other, saying nothing. The lights, she realized, were still on. He was breathing softly, like a little baby. She stroked his head.

"I love you," he said, nearly out of breath.

"I love you too."

"God almighty."

They remained entangled. Upstairs, a neighbor thumped across the hardwood floors, his footsteps landing in a mad rhythm. She heard, faintly, a record player, a swing song from before her birth. The neighbor was dancing alone.

"You have to work tomorrow," she said.

"I'll call in sick. Let's sleep in and get breakfast."

"I need to go into the *Raider* offices tomorrow."

"Why?"

"They want to tell everyone about the reward for the photograph of Vengeance. A big bounty."

"That two-bit clown?"

"Everyone is obsessed. He finally made the TV news. They keep showing the NYPD illustration. He looks like a sharp shooter in the old west."

"Another deranged lunatic."

"That's kind of redundant."

"You know, it is. But get breakfast first. C'mon. I need you."

"Saul Plotz doesn't always get what he wants."

"But he can try."

"We'll do breakfast this weekend."

"So many days."

"Just a few."

"I'd love nothing more than to wake up tomorrow and fuck you again."

"We'll have to start early. I need to be downtown by 9."

"We'll start whenever you want."

"You're just a little baby now, all sexed up. I love it."

He shed all his clothes and they slept together naked. She set an alarm for 7 a.m. Her dreams were light and peculiar, a struggle to remember phone numbers, a walk along the water at nightfall in a city that was just like New York that she nevertheless could not recognize. This did not trouble or disorient here. She only kept walking. When her alarm rang out, the bed next to her was empty. Saul had gone.

Panic collided with anger. She stood up, rubbing her eyes. Gray light waited behind her blinds. On her small dresser, there was a piece of paper with Saul's handwriting.

He had left to get breakfast. Be back in twenty minutes.

The anger, just seconds-old, suddenly seemed so absurd. In that flash of time, she had believed Saul fucked her and left her. But he *could* do it, since they weren't married, since he had no legal obligation to her. This realization, so obvious and so known, gripped her, and she sat back down on the bed. What bound them together? It was a question she had to begin to answer. They had known each other a half decade, shared in the most intimate acts, invested themselves in a relationship that had no name. No name, in this world, meant no identity. Are you boyfriend-girlfriend? Husband-wife? Engaged? They floated without designation and this never bothered her before. It wasn't supposed to. She was young, she had her photography and her tennis and her friends and she sure as hell wasn't going to define herself against the life of one man, no matter how well-intentioned, because all men natively sought control. It was evolutionary, she believed. Even Saul was this way.

But the question kept asking itself. There was a hunger, as time passed, to create a definition, and if this was done it would violate the pact she had made with herself to not be an appendage to another man, no matter how much she might love him. With Saul, given their age difference and his prominence, this would always be true. She would be Saul Plotz's girlfriend, Saul Plotz's wife, Mrs. Saul Plotz. Her mother had called her, one week ago, and asked when she was changing her name. Had the paperwork been finalized? She had become Esther Glass one day after her marriage, April 5th, 1940, it was a date she recited enough for her children to know by memory, like December 7th, 1941. For all the ways Mona disdained marriage, there was a begrudging admiration for the way Esther and Manny could cherish their own, the annual dinners out, the album of black-and-white photographs revisited every few years. It was just not the existence she wanted, a life framed against one day.

"I don't think I'm going to change my name," she told her mother.

"Oh God. Is it the women's liberation thing? Don't listen to the rabble-rousers and the radicals, Mona, it's a very good thing to honor a husband. It's living an honorable life. Don't listen to them."

"I'm not."

"But you are, dear. I know it, these are very chaotic and complicated times. Things aren't like they used to be."

"I'm not changing my name for him, or anyone."

"Don't be obstinate—"

"I'm not, damn it."

She regretted raising her voice. For one, it never worked. It would only enflame her mother more, drive her to spout ever more irksome platitudes about love and marriage, triggering another loop of yelling, her mother occupying a higher ground as the one who never cursed. Manny and Esther never ventured much beyond damn and damn was her father's word, to be paired with God, because Jewish men were less afraid of taking the lord's name in vain than their Catholic schoolmates. She liked that Saul let her curse, never questioned it, even tossed in his own. As a teenager, she had found a small, private liberation in curse words, fuck and shit and damn and cunt and cocksucker and motherfucker. Every word was so percussive, bullets fired through the lips, beauty in the rat-a-tat hate. On the tennis court, she cursed prodigiously. It could make Liv uncomfortable. Her ball sailing long over the baseline (*fuck*), a second serve going wide (*fucking shit*), a drop shot unreached before the second bounce (*you motherfucker*). Some girls grunted.

With her own mother, only de-escalation worked. If she knew this intellectually, it didn't mean she would practice it when she should. Sometimes, she just got so fucking mad at her parents. They were old, obstinate, they could only understand what they were taught decades ago, the passage of time holding as little meaning for them as the names of cold asteroids passing by outer rim planets. They liked Melinda because Melinda fundamentally thought like they did. She was the first daughter, the one who could accept the assumptions of the nineteenth century that bled into the twentieth. Melinda briefly considered being an actress. Then Dr. Harry Hyman came along. As Melinda Hyman, the apotheosis was complete. A marriage, Mona had come to believe, was asymmetrical fusion, one person entirely sublimated to the other, a new being wobbling forth into the world. Dr. Harold Hyman, though, did not have to become a Glass. He proceeded, as intact as he was before.

She heard the buzzer when she was done dressing. Letting Saul in, she hopped to the bathroom to wash her face and pee. She was done when he entered the apartment, holding a brown paper bag.

"I got you bacon, egg, and cheese," he said.

"You know how bad that is for you."

"I know how much you love it. I just got egg for me. Wasn't feeling the cheese. Enjoy yourself. There's a very delightful deli just a few blocks from here."

"It's fine." Touching the bag, she realized how hungry she was and how good the bacon, egg, and cheese sounded. "Thank you."

None of it was kosher. Her parents, despite their adherence to Jewish rituals, did not follow any dietary laws. Her father liked cheeseburgers. Her mother asked for kosher meat at the deli but wouldn't know or even object if they gave her something else. Mona devoured the sandwich. Saul ate his slowly, bite by bite, and she was done when he was only halfway. She could always outeat him.

"When do you have to be in work?"

"If I make it by 10, I'll have my ass covered."

"I'll have to be on the train very soon."

"Your big meeting. The masked vigilante."

"Yes."

"I hope you get that picture."

"I'd like the cash. I'm also curious who he is."

"Like I said, a lunatic."

"He's a response to the zeitgeist."

"A symptom of the times."

"Something like that. I don't know. I'd like an interview with him."

"Maybe he'll speak to you in tongues."

"Finish your sandwich."

"We all don't have your speed."

"We all should."

She found herself applying make-up, something she rarely did anymore. Perhaps it was the big day. Perhaps it was the unexpected presence of Saul, here in the morning. A man could make her do this.

They left the apartment together, smiling in the elevator, exiting like any American couple. The harshness of the morning, another day below freezing, didn't disturb her. Weather meant little against the future.

"How about I drive you to work?"

"What?"

"I can make it by 10 if I drove you. It's just Manhattan to Queens. If I'm late, so what."

"Won't you get in trouble?"

"Who's getting me in trouble? Rocky? I run the office."

He didn't say it to brag. It was a literal fact. The Queens office was his fiefdom. He was a benevolent lord.

On the radio, she heard Nixon's voice. The commentator said Nixon was in hot water today. She imagined the president, his jowls boiling, the fat of his skin melting off his bone. Saul rolled down the window to smoke and offered her one and she declined, not in the mood, she just wanted to sit by him and think. Traffic congealed at Ocean Parkway. She noticed he was smoking Kents now. The radio continued to hiss.

"What if we could do this every day?" Saul asked.

"Sit in traffic on Ocean Parkway?"

"No, us. Just go to work together. You and me."

"Here we go."

"What?"

"It's the same thing."

"You know, we can get a place. Your parents desperately want it. What kind of married couple doesn't have their own place?"

"My parents think you're just living with me."

"The cover is holding?"

"I never have them over. If I see them, it's a restaurant, or I go to their apartment. That's how we do it."

"And we'll just keep doing it this way."

"There's no other way."

They rolled onto the Prospect Expressway, a roadway her parents had told her was devastating to the communities that had to be moved for it to carry all these cars to Manhattan. She couldn't quite imagine all the building that went on before she was born and when she was a child, hardly paying attention to it. The roads, the bridges, the highways, the parkways, the beaches. All by an old man she had seen in the newspapers, Robert Moses, the so-called Master Builder. She only knew this city now, the construction complete, the paint peeling in the hallways, the roaches scuttering, the windows cracked, leaking dust and light. She was too late for consequence. A child grows, an adult settles, strength decreasing until death swallows the body whole. The city had reached full adulthood. It had nothing more to learn, nowhere to go. Al, who followed books more closely than she did, said there was a major biography of Robert Moses due out that everyone would be talking about, he had read about it in a magazine. Maybe she would read it. In the meantime, the Master Builder's Prospect Expressway bore them to the Master Builder's Brooklyn-Queens Expressway which would feed them into the Master Builder's Brooklyn-Battery Tunnel.

"I do wish there could be another way."

"You have obligations."

"If only I'd met you sooner."

"Don't say that."

"Why?"

"Because two children aren't the same as a mortgage and they're yours and I won't have the blood on my hands of a destroyed marriage. Or, if not the blood, the wreckage. God, Saul."

"I'm not saying that, or asking that—"

"But it's always the undercurrent! It's always there! You don't think I wish it was different? You don't think, on a morning like this, I don't think how nice it would be if we could just *date* and float around and be like everyone else? Do you think it's fun lying to my parents, as much as they piss me off?"

"I never said any of that, I mean—"

"This is what we are and who we are and Felicia is your wife and you live in Roslyn, Long Island in a very nice house and that is your *life*. When you die, that is your obituary. Married, father of two, Roslyn, New York. I am not in that obituary. I do not exist."

"You are my life, Mona. You're all I think about."

"You should think about other things! I love you too, but you should think about other things . . ."

She was surprised to feel a hot sting in her eyes. She shut them and opened up, pressing her lids until the tears disappeared. They were rumbling on the BQE, the crest that allowed her to see the Statue of Liberty and the full breadth of Manhattan, the Twin Towers and the Empire State Building. She strained to take in their enormity alone, to lose herself in the city rising to meet her. Saul had put his cigarette out. The radio was in a commercial break, shaving cream, rich, smooth shaving cream, and she clung to the enunciation of the man reading the ad, how he clenched his consonants and rolled over vowels and created a great American longing for cream on the face. In the darkness of the tunnel, Saul opened his mouth.

"I didn't mean for things to get so heavy."

"That's how it is."

"No, we should just have fun and enjoy each other. We always do.

Where are you again?"

"Where am I? In life? In the universe?"

"No, the offices of the *Raider*. Where am I driving you?"

"Franklin. Between Broadway and Church."

"Got it."

After another pause, Saul cleared his throat.

"So, play any good tennis lately?"

"I'm going into a tournament in the spring."

"That's great. You'll win."

"I don't know. A lot of experienced players."

"You're more talented, though."

"You don't know that."

"I've seen you play. And I've been to Forest Hills, I've seen the pros. You hit as hard. The talent is there. You even beat that man."

"He was a chump. He was weak."

"Maybe so. And you're strong. I'll come and watch."

"I don't know."

"I'd like to."

"It's a lot of nerves. A big tournament. I've only played in the park, against Liv and the others, basically."

"You clobber Liv. She's played in tournaments, yes?"

"A few."

"Then you've clobbered a tournament player."

They entered Manhattan, pushing into another wave of traffic. They weren't far now. Mona had the urge to bounce a tennis ball, once, twice, three times, from fingertip to cement to fingertip. The anticipation before a big serve, the rising heat in the core, the intake of breath—this she thought of now. This came to her. She wanted to follow through and smash the ball into the service box. There was nothing better in life.

Saul began to talk, the traffic building against them.

"I saw him once, Joe DiMaggio. At a restaurant. He was wearing a dark suit in a dark Italian restaurant, eating with two men. They had dark expressions."

"I can't imagine being like that."

"Like what?"

"He's not a person anymore. He's an idea, a longing, a song lyric. I saw *The Graduate* when it came out. I didn't understand it then but I do now."

"When you reach that level, maybe you don't bleed anymore. Maybe you're just gaseous. Maybe you just float."

"Wouldn't that be nice?"

"To not have a body?"

"There are no obligations anymore. Does an icon even go to the bathroom? He passes through walls, into memory."

"Mona."

"Yes?"

"I love this."

"We're at my stop."

The car had turned and they were slowing in front of the *Raider's* offices, pulling to a pump. Saul whistled.

"I hope you catch the masked man. For your sake. For money's sake."

"I'll do my best."

"Let's do dinner Friday."

"Let's."

He leaned over and kissed her. She found his lips and they held there, unwilling to move. Finally, eyes closed, she drew away.

"Let me know how it goes," he said.

"I will."

When she was through the front doors, nodding to the man at the front desk, she turned to see that Saul's car was still there, idling, as if he belonged to her.

4

Vengeance got hotter when the head rolled into Times Square.

For weeks, the *Daily Raider* screamed. HEAD'S UP. HEADLESS HORSEPLAY. SKULL YORK CITY. DEAD HEAD.

There was no photograph of Vengeance, but there were many, many photographs of the severed adult Caucasian male head deposited, in the dead of night, on the corner of 42nd Street and Broadway. Many photographs in many newspapers.

The head, eyes blown open, with bright red acrylic paint stroked across the bloodless forehead. The message was read first by an adult film distributor, then a hot dog vendor, and then, once whistled over, a droopy-eyed veteran cop out of Midtown South. They all gasped, and gasped again, and eventually—in the case of the cop, too dumbstruck to properly shield the head until a crowd had gathered—mumbled *holy shit* many times in a row.

In acrylic, the strokes unmistakable: *This Is Vengeance.*

"He wrote on this guy's fucking head!" Al cried out, waving around a *Raider* in Mona's face.

"He's proud of his work, I suppose," Mona managed.

Each day brought new revelations. Crumbs from the police investigation were selectively leaked to the *News* and the *Post*—the *Raider* was not a paper one leaked to—and Heed Ezekiel had to content himself, as much as he could, with rewriting what was already there, the details of a life cut short.

Mona allowed Al the theatrics of always reading from the paper, sharing what had been found, or what the NYPD was permitting, at this rate, to be found. Police sources were notoriously unreliable.

"This guy, his name is apparently Marius Shantz," Al told her as they sat around his grime-flecked kitchen table, a pretentious little cigarillo burning between his lips. "He was a lawyer."

"Why did Vengeance kill a lawyer?"

"I don't know. My guess is, he wasn't killed in Times Square."

What they, and the rest of New York City, learned: Marius Shantz, thirty-six, was a criminal defense attorney who worked out of the courthouses on Queens Boulevard. He was a regular at the bars there. He lived alone, in a one-bedroom five minutes from the courthouse. He was single. He was, apparently, bereft of close friends. Fellow attorneys spoke to his diligence, his ethics, his attentiveness with clients. He was a graduate of Fordham and St. John's Law, a lapsed Catholic, a native of Kew Gardens Hills who never strayed too far from home. His father died when he was twelve and his mother still lived in the apartment where he had grown up.

Poor Marius Shantz, the victim of Vengeance. Vengeance was now a killer. There was nothing Heed Ezekiel wanted more than a photograph of a masked murderer. God-willing, with time, he would be a mass murderer, the singular terror to drive the *Raider's* relatively meager circulation into the stratosphere.

The *Raider*, again, lagged the *News* with the latest break in the case. Their lead columnist, a voluble Sicilian who had penned several best-selling books and pitched a special brand of antacid tablets on network television for a number of years in the 1960s, had learned— *learned* was newspeak for a well-placed patrolman deciding to do a favor for an acclaimed columnist in return for NYPD-friendly spin in a popular tabloid for an undefined but lengthy period of time— that Marius Shantz had been interviewed in connection with a number of unsolved, brutal rapes in Queens, the Bronx, and Manhattan over a span of eight months.

Shantz was released. "He was released, Mona!" Al told her, barely able to contain himself. "They thought he matched the description. But here's the thing—*this* rapist wore gloves and a mask. No prints, nothing. No one ever got a good look. He threw girls up against the walls in back alleys. He cornered them on the way home from bars."

"And they interviewed Shantz because—"

"I was *getting* there, Mona." Al had another cigarillo and she couldn't wait for this phase—it was certainly a phase—to pass. "He matched a physical description and he lived not far away from two of the rapes. The rapist was described as six-two to six-three, lanky, spindly hands. Wiry muscle. Marius Shantz checked those boxes. But he had alibis. He was at court, at his law office, or home. They let him go. Besides, he had no rap sheet. No spurned lovers. He did his work and kept to himself."

"So Vengeance thinks Marius Shantz was the rapist then?"

"Looks that way, yeah. And now we *need* to find a way to get a photo of him. Ezekiel is hungry."

"Vengeance must have had inside information. He spoke to cops."

"Or he tailed Shantz around."

"Maybe." Mona reached over and tugged the cigarillo from Al's lips. He let out a mild yelp. "I think he may have his own inside source."

"Hand it to Vengeance at least for taking a sicko off the streets."

"Al, we have no idea if Shantz really did it. He was questioned by police. So what? He should die for that? We'd have to kill *how* many thousands of people, if that alone makes you guilty, getting questioned by a cop? I'm not handing anything to anyone."

Al had turned toward the window.

"Vengeance is a bad, dangerous motherfucker, then."

No one—not the police, not the public, not the inquiring press—had discovered the rest of the body of Marius Shantz.

Mona and Al were out every night for weeks on end. Often,

they separated, but at least once a week they decided they would stay together in Al's car. On these patrols, on these lobster tricks, they promised again that if one of them got the photo of Vengeance the reward would be split. Al ate very little, losing weight, his bones pushing against his skin. Mona guessed she outweighed him now by twenty pounds. She brought sandwiches on their patrol and tried to get him to eat. He was too focused, too trained on the night. Food could only matter so much.

"It isn't about the money anymore," Al said as they sat in the car together, at 3:20 a.m., on a desolate stretch of Stillwell Avenue, a short walk from the silent amusements. Just down the block, a bum was pissing into a trash can, his penis dangling in the dark. He sniffed and walked away. They were near the train station, hoping Vengeance would be there, somehow hunting for farebeaters. The station was just about empty. Most of the Vengeance sightings, however, seemed to happen at this hour, when the city emptied of all life and those who remained awake and outside offered themselves to the possibility of random death. Vengeance himself was random, a foot solider of fate, and Mona wasn't sure, in the bleary dark, how real he was anymore.

Al tapped the closed window. "The money. We're beyond money."

"Do you think anyone will find him?"

She noticed, after asking the question, Al was growing the beginnings of a beard.

"It's the pursuit now. Everyone in the city is keyed up. Is he here? Is he there? Is he of the world?"

"There are so many witness accounts."

"It's almost beside the point. He's real because we make him real."

"Self-actualizing a vigilante into existence."

"He was real and maybe he vanished. Or others are pretending to be him. You know, I dream of him now. He talks to me. Vengeance comes through the night. His mask hides a young face. He tells me it's going to be alright. That's all he says. Nothing else. There's a halo. It's like Jesus."

"Everything is like Jesus. I am going to sleep all day tomorrow. I am fucking tired. Then Liv wants to play tennis. On the clay. I hate the clay."

"You hate the bounce."

"It's not tennis."

"It's a form of tennis."

"Not the one I want to play."

"We never play what we want to play."

"Wait—do you hear that?"

Mona heard a faint cry from the Stillwell Avenue subway station. The echo reached their closed car window. She rolled the window down, peeking out. There was a rustle, footsteps, dangling change. She always had a strong sense of hearing, stronger than sight, and she leaned out further, trying to catch the sound. Her camera, she remembered, was around her neck. Al grabbed for his own camera, now lying in his lap.

"I hear it now."

"We should check it."

"Fuck it. Let's."

They left their car. It was spring, already into baseball season, and still so ruthlessly cold. An ocean wind slashed at her face. The amusements, off-season, were like vestiges of a dead civilization, wreckage on the surface of a moon. The Cyclone, the Wonder Wheel, Lunar Park. Her childhood stilled. Al walked around to the hood of the car and tapped on it twice, just to make noise. His emerging beard already seemed thicker. They crossed the street and entered the station. Mona sped in front of him, fear and dread and excitement sloshing together, powering her onward. They turned a corner, running past a shuttered newsstand and another bum sleeping on the ground, curled up in a whirl of blankets. He didn't stir.

She heard another cry. It was coming from the turnstiles.

One man held another by the lapels. One man wore a fedora, a mask, and a trench coat. She fought the human need to scream. Her hands trembled for the camera. Al joined her, sliding closer.

The other man was not a man exactly. Maybe twenty at most. He had long black hair and wild eyebrows, his lower lip shaking, spittle leaking out. He was terrified. Mona watched him through the viewfinder. When her flash went off, followed by Al's, the kid was dropped to the ground.

Vengeance was running straight for them.

"Oh shit, oh shit," Al said, turning.

"One more."

Mona needed one more shot. She pressed the button and caught Vengeance square, his mask consuming the entire frame. Al was grabbing her, begging, running, and she was with him, at first behind and then ahead, always faster. She didn't turn to see but knew Vengeance was close, only steps away, and they would somehow have to climb into the car and drive off without a vigilante catching and killing them. It didn't matter that there had been few reports of murders committed by Vengeance, the perpetrators of crime usually left alive enough to remember, through the blood and ache, his masked face. She could believe in this moment they would die.

"C'mon," Al said, jamming in the key and opening the driver's side, popping the lock for her, locking the door again, the key stuttering in the ignition. The engine flared to life at the exact moment Al's window began to shatter, the knife blade in Vengeance's hand colliding with glass. He was going to smash through it and slash and gut them both, watch them bleed out.

"The camera," the voice grumbled, behind the mask. "The camera."

"Our fucking photos," Mona said.

The engine was alive. Al crushed the gas pedal and they accelerated straight through a red light, swerving left onto Surf Avenue. He was going sixty, seventy, eighty, no cops at this hour, the car skidding past the aquarium and onto Ocean Parkway where he decided to blow another red light on the abandoned stretch. He was breathing hard, sweat rolling down his forehead.

"I think," he said.

"We did it."

"Oh my God."

Al was still trying to catch his breath. Finally, approaching the Belt Parkway overpass, he stopped at a red light.

"That was him."

"We got the picture."

"The money."

"It's bigger than that. Like you said."

Al was slapping the steering wheel.

"We did it! We did it!"

He began to laugh uncontrollably, bending over the wheel. She could see the smallest tears pushing out from the corners of his eyes. She couldn't help but laugh with him, just as hard. The light turned green and the car remained at the intersection. A truck idled behind them, honking, and Al rolled down his broken window to wave back.

"Let's get food and then let's gun it to fucking Manhattan. We'll wake up the boys on the night desk," he said, speeding up again.

"This is incredible."

She rolled down her own window, letting the cool air pour over her, this sleeping city suddenly so beautiful instead of sick, suddenly offering a slice of her destiny. They were crackling with energy, as wide awake as they ever would be. It was a moment she wanted to inhabit for the rest of her life. Her neck was fully out the window, Al accelerating again, fifty, then sixty, hitting all the green lights. They were young and alone.

At Cortelyou Road, only a few blocks from her apartment, he turned right, hunting for a bodega. His face glistened. They both needed food. A storefront, pale light and faded beer decals, beckoned, and Al parked in front of a pump. He killed the engine. She had forgotten how quiet this hour could be.

"He could've killed us," Al said.

"But he didn't."

"How, of all the guys looking, all the goons, the stringers, we got it—"

"Right place, right time."

"That's life, isn't?"

"Had I been born a decade earlier, in Germany, I would've been killed in a camp. Sometimes I think about that."

"We were born at the right time."

"Good enough time. Here we are. God almighty."

"Mona, you're wet."

"What?'

"I've just, I've never seen you sweat like this."

"Oh, really? That's right, you've never been able to stand me on the tennis court. And you're pretty drenched yourself."

Their breathing slowed. Neither of them were moving toward the door, readying to leave. In the distance, a siren wailed to an unknown destination. The city was in its last hours before full awakening, the clanking of vehicles and the explosion of daylight. She looked at him and he looked at her and there was the twin pull of two bodies, an electric tug that couldn't be ignored any longer. He reached toward her and she did it all without thinking, kissing him on the lips, and his mouth opened for hers like it had been waiting a very long time, far longer than she had contemplated such an act. He fell on top of her and she clutched at his back, thin but hard, feeling the pulse of his lovely weight. She wasn't going to have sex with him in a car but she could fiddle with the zipper of his denim, feel what he had, and she did, reaching with glee. He kissed her lips and her neck and unbuttoned her shirt so he could fall upon her navel.

"Oh God," he said.

It was only in the minutes after they had stopped, delirious and out of breath, that she considered in full what they had done together.

The friendship itself was over. In place of it would be something new, the bud of what would have to be named and classified, at least in her own mind. Al Falcone was someone she kissed. Al was a friend she had kissed. What would Al now expect? What would she expect from Al?

But the questions didn't have to be answered tonight. They were in the bodega, hunting for potato chips, asking the man behind the counter if he could make sandwiches. All night, lady, he said. All night. He was Italian, she could tell, the dark hair like Al, the rings under his eyes, the way vowels broke off his lips. So much overlap between Italians and Jews, two huddled masses in the berths of hellish ships bound for Ellis Island, destined for the ghettos of the New World. She leaned forward at the counter, waiting for her sandwich. When it came, wrapped in the white paper she knew so well, it tasted like a miracle, turkey and Swiss on a roll as the minutes ticked toward 5 a.m. Al asked for salami and American cheese. They ate together in the car, quietly this time, another siren wail in the distance.

"Let's go straight to the office," Al said.

"We'll give them the pictures."

"Ezekiel is going to be blown away."

When they reached the highway, the city rising before them, Mona lit a cigarette. She blew smoke out the window. Al turned the radio up, pop jangling in, an old Byrds hit. She closed her eyes, trying to let the music take her. Where? Did she want to leave? Fly through clouds? No, she was where she needed to be. And that meant she could feel this way about a time and a place that didn't include Saul. Guilt orbited her as they rode through the tunnel. She didn't belong to Saul, she wasn't dating him in any official sense, whatever that meant, they had their performative marriage and the delicious sex and their long bouts of conversation and he was actually married to someone else and she could repeat these facts to herself, one after another, like a catechism, and they wouldn't change how she now felt, the guilt gnawing deeper, the absurdity of its depth. She was free to be with anyone she wanted. Hell, she could tell Saul about it and he would have no right to throw a shit fit and maybe she should tell him just to test him, see what he did, see what type of man she really was.

Al, she could see, was not going to talk about what they did. Not yet at least. She would wait for him. He was humming along to the Byrds.

"The city is so quiet before morning," she said.

5

Mona couldn't resist. After she had bought the afternoon edition of the *Daily Raider*, a rarity rushed out purely for the photographs she and Al had taken, she called her mother and father. She resented, still, that she cared about what they thought. Calling at four, she knew she'd reach her mother. She would be in the middle of preparing dinner, a roast chicken or chicken pot pie or chicken soup for when Manny came trudging in from the office, the old pearl gray fedora still slouched on his scalp. There was only so much of the modern world they could take on.

"Hello? Glass residence," her mother said, still after all this time.

"Mom, pick up the *Daily Raider*."

"What?"

"Just get the newspaper. I'm in it."

"What did you do? Are you in trouble?"

"I take pictures for them, remember? I have the front page."

"Oh, how wonderful. Your father and I prefer the *Post*. But I will have him run down to the newsstand when he gets back. By the way, any leads on apartments? It's an awfully long time for a husband and wife to not live together, don't you think?"

"Oh, I suppose."

"Your father can try to find a realtor for you. I think it's about time. Marriages don't survive when you're apart."

"The point is, I'm on the cover of a newspaper, not what time it is to move into an apartment."

"It's a filthy newspaper. But I will see it when your father brings it. Thank you for telling me."

All over the city, on thousands of newsstands, was the photograph she had taken. In the end, Heed Ezekiel had chosen hers alone for the wood, which she learned was what they all called the front page. She had caught Vengeance straight on, flush, his two eyes small and black on the paper, a cloth mask tied tight around his face. The face consumed the entire front page. Ezekiel had chosen a simple, pun-free headline: THIS IS VENGEANCE. By now, everyone in the city who paid even passing attention to the news knew of the masked vigilante, his fury, his spray paint, his acrylic across a severed head. They knew of a man roaming the streets, bringing justice on his own terms. And now they didn't have to use their imaginations anymore, thanks to Mona.

"The girl beat you," he laughed through cigar smoke. "She beat the candy asses off every last one of you."

Her phone rang just minutes after she was done talking to her mother and she picked it up, dreading the voice on the other line. Her intuition, in this instance, was entirely correct.

"Mona, congratulations!"

"Thank you, Saul."

The black wings of guilt had spread; she could fathom a whole creature now, gnawing at her, sucking at flesh. She hated it and it was inarguable. Talking to Saul was a reminder of what she had done. And now what she wanted to do with Al. This didn't, however, change how she felt about Saul. She wanted him more, too. She wanted him in her bedroom. Al could come, then Saul. Or they could flip for it, bottle cap or coin. It was as comforting hearing his voice as it was confusing. She felt herself curling inward, away from the window, the phone cold against her ear.

"Mona Glass for *Daily Raider*. It says it right there, on the front page, in the little type. I bought five copies, just for me. You're a star.

Sonny Cannon is impressed too. You made us both into *Raider* readers."

"I got lucky. Me and Al did. We were on one of our patrols and we nailed him."

"Are the cops getting him now?"

"Funnily enough, he still hasn't been found."

Once the photograph appeared, the NYPD initiated one of the larger manhunts in their history, deploying scores of beat cops and detectives to Coney Island. Even to Mona, who had snapped the photo and watched as Vengeance slammed his knife into Al's car window, it all seemed absurd, especially for someone who had not killed anyone. But there was little more offensive to a paramilitary like the NYPD than another person claiming the authority and power of justice, deciding who should suffer and who should be left alone. Vengeance had killed without their sanction. He was still uncatchable, gone without a trace by the time twenty squad cars had descended on Coney Island. On the TV, they ran Mona's photo. They didn't need to name her—citing the *Raider* was enough—but she derived pleasure in knowing, in her own small way, she had joined history. Perhaps this was what Saul felt working for a governor who could be president, drawing strength from his proximity to power. She held the phone and breathed in. Saul began to talk.

"It's all they're talking about in the office, you know? Vengeance has his supporters. Marguerite, one of the girls in the front, was arguing the cops aren't controlling the crime so why not let regular joes do it? Even Sonny seemed open to that point. Strange times."

"What do you think?"

"About Vengeance roaming the streets?"

"Yes."

"God, I don't even know. I go back and forth. He could be sick. I don't want him killing innocents. A suspect isn't the same as a convict. There's a criminal justice system for a reason, you know? There's a certain catharsis in all this, I get it. The world seems like it's spinning out of control. You've got a president who's a criminal. What makes sense? Not much. So here he comes, an agent to bring some order, make some order. He follows impulses we all have."

"To want to do something. To feel like you are doing something."

"Exactly."

"He almost killed us, you know."

"Us?"

"Me and Al. We were out together."

"Oh right, Al Falcone."

"Vengeance swung his knife into Al's car window."

"He wanted to maintain the enigma. No photos."

"Like some kind of anti-celebrity."

A silence built briefly between them.

"Do you ever wonder where I am when I call you? I can't call you from the office. Too many nosy people. I can't call from home."

"You stand at payphones."

"I might."

"I can hear the city outside your phone right now."

"Listen for it, Mona."

"I picture you like this a lot, actually. Saul Plotz, lonely on a street corner, outside some godforsaken Queens diner where the tuna fish salads are made like clockwork at four in the afternoon. Where the waitresses are named Marge. Where ashtrays get overturned and no one sweeps anything up."

"So vivid, Mona."

"Am I right?"

"You are close. No diner here. Just an OTB."

"Damn."

"Well, I should get going. I just wanted to say I'm proud. Proud parent right here."

"Speaking of which, I told my mother about the front page. She's having my father pick up a paper. They don't read the *Raider*. All she asked about is when we are moving in together."

"We totally can."

"No we can't. And I like my apartment."

"I'll pay the rent on somewhere nearby. It can be your apartment, but it can be both of ours for your parents."

"There's only so much I am going to do for them. A wedding was enough. I like my apartment."

"They'll keep asking."

"And, eventually, they'll fuck off."

After saying goodbye to Saul, she went downstairs for a walk. She wanted to take in the newsstands with her photograph. She wanted the pleasure, the broadening of her ego. At the first deli she saw, she went inside and picked through the stack of *Raiders* left. More than usual seemed to have sold today. She still needed one for herself.

She ended up buying four, tucking them under her arm. Their rolled up weight pleased her. After so many nights turning the lobster trick, barely sleeping during the day, she could feel the adrenaline seeping away, a lull returning to her life. It was strange. What she could do was lean against a lamppost and stare at each front page, one after the other. She could take in the glory of her name, one she had disregarded or even found vaguely ethnic and ugly until it was there, in print, for millions of New Yorkers to see. She had not just joined history. She was a part of the future too. Running through the train station, pointing her camera at Vengeance, she never considered she was entering into a mass consciousness. She was now the media. Her pictures were for the crowds. She stepped back off the curb, keeping her eye on the newspaper.

And her name.

6

It was Al who told her Heed Ezekiel wanted to see her. He communicated through Al to reach her. That was his way and she realized it would not change. This time, she rode into work alone, no Saul to drive her. She joined the human tide on the subway platform, waited anxiously for her train, and forced her way in with everyone else, crunching between elbows and newspaper. She tried not think about what waited for her.

The door to Heed Ezekiel's office was closed. She knocked. She wished, too, she had Saul at her side.

"Yes?"

"It's me, Mona."

"Who?"

"Mona Glass."

"Glass, Glass—right. Open the fucking door."

She opened the door and saw him there, the usual ball of fury, the papers piled aggressively and indiscriminately. He appeared to be drinking some kind of juice. The ash tray on his desk was very full.

"Sit down, Mona Glass."

There was one seat facing his desk and this seat, like the desk, was covered in stray papers. She gingerly sat on them and waited for a reprimand. Ezekiel finished the juice and slammed the glass down. No reprimand came.

"You had a gentleman caller."

"Who?"

"He called the main line and asked for you. I had him patched into me. I figured, what does an anti-social vigilante know about the difference of gender in a voice? I've met women with deeper voices than me. And I know men with more frilly voices than you. Men who aren't even fruits. Men who go home and fuck their wives with heroic relish. But Vengeance wasn't going to be led astray. He asked for you. Demanded you. He reads newspapers. He knows photo captions. Discerning sicko. He said he will only talk with you. I asked him what he wants. He repeats himself. That's the conversation."

"That's it."

"Now you will call him and it will run in my newspaper."

"Right now?"

"Where else do you have to be? Are you stringing elsewhere? Are you one of these part-time social workers? I know you don't hustle. I can tell you don't. I knew women of the night."

"He left a number I assume."

Ezekiel slid her a crumpled piece of lined paper. Scrawled in pencil, in Ezekiel's swooping handwriting, was a phone number.

"Call it. Take good notes. He is talking to us because we've proven ourselves worthy of him. We won the hunt. This city will die but it will die knowing we won the hunt."

"Yes."

"You'll like his voice. I liked his voice. I found it soothing. It reminded me of my father's voice."

"He's older?"

"No! My deceased father's voice, when he was a young man, hurrying home from work to kiss me on the forehead. Vengeance speaks like a man who hasn't lived the life. But what do we know? We are all little mice in the dark. Now go call him."

"What phone should I use?"

"Phone? Use any phone."

"On the desks? But they belong to staff reporters. Won't they care?"

"Take an empty desk. If they aren't using it, they don't deserve it. Go write me five hundred words."

"Okay."

She set out into the office, warily walking among the cubicles, passing fleshy backs hunched over typewriters. At the end of a row of desks she found an empty phone and a chair to boot. A typewriter, an Olivetti, waited for her, next to a carton of cigarettes. A reporter two seats away frowned at her. She didn't recognize him. All she had for him was a slight smile, of the type that tried to tell as little as possible about the life she was leading.

"You new, kid?" the reporter asked.

"I took the Vengeance photo. I'm Mona Glass."

"Oh, celebrity. Very nice. Okee dokee. I'm just here. Minding my own beeswax. Not a celebrity."

She shook her head. The rotary phone was a bile green, the color of sickness. She dialed and waited.

There was breathing on the other line. She decided she would note-take on a pad left on the desk. She was too nervous to type.

"Yes?"

"Hello, is this—"

"You're Mona Glass."

"Yes . . . I'm Mona."

"This number was left only for you. It was not left for anyone else."

"Well, thank you. What do you want?"

"You aren't being a very good interviewer."

"You reached out to me. I'm a photographer."

"You took my picture. You attempted to disrupt."

"It was necessary. The public deserves to know what you look like. You operate in the public."

"You don't care about that. You took a picture for money. That's what you do. No need to make it more than it is."

"Tell me why you do what you do."

"There's a question."

"Why did you leave a message for me?"

"That's another."

"Tell me."

"Tell your newspaper. You need your money. Your bag of gold coins. How many for this?"

"You left the phone number."

"Like you, I wanted to understand what I dealt with that very night. I saw you. I saw your friend. I saw his fear, your fear."

"You ruined his window."

"You don't know what you ruined."

"What do you want? Tell me."

"For the bag of gold coins, here is your interview. There are layers of hell and I am below them, between them. I know darkness better than anyone alive and that allows me to confront it at its heart, in the deepest part of night, when death is closest."

"None of that answers my question."

"This city is failing. You can feel it. I can feel it. We all believe in it, still, we collectively will it to life, each and every day. But for how long? How long can we dream? How long will you dream, Mona Glass? Ultimately, I am for order over chaos, matter over anti-matter, creation over negation. The New York Police Department, which I know intimately, is a failed state. It is the Ottoman Empire on the eve of the Great War. It has exhausted itself."

"How do you know the police department intimately?"

"Finally, a good question."

"How do you know it? Did you know Marius Shantz was a rape suspect? What did you do with the rest of his body?"

"I *was* of the department, Mona. Turn that one over in your mouth."

To this point, she had been note-taking in a dutiful, nervous shorthand, ensuring she had every sentence of importance rendered as accurately as possible. Her hand stopped when Vengeance told her he had been a part of the police department. He was an ex-cop. It suddenly began to make sense. Only a former police officer could evade capture in such a way and only a former officer would be so darkly obsessed with justice. This was a story. This was a byline. She began to write slower, shaping the words, circling for clarity, ordering her memory.

"You were a police officer."

"I was a good little boy in blue. I shackled my share of lambs. But the real crimes lay elsewhere, out there, growing by night. I dreamed of zero, Mona Glass. Do you understand, in your young brain, what it is to dream of zero?"

"I don't."

"Zero crime. A world beyond it. A crime rate that decreases until none exists at all."

"You can't do that."

"Humanity is nothing without goals."

"When were you a police officer?"

"Only goals have meaning, Mona."

"Your goals can't be achieved. Especially now."

"Because of the chaos, the disorder, the lack of belief. God himself hiding, shriveling, afraid of the shadow he casts. That's why you think. You are more nihilistic than me, Mona. You lack like they all do. You see disease and you don't seek a cure."

"Why did you leave the police department?"

"I sought a cure."

"That doesn't answer my question."

"We're running out of time. In all senses. Do you want to know who I am?"

"Yes."

"You do?"

"Yes."

"Here's a rhyme for you. Take it down. Sing with me. You'll know the song, the tune." The line went quiet for a moment and Mona thought she had lost him, that he had cut the connection himself. And then: "*London Bridge is falling down. Falling down, falling down. London Bridge is falling down, my fair lady.*"

"What?"

"*Built it up with iron bars. Iron bars, iron bars. Built it up with iron bars, my fair lady.*"

"You aren't funny. And you don't know if Marius Shantz was guilty or not."

Vengeance hung up. Mona scrambled to write it all down, word-for-word, missing nothing. She ripped the paper off the pad and tucked it in her pocket. All she could think to do was return to Heed Ezekiel's office to tell him what happened.

"You got an interview?" Ezekiel asked after she arrived, knocking twice. He was in the process of packing a pipe with tobacco.

"I did. He said he used to be a police officer."

"That's tomorrow's wood. You bludgeoned my reporters' asses again. Go write it up."

"I've never written an article before."

"So write one. Open up the fucking paper, copy the format, and go. I want copy by 3:30 today, five hundred words."

She wanted to call Al. Al wasn't a writer either, he was a photographer and a painter, but he would know what to do. Again, she was faced with the dilemma of having no desk. She could ride the train home, write on her typewriter, and then hope to hustle the copy back to the office by 3:30. But that would be, obviously, a profound waste of time. There were typewriters here. There were desks here. She would have to take one and hope another man didn't come stomping back from a bathroom break or a lunch break or a smoke break or an actual assignment to see a young woman sitting there, hunched over a typewriter.

A pile of day-old newspapers lay in a basket against the wall. She grabbed one, opened it up, and took the first desk she saw that was open.

Many of the first sentences were puns. *Cat*-astrophic to describe the four stray cats found frozen in ice. She didn't want to use a pun. Though she had read, at this point, probably thousands of newspaper articles, she had never paid attention to the structure or the language. She had simply devoured the words and moved on. Now she perused the pages, trying to determine what alchemy went into the creation of an article, how the words arranged themselves to tell a coherent story. First, she had to figure out what the hell just happened with her phone call. The rhyme kept playing in her head. He had actually been singing. *London Bridge is falling down, falling down . . .* She didn't have the time to decode it, not now. She had to write.

Her notes were a scramble. What mattered most? What was new? Yes, that's how she needed to think. That's how Heed Ezekiel thought. There had been such an abstract quality to Vengeance, his speech one long, dark riddle with obscure insights and unreachable answers. He was taunting her.

But he had told her one new fact. This she could cling to. This she could run with.

She went to bed that night not knowing what to expect. It was only in the morning, when she woke up early to make the newsstand and grab one of the fresh *Raider* copies to roll off the truck, that she saw the headline.

Again, the front page.

EXCLUSIVE. MASKED VIGILANTE WAS COP.

Her picture, followed by her byline, a genuine one. A photo credit and a byline, on the front page. She bought as many copies as the change in her purse would permit, which was eight. The man at the newsstand, shaking his head, let her take them.

"You love that little paper, don't you? It's become quite a seller."

"I'm in it."

"Hope you didn't chop off any heads or bury any bodies alive like all the other people in it."

"No, I'm—" But she stopped. It didn't matter. She had to get home, pile up the papers, and bask in the achievement.

She dialed Al from home.

"I'm on the front page," she told him when he answered.

"Christ, congratulations. Again?"

"Vengeance spoke to me. Ezekiel made it front page."

"That's incredible. What did Vengeance say to you?"

"He was frightening, to be honest. He said he used to be a police officer. He also started singing to me."

"He sung to you. Wow."

"A rhyme. London Bridge is falling down. It's a clue. He wants me to know who he is."

"We should figure it out."

"It'd be another good story."

"A code to crack. The two of us."

The way he said it brought her back to Saul, and the phone call she had to make. He needed to know too. It was only fair.

"What are you doing later?" Al asked.

"Nothing much. Why?"

"I thought I'd come over."

She knew, from the sound of Al's voice, why he wanted to come over. It was a new Al, Al in masculine bloom, and she didn't know if she wanted this or not, if she was prepared to accept this arrangement of her life.

And there was Saul.

7

Saul was a regular *Raider* reader now, religiously hunting Mona Glass photographs, drawing closer to her this way. On days Mona didn't appear, he would roll the paper up and toss it straight in the garbage. The search for her name, performed with the aggression and clarity of a man that knew what he wanted, ensured he read the paper closer than most, whether he liked to or not.

One year was dribbling into the next. This was time. With Mona busy, he was home more now.

Summer, fall, New Year's Eve. Felicia took him to a gathering at Herb Weiner's house. It was there, in the pit of Long Island, that he had to steady himself in the bathroom, suddenly suffused with loathing he never quite knew before. He was unable to smooth it away. What had made this life bearable had been Mona—Mona needing him, wanting him, waiting somewhere in the ether of that delicious borough, Brooklyn, New York. A future with Mona, even in the most diminished way, was all he wanted. A pretend marriage could be a real marriage because there were other human beings on planet Earth who thought it was real. Hot pains shot up his chest. He sat down, sweating on Herb Weiner's toilet, his loafers kicking the linoleum. Outside, he could hear the jackals, the partygoers trading the same banal anecdotes, automobiles purchased, investments made, colleges their rotten little children would attend. After this, he would drive home to his cold house and wait for Felicia to come to bed.

They hardly spoke anymore. What do people say to each other? How does a conversation begin? With her, he was a proto-man, incapable of conceiving of the armaments of civilization he enjoyed so much with Mona. The references to the events of the day, the light banter, the jousting for position, who could make the better joke. He just loved hearing about Mona's life. He wanted to know about the tennis courts, the corpses photographed, the hum of a Brooklyn sidewalk. When he got home, he would tell Felicia they were moving back. Sell the place, buy an apartment in Brooklyn, maybe a little co-op off Prospect Park.

He dug his fingernails into the palms of his hands. He had never been this way.

Herb Weiner, he noticed, had toothpaste stains everywhere.

"In a minute!" Saul yelled, hearing a knock. One of the slobs wanted the bathroom.

"Hurry up in there," came the voice, barely masculine.

"One minute!"

He wasn't shitting. He was thinking. Out of an old, bad habit, he began to gnaw at his nails.

The man outside the door, when he opened it, wasn't someone he recognized. Bald, fat, slightly gray in the face, an amalgamation of ten different people he'd seen or talked to at the party, the man smiled coyly.

"Long time in there."

"Go fuck yourself," Saul said.

Unlike other holiday parties, there was no woman making cocktails. He was grateful that he could slip into the fridge for beers to ensure the swill of liquor and alcohol got him good and high. He had never tried drugs—grass or LSD—and it was in this moment, teetering ever closer to forty that he decided he had to try something. Except none of the squares had any here. No drugs at a Herb Weiner party. He drank furtively, aggressively, dodging conversations until it was inevitable that he could no longer, too many active Republicans seeking his ear about Rockefeller or Ford or the chances for the ticket in '76. He didn't care. He wanted to drink. His limbs were burning in a way he liked.

Three men stood around him. Two of them he knew: Alvin Glantz, a CPA and probable crypto-Nazi, and Buck Adams, an improbable WASP among Jews Felicia had sidled near. He tried to hide, for her at least, how drunk he had become.

"Yes sir."

"Absolutely."

"That's the stuff."

"Tell me more."

The night leaked away. A new year came, his vision blurry, Felicia kissing him dryly on the lips. Someone threw confetti. None of it meant anything, other than he needed to drink another beer. He drifted away, to a wall, leaning. Now it all was leaning, the room like a capsized boat. He stabilized himself. He remembered, somehow, he had driven here. This shithole. Felicia, who never drove, would have to get them home.

"You're a wreck," she said.

"You—you drive."

She shook her head. It was somewhere beyond, minutes or many hours. Herb Weiner had cake smeared on his face. Beer darkened the carpet. He smelled sugar and lipstick and Buck Adams' cigar smoke. Felicia was putting on her coat.

"Happy new year, Herb fucking Weiner," he said, swinging his right arm wildly.

"You're having a good one already, I see."

"Herb fucking Weiner. Enjoy the night."

Saul stuck his tongue out, holding it there in the brightness of the overhead hallway light, straining to see the glimmer on his tip. Felicia grabbed him by the elbow.

"Night night, Herb Weiner," he said again.

Felicia began to talk to him in the car. He was surprised to hear her voice. The car was moving, the night sky rolling away from him. He pressed his cheek to the glass.

"Drunk like that," she said. "I don't know what got into you."

"Me?"

"Don't talk. It doesn't matter. It's just embarrassing."

"Oh, bullshit."

"You pissed your pants. You know that."

He didn't know that. The warmth, which he had been ignoring all night, began to make sense. There was a bathroom trip where he had haphazardly unzipped his fly. Urine splashed out across his trousers. At the time, he just laughed and went back to the party. The droplets could burn through Herb Weiner's tile, for all he cared.

"Aren't you just uh, just a judgmental bi—"

"What? What are you going to say Saul?"

"All day, judging me."

"You ignore me. You ignore your family."

"I work *hard* for the family."

"It took you getting drunker than sin to talk to me more tonight than you have in two weeks."

"You don't talk to me. What do you offer? Huh?"

"Go to sleep, Saul."

He stumbled out of the car, nearly falling to his knees. The house raced toward him. He wanted, more than anything else, to hear her voice. To pick up the phone and hear Mona. He couldn't call with his wife in the house, with the kids and the baby-sitter.

He would wait until Felicia was asleep and call her.

"I'm staying downstairs," he mumbled to her when he got inside, sprawling on the couch, his head lolling away from the blank screen of the television.

"I don't care what you do."

He sat in the darkness. A half-moon peaked through the window, frost forming on the windowpane. The alcohol was not dissipating. It pulled tight on his skull. He leaned in, leaned back, flexed his fingers again. It was too early. Too late. He wanted to throw his body through the glass of the window and see what happened, test the proposition of his mortality.

He wanted to hold Mona in his arms. Below the rage and confusion, the churn of liquor and the broken memories of the party he never wanted to go to, was his longing. It took a state like this to make him realize it, linger on the reality of her life separating, slowly, from his own. She was not a college student. He was getting older. There would be men in her life—this was inevitable. He had children to raise. A wife he had to find a way to love. He tried to remember his wedding to his Felicia, what he felt that day, that year, the time building up to a young marriage, how powerful and necessary, for a brief moment, it all seemed. But he was chasing an existence sold to him between the pages of magazines, on the television, in the books he read, the ethereal concept of eternal romance. This he could see now, with the clarity of a decade melting away. Mona had thrown it all into relief. It was fun at first, the girl on the side, youth to grasp at, kiss and cuddle and undress. That's what it had been. Then it became everything.

All he wanted was her. To tear down his life and start over. He held his head in his hands.

On the fourth ring, she answered.

"Hello?" She was groggy. He listened for her breath, waited a beat, and began.

"Mona."

"Saul, it's late."

"I wanted to wish you a happy new year."

"Well, thank you. You too."

"You have a happy new year. The happiest."

"Are you drunk, Saul?"

He could've sworn he heard a snickering through the line. Not her snickering.

"What's that?"

"What?"

"I hear someone."

"It's nothing. I have to go to sleep. It's almost four."

"Who is laughing at me?"

"You're drunk, Saul."

"I don't want to be laughed at. I called, in a very caring way, to wish someone I love a Happy New Year."

"Let's talk later. I'm going to bed."

"I'll meet you."

"Don't get in a car."

"How the hell else will I get to Brooklyn, New York, USA?"

"Go to bed. I'm going to bed. Good night."

"Good morning! How else can I see you, Mona, if I don't get in a fucking car and drive out of this Long Island hellhole and come see you? How? Fly? Fairy dust? Do you know what it's like to miss you, Mona?"

"We'll talk in the morning, please . . ."

And then Saul heard a shuffling, a movement of the receiver, a little hiss, and another voice speaking to him. Mona's voice was distant, *not now*, but whatever plea she had made was ignored by the new voice, which he recognized immediately.

"Go to bed, Saul."

Al Falcone. That twerp was in bed with her. That little fucking dark-haired—he didn't even have words. The anger choked him.

"Put Mona on the phone."

"You're drunk, go to bed Saul. Good night. Good night!"

"You little goddamn rotten piece of shit, you get off the phone now."

Another shuffling, more breath, movements in loathsome shadow. He waited. Al Falcone's voice was gone.

"Saul," Mona said quietly. "I don't want to hear you like this. And if this is how you call me, how you talk to me, I don't want to hear from you at all. No one owns me. No one claims me. Good night, and Happy New Year."

III

Wander

1

Tad knew the Richard Nixon story because his father tended to repeat himself, not that he ever did it to brag. It was more as if the anecdote needed the oxygen of another listener to live on, a retelling predicated on the act itself to grant it life. His father meandered in and out of the past, from one cul de sac of memory to another, increasingly uninterested, Tad felt, in what was before him.

Or maybe that's how all adults were. He was meeting more of them. Teens were peeling away. That was only natural, when you were twenty and you already had the *used up* stench about you.

The story went that Richard Nixon took an office in the federal building downtown, right across from the courthouses. It was the same building his father worked in, for one of the federal agencies. The General Services Administration. Tad couldn't say what GSA did, only that it kept his father out late for a while and then didn't. For a brief time, he started to see a lot more of his father. Like magic, he was around to pick him up after school. He didn't have to rely on his mother, who'd rather spend the time at Herb Weiner's house, or old Herb himself, who so wanted to strike up lame, tired conversations.

How was school, kid.

Learn anything good, kid.

You get all A's, kid.

School was shit, like it was for all generations, Herb's included.

Nixon's too. The first time his father told him, he didn't care. It was only on the second and third loop that Tad, in his own way, started to enjoy the details.

His father rode the elevator with Richard Nixon at least once a week. They happened to be in the same wing of the federal building. It was a home base, a strange return to normalcy for a man who had been, not long ago, the most notorious human being on Earth.

Nixon only wanted to talk baseball.

"Seaver last night," Nixon said. "That fastball was cracking."

Another time, he told his father he had played football with the Hall of Fame shortstop, Arky Vaughan. No one remembered Arky anymore, but Arky, Nixon insisted, had been one of the greats.

Like all men of history, Nixon was diminished in the flesh. There was no screen to divide him from the masses, to enlarge him to haunting proportions. The rings under his eyes were not dark in a foreboding way. They merely spoke to a lack of sleep, this turkey-necked, shriveled man rolling in his sheets. His jowls were not cartoonish; they were mottled and purpling, like any man at the end of his rope. Nixon's suits, his father was surprised to note, looked like they were bought off the rack.

Neither of his parents, Tad was sure, really had too much to say about new things. He attempted, at times, to be as conversant as his father in baseball and politics, the religion of all American men, and that meant he soon could shuck it off altogether, hunt out a challenge. He liked his father more than Herb Weiner, at least. He was still sure his mother had carried out some kind of affair with Herb a few years back. It was possible they were still going. He didn't spend the time at home anymore to find out.

But if he had to choose, still, he'd choose his mother. His mother didn't elude him in the same way. Even if she kept secrets, they were of the open kind; he was sure he could be invited in. His father, no. His father left, came back, left, came back. He was easygoing, what they all called easygoing, as long as he got his way. And with Lenore, he got it enough, got the daughter he wanted.

Tad knew he wasn't what his father wanted. He always believed this, from the first time he could form these thoughts together.

What was it? What was the moment of disunion? There was never a single day, a single month, a single year. Never one memory to trouble him. As he got older, he decided it had to be an accumulation, a rolling together of senses. His father did not hug him as tightly. His father did not ask, after a while, how school went. There was a line of inquiry and then it closed. When Tad wanted to speak, he could see his father's face tightening. He'd rather be somewhere else.

There was one incident. A few years ago, his father had bought him tickets to a football game. It was the Jets, he recalled, and it was crucial for some reason. The tickets were a surprise, close to his birthday.

"Guess what I got you?" his father asked, his voice taking on a cheer usually reserved for phone calls or visits from friends.

Tad did not know. He was in his room, packing pieces of bubble gum into his mouth. It felt important, even vital, to chew three or four pieces at once, to see how far he could go.

"What?"

"Will you—you're going to choke on that gum."

He didn't believe it since he had never come close to doing such a thing. The gum, melon-flavored, fit with ease. But to appease his father and make it easier to have the room to himself, he decided to spit it out, back into the wrappers he had saved.

"The Jets are playing the Dolphins, Tad, and we're going. Fifty yard line. Exciting, isn't it? These tickets were really hard to get."

He didn't know how to respond. He could tell, from his father's voice, this was meaningful, either a gesture that he believed was important to his son or at least pleasing to himself. At school, he knew kids who pretended, all the time, to be happy or sad, who could manipulate emotions like clay and shape them to fit particular situations. It was a useful, even necessary, skill, one he could not dream of possessing. The Jets and Dolphins meant nothing to him because football meant almost nothing to him. Like other kids, he'd watch the Super Bowl, and he played pickup games if he was bored enough. Football had an advantage over boredom, in that sense, and it was a way to keep time from expanding too far.

Yet getting him Jets tickets for his birthday would have been like telling his father his birthday present was watching a new *Voltron* episode. His father would have sat stone-faced. An afternoon at a football stadium now seemed intolerable, the more he considered it, the more he watched his father's grin ease downward.

"I don't know, okay."

"Excuse me?"

Tad did wish he had a better answer. This was the part of molding and manipulating he was never good at, sensing what people wanted and giving it to them. That was the bulk of life, he was coming to realize, appearing agreeable and ready to accept the terms imposed upon you. People liked acceptance. They liked to feel their terms made sense. His father was no different.

"I don't know if I want to go."

His father breathed in, his grin still holding. To Tad, it was like the painting of a smile, almost real, the chips shedding away.

"This is a very exciting and important game, and I thought it'd be great for the two of us to go. These are great seats. You can really see all of the action."

Great, great. He should say it one more time. Tad wanted to spit the word out, hear how it held in the air.

"I don't want to see the action."

"You like football, don't you? We haven't gone to an NFL game in years and these tickets—"

"They're hard to get."

"A lot of people want these tickets. They're special, you know, and to sit there—it's not easy, and it's not cheap either."

"I don't want to go, I don't think."

The smile was gone. "Then what would you like to do?"

"I don't know."

"You don't *know*."

"Whatever it is, I don't want to see the football game."

"If that's the case, I'm going to have to give the ticket to someone else."

"That's fine."

Tad could tell his father expected him to capitulate at that point, like a child following a script on television. Young teenagers were supposed to be the jealous sort. The idea of his father taking his birthday ticket and giving it away was the kind of maneuver that should have provoked pleading, howling, keening, an absolute scene. You saw it on TV plenty. Tad certainly saw it. In the seconds after he told his father it was fine, he could wait for a reaction, slowly feeling that he controlled what would happen next. He had no sadness to betray, no disappointment. He did not want to go.

"This was your birthday present, Tad, really. It would be a nice day and you'd have a lot of fun. You always don't want to go to things and then you enjoy them later."

This wasn't true. It was never true. And there was a reason, years later, these bits of dialogue were coming back to him, the memory almost brightening. His father didn't understand the son in his wake. He was an explorer content to circumnavigate ponds. When Tad stared back at him, his eyes growing small, he saw what he regarded then as a strange mixture of arrogance and befuddlement. His father believed he was right, even as he was confused, even as he was wrong. He had to be that way, Tad supposed, to succeed.

It was never a way he was going to be.

"Then I'll do it," his father said softly. "I'll give the ticket away."

"You never asked me if I wanted to go. You just told me I was going."

"It's a gift, Tad."

"To you."

After that, they spoke even less, his father keeping later nights. He graduated high school and hardly remembered it, even though he was sober, always sober. There was a hardness to the days, something almost physical in nature, the sunlight colored like granite. He listened to the last two songs of one Beach Boys LP, which he had found in a garage sale. *I'm a rock in a landslide, rolling over the mountainside.* He hummed the melody for months.

In January 1989, he decided to drop out of college. His mother had wanted him to go to a private liberal arts college in the woods, the type where wine was served with dinner, professors ate out their female students, and novels were argued about as much as they were read. His parents had spent a summer touring these colleges, his father driving their family station wagon. First up north, to Bowdoin and Bennington, schools locked in the woodlands, mountains ominously lurking. Tad hated the cold, so no to them. In another spurt, they drove to Muhlenberg and Franklin and Marshall and Dickinson College, schools with unwieldy tuition bills his father was not willing to pay. He didn't blame him on that front. If college was a crock of shit, generally speaking, why pay so much for said shit? The schools bled together, their Doric columns and alternative newspapers and cavernous dining halls, the blinding emerald of the quads, the way cigarette smoke lazily trailed off the lips of the freshmen trying far too hard.

Lenore could go wherever she wanted. Her grades were good and her parents loved her. Columbia and the University of Pennsylvania were top choices. Columbia, because of New York City, and Penn, because it was nestled in downtown Philadelphia, a manageable metropolis. She was going to be a lawyer like her father. Tad, after bombing three years of high school and hustling up SATs just acceptable enough to dodge the horror of Nassau Community College, got accepted to Stony Brook, the state school in Suffolk County.

His father yelled at him for playing his records too loud. *Lenore is trying to study,* he said. *You're ruining Lenore's work.* Yet even this, Tad thought, was a put on, parenting as artifice. Saul Plotz didn't care all that much about what his daughter did either. He cared about his work and what he did after his work. He was a torpedo burying deeper into the murk, one unknowable mission in mind. Tad envied, in a small way, that kind of focus. To neglect so efficiently—what a father he was.

Though Tad had made the decision to drop out in the winter, short-circuiting the second semester of his sophomore year, he harbored no particular ill will toward the university. He was always able, on Thursday nights, to reliably procure good coke. In a sense, though he couldn't explain it to his mother and father, he was dropping out to *get away* from the sheer amount of shit he was putting into his system.

The school had no relationship to the space around it. The town of Stony Brook utterly ignored the university and the roads traveling outward could only be navigated by an automobile he did not own. The professors slouched apologetically, stumbling through the fog of their own logic, their tweed or billowy skirts bought second-hand, their degrees valuable only for this exile. Tad kept encountering construction sites but didn't know quite why: as far as he could tell, nothing was being built. There were pits of dirt, mounds of ruined grass, machines sitting idle, waiting for a signal from a bureaucrat or maybe God. Lenore would soon be off to Columbia or Penn and he was here. He found that funny.

The brutalist exteriors bred ferocious wind tunnels. When he wasn't snorting coke in Roosevelt, the cockroach-fed dorm he was assigned to live in, he was making his way between buildings, wind assaulting his face. What he liked most about coke was the energy. There was the anticipation before the rush and then the shot to his system, the rapid elevation of all he was—for those transitory hours, he was thrilled to be alive. He didn't want to die ever. The coke arrived through kids like Randy Richter and Isaac Niederman, Jews from the North Shore who came from far greater wealth. It took a state school, strangely enough, to tell him he wasn't that rich. For all the working class commuter kids who were gone from the campus, like clockwork, by 5 p.m., there was a contingent of implausible wealth, boisterous failures who couldn't parlay their advantages into seats at the Ivy League or Georgetown or Stanford. These kids could always be counted on for a Thursday night party. And Tad could always be counted on to show up.

He could say there was little guilt, no regrets. He liked the aspect of getting to write in college. He had always been good at essays and even taken his stab at the creative stuff, penning a few poems and short stories. One class, an introduction to writing remedial requirement he had to take because his GPA had spiraled so wildly in high school, even held his interest, tossing him into the loving melancholia of Virginia Woolf. But he sure as fuck wasn't going to stay in college for Virginia Woolf.

Now that it was spring, when he would have been ending his sophomore year had he stayed, he was beginning to think more on what he had given up. He was a busboy at the diner on Jericho Turnpike, the only white boy among the Hispanics, and they treated him okay, like a benign extraterrestrial they didn't quite know how to reckon with. Jewish kids from Roslyn didn't end up busboys in diners. His mother, predictably, was horrified. His father—he had to give old Saul Plotz credit for this—didn't flip out. He was accepting, almost warmly so, treating it like another inevitable development in the life of his only son. His mother, dejected, was already throwing her full weight into Lenore: she would be the family lawyer, she would be there to bail him out of jail one day.

Tad had to admit that he liked the rhythm of the days and nights. There were no Randy Richters or Isaac Niedermans to keep up with anymore, no parties to attend, no girls to try to please. He missed fucking—he had broken up with his only college girlfriend three months ago—but not much else. Existence cooled dully in front of him. He didn't see the point in turning into either his mother or his father. He was slowly saving enough money so he could never see any of them ever again.

It was at the end of March, just as the snow had completely melted off the pavement, when Tad heard his father on the telephone. He knew, immediately, he wasn't supposed to be hearing what he was hearing.

"You're going to keep it?" his father said. "You're going to keep it? You're going to keep it? Christ almighty. I can't."

Tad was home by accident. Twenty minutes earlier, he had left for the diner. Shortly after he got there, he realized he had forgotten his wallet. This didn't happen often. He had a compulsion for checking his back pocket. He told his manager, Big Dale Swallow, he had to run home, and for Juan or Eric to cover him for a few minutes. Big Dale tolerated him enough to let him go.

He opened the door just in time to see his father in the kitchen, sweat beading his forehead, his hand curled around the phone. The words had already left his mouth. His father always had a loud voice, one that carried when it needed to. One that, by accident, could find its way through walls. He must have known something because he quieted. He sensed his son's arrival and Tad couldn't do much to hide it. Like his father, he was a producer of unintentional noise, his feet clopping on carpets.

His father hung up the phone.

"Tad, you're home."

"Sorry, I forgot my wallet."

"No problem. Go ahead. Just wrapping up a work call."

His father didn't take calls from work at home. They both understood the absurdity of the explanation. Tad could challenge him, ask what was really going on, kick it off in a casual way or just brandish the blade of his accusatory voice. He wasn't afraid of either of his parents. They were humans like him, only older, their wisdom faulty. But he couldn't speak. His lips had drawn together. His chest was hot, his throat dry, his arms and legs locking into place. The kitchen, beneath a dim florescent bulb, began to fade, losing the remnant of its tired color. He stepped backward. He needed water.

"I need to go to the bathroom," he said quietly.

In September, Tad moved into an illegal basement apartment off Jericho Turnpike, paying rent in cash to an Indian immigrant who owned the upper two floors. No windows, a barely functioning bathroom, no functioning kitchen. There were two crucial upsides: no parents and an ability to pay the rent while socking away money for savings. He was living in a way that could feel outside of time, the only markers food and water and work, the diminishment of sunshine and the arrival of night a daily coincidence he could shrug off. He lost weight. He stopped snorting coke entirely. He didn't have a phone.

Language retreated to his head.

His parents tried to visit him but gave up. How could they get him if he didn't have a phone and he wasn't answering his door? The doorbell didn't even work. Fall arrived and he didn't notice, only that the sweat on his chest and between his legs continued to diminish. He understood what it meant when it was said one lived in the shadows. The phrase always created a cartoon in his head, creeping darkness off the side of building, but now the lack of physicality took on a new meaning, his bones having the weight of air, his eyes disappearing into the hulls of his sockets, his thoughts petering into instinct. He slept deeply, without dreams.

In October, he decided to pay his parents a visit.

There was no explanation. He didn't need them anymore. He could go to work, pay his rent to the Indian, and never need anyone again. Lenore was at Columbia now, preparing to seize the kind of social capital his parents longed for all their lives and his father, in some sense, seemed to attain. He couldn't hate them for what they were. They knew of no other way to live. It was late October, around the time of the World Series. His father tried so hard, over many years, to make him care about baseball. They sat on hot, sticky seats at Shea Stadium, the sun browning the back of his neck, the air smelling of ketchup and stale popcorn. His father held a scorecard and tried to give the squiggles meaning. *Look here, Tad. This is how you score a fly out to left.* All he really liked was listening to the crowds, their odd, collective rhythms, the way they almost sounded like the innards of some demented, enormous machine. The game meant so little. But his father tried, didn't he?

Tad hadn't seen them in a month and a half and he lived two miles away.

He decided to go on Thursday, when he was off. He entered his car and turned on the radio, hearing gospel music. The station was alien to him. He couldn't recall ever roving on the dial there but his body could perform actions without his mind following, the strings not always attached. There was nothing in particular he had to say to his parents. He was hungry and he imagined reaching into the fridge he knew so well for some sliced meat. His father was drawn to cold cuts, turkey and salami, lining the fridge with the salted flesh of dead animals. Whatever moral objections Tad could summon against the consumption of meat were outweighed by the sheer taste, the delight that came with well-cooked, well-cured burgers or steaks or venison or deli turkey. He loved the smell. On Jericho Turnpike, driving without thought, he could see how much he had been denying himself. An urge almost came, before he suppressed it, to sprint to a phone booth and call Harold Shaw at school. That coked up piece of shit. He could call Harold Shaw and tell him to fix his life, fix his face. Fix all of it.

"Watchit, buddy," a bald head shouted to him through the window, trying to change into a lane he already held. Tad just waved back.

There had been times when rage would overtake him, a feeling so hot as to be beyond description, language exchanged for action. He could punch his way through drywall. He could smash mirrors, shatter lamps, crash his trembling foot through a table. In the moment it all made sense, the universe coming together. There was a dark beauty to the way his body could cut through space. But it was destruction and it got him nowhere. He had turned twenty and he had no idea what the future could possibly hold for him. He didn't understand the people he still called friends. His mother and father would never know him. The world was light and he was the void, the anti-matter—this he began to think as he drove. He knew he wanted to feel differently but didn't know how. Soon he would be at the house he grew up in, knocking on the door, entering, waving, maybe even smiling. Lenore would or wouldn't be home. He didn't know what he preferred. In the living room, maybe, his father would be reading a book, a cigarette burning between his lips.

He stopped a block away, parking his car next to a sprawling white house with colonnades and a porch. He smelled the money pumping through it. As he leaned out of his car, he spat, watching the saliva dissolve on the asphalt. It was warm for October and he was glad, sunshine and clear skies. He began to whistle. What could he say when he got inside? Hi Mom and Dad. That was all. What did he want? That would be their inevitable questions. He knew his mother, in particular, was suspicious of him, quietly unsure if it was her DNA coursing through him even though they looked so much alike. Same nose, same eye color, same hair color, same way of chewing food. Lenore actually looked more like their father. She narrowed her eyes over text in the same intense yet slightly befuddled way.

Tad began to walk. The street was wide and empty, like it always was, the cars shelved in their garages. No one walked outside because that's not what anyone did here. You went into your garage, entered your car, and drove. He was the outlier in the street, the lone body against the sun. This was how the desperadoes felt in the Old West, their guns drawn, singular in their walk toward death. He wasn't going to die. He was just going to say hello.

He hooked his fingers in the beltloops of his jeans. He was a gunslinger.

When he looked back on this day, years later, he would consider words like coincidence and serendipity, words to explain what could not actually be explained. He would remember how large and empty they really were. As he transitioned to a new way of living, he would think these were lazy approximations of God and how He was the sole guide of fate. In that moment, still the young gunslinger on his way to the house he had grown up in, he had no thought of God. There was only the usual enigma of his immediate future, a vastness trending, always, toward death. He was only certain he would die.

The house looked at it always did. Like the others, faded white clapboard, the gardenias his mother meticulously watered, the windows with their curtains drawn. She didn't want the neighbors looking in.

It was only him looking in now. I'm here, he almost shouted. I'm here.

And then his father walked out the door, directly down the front path to where his only son was standing.

Tad couldn't breathe. His father saw him and smiled in a way that was jagged and strange, like a distant relative attempting communion through a faded family photo. He was sweating, a red tie knotted tightly at his neck, his trousers dark blue. It was late afternoon.

"Tad," his father said, stopping. Tad had cut him off on the way to his car. He had been intending to leave. Where would his father drive? In the bulge of his trousers, Tad could detect a pack of cigarettes.

"Hey."

"You're home—I mean, it's good to see you. How are you?"

"I'm pretty good. Just came to say hello."

His father rested a hand on his shoulder, ruffling the sleeve of the pullover sweater he had decided to wear. He didn't know what to make of this gesture. He knew many thoughts were competing for space in his father's mind. He knew his father intended to get to his car. He was simply in the way.

"That's great. It's really great to see you."

"Is mom home?"

"She's out, out shopping."

"Lenore?"

"At school."

"Right."

"Well, I've got to get going right now. But your mother should be home soon. She's making dinner. I need to run a few errands and I may be out a bit late. You should stay for dinner. She would like that."

"I might."

"You look well."

"Thanks."

"I really ought to get going. Come by tomorrow. I should be here."

"I'll try."

"It was good to see you, Tad."

"Good to see you," Tad murmured, his father rushing past him. He climbed into his car, his features shrinking behind the windshield. His father was always hurrying to places away from where he was supposed to be. As much as Tad could resent it, he was getting old enough to understand this was what adults did. To be an adult and shed the dead skin of childhood meant to enter into tangled arrangements beyond explanation that would define your very existence until death.

Once his father's car had left the driveway, he sprinted to his own parked car down the road, his sneakers hardly touching the ground. He ran like the baseball players of his father's lost youth, Mays taking third, Mantle soaring toward the monuments to nip a fly ball from the air. And, of course, the Duke of Flatbush. He hardly cared for them but knew them all and even their statistics because his father had weaved their stories into his childhood. They clung to him as he entered his car and began to drive, following his father's familiar license plate. He decided he was going to tail his father as far as he would go.

Tad knew he was heading to the city. He kept pace at the traffic lights, careful not to fall too far behind as his father's car drove in the direction of the entrance ramp for the Long Island Expressway. He was due at the diner in an hour, the start of an eight-hour shift, but this would take precedence and if he was fired so be it, there were other diners and other ways to scrape together a sub-minimum wage. He didn't know what he would find at the end of this drive. He only knew he would keep driving, onto the highway and wherever else. His father's car sped, weaving into the left lane. He would speed too.

Like father, like son.

Traffic slowed, as it always did, when they cut into Queens. The brake lights multiplied. His left foot danced from the gas to the brake and back again. He strained forward, peering into the bleary dark. Trucks threatened to block his view, obscure the car, the New York license plate he needed to tail. His father's plate was HV42321. He repeated the letters and numbers to himself like prayer.

He liked the mindlessness of highway driving, especially when cars cleared out of his way. Manhattan loomed now, remote and glittering, each spire like a haughty goddess rendering judgment from the sky. They were passing the Brooklyn-Queens Expressway and heading straight west, to the Midtown Tunnel. Cars slowed again, an epidemic of brake lights. He needed cash for the toll. His father changed lanes and he slid over, one hand on the wheel, one hand in his back pocket, shifting for his wallet. Father and son, paying tolls together, one after the other. Saul Plotz to Tad Plotz. Tad, he had to explain to anyone who cared, was his real name. His father gave him three letters, percussive, firing from his lower row of teeth. It was short for nothing. He was Tad. He spent years of his life telling people he was not Theodore or Thomas, his existence whittled down.

They were through the tunnel together. Tad wondered if his

father suspected anything. He knew what Tad's car looked like.

Manhattan was where work was but Manhattan at night was not where his father's work should be. There was nothing for a federal employee to do at night. He wasn't essential enough. He wasn't fighting crime, putting out a fire, hauling trash, cradling a body riddled with gunshots. Maybe it was a lover squirreled away in some apartment somewhere. That was the easy answer. Men of his age needed a second woman to tell things that couldn't be told to the first. They were the keepers of secrets, the winking confidants, the true loves who could never be true loves because this sort of epoch had not allowed it.

Tad conceived her as he left the Midtown Tunnel: urbane, elegant, a few years younger than his father because men of that generation could not stomach dating older women. She was tall, dark-haired, worked for an advertising agency or a bank or maybe was the great-granddaughter of a Vanderbilt. She laughed harshly, smoked aggressively, and wasn't afraid to give head. She was a Simone, a Julia, a Belle. She could not be Jewish, Tad decided. His father wouldn't flee one Jew for another. What kind of logic was in that?

They swerved deeper into the occluded city. They were slashing among side streets, then avenue-bound, downtown. He wouldn't lose his father. Yellow taxis spun past them, buses in haunted light, neon glowing on all sides of them. Women on the streets, laughing into their lovers' ears. It was all painterly and he had to smile.

In front of them loomed a hospital.

His father's car jerked down a cratered street and into a parking garage. Tad followed, realizing he'd have to burn his meager cash supply on parking. What was so abundant where he grew up was a commodity here, like paying for the privilege of breathing air. He saw his father's familiar hand take a ticket from the booth attendant. The car descended down the ramp and all he could do was watch, not even looking at the attendant who wordlessly passed the ticket over. What he needed to do was park close enough to follow on foot but not close enough to be seen. When his father turned left, he decided to turn right.

Tad knew the sound of his father's loafers, the click clack over the floorboards of his childhood home, the lightest scent of tobacco and aftershave. He listened again for the one-two thump, an echo off the grim cement, and when he heard it he began to follow. His father was a hundred feet ahead, cigarette smoke trailing over his shoulder. A van came trundling into the garage and his father dipped to the side, onto an embankment. Tad was surprised at how limber he was. Inside his middle-aged body lay the ghost of the boy he had been and sometimes, maybe, it could materialize at the strangest time; he saw his father in center field, fifteen years old, roving under a fly ball. Tad was never that kid, someone who wanted to catch a baseball out of the air.

The hospital was a wall of light, like the hull of an extraterrestrial craft crashed to Earth. Tad had been a healthy kid so he was grateful to not know hospital protocol, the way people walked and talked within its walls, how nurses scrambled to patients, what food could be consumed according to custom, how to manage a tombstone smile. Once, when he was six, he had been transported to a Nassau County hospital with a bad stomach ache that could have been appendicitis but wasn't. He was discharged after one night and the memory became a dream.

There was a sign-in desk where his father was hunched, talking. Several women in white sat behind, their faces blank. The freshly waxed floors had the shine of unreality. Tad lingered at the sliding doors, letting bodies pass him, wondering whether they could walk through him. Maybe he was the ghost. His father hurriedly wrote something and began jogging down a hallway, Tad's signal to move.

He was at the desk ten seconds after his father, with no words coming from his mouth.

"Yes?" The woman at the desk asked.

"That man, um—"

"Excuse me?"

"Was that Mr. Plotz?"

"Do you know him?"

"He's my, uh, I was supposed to meet him. My father."

"Can I see ID?"

Tad's hand trembled over his wallet. He hated the photograph of himself on his driver's license, a frail teenager with a drained expression, his eyes blurred like stones sunk to the bottom of a pond. The woman looked at the license and saw the last name.

"You said you're his son?"

"Yes. Tad Plotz."

"Well, congratulations. Go join your father in the maternity ward."

Tad didn't understand her the first time. The words passed through him without meaning, randomized sounds his brain struggled to rearrange.

"Excuse me?"

"It's on the third floor, the maternity ward."

"Oh right."

He knew he wasn't actually staggering backward, like a man in a cartoon. He was turning and walking away. It was a slow, easy walk, the colors of the hospital dissolving, the sound slipping as he entered the dark. The words began to take form, making images that would harden into implications: antiseptic wallpaper, sharp overhead lights, the woman his father had given a baby to, his hand around hers. His heart felt light, as if it could float away altogether. All of him was like that, the more he considered it: an insubstantial body that was little more than a symmetrical arrangement of skin and bone and flesh. The garage attendant seemed almost surprised to see him. He would pay the hour rate for fifteen minutes. The cash disappeared in a slot.

He sat uselessly behind the wheel of his car. All he could do was back out and drive away.

2

The news existed in that dangerous moment between what the past had been and what the future would always be.

In the months leading up to when her life would change forever, Mona was in a mood of taking stock. The decade was ending. As she aged, she became increasingly interested in numbers, attaching growing significance to them as they came to define what her life would be. Soon, she'd be forty. That was halfway to eighty, nearly halfway to a half century, arguably closer to death than life. She didn't *feel* it, not in the way her friends did, griping about leg or back pains, the creeping cellulite, wrinkles fanning out. She wasn't old because she was winning tennis tournaments. Friends would remark she should've gone pro but she wasn't interested in any tennis paycheck beyond the cash prizes and the value of a trophy, the lure of fame never serious enough to provoke any kind of lament. And besides, most people didn't get to be Martina or Chris or Billie Jean King. That was a lottery life.

She was content to play tennis, take photos, and then cherish the memories of playing tennis.

After the *Daily Raider* folded, she had bounced to the *Post* and then the *Daily News*. For a time, she contributed to both, floating between assignments, making enough money on shootings, robberies, and building fires to pay her rent. She was always the girl who had taken the Vengeance photograph and later interviewed him. It was enough to build a career, or the shadow of one, hustling for photos and waiting for her credit in tomorrow's paper.

Life had been okay, even good for the most part. The worst year was 1980. Within five months, her father and mother died. Her father dropped dead from a heart attack at dinner. He was eating chopped liver. Vic was there, the only child who still regularly ate with him, still wearing his USPS uniform. He would tell her that dad was dead by the time the ambulance showed up, not breathing, his eyes still open.

Her mother's pancreatic cancer arrived on cue. She hadn't been feeling well at the time of the heart attack, a queerness in her stomach and stool, and it was a doctor's appointment, prompted by her husband's sudden death, that delivered her own death date to her. She was told she had less than a year to live. The cancer could not be stopped. In October, shortly before Mona's birthday, she died at Maimonides, Melinda, Mona, and Vic standing over her.

This time Mona cried. She left her siblings, ran downstairs, and sobbed in the parking lot, her back against a stranger's automobile.

Then Mona traveled. With Liv to Morocco, with Al and Liv to Paris, once alone to the Soviet Union. She took photos with an old polaroid when she went abroad. It was easy, in a new country, to forget she was mortal.

New York City was changing, that she knew, and she could see it most when she returned from a trip. Certain bars and restaurants would disappear, the landlord content to keep it vacant until the property escalated enough in value for a better-heeled tenant, like a bank or a McDonald's, to suddenly take its place. New construction filled once vacant lots. Graffiti vanished from brick walls and train hulls. Her rent began to edge upward at a steady year-over-year trajectory she was not used to, especially when the management company, back in the '70s, had struggled to fill units. There was a time she felt she was almost doing them a favor by mailing a check every month.

That time had passed. Old men and women left their apartments, either to Florida or cemeteries. In came younger residents, those born a full decade after Mona, paying rents that would have been unimaginable when she moved in. The men commuted to work in dark jackets and bright red ties, their hair gelled against the wind, and the women joined them in gray suits, complete with shoulder pads. They didn't smile in the elevator and didn't have to. They had money.

Then Al asked to marry her. They had just gotten back together, one more reconciliation in a decade that had been, among the rise of Reagan and the alleged resurgence of New York and the dispersal of her credited photos of maimed and burned corpses in the city's tabloids, a time for habitual break-ups and reunions with Al, now an artist living off Tompkins Square Park, painting in a den of crack addicts. She loved him enough and he really loved her and Liv encouraged a marriage, since they all got along and it was inevitable anyway, right?

They were at an ancient, excessively expensive bistro in downtown Brooklyn, the sort of place that wanted to remind you men ate steaks here when women couldn't vote. Al was sweating, his hand wrapped around his cloth napkin, a plate of oozing spaghetti cooling in his wake. She poked a chicken cutlet with a heavy silver fork. String music played from hidden speakers. The waiter repeatedly badgered them about the wine list. The carpeting had the hue of the wine list spilled and dried on the floor. When Al spoke, she looked at him and then at the window, where trucks crawled on a narrow street of faded cobblestone.

"Mona, I'm ready to take the next step. I'm ready."

"You're ready?"

"Mona Glass," and there he was reaching into his pocket, the velvet-lined box in his hand, a smile breaking slowly across his face, "will you, uh, will you marry me?"

The boy she had first kissed that night chasing Vengeance, that thrill in the car, wanted to marry her.

"Al," she said.

His eyes were wide and waiting. They had been friends, then lovers, then friends, then lovers, a whirl that had grown comforting, the background noise to a life. Marriage was stillness. Al had quit the amusement park, stopped doing the books, pursued a passion. He would never be famous but he would have a career. A gallery wanted him. Al didn't need marriage any more than she did. But he wanted it and he was here with this ring, thousands of dollars thrown into the void, and she needed to answer him.

"Al, I, I don't think so—"

"You don't?" And he withdrew the box just as quickly as he had brought it out, his face hardening. "Oh, well, I was thinking, we've been getting along . . ."

"I'm never getting married, you know that. I've said that."

"You said that to other people."

She knew what he meant. There had been a person she turned down for marriage and one she still thought about, just about every day. He still called. Once in a while, they'd get dinner. Once in a while, he'd come upstairs.

"I can't."

"Think about it, Mona."

"I have."

"You didn't think very long."

She reached out and took his hand. "Aren't you happy as we are? Isn't this good? Don't we have fun?"

"We do."

"Marriage means, I don't know, we are fused into one body before God."

"I want to spend my life with you."

"We are."

"You know what I mean."

"I just can't, Al, I'm sorry. I like what we have. Don't you like what we have?"

"I love what we have, Mona, that's the point."

They finished the dinner in relative silence, passing banal remarks about the taste of the sauce and the hardness of the rolls, how a waiter seemed to walk on his toes. Al paid the bill as she protested. They walked to his car because he drove. She should have known, when he offered to pick her up at her apartment and drive down here, that something was afoot.

He drove without speaking and she hated how his shoulders were slumping, the way in which he, like all men, wanted to shame her into giving him what he wanted. If she felt poorly enough about herself, she could wed him. She strained to see why he really wanted to do it. Was it for an ideal? His pushy Italian grandmother, now on her deathbed? A love so overpowering that it needed to be recognized by the State of New York? At her apartment building, he sighed deeply and rolled down his window, lighting a cigarette and then blowing smoke, delicately, into the night. He was always handsome in a haunted, underfed way, and even now she wanted to take hold of him, cradle his body against her own.

"Well, it was a good dinner," she said finally, knowing it was nothing close to what Al wanted to hear.

"The sauce was a bit heavy," he said, rolling up his window and driving away.

It was Saul. Always Saul.

If she had to explain it to Al in a way that would enrage him most, she would say that she could not marry him because this would make it harder for her to see Saul Plotz, the older man with the other family he would never leave for her. There was a stasis to her life, Saul and Al, that she was not willing to disrupt as she neared forty. Her parents, before they died, couldn't have believed in her marriage to Saul anymore—though she still wore the ring around them—and they had stopped asking long ago when they could visit the new apartment. She said Saul had moved into her apartment and she tried to keep them as far away from it as possible, going over to visit them in their new Bay Ridge co-op or getting dinner somewhere close to them, a diner or a Greek restaurant. If her parents managed to get inside, she tried to sling one of Saul's old windbreakers over a kitchen chair to create some faint impression that he really lived there.

Al told her, a few months after his proposal, that he was moving to California. He did it over beers on a Friday night, Liv at his side.

"Los Angeles is the place to be now," he said. "New York is getting played out."

"LA is a drag," Liv said, trying as hard as she could to hide her disappointment.

"You think the art scene is better out there?" Mona asked.

"I need to go for a while. Clear my head. I have some contacts. There's a gallery that's hunting for the sort of stuff I'm doing now. Color Field. You know Frankenthaler?"

"Of course," Liv said.

Mona didn't know Frankenthaler.

"I'm going in that vein and, anyway, it'll be good for a change of scenery. What are we, thirty-seven, and we've been here all our lives? I visited a friend out there and the weather doesn't get you down and you can go to Dodgers games and why not?"

"Where will you live?" Liv asked.

"Plenty of cheap apartments. I have a cousin out there who's going to help set it up."

"You Italians and your cousins."

"You Jews and your . . . accountants."

"Good one."

"You'll like L.A.," Mona finally said, setting down her beer.

"Will I?"

"You will."

On the day he left, he called to say he was going to the airport and Liv would drive him, no need to take him to JFK. Mona told him to enjoy the trip, that she would come out and see him soon. Al said she could come anytime once he got set up. He was also going to take a job at a gallery, in addition to showing his paintings. She said she'd like to buy one.

"Sounds like a plan," Al said.

She spent the next year convincing herself she didn't force her friend and lover to Los Angeles, where she was unlikely to see him anytime soon. Liv tried to plan several trips but all fell through for unrelated reasons, an illness or a scheduling conflict or an unexplained cancellation on Al's part. She understood, soon enough, that Al couldn't see her again.

And Saul seemed to implicitly understand too. He began to call more and they were making dinner dates all through the summer and fall of 1988, Saul telling her about the foreign travel he was getting to do on behalf of the federal government, enjoying free lunches with Soviet diplomats in a half-hearted attempt to ferret out secrets. His Soviet counterparts would seek one benign tidbit to bring back to their bosses and in exchange Saul would offer something up, a half-truth they knew was a half-truth, a morsel to satisfy those who decided how generous their pensions would ultimately be.

"This is the Cold War now," Saul told her.

They had over a decade together, uncountable dinners and hours in bed, along with a fraudulent wedding. Her love was rooted in the familiar, memories joined to the emotional and physical language of her life, his scent and voice and touch as essential and knowable as the breaths that left her own throat. Chasing him away always brought him back. She would never marry him, never share a house, but she could have him on a Saturday afternoon in August in her apartment, naked and laughing in her bedsheets. She could coil herself around him, feel the beating of his heart and lap at the nape of his neck, drawing close enough for his blood to almost rush into her own. In those moments in her bed, she believed she had all of him, his deepest core, and that was enough to carry her through the days when he was gone, off again to his family in another county and a wife that still existed, after all this time, as a figment beyond approach, a legend without a corresponding tale.

Felicia Plotz, right there in a phone book. Mona could call anytime she wanted.

On her thirty-ninth birthday, Saul took her out dancing. There was a tango class and he had two free tickets, a gift from work. Like teenagers, they necked in the car afterwards, and then fucked in her bed. They fucked again in the morning. It was Sunday and she asked, too casually, if his family would miss him on the weekend, when he was expected to do whatever it was suburban fathers did, take the kids out for pancakes or mow the lawn.

"I told them I was in Europe," Saul said. "And besides, Tad and Lenore don't ask after their old man anymore. They have other concerns."

"That's sad."

"I don't know how much they ever really cared. Well, they do. We love each other. But, I don't know, I never figured it out."

"Figured what out?"

"How to be a father. There's supposed to be a mystical bond that forms and you do everything correctly for them, selflessly love them, and I never figured it out."

"You're a good father."

"You don't know that."

He said it playfully, a grin lighting up his face. But the truth of the words, however he chose to emphasize them, cut at her slowly as they day wore on, as they ate eggs and bacon for breakfast at a diner and took a drive down to the Coney Island boardwalk to stroll among the fidgety seagulls and Soviet emigres. They passed the parachute jump, the android appendage in the sky. She imagined phantom jumpers, men and women and children falling to the planet, their sneakers skidding on the sand. Recently she had stopped smoking but now she wanted one cigarette, that poisonous relief. Saul was smoking less too. They walked west, away from the park. Blunt brick apartments met them.

"I do have to go to Europe, for real," Saul said. "Just a week."

"What will you tell your family then?"

"I have another trip. It's precarious. Who knows how long the Soviets will last."

"They seem built for the long haul."

"Everything seems that way until it isn't."

3

Mona was shooting for the *News* now because they were willing to pay a slightly higher rate to keep her from the *Post*. When a snowstorm hit, they had her in the streets for seven hours, shooting men digging out cars and cops directing traffic and kids sledding in the park. It was easy work and she was happy for the reprieve from bloodied corpses. Though she had been doing it now for a decade, she had no grand theory of photography, no lessons to pass on to others. She was good because she was always good and just needed to uncover this skill that would launch her into delicious motion, charging after a corrupt politician or breaking through a police line or rushing toward a flaming house on the verge of collapse. Winning on the tennis court or beating out the other photogs to get the best shot—it was all small, beautiful glory.

Saul visited her in January, on a Sunday she was off. He came bearing gifts, a box of chocolate for no particular reason and a *Sports Illustrated*. It was a quiet news cycle, just after the holidays, and she didn't have to worry about the phone ringing from the photo editor on an off-day, begging for extra help. He undid his tie and she unbuttoned his shirt. They had sex on her couch. This was the aggression she liked, the real Saul beating beneath the father and bureaucrat. She felt him shudder inside of her. When he was done he fell off to the side, like always, exhaling heavily. She traced a finger around his neck, drawing an invisible line down to the dark hair curled in the valley of his chest. If she was told, in that droplet of time, she would never be able to go anywhere else again, that she would die on that couch in the arms of Saul Plotz, she would have accepted her fate.

Two weeks later, she missed her period. She didn't think much about it. She was almost forty, getting to that time, and she had heard enough gripes from Liv about irregular periods, no matter how clockwork her own body was. It was true she was technically not on birth control, since she had assumed, at thirty-nine, she was unlikely to bear any children. She knew of no thirty-nine year-old mothers of newborns. Men could impregnate women at any age but it got harder as they got older and she had sex with Saul so many times and of course a missed period didn't mean anything had come out of it *this time*, it could mean the period was late or her body was failing her in some other mysterious way.

On a Friday night, out for drinks with Liv and a friend from Liv's work, Audrey, she threw up after one beer, hocking spit and light bile in the bathroom. When she was done, she was still nauseous, the table slanting away from her. Audrey asked her if she had something rotten to eat. Mona nodded, her hand trembling around the wine glass. After ten agonizing minutes, she said she would have to go home.

Another week passed. Her head continued to throb. On Wednesday, she threw up again. Her body felt like a tender and baffling inheritance, a sudden accident. It was never like this. Shooting a crime scene, dominating on the tennis court, making love—it always did what it was supposed to do. Perhaps she was really sick. Her mind hunted through scenarios. A friend of Liv's, just a bit older than them, had found out recently she had breast cancer. A lump. Stage two. There were no lumps on her own body, thank God. On Thursday, she stared at herself in the mirror, paler now, strands of dark hair matted on her sweat-dappled forehead. On Friday, she stared again.

She felt like shit.

"Saul, I don't feel well," she said on Friday morning, calling him at work at the federal building.

There were voices in the background. Men hovering. He whispered he would call her back. Fifteen minutes.

She waited twenty. "I don't feel well," she said again, this time with less feeling. In an hour, she had to drive to a Koch press conference in Queens.

"What's going on?" He sounded upbeat, Saul-at-work, the affect of a salaryman coming into his own.

"I feel horrible. Something is wrong."

"What's up, Mona? Tell me."

"I threw up and I feel dizzy."

"Probably the stomach flu that's been going around. I read in the *Times* yesterday we're in the midst of a bad flu season. Worse we've seen in a while. You see a doctor?"

"No."

"Rest and drink lots of fluids."

"I was going to go to the drug store."

"Sure, get some medicine for it, you know, what's the brand—"

"A test, Saul."

"What?"

"You know."

"I don't."

"I need to find out."

"That's ridiculous, of course it isn't—it *can't* be."

"I don't know."

"Okay, let's calm down. You know, might as well. After you get the negative, you'll see it's probably something bad you ate. Or the flu. Call in sick to work."

"They need me to shoot a Koch presser. I can't. Talk to you later."

"That fucking asshole. Okay. Let me know how it all goes."

At Genovese, Mona bought a kit. She remembered once, eight years ago, worrying about it after a night with Al when his condom broke but she never had a feeling like this in the days afterward and her period showed up, one day late, putting her fears to rest. To show the cashier, an elderly woman with horn-rimmed glasses and spidery fingers, this was an ordinary day, she added M&M's and deodorant, slipping in both over the kit and letting the cashier ring them all up together and throw them into the same plastic bag. The cashier's hand paused over the kit, a small shadow cast on the packaging. She tried to make eye contact with Mona but Mona wasn't looking at her; she was pretending to survey the row of gum.

Without looking directly at the cashier, Mona pushed across a ten dollar bill. The cashier achingly made change. Mona was scrutinizing, as best she could, the price of a pack of cigarettes. All the items were safely in the plastic bag. The change was made. Outside, she finally let go of a breath and watched the traffic grumble by, the every day ferment that couldn't stop to judge her. New York's indifference cut both ways and today she was thankful. Even the cashier, in her judgment, wouldn't care in another hour.

Mona peed and waited. She didn't have to wait long.

"No, no, no," she said to her empty apartment, her empty apartment not even sighing in reply. "No, no, no, no."

If she spoke each *no* into existence, the test could change itself. And if the test could change itself, she could change herself. Her body, always so reliable, the deliverer of so many tennis victories, the vessel of *un*-sickness—when had she last felt a cold, a fever, a sore throat?—was now what would undo her. She stared at the test and flung it away, off into the garbage or a pocket universe of absent matter, she couldn't say. She fell back on the couch.

A child growing inside of her. A smaller version of her, of needs and wants innumerable, eating away, drinking away, taking what she was to make *it* stronger. How do you raise a child? How do you make sure it doesn't become a deranged killer? This was her next thought, incongruent but real, her failure launching a new psychopath into orbit. It wasn't just the genes that made them; they all had unfit parents. She couldn't argue to the empty apartment that she was fit. She was fit to run and jump and take photographs, not gently nurture a beautiful boy or girl into being. She was Mona Glass. Mona Glass did not raise children.

So a decision was made, yes, she knew what to do. Saul would agree. Easy enough. She began to pace. The sickness had melted away. There was the street, the people, all those lives like stars in the sky, each clinging to galaxies she could only dimly apprehend. Some of them had children. She touched her stomach. Now, well, she *could*—there was, waiting inside of her, nothing and everything. Love enfolded in fear. Hope in terror. She continued to pace. In the corner of her eye, a pigeon was taking to the windowsill, surveying what she had become. What if she . . .? Why *couldn't* she?

She couldn't because she was Mona Glass and Mona Glass was not the mother of human life. It had never been this way, therefore it would never be. It was not the narrative that played inside of her, barely at a whisper, just audible as she pounded through her days. A baby, a child, a teenager, an adult. The years pooled at her feet. She wanted to say *no* one more time, shout it out. The word caught in her teeth. She couldn't say it again.

There were other narratives too, other whispers of logic, hints of ambition. She paced faster, the pigeon flying away. There was Saul. What would he do? Saul could not be a father. Saul was already a father. His narrative had hardened. It was impregnable, with its marriage certificate and mortgage documents and life insurance policies, paperwork that certified it was real and it would always be real. She did not want it, anyway. She was not going to remake herself for him. She did not want to be shuttled into the suburbs, in secrecy or in the open, to become a figurine in a window, smiling in faint sunshine.

It was all much easier when she could believe it was a stomach flu.

4

Saul offered immediately to pay for an abortion. It would be Mona's second. When she was twenty-seven, she had visited a doctor after having sex with a man named Bruce, a tennis instructor she had been curious about. They only saw each other for about a month and she wasn't taking birth control regularly. Bruce, who was forty, refused to wear a condom. The doctor she saw in Manhattan had been recommended by Liv's cousin, who had an abortion performed as well. It was quicker and more painless than she thought. She didn't want a child and wasn't ready for one and Bruce sure as hell wasn't going to be in her life any longer. She stopped seeing him without even telling him what happened.

"I know a very good doctor," Saul said on the phone. He was at work, his office door shut, no noise emanating around him.

"Where?"

"Manhattan. I'll get an appointment for you this Friday. Mickey Berman. I went to law school with his brother. We'll get you in."

"I don't know about this Friday."

"You want to do it soon, don't you?"

It was a question that she couldn't immediately answer. A pregnant Mona, a birthing Mona, a Mona so opposite what had been, until a day ago, the conception of who she was. The narrative could not include a child. She was almost forty. She wasn't actually married. Saul had his own family.

None of what she was about to say made any sense.

"I don't know."

She could see him through the phone, the way he painfully yet calmly sucked breath in, telling himself he could steady his tone, no matter what she said to him. She saw him adjust his tie, fiddle with his belt, stare out his twenty-third floor window to a humming Broadway, maybe press his fingers to the glass and feel the warmth of sunlight on his skin.

"What do you mean, Mona?"

"I may not go."

"Are you busy? Berman could get you in next week."

"I don't know."

"What don't you know?"

"Saul, this is a huge decision."

"But we've decided."

"We have?"

"I thought so, I mean . . ."

"Okay, how about we talk about this?"

"We are. Right now."

"In person."

"We can do that. We can get dinner Friday night."

"Friday night then."

Mona met Saul near his office, slipping into a diner on Church Street. Saul came minutes after she sat down, wearing his tan trench coat to guard against the possibility of rain later in the night. He sat down and smiled, his face creasing, his hands nervously finding the laminated menu. He started to talk like he always did, cramming the silence with his words, the old motormouth, telling her about the Georgian consulate and how the cafeteria in the federal building couldn't make an egg and asking if she was enjoying going to Koch press conferences because that loud bald asshole was going to lose, one way or another, the city was sick of him. A plump waitress couldn't even stop him—he muttered hamburger and fries, medium rare, then went right on talking—and he seemed to be hungry for more breath, so his words could overtake them both, transport them away from what was coming.

Mona opened her mouth.

"I wanted to tell you something."

"Yes?" Saul was drinking his cup of coffee, his other hand searching for a sugar packet.

"This is a huge decision."

"You want to see a different doctor? Berman is good. I can find someone else though."

"No, I don't."

"Who do you want to see?"

Mona took a large drink of water, feeling the ice slide around the inside of her mouth.

"I don't want to see anyone," Mona said.

"I'm trying to understand."

"I'm keeping it."

"How?"

"What do you mean? How?"

"I don't quite understand how this is even being considered."

"I think I want to keep it."

"You have time to decide."

"I am thinking about what it means to be a mother."

"It means a lot, Mona, it's a huge, huge thing, it's major, and I don't know—"

"You don't know if I can do it?"

"That's not what I mean. I just want you to think about what it means for us." He dropped his voice to a whisper. "For us to have a child."

"You already have a family. I know that."

"I want to be there for you, always. God, I love you. I've known you now, what, almost twenty years? I'm gonna be fifty. I just, I don't know how'd this even begin to work."

"I'd raise the child."

"If you keep it."

"You can be involved how you want."

"It's remarkable Felicia doesn't know about you. That's remarkable enough."

"Felicia probably knows about me."

"What?"

"Don't be so alarmed. Women know. Even me."

"Well, let's think about it. A week or two, okay? Let's just, we need—we need to really think about it."

She would think for his sake, decide again, posit scenarios, evaluate the twin paths her life could take as she ate dinner, went to work, played tennis, and lay awake at night. But each day that passed, she knew. It was knowledge on the scale of a dream, with its own logic she couldn't quite name. Perhaps she could call it a longing, though she had never had it before and the word connoted exactly that: wanting what had already been in existence. Instead, the feeling had simply appeared. There would be a person growing inside of her.

Saul didn't call for several days. When he did one afternoon, just as she was sitting down on her bed, a magazine in hand, he was not prepared for the finality in her voice. She could hear him cracking, the uncertainty and fear, the American male terror of *what does this mean for me?* He was a child again, in a way that disgusted her this time. The child who had struck out, the child kicking sand.

She didn't need him for this.

"You're going to keep it?" Saul said. "You're really going to keep it?"

"I am."

Saul was sick and Saul was sorry. He was sick, literally, stricken with a rare cold that wouldn't quit. Mucus practically foamed from his nostrils. His throat ached. Tissue boxes were raided and discarded within the day. His body was a floating hotel of aggrieved germs, his office a growing disaster zone. He kept coming in. He couldn't stand being at home.

He was sick because he knew Mona was having this child and he was comprehending how punishing his words to her had been and how, whenever he called her, her tone had drained of all lightness. She was a businesswoman, dealing in facts, figures, and trimesters. He was the dispenser of sperm and nothing more. Mona, politely, wasn't allowing him to make any kind of amends, even as he quietly, and then more persistently, began to ask that summer about what kind of role he would have in his child's life. Yes, *his*. He couldn't be at every baseball game, dance recital, or spelling bee but he'd be something, somewhere, this child wouldn't grow up not knowing his or her own father, he wasn't dead nor beat. And well—he wouldn't say this out loud, not yet anyway—but maybe he wanted another *shot*. He'd fucked up with Tad, his only son, a college dropout now living in some basement apartment off Jericho Turnpike. Tad wasn't turning it around. He saw it in the boy's stare, the way he shirked eye contact, how he seemed so terrified just to be alive. Lenore was fine, she'd get into law school and make money but he couldn't profess to really know her, to have accomplished a significant father-daughter bonding moment the television told him would happen by now. Lenore was closer to Felicia, that was okay, and Tad was closer to no one, which was not okay but also not likely to change anymore.

That's what he wanted to tell Mona, as the days burned on. He wanted a chance with the new child. He was going to be fifty. He had learned something. His initial reaction—kill it!—was gut, nothing else. The logistics were now getting turned over in his head, the money and the visitations, how he'd maintain another secret from his wife and children. A child could be kept as quiet as a mistress. And he'd visit! Maybe weekday afternoons, some weekends, a stray holiday, and attendance at soccer games or whatever the child wanted to do. He'd support all of it. Trips to the toy store, drives to the children's museum, videotapes of popular TV shows. A cash allowance.

He would give—give himself. He would love.

I'm sorry, he cried into the phone, the invisible one held in his hand. Forgive. Forgive me.

Mona consented to meet with him. She transformed from a person who was not visibly pregnant at all to one assertively so, her belly announcing itself in every diner and coffee shop they sat down in, the waitresses smiling approvingly, wishing her all the best. It helped Mona didn't look her age, more of a thirty-two or thirty-three year-old having a baby than someone nearly forty. She was another mother-to-be and he was the father, the husband, in his tailored suits that tapered down his wide, welcoming shoulders. Soon, she said, she would stop playing tennis. *You're still playing?* He almost spit his coffee out. Still winning, she said quietly.

"Do you know, uh, what kind of baby—"

"The gender?"

"Yeah."

"I'll find out when the baby is born."

That was it, his matter-of-fact woman. He tried to remember what Felicia was like, how she had evolved from giddy and expectant mother to bloated and miserable, the second pregnancy worse than the first. He knew he hadn't given enough of himself to Felicia, he was always closing off more of who he was, each year revealing less.

What Mona actually wanted, he couldn't say. She was merely polite with him and it was breaking his heart. Actually breaking it, because he had never known the feeling before, forty-nine years without this kind of rejection. He never cared much if girls in high school or college dumped him. With Felicia, it was a quick and tidy courtship, and when they fought in later years, he was never going to lament it for long. There was a literary quality to heartbreak as described that he never took seriously. He had friends who cried over women but they were more terrified of being alone than anything else. When you cut away the melodrama and the angst, the soft moaning for their beloved, that's what you found: men who couldn't hack it on their own. If he hadn't found Felicia, he would have had an agreeable existence as a bachelor, that he was sure of, he could be at home with himself, throw his feet up on the desk and read a good book or just watch clouds change shape in the sky. He had no problem inhabiting his own mind, carrying on phantom conversations, remembering World Series lineups from forty years ago.

But yes, he had to concede now, hearts could break. It was almost September. She'd be due in October. He took a day off and went to the beach alone, bringing his transistor radio, three newspapers, and one of the new Roth books where Roth was the main character. He drove down to Manhattan Beach, away from the rush, and sprawled out in the sun, smoking and reading and moping. There wasn't another word for it. He wasn't artful but he was sincere. He made his way through an entire pack of Marlboros, returning to an old habit he had been trying to shake. God, it felt so good on his teeth, down his lungs, blowing columns of smoke into the salty wind. He watched the tide go out, seaweed and seashells and dead horseshoe crabs peeking from the blackened sand.

His best sleeping came on the beach. For an hour, twenty minutes, or even five, he believed he could slip outside of time. He broke with reality in the heat. His eyes closed, he could live the interstellar existence the people on Earth would never know. In the aphotic dark, the trace of dead starlight all around him, he could leave behind his marriage, his children, his failure. How he treated Mona. The shapes behind his eyes were like the remnants of galaxies, exploding remnants of mystical color. He was coming home.

When he woke, he was still shirtless, still sweating. Manhattan Beach was unchanged. He was deeply tanned, as always, since he never wore sunscreen. If he went bearded, people thought he was an Arab. At least in Jerusalem, they did. He imagined a phone shooting from the sand, hitting his outstretched hand. The only line it connected to was Mona's.

"Help me," he would say, his lips dry.

In the end, he was there. Of course he was. She could only be so angry as he was holding her hand as another human being roared out of her.

A nurse with frenzied hair but calm eyes. And Saul Plotz.

"Push," the nurse said. "Breathe."

Push and breathe. So easy at any other time, two of the most obvious actions a body can take. She breathed as she rushed the net, pushed—well *brushed*, really—with her racket. She had said no to the epidural because she had been told it would take longer and she didn't want to spend a moment more in this hospital than she had to, not after watching her mother die. Yes, she would endure this radical pain, the cramping in her abdomen, groin, and back. She would feel every inch of her body ripping apart. Hot bands of muscle spasm pain shot through her. The nurse's voice began to fade.

She found Saul's eyes, their warmth and hopefulness. His mouth was moving but she couldn't hear what he was saying anymore.

Hours, like broken bodies, dragged by. She watched a clock, a classic with a bone-white face and black numbers, two elegant hands inching behind glass.

Breathe and push, breathe and push.

When the baby emerged, bloody and screaming, Mona couldn't believe it at all. The nurse brought the creature to her and immediately Mona wanted nothing more than to hold her, him, it—what was the gender?—and never let go until she died, the baby crying in her arms, rocking back and forth. My baby, she said. My baby.

He's a boy, the nurse said. Eight pounds, nine ounces. A healthy, baby boy.

Saul stood over her. He was almost beatific, the overhead florescence haloing his corduroy jacket. She looked at him without saying anything.

The baby cried. She would never let him go.

5

No name came to her. For all her anticipation, the readiness to raise a child and commence a new phase of her life, the final phase—she would, until her dying breath, be a mother—she never stopped to think what exactly she would call her son. There had been names drifting in and out of her consciousness. None stuck. None felt right.

And there was the birth certificate. Father. There was a father, yes, and he could easily be put there, she was being asked, father, first name, last name, and she gazed toward a window facing the waterfront, the East River enormous and silent.

The baby's last name would be Glass. There would be no father. She would make a name for the father.

Howard Strawberry, she told the nurse, mashing up two star New York Mets. That's the name of the man who was with you? The nurse squinted, just slightly, when she asked the question. Mona's voice began to shake. No, not him.

Oh okay, I apologize, ma'am. I thought he was the father.

He—

So I'll put Mr. Strawberry down as the father.

Does it matter who's there?

Excuse me?

I mean, if it's a name, any name, not a real name . . .

Not real?

There's no—no Howard Strawberry, exactly.

It needs to be a real name.

Leave it blank then.

Blank?

Yes. I'm the mother. That's it.

The baby's name?

His name, yes.

What will we put down? You have a few days but I'd advise doing it sooner rather than later.

His name. Well, his name is Emmanuel.

Emmanuel?

Yes. Emmanuel Glass. Emmanuel Esther.

Esther, that's . . .

A woman's name. But it will be his middle name.

Okay ma'am, we'll get that processed for you.

Processed, Mona thought. My boy. She held him and said his name silently to herself.

IV

Libra

1

"The dinosaurs," the boy asked. "What happened to them?"

Morah Klein leaned forward, her lips pinched together. He never liked when that look appeared on her face, like a cloud was passing over her. Sunlight, then shadow. She took a step toward him, her small shoes thudding on the carpet.

The other boys and girls swiveled their heads toward him. They were old enough to know what trouble looked like.

"What are you asking, Emmanuel?"

"I read, I saw—" He strained to remember how the fact first entered his head. This suddenly seemed essential. "An asteroid hit the Earth and killed the dinosaurs. Did the asteroid come before or after Noah's ark?"

"I've never heard of that."

"Did the dinosaurs fit on the ark?"

Morah drew her breath in, the room of boys and girls joining her, all of their breaths one except his own, which came hotter and faster as if he were running out of air altogether.

"No, Emmanuel. They did not. The Torah does not speak of dinosaurs."

The class began to snicker. There was still one more hour, snack time and story time behind them. This was raw instruction. This was the learning of a faith.

There was little he hated more than being here.

Morah spoke to the students she liked more. Sarah and Ezra and John and Samantha. The only student she probably liked less than Emmanuel was his friend Carmine. There were twelve of them in all, gathered into the backroom of the Bay Ridge Jewish Center from nine to noon, every Sunday. He was sure he liked it least. He hated sitting still, hated Morah's stare, how she sought out ways to expose him for not knowing what he was supposed to know. She wanted to teach them a new language, Hebrew, and the symbols, like spilled ink on the page, greatly confused him. *Alef, bet, gimel, dalet, he.* He tried to commit them all to memory for each Sunday. On Friday, on Saturday, they seemed to stick, but by Sunday—maybe it was the alchemy of a Brooklyn Saturday night—they were gone.

He liked Hebrew School even less than kindergarten.

Morah told them about the ark and at least this was a story, without rules he needed to memorize and repeat back to her. The animals entered, two by two, and it rained for forty days and forty nights. Hashem was punishing the people for being wicked. Why? Morah said the world had grown immoral. *Immoral* sounded like Morah. He pondered the word and the word led him to the image: rainfall on a desert, a sea rising over a hill, filling a canyon, covering a mountaintop, thousands and thousands of feet in the air, higher than an airplane, Noah's ark bobbing over the immoral, flooded Earth. Hashem had done exactly what He was supposed to do.

Morah said this was necessary for the good people to be born. But what about the others? He imagined boys like him, mothers like his mom, places like Brooklyn, water rushing down lungs until the world went black. All these people and all of them immoral. Did that mean today, in the modern day, they were not wicked anymore. Would there be another flood?

He was too afraid to ask.

"Hashem spared Noah and his family because they followed His word. Hashem is our guide, always. He knows what's best for all of us."

He had heard a lot about Hashem in Hebrew school. This was the same as God, the God that his mom, when she got angry, "damned." *God damn it*, she would say. Usually on the telephone or when she took him to the tennis court, smacking little green balls for two hours. The game was not as fun as baseball but he liked to pick over the balls themselves, dig at the fuzz with his fingernail, smell a fresh batch that cracked from a long, narrow can. They had letters and numbers. Penn 3. Penn 2. Wilson 1. He sat on the bench and watched his mom. This was on Saturday and on Sunday he went to Hebrew School.

He asked mom, more than once, to play tennis on Sunday and take him so he didn't have to go to Hebrew School.

"But don't you like it there? You're learning so much."

"No, I don't."

"You'll grow into a smart boy there. Pay attention. It's important to know where you came from."

"From the Hebrew?"

"The Jewish people, Emmanuel. We are Jewish."

In the neighborhood, this meant he didn't celebrate Christmas. On his teeball team, Mikey Pergola and Frank Doyle asked him if he believed in God if he was Jewish. "You go to hell if you don't," Mikey Pergola said. "I believe in God," he answered Mikey. "God is Hashem."

"*Hashwhooo?*" Frank Doyle belched.

"Hashem," and he hated himself for saying it.

When he started teeball, he played for a league called the 68th Precinct. This was also the police precinct and they sponsored the league. Frank Doyle's dad was a policeman. His mom stayed at home and cooked.

But *his* mom took pictures and his dad worked for the government. He still didn't quite know what "worked for the government" meant, except it was something important. Maybe like working for Hashem. When he played teeball, he tried not to think about Hebrew

School. Next year, the adults would pitch to them. Later, when he was older, he would get to pitch himself.

On the Sunday he asked about the asteroid killing the dinosaurs, which made him feel sad because he wanted to go to a zoo and see a dinosaur, he finally came home for lunch. Mom picked him up, fresh from tennis, and he rode in the booster seat in the back, too old for it on a technicality but short enough and desirous enough of the plush dark blue seat, the only he had known, that his mom wouldn't take it away. She asked him how school went. He said it was okay, just okay, and started to stare out the window, his finger drifting upward.

"Don't pick your nose!" mom jumped. "It's a yucky habit. Did you learn that from your father?"

"No mom."

"Don't do it."

He decided, as the car was moving, to tell her what happened.

"Morah got mad at me," he said quietly.

"Why?"

"I asked about the dinosaurs, if they made it onto Noah's ark."

"It's just a story, you know."

"I know."

"The stories are for instruction. They aren't literal. Do you know what I mean, Emmanuel?"

Literal. A word like *immoral*, enormous and beyond his understanding, like a deity in the sky. He concentrated and tried to see what appeared behind his eyes, the image and its power. When nothing came, he said he did not know.

"Literal means it actually happened, word for word. If you told your friend Carmine I drove you home today, that's being literal. The stories from the Bible—the Torah, they aren't exactly literal, they're used for instruction."

"The dinosaurs were real. I saw the bones at the museum."

"Yes you did. They are literal. But the story of Noah—you won't see Noah's bones in a museum. It's not a literal story. Do you understand?"

"Like make believe?"

Mom waited. He always hated silences like these.

"Yes, something like that, Emmanuel."

It was the season of questions. He didn't know why they kept coming. On the wall of kindergarten, he studied the calendar, the year in striking bold: 1995. Each day, he wanted to know more. There was a longing that was difficult to name, that wasn't easily satisfied like it used to be. In kindergarten, with Mrs. Stryker, he was Emmanuel Plotz. In Hebrew School, he was Emmanuel Glass. When he asked Carmine, who was in kindergarten with him too, if he got different names for different places, he laughed.

"I'm Carmine Asher, wherever I go."

Glass and Plotz, Glass and Plotz. He knew how to write both names, the snake's curve of the G, the Z like the beginning of a lightning bolt. One day, in the fall, he asked mom why they were different when he went to different places.

"Your last name is Plotz."

"Oh, okay. But in Hebrew School, Morah says I am Emmanuel Glass."

"Don't worry about that. Plotz is your last name."

He did like Plotz enough and it was dad's last name. His mom was Glass. Most of his friends had parents with the same last names, like the Doyles and the Pergolas. Carmine only had a mom and she was Victoria Asher.

During naptime, he got a bloody nose. It started when he couldn't find his Power Rangers blanket, with the Red Ranger featured prominently, to bring to his cot. Mrs. Stryker didn't like it when you delayed getting to your cot so he worried about getting in trouble. Mrs. Stryker was a big, old woman with dark, thick glasses and heavy lipstick. Her perfume always made him sneeze. Her favorite words were "be quiet" and "listen up" and when she talked, it sounded like gooey, sticky fluid was caught in her throat. He was nervous, bracing for Mrs. Stryker's yell, when he saw Vito Ricci, one of his classmates, wrapped in his Power Rangers blanket.

He stood over Vito, waiting for him to hand back the blanket. When five, ten, and then twenty seconds passed, he asked again. Vito was turned away from him, in the blanket.

"That's my blanket," he said, louder this time. "It's mine. Give it back!"

Vito flipped his body over, his eyes shooting open. He had been napping.

"I like this blanket," Vito said. "Mine now."

"It's mine, Vito. Give it back. My dad bought it for me. You stole it."

"I don't care. It's mine now. Go away."

He reached down and began tugging at the blanket. Vito rolled it tighter, yanking it back, his body rocking away from him.

"I want my blanket!"

"Shut up!"

Vito was thin, taller than him, and his knuckles protruded hard from the flesh of his pink fist as it hit him. He had never been punched in the face before, and he tumbled backward into the cubbies, saliva and blood exploding out of him. He was crying too hard to see Vito anymore or Mrs. Stryker bellowing, the chairs shifting and the footsteps pounding toward him. He was still crying when Mrs. Stryker took him by the hand, harder than he liked, to the nurse's office.

"You shouldn't provoke that boy. He's a bad seed," Mrs. Stryker said, sitting him down. He was pressing a tissue to his face to keep the blood from gushing into his mouth. The nurse gave him new tissue. The cries came up from his belly to his throat, the pain total, unlike any he had known. There was a wildfire raging between his eyes.

"You will be okay, Emmanuel," Mrs. Stryker said.

Saul picked up his son from school at one, almost two hours

before he usually got there. He was in his office, just done with talking to Sonny in D.C., when he got a call from a harried Mona, telling him he needed to get down to the public school in Brooklyn. She could hardly finish the sentence. *Emmanuelgotpunchedinthenose.* Saul needed to go because the *News* was yanking her to Chinatown for a crane collapse, they needed her on the scene as soon as possible. She was driving to Manhattan and he had to get his ass to Brooklyn.

"His nose is bleeding, Saul."

She sounded like she was going to cry.

He told Meryl, his secretary, he was going out for the afternoon. He had a 3:00 she could cancel due to a family emergency.

"Is everything okay, Mr. Plotz?"

"It'll be fine, yes."

It was lovely and strange to be a father again. Five years—where had they gone? He bounded to the elevator, no longer the speed-walker he used to be, huffing for breath as he jammed the lobby button. It was at this elevator bank, this very one, he talked to Richard Nixon about baseball. A world-historical figure reduced to grumbling about the Mets' starting pitching. Dick knew his stuff. At first, it was like a figment of his imagination come to life, Nixon having loomed so large over his consciousness since he was a teenager trying to follow politics on his black-and-white Philco. Like talking to a Smurf or Bugs Bunny. Eventually, after enough encounters, he began to see just an old man in an oversized navy suit, the fatty flap of skin quaking beneath his chin as he recalled, with photographic precision, a Mets-Cardinals showdown.

"I wanted to play center field for the Brooklyn Dodgers," Saul once said to him.

"The tragedy of life. We don't always get what we want."

Nixon died last year. Now Saul was riding the elevator with several HUD guys, nodding politely and checking his watch repeatedly. He had to get to Brooklyn. His son's nose was bleeding. Some kid— some kid he would throttle right now, throw against the wall of the elevator—had hurt him. His quiet, gentle boy, with Mona's springy hair and milky skin color and no one's reddish blonde hair. It was hard to imagine who would want to hurt him and how that could be, such evil coursing through the world.

But how many times had Saul been punched on the playground as a kid in Brooklyn? Different times. Saul could take it.

Saul climbed into his Toyota, parked near the elevator in the underground garage. As a top grade, his prize was a close parking spot, along with dozens of NYPD parking placards he could distribute to friends and family. Mona had two, in addition to her press plates, which gave her special permission to park in designated spots for New York journalists across the city.

To his right, as he swerved onto Centre Street, were the Twin Towers. When they were first built, casting ever-widening shadows over a desultory downtown, he was deeply skeptical of what they were becoming. A megalithic assault on the blue sky. Gargantuan, otherworldly syringes jammed into the soil. He was nostalgic, in those early years, for what the Towers had displaced: Radio Row, Little Syria, the clutter and the clacking that signaled to him a childhood he hadn't yet lost. The salesmen with their overgrown mustaches and hunting noses, moon-faces wide behind mountainous counters. Streets so narrow you had to turn sideways to pass an old lady with a pushcart and a ten cent umbrella. But the Towers continued to rise and soon they were here, inarguable in their might, immortal and faceless. He accepted them, as any man would accept a god. Mona's friend Liv, after losing her secretary job, started up at Windows on the World and was now a manager, making a decent living from what he could tell. He'd even taken Emmanuel up to the observation deck.

Saul drove over the Brooklyn Bridge, heading toward the Brooklyn-Queens Expressway. He didn't want Emmanuel to be sad and alone, in pain. He was a boy who was afraid of the dark, resistant to the unfamiliar. Tad was a little like that as a boy, though he'd grown out of it soon enough, evolved into something fierce and ultimately unknowable. How much of that was Saul's own fault? Part of it. All of it. He felt sick anytime he thought too hard about his oldest son.

Tad hadn't spoken to him in five years.

The last time he saw Lenore, two months ago, she urged him to not feel guilty about Tad.

"He's troubled, dad," she said. "He needs to figure things out."

"Five years. At least you know he's alive."

"He sent a letter to me early in the year. I get them maybe once every few months. He mostly says he's been on the road, you know? He last said he was working at a record store in San Francisco."

"San Francisco? What's in San Francisco?"

"The record store he works at."

"Jesus Christ."

"I may see if I can see him at some point. I ask to meet in my letters and he ignores me. I've gotten letters postmarked from California, Colorado, Michigan, and Illinois, just off the top of my head."

"I wish I understood him."

"We all do, dad. You're doing your best."

He couldn't say if Lenore was telling the truth. Like her mother, she was a practiced diplomat, masking whatever raw emotion built inside of her. She would have made a good press secretary. She understood implicitly the value of spin, of telling others what they wanted to hear or making bad news more palatable. It was possible she blamed him, thought him a helpless, absentee father scrambling to make up for time that was not just lost but dead altogether. Time that would never get clawed back. He tried to imagine what Lenore would say if she knew she had a half-brother. What he tried to do was give his weekday afternoons and whatever other time he could steal away to Emmanuel, telling Felicia, when he arrived home in the evening, that he was on a later shift, undertaking a time-intensive, years-long project with no definite endpoint. He said he needed to visit the United Nations, which used to be true but wasn't any longer.

That was the advantage of government work. It was vague enough and useless enough, while seeming pivotal to the lifeblood of a nation, for him to create flexible hours for his other life.

He sped on the BQE until he hit a rough patch at the Gowanus Expressway, the trucks slowing to a crawl with a lane, as usual, shut. He smashed the horn. It was a meaningless action, like crying into a black hole. All the suffering in the world couldn't compare to his child wounded.

Did he feel this way about Tad? A memory, unprompted, returned: Tad, six or seven, tumbling off his bike, not long after he had learned to ride without training wheels. The boy had hit some divot in the pavement, careening from the sidewalk and slashing the skin on his right arm open. Tad lay there stunned, too shaken at first to even cry. It was when he saw the long streak of blood on his forearm, sickeningly bright in the afternoon sun, that he began to wail. It was a cry from the deepest part from his stomach, a despair that was almost existential, Tad experiencing a tragedy of being. Saul ran to his son, doing what he could to comfort him, lifting him up and carrying him home. He would have done anything to unwind time and make him whole.

His own father, a sullen Brooklyn tailor who spoke fluent Yiddish, would have never done such a thing. The parenting of his childhood would be unrecognizable today. Had he showed up bleeding on his doorstep, his father would have told him to not drop any blood on the carpet. His mother would have clicked her tongue and gone back to her sewing. Neither his mother nor his father wanted any kind of reach into his life. They were not curious about his wants, his desires, his fears. He was an object they had an obligation to see into adolescence—clothe, feed, speak to from time to time—and then cast away. Even Mona's parents, in their obsessions, displayed more love, attempted to control her life in a way that would be, in their view, beneficial to her.

But what he had done—carried Tad home—could not have

taken place on a 1950s sidewalk. The children today needed parents. Maybe he had needed them too without realizing it, a pat on a back on the way home from the basketball court, a kiss on the cheek and a congratulations when he got an A on his report card.

Tad was gone now. He was somewhere across America. There was a decent chance he would die without talking to his son again.

The hardest part was explaining it to others. After telling Sonny Cannon and Izzy Locker, two of his oldest friends, he didn't bother telling anyone else. It wasn't as if there had been a decisive break. Tad simply took off, in the fall of 1989, and didn't say where he was going. Saul and Felicia drove by his apartment and saw it was vacant. The landlord said Tad was on a month-to-month lease and decided to go. The first letter came in 1990, addressed just to Felicia, to explain he was okay, that life was better, that he needed to be "with himself" and "of himself" for a while. The postmark was Connecticut. Afterwards, Lenore would get the letters. He said, in the third or fourth letter, he never wanted to hear from *his father* again. That's how he said it. Not Dad, not even Saul. The implication was that he could still speak to his mother and sister.

He hated to admit it but it would have been easier to tell his friends and colleagues at work that his son was dead. This would elicit nods of sympathy. It was simpler to process a death. A person gets erased from the Earth, we're all sorry, here's the flowers and my condolences. But no, his son was alive, perhaps quite healthy, breathing somewhere on this American land. He was not erased. To tell someone your son won't talk to you connoted lasting failure, a character flaw so enormous that it had to belong to literature. Did you beat your son? Were you an alcoholic? Did you psychologically torture him? Are you one of those sick and twisted people?

He drove on, closer to the little public school in Bay Ridge. She had taken over her father and mother's apartment when they both died. His own parents were long dead, twenty years gone. His father had a quick and brutal descent into senility. His mother died crossing Ocean Parkway, flattened by a truck turning with the light. That always saddened him most, how ludicrous her death had been. She was only sixty-six. To live that long, to witness a Great Depression and a World War and then labor under the threat of nuclear annihilation and then die *that way*, in the most banal fucking manner imaginable—the truck, with Jersey plates, had been transporting crates of juice—was too much for him to consider without shoving his fist through the windshield.

There was no parking by the school so he double-parked next to the schoolyard, risking a ticket. The public school buildings could always trigger memories in him because their edifices had changed so little since he own childhood, generations of kids crowding into the same squat buildings with caged windows and black fencing lining the perimeters.

The security guard at the front desk nodded without interest, telling him to sign in and proceed to the fourth floor, where the nurse's room for the kindergarteners was located. Room 409. He wrote his name, barely legible, and the time of his arrival. He found himself sprinting up the stairwell like he was twenty-five, his arms pumping out and his dress shoes slamming the marbled stairs. He spun on his toes back from where he came, watching the rooms roll by until he saw an open door with no number, this was close enough, and barged in to begin yelling "I'm Emmanuel's father!" when the woman behind the desk stood and nodded and smiled and motioned for him to lower his voice.

"He's here, Mr. Plotz, and he's doing well now with ice. He has an abrasion—"

"Where is he?"

Everyone was an enemy to Saul. The security guy at the front desk, the kid drinking water, this placid nurse. All of them failed to keep his son safe. Emmanuel came slowly out of a second unseen room, a pack of ice pressed to his face. There was swelling and dried blood. Saul bent down, wrapping his son in a firm hug.

"Are you okay? How are you?"

"Vito punched me but now I'm okay."

Saul wheeled around to face the nurse, speaking through gritted teeth like an old Western anti-hero. "Who is this Vito kid? Is he being expelled?

"Sir, I don't handle discipline. He's likely with the principal now."

"If he gets near my son again . . ."

"You should take it up with the principal."

Yes, he'd call the principal. The teacher too. If this wasn't rectified, if his kid was picked on and abused in a kindergarten class—where the hell was the supervision anyway?—there would be more than hell to pay. Jobs, careers. He would go after all of them. Izzy could recommend a good lawyer. He'd get in the courtroom himself. He'd get a battery of fucking attorneys. This goddamn school. Why was Emmanuel in this public school anyway? Sure, he himself had gone to only public schools but that was eight million years ago, different world, Kennedy was alive for all four years he was in college. Emmanuel needed a class with ten kids instead of thirty in one of those schools where all the kids called the teachers by their first names. Emmanuel would get all the advantages he never had. There was no such thing as private school, where he came from. You went to the local public school or you didn't go to school.

Emmanuel wasn't crying as they left the nurse's office, holding hands. The boy seemed content now. "I'm a little hungry," he said.

"What would you like? We can get lunch. Do you want pizza?"

"I'll eat a grilled cheese sandwich at home. Can you make it like mom makes it?"

"Of course I can."

He didn't quite know how Mona made it. They would share dinners together with Emmanuel on weekdays, crowded on a dining room table with newspapers, press releases, and photos saved from Mona's work, along with excess fact sheets and copies of policy reports Saul had left behind on his visits. Dinner was usually takeout or something already prepared at the local supermarket for $5.99: a meatball dinner, vegetables and stew, lasagna. He was in charge of buying these meals. He always wanted to buy things Emmanuel would like, that would bring a smile to his face. Mona, still playing tennis three times a week, wanted him off the "sugar crap" and the "carbs crap" but allowed Saul these purchases. She wasn't a cook but could always find time to steam vegetables. What she said went: parenting was a partnership only in the sense that there was a senior partner (Mona) and a junior partner (Saul) who could offer opinions to be taken under consideration.

Emmanuel was quiet on the car ride home. He didn't seem to be in pain anymore, though that didn't mean he wanted to talk. The boy could be this way. He stared out the window, silently regarding the quiet streets of single-family homes, this suburb in the city. It was unusually warm for early February, though Mona had still bundled him in a boy's ski jacket, the hood flopping over his head of curls. He tried to remember what it was like at that age, the thoughts that floated across and held him: the world, then, could be enormous and wondrous and terrifying. Childhood friends were folk heroes, bullies worse than European fascists. There was so much you didn't understand yet so much you were powerfully certain of, like the best flavor of ice cream or your favorite ballplayer. He could remember the slowness of late winter and early spring, how his body begged for the planet's warming. Time was a thick liquid drip.

It was early enough that he could find good parking across the street from the co-op. Mona visited her parents there, in the last years of their lives, at least twice a month, sometimes more. For all her resentments, she was more dedicated to her parents than he had ever been to his own. And he hoped Emmanuel would find the time for him when he aged out of relevancy, skulked on a dusty couch in front of daytime television, his face like Yogi Berra's catcher's mitt. He'd left his parents alone and then they were dead. He wasn't sure if he deserved more from his own children but he wanted it.

In the apartment, he sat Emmanuel down on the couch and turned on the TV. He knew to flip it over to Cartoon Network.

"I'll go make you your grilled cheese."

"I'm thirsty."

"I'll pour you a cold glass of milk."

"I kinda want soda."

"Would mom let you have soda?"

"I don't know."

"I don't think she would."

"She's not here."

"Rules are rules, little guy. I don't make them."

Mona kept ginger ale in the fridge, mostly for Saul's benefit. She'd sworn off soda. Instead, she froze water in canteens with lemon and let them thaw later on. Emmanuel was expected to avoid soda. Saul was hungry himself. As he put the butter in the pan, he dug in the fridge for some grapes, a slice of bread, and a few pieces of rubbery packaged turkey.

Emmanuel seemed to enjoy the sandwich. An unrecognizable cartoon played on the TV. Saul hadn't followed the world of animation since Yogi Bear. There appeared to be robots of some kind fighting each other. A bit much, he thought, for a five-year-old.

The phone in the kitchen rang. Saul went in a near sprint to the wall phone, picking it up out of breath. He forgot to say hello.

"Saul, is that you? You're home? Good."

Mona.

"Yes, I got Emmy and we're here. He's doing okay, pretty well, all things considered. I made grilled cheese."

"Ugh, we can't keep giving him such fattening foods. How is his nose? Is there swelling? What happened with that kid?"

"It looks like just a bruise. I'm trying to find out from the school. If they don't suspend, if there isn't a severe punishment, they'll be hearing from me."

"I'll handle it. You just watch him. I'll be home as soon as I can."

"Okay, he's just watching one of his cartoon robot shows. They're kind of entertaining, actually."

"Can you stay there tonight? Past six?"

Past six, past six, well, shit, no, he couldn't really. It was a Wednesday. Felicia was expecting him home by seven. He'd already stayed out later than he should a week ago. And fucking Herb Weiner was coming over for a dinner party. Twenty years later, he couldn't be free of the Roslyn yokels. They were all stubbornly alive and locally relevant. Herb's kid was supposed to come too. He was a bond trader or something like that. Saul didn't have to handle the shopping or the cooking but he sure as hell had to be present, had to be mildly entertaining, needed to put up a front for Herb and the others from the civic. He wanted, more than little else in the world at that moment, to say yes to Mona and negate the reality of tonight's dinner, the flaccid conversation over cold plates of hummus and wet salad.

"I can't tonight, dear. I wish I could."

"Saul, I need you this time."

"I want to—I mean, I need to, I would . . . I have to be back out east. Felicia—"

"Yes, of course. Okay. I'll try to swing a babysitter."

"I'm really sorry."

"It's fine. It's my responsibility anyway. Liv invited me at the last minute to a party to meet the new guy she's dating. First since the break-up, really. She wants me there. I hate things like these."

"I don't blame you. I wish I could be watching Emmanuel tonight. If I could I absolutely would."

"That's the story of your life."

2

Mona found a local high school girl to babysit Emmanuel. She spent about ten minutes pissed at Saul on the train ride uptown, thinking about how unfair and infuriating it was that he couldn't stay past 6 p.m. Her anger subsided as she considered their past, in its enormity. She remembered this was the only way it could be.

When she had given birth to Emmanuel, she had never been more certain or terrified. The certainty came from the well of who she was, what she wanted: to be a mother to this child. The terror was everything else. *Could* she be a mother? What if the child didn't love her? How did people raise children anyway? Even if the act of childbirth happened every day, all across the world, she wondered whether she was missing what all these new mothers had, an ineffable something. She worried until the pain was too intense and Emmanuel arrived and she was in love.

When Emmanuel was born, she told herself Saul would have a role in his life, that was only proper, but it would be on the terms she set. He spent his first years as a Glass. She couldn't forget that at first he was the accident Saul wanted to make go away.

It still surprised her how much she clung to her child. Emmanuel, she feared, was a transitory miracle, to be snatched away or erased whenever God, someone she had spent little time appeasing in her life, deigned to do so. She whispered prayers in the shower, before bed, on the way to the train. *Please protect Emmanuel.* If he toddled in the park and fell, like all children learning to walk, she would gasp with pain, racing to his side, asking him and asking him and asking him if he was okay, if he needed anything, if he was hungry or thirsty or afraid or still in pain. And the boy would only smile, laugh, *okay mommy,* and continue his pigeon-toed walk across the rubberized playground mats, forgetting he ever fell at all.

Melinda demanded she give the boy Saul's last name. Eventually, she had learned her marriage to Saul was a farce and after judging her severely, in her fine-tuned patrician manner, Melinda barked that the least Mona could do was not have a son who carried around her mother's name. It offended her traditionalist sensibilities. Melinda and her doctor husband were firmly ensconced on the Upper East Side in a small two-bedroom apartment on Second Avenue and the veneer of their lives—Melinda's two sons were attending Ivy League schools and Dr. Harold Hyman was a deputy to the health commissioner—enabled her to render judgment in this way, like a penny-ante goddess handing down pronouncements from the mount. Mona also knew Melinda wasn't as wealthy as she wanted to be, that Dr. Harold Hyman drew a public salary and never earned the exorbitant fees of other neighborhood doctors. Their Hamptons retreat was little more than a cottage, and Melinda knew she was running out of time to achieve her dream of a life behind the hedgerows, the Mexican maid preparing her three meals a day. That was Melinda's existential despair, at the half century mark: my husband won't ever be rich enough.

It was Liv, newly divorced, who told Mona her older sister made a suggestion worth heeding.

"Do you want Saul in Emmanuel's life?"

"I do."

"Let him be a Plotz then. I don't even know if Saul cares or not. He's probably just thankful he gets to see Emmanuel sometimes. But it's a gesture, a concession maybe. It may even smooth Emmanuel's path in a way, when he starts asking questions about his mom and dad."

"Questions? Oh God."

"How his mom and dad are not really married. How his dad is older than the other dads. Why he has his mom's last name."

"The last one, these days—it's not a big deal."

"It's not. But it can be a small way of welcoming Saul in, you know?"

"Saul will never leave his other family."

"But you are the one he loves. You know that."

Emmanuel Glass became Emmanuel Plotz. She considered, for years, changing the middle name too, because he was a boy with a girl's middle name. At five, he hadn't yet noticed. But he would or a bully would. If the bully noticed first, he would get hurt on the schoolyard. Physically or emotionally. In her idle moments, she considered masculine replacements for Esther, her mother's name. He could be an Ellis or an Edgar. None, though, felt like they belonged to him.

It was her idea to put him in Hebrew School. Vic had a bar mitzvah but girls didn't get such treatment, not in Brooklyn at midcentury. She was utterly without religion, exiled from the Torah and the Talmud, unable to even read the dreidel. It suddenly seemed important to her for her son to get a Jewish education.

"Why?" Saul almost laughed. He was, at his core, an unshakable atheist, a closet Marxist with the opium of the people quote frozen inside him. Like most men of his generation, his Judaism was limited to the wrathful Yiddish phrases gleaned from parental arguments, as well as the prolix novels and cinema expelled by fellow members of their apostate tribe, the motormouths spurning their immigrant forebearers. Hebrew School wasn't his bag.

"I think it can be good for him. You got to have a bar mitzvah. You went."

"I didn't enjoy it. The only thing I remember is the family dinner afterward. I asked to get Chinese food and my mother told me that was very disrespectful, on a day like this. We ended up at a red sauce joint in Queens."

"Perhaps Emmanuel will have a different relationship with faith. Or he'll try."

She was taking the Lexington Avenue line to East 86th. It was finally a chance to meet the man Liv had been seeing for several months, the enigmatic Port Authority chieftain who got breakfast almost every morning at Windows on the World. Liv still prowled the floor and checked on the waitstaff and this led her into occasional chats with customers. As the curious extrovert, she liked to latch onto snippets of conversation and hear how other lives were conducted, or at least acted out on this stage in the sky. Eventually, she noticed the man in his fifties dining alone, always in a gray or navy Brooks Brother suit and with hair impeccably coifed, his thin face without even the hint of hair, every last sprout aggressively shaved away. His smile was unexpectedly bright. They talked, at first about the weather and roasted coffee and the way umbrellas threatened to poke you in the eye on rainy days coming out of the subway. His name, she learned on their second chat, was Grayson Moegenborg, and he was not merely a Port Authority staffer or "man"—he was the executive director. He had, Liv learned, worked in banking, rising to vice president at Goldman Sachs. He took a pay cut for more power. That's how Liv put it.

The Moegenborgs, Liv said, were old money, Germanic aristocrats who never got enough credit for guiding the destiny of the world's greatest and most frustrating city. His great-grandfather had been the president of a railroad that made millions and killed the Chinese peasants who built it. His grandfather ran an armaments factory during World War II and turned to collegiate philanthropy during the great American expansion, endowing a small, liberal arts college in the Midwest he had taken a fancy to during business trips to the region. His father was an investment banker, a Columbia trustee, and member of various public-private civic partnerships. None of this seemed to bother Grayson, who was comfortable enough with a family name on red-brick buildings. But Liv insisted he wasn't pretentious. His confidence, she said, was *hushed*.

Mona began the long slog to the far East Side, East End Avenue, not very far from where Melinda lived with Dr. Harry Hyman. It was a neighborhood of bankers and Jewish grandmothers, apartment towers walling off the sky with their silent girth. This was a part of Manhattan beyond tourists, sidewalks emptying at dusk, the gurgle in the street limited to taxi cabs and MTA buses, the commuters with faces like faded watercolors. As she walked, she saw doormen in their museum piece lobbies, their bloodless stares passing through her. On every block, there was a dry cleaner and a parking garage. The automobiles and the dress shirts were always well taken care of.

Grayson's apartment faced Gracie Mansion, the mayor's residence. Maybe she'd see that fucker Giuliani. The building was more modern than she anticipated, a geometric assemblage of high glass windows and sleek terraces, gleaming enough to not seriously belong to the city's lurching past. It was either the most glorious building on East End Avenue or one of twenty; nightfall was an impediment to rendering a final judgment. Across the street, a few men and women in overcoats walked their dogs. The dogs barked almost apologetically.

She told the doorman she was here for Grayson Moegenborg, stressing the *borg* like she was asking after an android or Björn Borg. The doorman asked for her name.

"Mona Glass," she said reluctantly.

He peered down, his eyes narrowing on an unseen list.

"I see you there. Go right up to the top."

Liv told her Grayson had the penthouse. It was like a fairy tale, a lark, the wealthy savior as a deus ex machina, except Liv didn't need any saving. She didn't require a god out of a machine. She was one of the least self-pitying people Mona knew.

The elevator opened straight into the apartment. It was the first time, in her forty-five years, she had entered a penthouse apartment. She knew, from TV and the occasional novels depicting the interior lives of the rich and famous, elevators led straight into homes. But it was always more striking to have a so-called lived experience match a theory: people really did exist this way. Grayson Moegenborg couldn't be troubled to leave an elevator and walk down a carpeted hallway to his apartment. The exertion was unbecoming of old money. In retrospect, she was surprised there wasn't a velvet-gloved elevator attendant to guide her up into the sky.

She was in a slim hallway, the sounds of the party distant and above. She could hear the mingling of voices, laughter and the clattering of silverware. A small stairway of sanded wood led upward. She walked onto the penthouse floor, a vast space reaching out toward floor-to-ceiling windows revealing the black breadth of the East River. It was a home for someone who could not stand to be alone, who needed to clutter his shining floors with personalities. She recognized no one.

When Liv asked her here, she imagined, for some reason, the party wouldn't be this. There were dozens of men and women crowded together, gabbing in clusters, fluttering from point to point on the sprawl of tile like little indolent moths. A wine bar kept them hydrated, islands of cold cuts and elegantly sliced cheeses filling their toned little stomachs. Liv was somewhere. Mona passed through crowds, hunting first for a glass of wine so she could seem plausible, one more actor on this glittering stage. Once she had her red wine, she began the search, covering each quadrant of the penthouse, stopping only to gather a plate of cheese and small red grapes. The party called to mind the numbing gatherings of high school and college, the hordes of people she never knew and didn't want to know, shouting to be heard over the din of rock music and marijuana smoke.

She swallowed grapes and waited. In the corner of the room, a man began to play a piano. More people continue to arrive, laughing and kissing one another, forming new clusters of warmth. They seemed, from what she gathered, to be people who worked with Grayson in government. She considered that there was no logical occasion for this party, no holiday or birthday or change of season. It was merely early February. But the rich didn't require occasions to celebrate—they lived lives free of news hooks. They had money and time to gather and they did. Tomorrow morning, the *News* wanted her to shoot the chancellor of the Board of Education's tour of a new special education school. None of that had any relation to what was happening in this room.

Liv had materialized near the wine bar, out of a jacketed horde that must have come together for Grayson. Mona walked toward them, smiling hesitantly as she made eye contact with her friend. She had to admit Grayson looked particularly good tonight, better than in a grainy *Times* photo, and he was imbued with that nameless magnetism which always seems to find itself more in the rich than the poor. He was a man at home in his money and name. That was clear.

Mona approached and Liv raced to hug her and kiss her on the cheek.

"You made it!"

"Of course. You told me to come."

"Mona, love, please—this is Grayson." She turned to him, nudging his shoulder. "Honey, say hi to my best friend."

"Grayson Moegenborg," he said with a smile, leaning in to also kiss her on the cheek. Mona would have preferred a contact-free greeting, if such a thing were possible.

"I'm Mona Glass," she said quietly, failing to lend her name any kind of meaning. It did not grace the edifices of any buildings.

"Mona and I go back to college," Liv said. "She's unbelievable. She will kick your ass. Right now, she's the best the photojournalist this city has. I was telling you about Vengeance, honey—"

"Ah yes, that '70s vigilante! My father hated him so much. I rather enjoyed him, to be honest. Right before Son of Sam. He wasn't killing anyone so, to me at least, he was a friend."

"Mona got the exclusive photo and interview with him. You remember all those pictures, what a sensation they caused?"

"Of course. It was the talk of the town."

"Mona Glass."

"So I am in the presence of a real New York institution," Grayson said, without a seeming hint of irony.

"I wouldn't say that," Mona said.

"She'll demolish you on the tennis court too."

"I've heard you're quite good," Grayson said. "I played in tournaments in my youth. Now, it's strictly recreational. The game drives you hard. Body and mind."

"It does," Mona said, hunting for something else to add, any stray fact about the sport she played obsessively, week after week, day and night. She was sure, at this point, she was the best over forty female tennis player in New York City.

"Grayson, I'm going to leave you to talk to Bobby and Rick over there. Mona and I are going to do a little catching up. You be good, okay?"

"I'm always good, as long as you're around."

"It was nice to meet you," Mona said.

"Likewise, Mona Glass. I'll look for your name in the papers. And maybe we'll find time for a game. I'd like to test myself."

Liv took her by the arm and they walked across the floor, toward the windows with the full view of the East River. They stopped at the wine bar to refill. Now a mother, with relatively little time to drink alcohol, Mona's tolerance for wine was exceedingly low, two glasses enough to blur the edges of the crowd. Liv touched her elbow and pulled her gently into the corner, where they could see a tide of brake lights from the FDR Drive.

"What did you think?" Liv asked.

"He seems nice."

"I love him, I really do. His world, I can take it or leave it."

"You mean this?"

"I loved it at first. I know I want to be with him, stay with him. He knows I don't want his money. If anything, he knows the money is an impediment to us getting closer. He knows I am mildly disgusted by it."

"It didn't draw you at all?"

"His looks drew me, Mona. I wanted to fuck him. And he's nice, once you peel him back."

"Oh, no, of course, I didn't want to make you out as some kind of—"

"Gold digger?"

"No, I wasn't going to say that."

"Mona, dear, loosen up. I'm kidding. Look, he's fun. He's good for me. I can be serious with him and I can be not-so-serious with him. He likes a good jag. We can drive up to Connecticut, walk around apple orchards, get drunk. It's a bit like playing pretend. But it's nice."

"Well, it was good to meet him."

"You seem disappointed. I know I look at ease here, but I'm not really. I don't know these people either. They've never set foot in Brooklyn. You'll like Grayson though. Maybe bring Saul for a double-date sometime? Saul probably knows Grayson anyway. They both swim in those Republican political waters."

"I don't know if Saul would do it. You know, Grayson could know his wife too."

"There is a small part of me," Liv said, leaning in closer, "that fantasizes about Saul dumping his family and coming to you. I know he wants to. He can just get a divorce. The kids are grown, right?"

"I don't know them."

"Well, of course, but I mean, they're in their twenties. They can handle shit like this. Daddy gets a divorce. What's stopping him?"

"He's stopping him."

"You really think that?"

"If he wanted to, he would have done it. That's the truth. And I'm still pissed he couldn't watch Emmanuel tonight. I needed to get a babysitter I barely know. I worry about these babysitters. Do we really know who they are? They can lie. They can be irresponsible, pedophiles, killers—"

"Whoa, slow down there. When did Mona become such a worrywart?"

"I worry about my son every day. That someone is going to hurt him. Snatch him away. The world is sick."

"I don't have any children so my advice is maybe of the grain-of-salt variety. But we grew up without adult supervision, right? My friends and I would just drink in the back of cars in Nassau County parking lots. I smoked marijuana at fourteen. You were a little savage beating up boys during football games in Prospect Park. Were your parents out in the street or in the parking lot watching you all the time?"

"Not technically, no."

"And you turned out fine."

"The world has changed, Liv. It's not like when we grew up."

"It's probably better, honestly. When I was thirteen, I thought Cuba was going to nuke New York."

"Cuba wasn't going to mug you, throw you up against the wall and take your life for train fare."

"You never used to talk this way."

"I just want Emmanuel to be safe. Saul should be watching him."

"He had to go back to Long Island."

"Of course! This is how it is. He can have his cake and eat it too. He can play nice and normal dad to two different families."

"Look, I've been a critic of Saul, myself, but it's not like he has it so easy! Didn't his adult son just disappear or stop talking to him? That must be rough."

"I'm sure it is. He also has a son here who's at home with some sixteen-year-old that Victoria Asher thinks is great. She's a nice woman but she's a bit flighty. I don't know. I think I'm going to go home."

"Mona, stay a little longer."

"Yes, stay," came the voice that belonged to Grayson, who had sidled up next to them, drink in hand. "We're going to do a charity raffle in a few minutes. We'll also be rolling out the dessert bar."

"That's all very nice," Mona said. "It's late for me. I need to get back to Brooklyn."

"Listen, if you stay later, I can have a car sent for you. No big deal. Just let me know.

"I'm okay, Grayson. Thanks, though."

"I do have to ask and pardon me if I'm prying too much . . ."

"Yes?"

"That picture. How did you get it?"

"What do you mean?"

"The great and terrible vigilante, Vengeance. You were pretty young then, and you beat out all those photographers."

"Right place, right time."

"I want to hear about it."

"I'm a little tired . . ."

"Come now, you're practically famous. I'm all ears."

Why did Grayson want to know? Did he have an actual interest? What did the people who have everything think about? He had infinite time for the past. He could loll on the shoreline of a memory, waste hours on idle recollections, drawing no conclusion other than time, quite obviously, had passed. Her existence allowed no such gaps. She was racing to burning buildings or dead bodies or mayoral press conferences and trying, in the meantime, to raise her only son. Though she wasn't, in the literal sense, a single mother, she perceived herself that way and the burden felt accordingly allocated to her. Saul did what he could. Saul had real love for her son. That was undeniable. And he was always ready with cash for dinner, a treat, a toy, whatever Power Rangers action figure or rubber dinosaur or little baseball mitt Emmanuel quietly desired. He was not a boy who made demands, who tested boundaries. She sensed he was just thankful to be here, on the planet with her. God, she missed him, at home with whatever feckless fucking teen Victoria Asher had recommended to watch her son. Saul should be there. Saul should be watching him.

"There's nothing to tell, Grayson. I was working for the *Daily Raider*. They were desperate for a photograph of Vengeance. Everyone was. My friend from the paper and I were hoping to catch him. We got lucky in Coney Island. I took the picture. Then Vengeance began calling the office. I took the calls. That was it."

"They never found out who he was."

"No, they didn't."

"One of the profound mysteries. That crank got away. I always wondered how."

"The city can be an enigma. You find a way between the lines, you can disappear."

"What does that mean?"

She could tell quitting this conversation wouldn't be possible as long as Grayson, a man used to posing questions and getting immediate answers, kept questioning her. For Liv's sake, she couldn't tell him to fuck off. It was a time to go home and she wasn't riding in his black car.

"It means, you've got a city of eight million people, maybe more. You've got roads and side streets that you can spend fifty years here not exploring. You have worlds enfolded in worlds. Entire lives lived between avenues. There are ways to disappear. I was never shocked, truthfully, he was never found."

"If anyone was going to crack the mystery, it was Mona," Liv said.

"Who was the friend with you that night? You said he was with the paper."

"You mean . . ."

"In the car. You mentioned your friend, with the *Daily Raider*. It was a rollicking, alien little paper. I read it voraciously. The bylines and headlines will come to me in dreams. I remember your name in the photo credits. I'm sure I'll remember him."

Al Falcone. Christ, she owed him a phone call. Last she checked, he was still in L.A. When had they spoken last? 1992? 1993? It was hard to think about how people could slip out of her life. There was a reason Al left and she didn't like to think about it too much because she still wanted his friendship and would never have it in the same way again. She knew if they spent too long on the phone he would ask her a question she did not want to answer.

"Al Falcone."

"Falcone, yes! Is he still working with you?"

"He's in L.A. Not in the business."

"Ah, I know there's been such a churn lately. The business is dreadful. My friend Carter Burden used to own the *Village Voice*. Carter was a character. I've always loved newspapers, from childhood. I remember the '40s, when there was a daily newspaper covering everything imaginable. You could read a broadsheet on how to properly cleanse your nostrils of snot. I've admired the people who do the work, the journalists, those like you who prowl the streets. It's a singular mindset you need to have."

"I don't know. I go out and take pictures. It's not much more complicated than that."

"Well, I hope you stay in it. It's a shame Falcone left, and others too. I remember the *Raider* shuttering. Those Brits got sick of losing money."

"Those Brits didn't care about journalism."

"Fair enough, Mona Glass."

Liv offered to ride down with her in the elevator. It was late, almost ten, and she would probably end up spending an obscene amount of money for a cab to take her from the Upper East Side to Bay Ridge. Grayson had offered his car but she couldn't take that kind of charity. He struck her as the sort of person who could remind her, months or years later, that she had accepted a favor. She didn't know what to make of his interest in her career, if it was earnest, a party act, or something else entirely, some attempt at sleuthing into her past.

"He took a real interest in you," Liv said, almost hopefully.

They were in the elevator alone.

"I wonder if he actually remembers Al in that newspaper."

"His memory is amazing, I'll say that much. He can't forget names, faces, dates. It may be photographic."

"Is he the one?"

Liv burst out laughing. The elevator doors opened for them.

"Oh gosh, the one? Does that exist? It does for you, Mona, I'll say that. You may be pissed at him half the time but Saul is it. No one else. For me? Grayson will do. I feel it. There's something about him. I can't quite describe it. Whatever hard-to-name thing that turns you off with him, and I see it in your eyes, that kind of thing—it draws me. I can't quite explain it. Before, I said the money was an impediment, and I think that's true. It'd be easier if Grayson didn't throw parties like these, if he didn't have so many friends, if he didn't live a life so far beyond the reality of whatever it was we grew up with. I don't know if Grayson's ever been on the subway. But I love him."

"If you love him, I support him then."

"We'll see where it goes, right? Life with him is fun. But you're okay getting back? That babysitter, she must have put Emmanuel to sleep, shit, *she's* probably sleeping . . ."

"I'm getting a cab. Actually, that one, right there," Mona said, flagging down a yellow cab slowing at a red light on East End Avenue. She waved to Liv and dove into the backseat, the wine still swishing somewhere in her blood.

3

Tad would come to each town and try to work. That was the idea as he passed through one-story motels or rentals near trailer parks, apartments with brown water in the tubs, toilets that did not flush and never would. He worked in three different Walmarts, each more gargantuan than the last, stores that could swallow societies, all with the acre of parking. He did his best thinking walking across these lots, to his car parked far from wherever he may have to utter words to another living person.

Each year, he felt less of himself, a shadow replacing a limb, his breath disappearing inside of him. There were days he was sure he didn't exist. In one town off I-80 in Ohio, he shot heroin in an apartment without running water, the fogged windows facing an abandoned train depot. The rush was undeniable, his breath like fire on his lips. He dreamed of new needles puncturing skin, wild for his next fix, unable to understand why his dealer only carried so much.

The habit could die because his resources limited him. He had no fondness for food or liquids but he was not ready to die. Shivering, crying, he spent six days beneath the covers he had draped over the air mattress he deflated and inflated in each new town. His fingernails crushed skin. In his careening dreams, he could meet them all: his mother and sister and father. At the needle's tip, just before waking, he saw Long Island.

When he was well, he drove west.

He wrote letters when he couldn't imagine what else to do with his day. They always went to Lenore. He waited tables at a Friendly's in Indiana, absorbing orders without the need of a notepad, assigning meals and patrons to little empty rooms in his mind. He stayed there for a year, the hunger receding. He didn't need to inject himself. He could drink or do nothing. Withdrawal was an assault on his body, aching and retching, and he couldn't be sure why he made it through until he did. There was an older waitress he had sex with, a woman who wanted to nurture him back somewhere. He didn't tell her when he left town, no phone call, no note.

Hellos and goodbyes, he could not abide.

The last decade of the twentieth century only met him at odd hours. Mopping the floors of a Sears in Missouri, he first heard a couple, in hushed tones, talking about O. J. Simpson. He remembered the Buffalo Bills running back. Two nights later, on a bar TV, he learned of a trial, an alleged murder that took the country by the neck and did not let go.

It was on stray newspapers underfoot, in a Dollar General and a Walmart, that he learned about a bombing at the World Trade Center and another in Oklahoma City two years later. Both beneath his sneakers, the very same pair of New Balances, headlines peeking out from under the peeling sole.

He sensed he had escaped the drug too swiftly, that it would call to his body again. He sensed these years, now that he was free from that hotel room and the nights that tore him open, were too easy. He was making money and free.

Wherever he went, he was Tad Plotz. He carried his name with him. There were opportunities to invent an alias, to forge documents or start calling himself by whatever he dreamed. A gas station, a Sears, or even a Walmart didn't care too much about who he had been, what he had done. Could he stand upright and perform the task? Could he smile at check out? In the newspapers that drifted before him, he learned of the economy's strength, prosperity with no end point. It was like being told God was healthy. He couldn't see God or hear God so why would His health matter? One year became the next. His wage rarely changed.

He drove to rural Michigan, north, near the Upper Peninsula. The cabin he found didn't have heat. Snowfalls came in April. Sunshine, hail, nighttime chills to bring him to his knees, his lips blue. The woman who owned it told him all he had to do was pay her $75 in cash every month. The toilet backed up and the pipes froze.

Sometimes he thought about his father's child.

In the depths of night, his back creaking on the cot, he could weigh the purpose of his flight. The last time he saw his father he was driving behind him, on the way to the hospital. Parts of his life gained light, gained sense: his father's absences, the inattentiveness at dinners, the slapdash attempts at connection. His father loved from a distance. It wasn't until that moment, racing from the hospital to his car, that he realized he wanted a father at all. Other friends had drunks for fathers, fathers who beat them or beat their mothers, fathers that divorced and left altogether. Long Island was awash with lonely young boys and girls with mothers and fathers parenting in separate homes, initiating strained conversations over parallel dinners, how is school and are your friends nice? He had a father. His father never hit him. His father never told him he was stupid.

The cot in the cabin was too small. They all were.

Saul Plotz was always choosing elsewhere. Whatever Tad offered, it wouldn't be enough. So maybe Tad chose elsewhere too. That was it, he figured: he was where he was meant to be, in the darkness of a hidden cabin, his bones at a steady ache. He would be nowhere else. When he died, in an unfathomable number of years—even minutes from now were hard to imagine—he could only be here, in his pit without light. Where else did he deserve to be but here?

He told Lenore he couldn't promise a letter would be returned. He may be gone by then.

Time only moved with heat. The growing sunlight told him it was summer. Small black insects swarmed his eyes. He found a lake heavy with algae, the waters thickly green. Sitting on the bank, smoking the occasional cigarette, he remembered he used to shoot heroin and this memory triggered a hunger that wouldn't be satiated until he made a score but there were no scores to make on the shore of an unnamed lake in an unnamed woodland, the sky so naked and empty of clouds. When the longing was deepest, he could forget his name. Tad Plotz meant nothing against it. The memory of the high: a world beyond death, the extradimensional force that could take hold of him and never let go. Later, in the hours and days when the drug exited him, he could vomit and shit and sweat so hard he was blinded, the nausea choking him. Sometimes it was gone in a day. Sometimes it took weeks.

In the mirror, his pupils could be as large as almonds. He retched over the bowl-shaped sink, his insides crackling. The paleness of his skin could unsettle him, make him think that he had died already and was watching a replay of his life from a coffin deep underground, the memories a loose static in the hollow of his skull.

In the summer, he felt better. He spent a lot of time by the lake. Occasionally, a rowboat would make its way across the stagnant water. On the opposite shore was some kind of campsite where civilization continued. Bodies as small as gnats flitted on the shoreline. More boats began to come, even one with a motor. They never quite made it to him. His lake, he came to understand, was the outlet of a much larger sister lake, and he was living somewhere beyond their acceptable boundary. He was outside of time and place. There were no other cabins on his side of the lake. He imagined the cabin's architect, some thickset man of the midcentury, his jowls dark and loose, his fingers calloused, his nails yellowed. Sometimes he expected the ghosts of Indians to ambush him. At night, there was a howling he couldn't place.

There was no way to send or receive letters here, the post office fifteen miles away, so he wrote letters to himself and tore them to pieces. Whenever a memory creeped, he wrote it down and destroyed it. Saul Plotz, Felicia Plotz, Lenore Plotz. Father, mother, sister. A family unit among billions, one data point soon to be erased and forgotten. He forgave Lenore. Her name could stay.

In his last trip to the nearest town, he bought a spiral notebook. His hand trembled, clenching a 50-cent pen from a dollar store. In the semi-dark of daytime in the cabin, he sat on the edge of his mattress and shook. A writer created history. A writer lived outside of history. He would never be a writer in the sense of how the role was understood at the end of the twentieth century, but he could live beyond history too; the last man next to a lake with no name. He could alone make symbols on his white paper. If he stared hard enough, his eyes trying to cut open shadow, the symbols could leave the page. They could float to the lake and disappear.

He was sure he spoke to no one that summer. In the dollar store, his mouth remained closed. If a cashier attempted conversation, he nodded and walked away. Had the town had enough people, he would have attracted suspicion. The human voice, he believed, was a distraction. He merely had to disappear. Once he stopped hungering, he began to focus on that. A body, no body, had to exist.

The heat held the cabin. It surprised him, up here, how one August day could confront him and not let go. There was no relief. The shoreline's dust was exhausted on his sneakers. When he touched the water, he only felt sun. Bottles of water, purchased in town, were finished in minutes. Out back, he gazed down the well and found the darkness hot and empty. Day and night, he sweated. This was raw, native heat, the kind that came at history's edge, the crust molten, fire deluging lakes and canyons. He could lay on his back, naked on a bed of leaves and sticks, and imagine there was no summer, no fall, the heat sucked back into the desolate blue.

His skin reddened and darkened. At the close of August, he walked the lip of the lake and circled beyond the shoreline into raging thickets and bushes untamed for any human body. The branches cut at him. He didn't know where he was going or why, other than that he needed to walk and he was sick of boiling potatoes and swallowing black beans from cans.

At a clearing, he saw a tent. There would be someone inside. He was thrown into his past, when he shaved and tucked in his shirts and combed his hair in a dorm room mirror, applying light gel. He couldn't understand why this self-consciousness was returning. He had no self to be conscious of anymore. Perhaps it was simply the chance encounter with another person. Even now, he wanted to present, to act. There were no mirrors in the cabin. His beard, a dark cloud hanging off his thin cheeks, would be his first identifiable trait to the stranger, a way to define him against the canopy and sky. He would be the man with the beard.

He walked toward the tent. The brush thickened at his feet, slowing his approach. A small robin fled a branch above and nearly flew into his face. He had forgotten, at least, how hot he had been. The sweat was drying. As he came closer, he saw the tent was a mossy green, like something the military would pitch. He had never camped as a child. It wasn't something New York Jews did. There was a lunar quality to it that had repelled him, his younger self unwilling to suffer on a foreign landscape for recreation. Now, he was effectively doing it, though he couldn't consider his existence on those terms. Camping implied an impermanence, an eventual return to civilizational affluence. Camping would transition to a state of non-camping, an automobile in the driveway, ravioli in the microwave, the TV tuned to the NFL. He could not see what came after this, the flies hanging fat and hungry above his eyelids.

He could not see what else there was other than his body in motion toward the stillness of the tent. Another robin escaped the brush and he wished he could reach out and catch it, cradle the bird before letting it join the sky. His steps seemed louder as he approached, even though he was trying to go softly on the leaves.

All he wanted was for someone to talk to him.

But what of disappearing? He couldn't do that if he heard a voice and spoke with his own and validated his flesh-and-blood existence, the body always getting in the way of the mind, the mind poisoning the body. Both had failed him. Neither worked in union. His palms were damp, his chest tight. He stooped down to open the flap of the tent.

There would need to be a voice. There would have to be a voice. He remembered his one semester of Latin, in ninth grade. Vox. He wished English had simply ripped the word from Latin, not polluted it with the i and c and e. All the meaning was there. A civilization, maybe a better one, had invested in it already, lent it the necessary power. He didn't need pygmy words.

A sound, music. He heard it, but it was only inside of him, a tune of memory. Jangle-pop of the late 1960s, one of those shaggy bands, his father's rock. There was a record player in his childhood living room. He was there now, twenty years peeled away, the vinyl at his fingertips. The ghost of cigarette smoke drifted overhead.

He smelled, in the present, something awful.

The tent was not empty. Wrapped in several filthy blankets, smeared a dark brown, was a body. He couldn't see the face because it was turned away from him, staring out into the other end of the tent. Dark, wild hair sprung from the skull. Even in the most wretched dens, a needle in his flesh, he never smelled a body like this.

"Hello," he said, knowing the body couldn't answer.

He reached out and turned it over, shoving blankets until he could see. He was surprised by how light the body was, almost like a child's. In the face he saw a man not much older than himself, the thin skin drained of color, the jaw sagging to reveal rotted teeth. Flies dipped in and out of the strands of hair. He saw a flicker of tongue, pale red, in the crumbling mouth.

The eyes were still open.

Dried blood was below him, all over, a continental drift that began at the sheets wrapped around the body and continued to the tent's floor, darkening the nylon. He struggled away, back to the flap. The scent seemed to worsen, enlarge itself, take hold of the entirety of his body. A tooth from the mouth had fallen and lay, like a withered seed, on the blanket. Now the tears came. Each drop inched out and rolled down his cheek, one and two and three.

Was the open mouth smiling at him?

Back in the light, he threw both hands on his knees and heaved out the beans he had eaten for lunch. After the mess, he pushed out acidic saliva and bile, his heart slamming his chest so hard he was sure that his bones would break. His tongue burning, he fell back against a tree trunk. He was tired, more tired than he had been in weeks, a crashing on par with a withdrawal. If not the same physical symptoms, then the terror. He slid down the tree, unable to move. The body had been there days, maybe a week, stewing in the hot tent, the blood drying in the fabric.

This person was killed there or killed elsewhere. He imagined a band of boys ferrying the body out to the most remote point in their Michigan town, three or four sandy-haired children with sun-scorched muscle, death in their hearts. The image wouldn't shake. He saw them laughing about football and girls, blood dried in their fingernails. He saw them going home, joking about the tent and the filthy sheets, how they were able to defy to God. No one saw them. No one knew.

Tad started back, hoping to find these boys. They wore varsity jackets. Red felt, script letters, All-American blood. He was shaking despite the heat, a thunder bolt chill in his chest. A branch slashed at his leg and he stumbled, staying upright just enough to keep moving, his breath short and broken. Sweat crusted in his eyes. Their names—the boys all had names. Buddy and Chet and Richie. They all had sweethearts back home. The sweethearts knew too, were turned on by it, begged, gasping, to hear the story again. Tell me how you did it. Buddy and Chet and Richie draped their varsity jackets on their sweethearts' supple shoulders. Blood dried on the lettering.

Tell me how you did it.

At the cabin, he collapsed.

4

Mona needed to get back to Brooklyn for Emmanuel's tennis lesson. She had become increasingly determined to give Emmanuel what she didn't have. This began with the attention of a coach. To this day, she had not taken a single tennis lesson. She never played for a high school team or a college team because neither institution had been required, by law or otherwise, to offer athletics to women. She had been entirely schooled in the parks, gleaning advantages through observation and practice, modeling her approach on what the winners did, in person and on TV. Look at how Billie Jean King hits an overhead, Martina Navratilova serves and volleys, Chris Everet shifts her feet. But there was the lingering wonder—what *could* she have really been with mentoring and training? How much potential was squandered? She loved her son and therefore her life and playing tennis professionally was always, until a short time ago, a fool's errand of compensation, a hunk of prize money for the winner and so little for everyone else, the lucrative sponsorships largely unavailable to women. It was all tragically unfair but life was tragically unfair and she never, really, believed otherwise, even in her more idealistic spurts. What training and tutelage could have done, then, was made her a better tennis player for her own sake, the sake of dominance of another, the transcendent physicality of the task itself. That was enough.

If she couldn't unlock it for herself, she would for Emmanuel. He had some aptitude. He could throw and catch a ball, hand-eye coordination innate. He looked so small on the tennis court, the racket head seemingly as large as his body, his little, doughy legs chugging after the ball as it bounced away from him, one, two, three, four bounces and *swing,* all of him whirling like a wooden wind-up trinket on some cobbler's shelf. He had a natural two-handed backhand, his stroke aggressive, almost angry. She still hit one-handed, the fashion of her youth, and was happy that the old pro she had brought him to was willing to school Emmanuel in contemporary technique. It was forehand and backhand, *brush up on the ball, keep your eye on it, bend those knees,* her tone unchanged from adults to children. Sylvia, the old pro, was a successful amateur player in the 1960s, and told Emmanuel to hustle. Sometimes she blew a whistle to make a point. *Hustle.* No one had told Mona to hustle. It was understood, as long as she could remember, you had to run out every ball, reach every shot, try harder than anyone. It was the only way to win. She had come to realize that with the passage of time, she was skeptical of her own talent, afraid that somehow, one day, it would disappear. She was more dedicated to fitness at forty-five than she was at twenty-five, biking every day, running four to five times a week, playing tennis every day that her schedule permitted. Her talent wouldn't vanish if she maximized her strength and stamina. It would have to be trapped inside of her, forever.

Saul took Emmanuel to a Yankee game. The drive to the Bronx was a bigger shlep and free parking wasn't a possibility, unlike Shea, where he could reliably jam his car under the Van Wyck Expressway and walk across Flushing Meadows.

"Why didn't you become a baseball player?" Emmanuel asked Saul one day.

His son was seven. He readied to explain the tragedy of physical limitations—at no point was he destined for a future as a professional athlete, unlike Mona, maybe—and how he was never blessed with talent and if you don't have it at birth, you'll never have it, and every professional athlete was the best player on their little league and high school teams, not just the best but so utterly superior that teammates and classmates and fans would spend the rest of their lives talking about your feats, fusing their formative memories with your own and making them nearly interchangeable, trying and failing to fathom your lifestyle as a multimillionaire compensated for blood-and-flesh alchemy.

"I don't know, it was hard to do," was all Saul said.

"Well, I'll practice hard and be one."

"You can do anything you put your mind to."

He did believe utterly in his son. He liked to think, at one point, he utterly believed in Lenore and Tad too. Lenore at least would lie to him and say that he did, that he was such a giving, good father, the best there ever was. Lenore knew spin. She was a successful white shoe lawyer now. She was married and would soon give him grandkids who would grow up in suburban Virginia, not so different than how Lenore grew up on Long Island, with a backyard and a public school funded with generous property taxes.

It had been a decade since Tad spoke to him. Lenore assured him that he still sent her letters and sporadically consented to phone calls. She hadn't seen him in person at all. Tad's departure was what bonded him to Felicia, still his legal wife after all these years. The hole that opened up in them both had equal depth and sorrow. If there was a difference, it was that he had somewhere to retreat to where Tad's disappearance meant little because Mona and Emmanuel didn't know him and never would. It was wrong, then, to keep referring to them as his counter-life, as if they were the parallel existence unfit, in his mind or anywhere, to be the default, the reality from which all possibilities sprang. Felicia had become his counter, the body he slept by, soundlessly, at night, and waved off in the morning on his way to work. He could no longer imagine her interiority, what thrilled her, what terrified her, what thoughts took shape as she drank coffee, drove to the gas station, and took tea with the civic association and school board members. He knew she spent many afternoons and evenings at Herb Weiner's and he didn't begrudge it, not anymore, at least. Whatever they did—he couldn't imagine it, truthfully—would be done, with or without his intervention.

His counter-life, yes, was his life, the only one, where color seemed to explode and he could laugh and shout like a much younger man. He was almost sixty. Time's passage still confounded him, the speed at which it all went, the decades passing from him like mist, existing to him as peculiar after-image. Did he really live all those years? Had Tad truly been a child? Had he now known Mona for thirty years? Was this a dream, to be fifty-nine and sitting at Yankee Stadium, the second version of the ballpark, Mickey Mantle dead, all the men arrayed on the field unborn when he had graduated high school? Emmanuel, next to him, urging on his team desperately, breaking into a wild cheer when finally the old slugger Chili Davis slammed a home run to right field, the first hit off Pedro Martinez. Out of obligation, Saul stood with the other fans, clapping politely, Emmanuel slamming both hands together and screaming as loudly he could, *let's go Yankees let's go Yankees let's go Yankees,* and he turned and put his hand on his son's shoulder and said *alright, here we go* and he could be a Yankee fan for his son, watch them run roughshod over Pedro Martinez, who may have been the best pitcher he saw since Sandy Koufax.

Saul's cellphone rang. It was a new contraption, one he was still unused to. He remembered when he got his first beeper and that seemed to be enough of an intrusion. Having a person being able to call you wherever you went seemed to violate, for him at least, the sanctity of outdoors, the freedom to circulate without the gray gears of his work life catching him. At this hour, it probably wouldn't be someone from work, unless it was an emergency, and he had very few of those. He was planning to retire, take his pension, and spend more time with Emmanuel and Mona—as much time as was possible without Felicia knowing. Because it still mattered, four decades on, how his wife perceived him. If he was going to divorce her, he should have done it a decade ago, before Emmanuel's birth. She would crush him in court if they did it now. At the bare minimum, half his federal pension would go to her. She had the moral and financial high ground.

It wouldn't be her because she never bothered to call his cellphone. She just waited for him at home, setting dinner, letting the TV run. Without children, his Roslyn house was an alien enormity, hollow rooms and echoing floorboards and windows that threw light onto carpets free of toys, footprints, and grime. He was excited most when he left, driving into Manhattan as the sun rose, returning from Mona's in Brooklyn when it was dark. They spent, at most, ten minutes speaking to each other on a given day. He ate dinner alone, on the couch, and went to bed with a newspaper armoring his face.

His cellphone didn't recognize the number. He had only Felicia and work numbers saved. Calling someone like Izzy Locker or Sonny Cannon on a cellphone seemed incomprehensible. Emmanuel, he saw, was reciting Yankee career batting averages from memory to a kid sitting next to him, a stranger who was now a friend. Taking the phone in hand, he smiled at them both.

"Mr. Saul Plotz?"

"Who is this?"

"I'm calling from North Shore LIJ. Your wife, Felicia Plotz, was involved in a car accident tonight and I am sorry to say she's in serious condition. She's currently in surgery . . ."

Saul took his son's hand without speaking, leading him up the aisle on the third base side, where he had splurged for a real sight line. Chuck Knoblauch struck out, unaware that Saul's wife was in a medically induced coma, his woe reserved for his inability to connect with Pedro's fastball. The organist, playing one of those canned ballpark melodies, didn't seem to care either. He pushed his way through crowds on the concourse, slipping between the mindless gaps of flesh, hurrying as fast as he could without alarming Emmanuel further. When he began to ask where they were going, why they were leaving early, Saul told him it was an emergency for work and he was really sorry and he would make it up to him with another baseball game this year, they'd hit Yankee Stadium again before the end of September, and Emmanuel asked, quietly and reasonably, why work wanted him so late.

"I agree, it's very annoying. Work can be very unfair."

Emmanuel gazed up at him in his floppy Yankee cap, last year's World Series patch from 1998 sewn on its side. The boy was more perplexed than disappointed. He was being whirled, in the bottom of the sixth inning, out of a ballpark. Saul had never taken him home early before. Mona resented crowds and liked to beat the traffic but the massing of bodies never made Saul uncomfortable, the constriction of space. Crowds meant action, the exhalation of a society. He loved ballparks the day of a big game. Now, as he raced to the street lot he stashed his car in, they were an impediment. Felicia did know he was at a baseball game. But his companions, he said, were friends from the federal building, not his son. He tugged hard on Emmanuel's hand, too hard, and the boy let out a small yelp. "I'm sorry, buddy, I didn't mean it, we're just in a hurry." It would be two hours before he got to North Shore LIJ. First he had to drive Emmanuel home to Bay Ridge, in the southwest corner of Brooklyn. Then he needed to get his ass right back on the Belt Parkway and swing around east and then north. If he was lucky, he wouldn't hit traffic. Luck like that, though, did not exist in New York City, any time of day or night.

If he didn't want to go home to Felicia at night, he also didn't want her to suffer or die. She was the mother of their children. She deserved better than this.

They shot down the east side of Manhattan and then through the Battery Tunnel, into Brooklyn. The radio crackled and dissipated as they rode underwater. A double-lane became a single due to construction and he was slowing, his luck run out. The sea of taillights swelled, beady red, and he wanted to punch the windshield.

"Hi dear," he said, the cellphone unnaturally pressed to his ear as he slowed at a red light. "We're home a bit early. I'm going to bring Emmanuel in and then let's talk for a few minutes."

"Talk?"

"There's something I need to tell you."

"What is it?"

"Not about him. He's good. Something else. We'll talk outside, okay?"

"Okay then."

"I'll be pulling up in the front."

He finally parked in front of the pump at Mona's apartment building, putting on his hazards. "Alright, Emmy, let's go inside."

They walked together through the small courtyard and into the lobby, where Saul nervously punched the button and waited to be taken to the third floor. Mona's lobby always had the faint of smell of cigars, like something out of his childhood.

"Did you guys have a good time?" Mona asked, opening the door.

Emmanuel immediately ran inside, waving his program. "None of the Yankees hit *anything* but Pedro was great, historic, Dad said, we saw history."

"Pedro is a special pitcher," Saul said.

"Only Chili Davis got a hit. No one else. It was a home run," Emmanuel said, lament in his voice. "I wish more of them hit."

"We'll get to another game before the year is out," Saul said. "Now, your mom and I are just going to chat outside for a few minutes. I'll see you tomorrow after school okay, Emmy?"

"Good night, dad."

"If the weather is good tomorrow, let's go out and have a catch at the playground."

"Yes!"

He walked with Mona down the hallway and back out into the

courtyard, the air suddenly cooler. He was no longer smoking but hungered for a cigarette in a way he hadn't in years. Mona had quit too. She was turning fifty, much older than he had been when he first met her, when he felt so old, the square among hippies but now the hippies were graying too, getting fat, settling down, unwinding into the sort of people they could never believe had cogent, constructed thoughts worth taking seriously. Youth was ugly in that way, ugly with disbelief—not us, we won't grow old. But he was always ready. He knew it was coming. At thirty, he anticipated the forehead wrinkles that so dominated his skin, the vanishing of one self and the gradual emergence of another, the one a whole new generation of human beings would know as the *only* Saul Plotz, stooping, rogue hairs sprung from his nostrils. He avoided mirrors.

Mona, though, was still beautiful. Always herself. Time would never weaken her. He fished in his pocket for a phantom cigarette. She waited for him, since he was the one who summoned her, and finally he began to speak.

"Felicia was in a car accident."

He hated how his wife's name sounded in Mona's presence. Though she never appeared to resent the few times his wife would have to come up in a conversation anymore, he still believed it was an affront to mention Felicia. For all his dedication to his life here, in Brooklyn with Mona and Emmanuel, he had never left Felicia. He had never even told Felicia. He used to tell himself he stayed with his wife because Tad had left them both and she didn't deserve to lose a son *and* a husband. She was not a sinner, she was not lousy, she was not someone who had, in any fundamental way, wronged him. In certain moments, he could convince himself of his offbeat nobility, that by not telling her and living two lives he was both sparing her while giving another boy the father he deserved, blessing him with a childhood free of strife and consequence. Emmanuel played ball and ate chocolate ices and watched Saturday morning cartoons.

"What?"

"The hospital called tonight. Northshore LIJ."

"Well, why are you still here talking to me? *Go.* She needs you."

"I just wanted to tell you. It's why we left the game early."

"Is she okay? How serious is it?"

"I don't know. I don't know much. God, I hate hospitals. They remind me of my parents."

"I feel the same way, Saul."

"I may be out of touch for a while."

"I understand."

"I'm still getting Emmanuel after school. And I am having that catch. I promised him. But I'll probably have to jump back to Long Island after."

"She needs you now. I wouldn't wish that on anybody."

He brought her close and kissed her. She looked up at him, a sudden distance in her eyes, like she had spied some weather formation over his shoulder and was more interested in what hung there now.

"I love you, Mona."

"You too."

He left her there in the courtyard, rushing into his car and speeding off into uncertain night.

5

In the future, Emmanuel would cleave his childhood into two parts: before private school and after.

Until he was nine, he attended the public schools in Bay Ridge and Dyker Heights, Brooklyn neighborhoods that weren't well known to anyone who hadn't grown up in them. He relished the white noise of this time, the shouts bouncing off cafeteria walls and schoolyard pavement, exploding games of tag and handball and kickball and dodgeball, a summertime that seemed to swallow up other seasons entirely, hot spring and hot fall and the sweat drying and crusting on his eyes. It was true, the teachers said, he didn't talk much in class. He wasn't interested. There were enough children to answer questions. He preferred a desk near the back to stare out a window and contemplate the games he was going to play, the ultimate prizes he would claim: a future in Major League Baseball or, as a default, an astronaut walking the surface of Mars.

When he was eight, he pitched to his mom in the parents vs. kids baseball game in the Parkway Youth Organization, where he was playing for the summer. He had made the all-star team, the travel team, and he was a tough little left-hander. He liked hitting even more than pitching. The coach, a well-meaning auto mechanic, was the only non-screamer in the league. There was tension to the games, bodies crushed against fencing, cyclone barbed wire cutting them off from a small chemical treatment plant. Fistfights among parents happened several times a year, over manhood challenged or a blown call by the teenage umpire. It was the sort of local sporting exercise that was probably on its way out: organized, but not organized enough to sever its ties to the street. There were rumors of mafia sons joining squads, all named for Major League teams, even though the jerseys merely said "Parkway" in an old-fashioned script, colored red, white, blue. In the small clubhouse where the commissioner, a retired bus driver named Pete DiSapio, drew up schedules and assigned teams, there were occasional bets placed, the transfer of cash in secret lending meaning to these hot days out of view. Commissioner Pete smoked cigars, his belly jutting out, his digraphs crushed. Throw the ball was *troh da ball.* The plural of you was *yous.* He was never seen without his PYO hat. In the little clubhouse was the photograph of the lone PYO alum to reach the Major Leagues, a mediocre left-hander for the Padres and Giants in the Day-Glo 1970s, an Italian boy who made good.

Emmanuel loved it all. His teammates were angry and they cared about winning. They played spikes up, elbows out. They picked at scabs to watch them bleed. They had his back when he took the mound, shouting down shit-talkers in the opposing dugout. *Rally rally, the pitcher's name is Sally. Pitcher in the hole, ten feet deep, can't get out cause he's got noooo heat.* Sometimes he would imagine standing in a ten foot hole, the cool dark on his face, straining to escape with nothing but a fastball.

When he was eight, he pitched to his mom. She was the only woman on the parents' squad. Jason, the third baseman, snickered as she came to the plate. "Nice and easy to Mommy," he said, pounding his mitt. The parents didn't seem to know what to do either. Not all of them knew how to play well. For every muscle-bound dad like Nicky Petric's, who once played baseball for a college and still liked to take swings in the 80-mph batting cage, there were three who were too winded or afflicted with bad backs or creaky knees to intimidate. But they were all fathers and therefore on the field without question.

His mom was a constant presence behind the chain-link fence in left field on game days, her beach chair out, sunglasses on, a newspaper unfurled. This did not mean, though, they knew what she could do. He knew. Jason pounded his mitt once more. "Strike Mommy out."

He wanted to turn around and hurl the ball at Jason's face. His mom was in the right-handed batter's box in a small crouch, her bat just off her shoulder. It was too small for her. He could see that several of the dads in the dugout were laughing amongst themselves. Nicky Petric's dad, for fun, had laced a double in the gap in the last inning. "That lady is gonna hurt herself," he heard Dan Morrissey's dad say out loud, with enough effort for everyone to hear. As he squinted in at his mom, he saw she was actually using *his* bat, the red Black Magic, waggling it softly. Her sunglasses were still on.

"So bored," Jason groaned. "Just pitch already."

He got into his wind-up and fired the first pitch, as hard as he could, high and away. The ball clattered against the backstop.

"Nice and easy," said his coach, clapping his hands.

"I couldn't pitch to my mother," he heard Dan Morrissey's dad say. "She'd be telling me to clean my room."

"My ma stayed in the kitchen. That's where mas should be," said Vinny Black's dad.

"A dyke in the dugout, maybe, but that's about it."

"Yeah."

His mom was still standing in the batter's box, unmoved. He would try again. With her sunglasses on, she always seemed especially severe, a dislocating blend of fury and disinterest. He decided he would slow down his wind-up but come just as hard, maybe harder.

He had to throw her a strike right past her.

When the ball left his hand he knew it was headed down the middle. He had gripped it across the seams, what they called a four-seam fastball, straight and true. He followed through like the coach had said, his arm falling forward, his legs splitting into a fielding position. His PYO cap came tumbling off his curls. The ball, he believed, had left his hand harder than any he had thrown before.

The aluminum ping of the bat woke him. It was the loudest he had heard on that field, and that included the double Nicky Petric's dad smacked into the fence. The ball soared in a high, debilitating arc, so high it looked like it had been intentionally tossed straight up in the air. It was over the left field fence and onto the big kid's field, where the teens were practicing for a game later that afternoon.

"Holy shit," Vinny Black's dad said.

They were clapping and cheering for her and he wanted to do the same, to fight off the wicked shame of surrendering a home run to his own mom.

"Emmy!" she cried out, touching first base.

Jason, he saw, was lightly applauding.

He knew he had done something incredible, that he had been, for the first time, a participant in some kind of history. His mom touched second and third in a slow jog, like a slugger who had done it many times before. All the boys were thinking the same thing: they had never seen a baseball hit so far.

After the game, he began to feel proud. His teammates were done with their jokes. The dads had rallied around her. Their deeply-held convictions of gender had been shattered, for an afternoon at least.

A year later at the same field, his mom made him cry. Her temper was unpredictable, but usually tied to sports. He had seen her smash tennis rackets in frustration and shout curse words at players. With him, she wanted the best. If he didn't give his best, she would let him know. One year after giving up the home run, a Parkway coach asked if he would like to play for a while on the bigger kid field, with the older team. He was nervous.

"I don't want to go," he quietly told his mom.

"What do you mean?"

"I like it here."

"This is an opportunity to play with the 11-year-olds. It would only be temporary. They want to try you out, see what you can do, and if you do well you will move up."

"I think I want to stay."

"Stay?"

"Stay with my friends."

"Opportunities like this don't come along often, Emmanuel."

He knew the simmer of her rage. It came on suddenly, her sentences like little pellets out of her teeth. She could get loud but she didn't have to. Behind her sunglasses, he knew her stare. He was afraid of so many things and other than reptiles and crowds—she didn't like to be hemmed in by people and she hated snakes—she didn't fear much of anything. He began to sniffle and he knew that was a mistake.

"You have an opportunity here. You should play."

"I don't want to."

The little field with the cyclone fencing was his field. The rough, grave dirt, the lightly-painted foul lines, the way his cleats sunk into the batter's box. He knew it all and wouldn't leave it behind for larger people he did not know. Change inherently disturbed him. At nine, he was already in the private business of predictions, attempting to as accurately forecast his life as he could, down to lunches and lights-out. He would know as much of the future as he could. And the future on his field was one he could understand.

"You are going to disappoint the coach. You are going to disappoint me."

"But I don't want to . . ."

His tears, slowly rolling down his cheeks, did not move her. He had never seen his mom cry. Once, he remembered being at his friend Scott's house and watching as Scott's mother cried into the phone. She was talking to someone, slowly and intimately, her voice barely at a whisper. Scott's father didn't live with them anymore. The cord of the wall-mounted phone wound around her smooth index finger, the light from the kitchen window shining off her ring. Though his mom hadn't said it, he knew she viewed crying as an admission of failure, of something broken. He never asked Scott why his mother cried. Part of growing up was learning not to ask questions.

"Emmanuel, you're going over there," she said.

He could hardly see her when he looked up. The tears had blurred his vision, rendering the world a mash of color. He could only tell there was a sun hanging somewhere above him.

"Stop crying, Emmanuel."

He couldn't form sentences. Only recently, he had seen the phrase "tongue-tied" in a book he was reading and asked his mom what it meant. It means, she said, you can't say what you want to say, like your tongue has been tied. But how did one tie a tongue? The flesh was twisted against itself? He now understood. No words would form. Language was like muck in his teeth. He could only breathe between tears.

"I don't want to go," he finally said.

"If you don't go," she said, "I'm not going to talk to you for the rest of the day."

She kept her word. After the practice with friends, in which he hit baseballs with a hollowness in his stomach, she silently walked him to her car and drove home.

"I think I may have the Beefaroni in the cupboard for lunch. I'd like that," he said from the shotgun seat.

His mom had no answer for him. Behind her sunglasses, she was inscrutable, like an agent carrying out a mission that transcended language. Her mouth was fixed. At the red light, she seemed to breathe, but otherwise would not move.

"I can heat it up in the microwave myself," he tried again.

Nothing. She continued to drive through the familiar neighborhood, the leaf-blown streets and the attached houses, windows advertising decals of whatever holiday was upcoming. He saw stars-and-stripes for July 4th. The more time passed, the more he failed at deciding what exactly he should say or do next.

The silence was like a fist closing in his throat.

She parked the car. He only knew to get out because she got out first. In the backseat was his bat bag and cleats. Often, she would grab it for him. Now, she simply departed, crossing the street to the apartment's courtyard, with the flagpole and the trimmed hedges and flower beds. He was left there to scramble in the backseat for his equipment. The bat bag kept sliding out of reach.

The side entrance to the building where they always entered required a key. He sped up to catch her, to make sure she didn't just shut the door on him. What he saw was her back through the closing glass door, his hand firing out to catch it before it latched shut. Another moment and he would have been locked out. He followed her, panting, beginning cries of "hey mom" and then "mom" as she ascended the stairs, on the way to the third floor. She hated elevators and always walked. Each "mom" was louder than the last and all that was returned to him were his own echoes off the walls of the stairwell.

His apartment door closed on him. At least she had left it unlocked.

"Please mom, talk to me," he said in a voice he couldn't recognize, tattered and cracking, his tears burning behind his eyelids. "Please mom."

She was in the kitchen opening the fridge, reaching for a canteen of cold lemon water. She drank it not looking at him, her sunglasses still on.

"Please talk to me."

The cut scenes of a new life played inside of him in terrifying succession. Disowned, orphan, on the street begging for a meal, nights in a makeshift cardboard box. Or, more simply, a lifetime of silence, his teenage and adult years passing without ever hearing another word from his mom. His dad would join her. He would never hear from them again.

"Please, please."

She drank her canteen, refilled it, and drank again. The day was a slow broil and the only air-conditioning unit in the apartment was in his mom's bedroom. In the living room, he turned on a tower fan and sat, thinking. He needed a plan. He had no plan. With nothing left to do, he turned on the TV. Midday, he flipped to Cartoon Network. He couldn't focus on the show, *Dexter's Laboratory*. He couldn't lose himself in the artifice of a cartoon. Older men and women drew these characters in some stark, hidden room for his amusement and he couldn't be amused anymore.

"Mom, I think I'll heat the Beefaroni now."

She was in her bedroom, eyes closed. Midday, she could enjoy a nap. She believed in naps. It was like a religion to her: rejuvenation achieved through short bursts of sleep. He was different, naps disoriented him, daymares dripping out of his wobbly consciousness, his dried saliva always tasting like cotton. Nudging the door open, looking carefully inside, he watched his mom. Sleep was now his hope. She would wake up and forget this ever happened.

Old men drew pictures and animated them to entertain him. They knew nothing of his life, but they tried to anyway. He watched TV.

He would remember it, years later, as one of his more painful days, though he suffered no physical or emotional blows of the like he would know in his future schooldays. Each hour, he would try to speak to his mom and she would say nothing back, continuing on with her daily tasks: washing her face, clipping her fingernails, boiling water for plain pasta and Romano cheese. This is how the dead feel, he thought. Hell was not the firepit beneath the ground, a scaly red being torturing souls with pitchforks. That sort of suffering was eventful. Punished souls did not really travel there. Instead, he was now convinced, they remained on Earth to hover uselessly among the living, their actions unseen, their words unheard. The torture would not be something as trite as scalding metal jabbed into flesh. It would be far deeper, everlasting, the pain of a permanent exile—life played out on a stage without you. He would be doomed to watch.

"This Beefaroni is pretty good," he said, slurping at his heated up food from the can. He was standing in the kitchen, leaning over the bowl. His mom was still in her bedroom.

"Really really good!" he shouted.

He retreated with his bowl to the glow of the TV, watching the afternoon fade beyond the living room window. Cartoons continued to play. He wanted the TV, in some way, to acknowledge what he was feeling. He wanted the characters to leap from their two-dimensional planets and throttle his own.

The Beefaroni oozed like alien intestines in the large bowl.

At 5 p.m., he closed his eyes. What was beginning as a nap, he decided, would take him into tomorrow. Tomorrow was the only promise he had. He would have to embrace what he had now, this murmur of the TV, the blaze of afternoon sun, his body sinking deeper into the couch. Sweat was caked and dried, grime deep in his pores. He felt ancient, mummified, a thing ripe for burial, a disappearance in a hot cloud of dust.

"Emmanuel."

He didn't believe it at first. Unsure if it was dream logic, he waited. His eyes were closed, his head turned into the couch cushion. The TV continued to whisper.

"Emmanuel."

It was his mom's voice. He couldn't resist any longer. His body spun, his eyes opening to the light, her face free of sunglasses.

"Mom."

"You need a real dinner. Let's get up."

"I'm sorry, I'm sorry that—"

"I overreacted, okay? I'm the one who is sorry. I wanted to see you on that field with the older kids because I know you can succeed there and I want you to believe in yourself. I want you to have that kind of courage. My parents never pushed me. I had to push myself, and it got lonely. But I pushed too hard."

"You did say you wouldn't talk to me for the rest of the day."

"I've got some salmon in the fridge. Do you want me to make some, then we'll go out for ices?"

"I'd like that," he said.

6

Mom had sayings. There seemed to be more and more of them, each to fit a particular situation. "Forewarned is forearmed," she said when he forgot to put on sunscreen before a trip to the beach. She would always have more—she was always prepared—and brought it herself. Others: "If you live with the wolves, act like the wolves." "Only the paranoid survive." "If you ever forget you're a Jew, an anti-Semite will remind you." She was always in motion. He could hardly keep up. Jogging or tennis or driving him to practices, yelling out windows, honking horns.

Jesus Christ. It was in first grade when he learned this was the name of an actual person and not a curse word. Igor, who was also Jewish, told him. "We don't believe in him but a lot of them do," he said, pointing to the room of children. Igor always seemed to know more. Jamal and Robbie believed in Jesus. Who was he? "He's the reason for Christmas," Igor said. Emmanuel didn't quite understand, though he loved Christmas. The lights, the music, the treats. In second grade, he would write a Christmas poem that dad loved.

Christmas trees stand,
Soldiers lead a band,
The snow gets deep,
People go to sleep.

Mom rarely used *Jesus Christ* towards him. She saved her mean words for the tennis court, for the people on the telephone, the drivers who were too slow. One time, she was trying to play a match on a court she had a signed up for, her Parks Department permit in hand. The man, who had a big belly, wouldn't move. "You want the court so bad, have it!" he finally shouted, wobbling over to a garbage barrel and tossing it on the court. Dark liquid and trash spilled out, rolling toward the service line.

"Jesus fucking Christ," mom said, running closer to him, sticking her finger in his face. "You fat piece of shit. Clean up my fucking court."

What amazed Emmanuel was how the man, who was larger and hairier than his mom, with a sardine smell he wouldn't forget, eventually backed away. There were no fists thrown, like in his schoolyard, where kids could tackle each other on cement over stolen Lunchables. She never laid a hand on him. She never needed to. Whether with him or the hairy man at the tennis court, intimidation was enough.

The man skulked away after trying, and failing, to push the trash can wholly off her court.

Sometimes she would bring a newspaper but it would lower whenever he came to the plate. On weekday afternoons, if possible, dad would come too, in his coat and tie from work. He always wore loafers and pressed pants, unlike the other dads, and he was older. He noticed this more each year. The other dads had dark hair. His dad was already going gray.

In September, he started at the new school. He would soon be ten. What he wanted to say to his mom, who was adamant it was time for a change of scenery, whatever that could mean, was that life began when he left the classroom, that everything that made his elementary school what it was, and what would make junior high with his friends even better, happened when the bell rung and he ran out, almost breathless, into the schoolyard. Jamal, Igor, and Robbie would all go to the local junior high together. So would the friends he made in third and fourth grade, like Scott and Ganesh. They would all be together without him.

"This school is a great opportunity," his mom told him after a trip to the admissions office. "You are going to really enjoy it."

"I like my old school."

"You'll like this one better."

Bridge Prep Country Day School, located on the border between Bay Ridge and Dyker Heights, had existed since 1854. It was a stretch of time beyond comprehension. There were Bridge alumni who fought in the Civil War, who died not knowing what indoor electricity was like. When he was a younger, he had gone to summer camp on Bridge's vast campus, with its two duck ponds, a fitness center, tennis courts, a performing arts center, a separate science building, and a backfield looped with a running track, baseball fields tucked into the corners. The track circled the football field. Whatever acreage it was, it was larger than any he had ever seen within the city. The campus was like an urban glitch, barely able to be reconciled with the density just a few miles away. He was starting there in the fifth grade and would be expected, somehow, to be there for eight years. That was how it worked at Bridge Prep Country Day School.

What he found out quickly was that he was one of the few kids from the actual neighborhood. Most were bussed in from Manhattan, Staten Island, and the parts of Brooklyn he only knew from day trips, like Park Slope and Brooklyn Heights. Their parents did not take photographs for newspapers or work for the federal government. They were bankers, doctors, owners of ubiquitous businesses (one was the scion of a snack food empire), or engaged in other financial dealings he only dimly understood. There were celebrity children too: the son of a New York Met, the daughters of an otherwise populist civil rights leader, the daughters of an Oscar-winning actress, and the son of a legendary folk singer who resembled, almost exactly, the folk singer himself. The school was not so much a breeding ground for future greatness as a ground on which the offspring of great breeders trod. No one was sure exactly what any of these children would do, only that they would die as they came: very rich.

The distinguishing feature of Bridge Prep Country Day School was a white clock tower. It appeared on school brochures, sweat-shirts, and letterheads. It loomed from every quadrant of the school. There was supposedly a way inside and upper classmen knew how to get there, to hide away and sneak a beer or something more. A school like Bridge Prep ultimately needed a clock tower, he figured. It was the only symbol that would do.

At lunch hour, or whenever he had a free period, he retreated to a concrete wall facing the school's sprawling fitness center and pounded a pink rubber ball into the ground. This was called Chinese handball, one bounce before the wall, and he could always play it alone. He shuffled in his polo shirt and khakis, the male dress code on non-chapel days. On chapel days, with blustery addresses from the headmaster and the head of the middle school, boys wore jack-ets and ties. Occasionally, he would defy dress code and wear white sneakers instead of dress shoes. His only moment of real enjoyment during the day was running across the cement in his sneakers to smack his pink handball against the wall. At lunchtime at the end of September, Jake Katz grabbed his ball and chucked it into onto the roof.

"Pink is for faggots," Jake said, walking away.

7

Liv was adamant: Mona was going to celebrate her fiftieth birthday in fucking style.

"We're going to the top," she sang over the phone, from Grayson Moegenborg's apartment.

Defying Mona's expectations, Liv and Grayson remained a couple. They wouldn't marry because neither wanted to—Liv said it would be a jinx, and figured it precluded any awkwardness over someone like Grayson nudging her to sign a prenuptial agreement. "He gives me what I want anyway. And I don't ask for much," Liv said.

The October party was at Windows on the World, where Liv now earned a comfortable salary overseeing the staff and Grayson worked thirty or forty stories below, as the executive director of the Port Authority. It was strange to always see his name in the newspaper. He belonged to Liv but to the public too, this second self playing across the municipal stage. He appeared on NY1, gave feisty, barbed quotes to the tabloids, and made sure to be photographed, Liv on his arm at the society dinners, galas, and fundraisers he was a required presence for. From afar, Mona enjoyed their life. These sorts of functions—in which dress and manner took such priority—would never be where she wanted to be, but they were delightful enough for Liv. And she seemed happy.

Her fiftieth birthday, at a steep discount, would be at the top of the World Trade Center.

She had decided to call Al. It had been several years since they last spoke, Al still in Los Angeles, painting or operating galleries or doing whatever it was he did in a city she had still never been to, always sun-blasted and remote in her imagination.

The first number she called was answered by a stranger. "I think he moved out around six months ago. I remember him a little," the woman said.

"Do you know where he is now?"

"Beats me."

She called the last gallery she knew that he worked at.

"Oh, Falcone, yeah," the man on the line answered. "He's been gone a while. I think he's over at Marney's now."

"Marney's?"

"Her gallery. Give her a ring," and he passed her another number.

No one picked up the first time. She waited a half hour and tried again. No, Al Falcone didn't work there anymore, the woman said. None of the people who spoke with Mona on the phone seemed particularly excited about Al. This saddened her slightly. She expected his name to elicit warmth and familiarity. *Al Falcone, that talented sonofabitch.* Instead, like most people, his name was another that had slipped in and out of memory over the course of a decade. The woman at Marney's said she thought someone named Cristobal may know, to try back after three.

"After three, got it."

Three in Los Angeles was six in New York. Saul and Emmanuel were both at home, eating turkey burgers they had heated in the microwave. The TV was turned to ESPN. She could only focus on Al, where he had really gone. He didn't fly into New York, as far as she knew. The idea of him actually coming to her birthday party seemed laughable. There had been a time when he mattered to her as much as anyone else, when they were young in the bruised dark of a Brooklyn morning, chasing a vigilante for a photo. The identity of Vengeance, she remembered, had never been uncovered. It was one of the mysteries of the city, this '70s crime-fighter and decapitator of Marius Shantz receding from collective memory, from the haphazard reach of law enforcement. He could be dead. It had been one of her links to Al, perhaps the most important one, the quest they undertook with such abandon for the *Daily Raider*, a tabloid thirsty for violence. Saul would never have chased anyone like that. He belonged, fundamentally, to the daytime.

She called again, after three in L.A. A man answered the phone. "Yes?"

"I'm looking for Al Falcone."

"Who is this?"

"I'm a friend. My name is Mona. I wanted to speak with him."

"I can pass along a message."

"Do you have his number?"

"I know Al and he likes to keep to himself. He burned out pretty bad, a few weeks back, and he's really taking a break."

"A break from what?"

"Oh darling. Al is a good, quiet boy now. It's almost the year 2000. He can't party like it's 1990 anymore." She heard small, light laughter.

"I knew him from back in New York."

"You seem like a nice enough person. Let me head over to Al tomorrow. I'm supposed to see him for lunch. I'm one of his few industry friends, so to speak. Give me your number and if he wants, maybe, you'll get a call."

"I'm inviting him to my birthday party."

"No alcohol!" Cristobal cried out, laughing again.

She heard the phone go click.

Five days later, Mona came from shooting a Giuliani press conference to find a familiar voice on her answering machine. She played it twice to make sure it was him.

"Hey, it's Al, hope all is well. Cristobal said you were looking for me. I guess I missed you. You can give me a ring, 213-802-4319. Sorry, I moved a while back and forgot to tell you. I forgot to tell others too. Well, talk soon."

She called immediately. On the fifth ring, she heard him.

"Hello?"

"Al, hi, it's me. Mona"

"Mona, wow, yes. How are you?"

"I'm good. It's been so long."

"Years and years. Jesus, yeah, it's great to hear from you, really."

"You were hard to get a hold of."

"I've been moving around. What's new with you?"

"I'm shooting for the *Daily News* now. I decided to go on staff for a while. Higher pay, though I hate being chained to them. Emmanuel is starting at a new school so we're getting him ready for that. Things are crazy, as always."

"And the tennis is good, I hope."

"Every Saturday and Sunday, unless they throw me on the weekend shift, which they like to. I may quit at some point. I think I'm ready for a change."

"You like routine."

"I'm going to be fifty. We're fifty. Did you think we'd get here?"

"I never believed in fifty. I saw twenty, thirty, then death. But I'm here. We got old, Mona. We're walking into another century."

"Now I remember why I called you. My fiftieth birthday party is coming up. Liv is having it at Windows on the World. She practically runs the whole place. She's getting me a discount."

"That sounds like a lot of fun."

"I want you to come."

"I'd like to, yeah—definitely would. But that will be a tough week for me."

"I didn't tell you when it was."

"I remember your birthday, Mona. I'm assuming it's around that week."

"Why is it a tough week?"

"Just busy, that's all. L.A. isn't as laid back as it seems."

"Are you still painting?"

"A bit. Working. I have a few projects."

"You seem like you're hiding behind your words."

"It's been a long time, Mona."

"And that means I may want to talk to you or even see you."

"I'd like to see you too. We're our last link to our twenties. City College, taking pictures of corpses for the *Raider*, Brooklyn—I see it so clearly, every day. The past lives in full color in my head, it's not even the past. Of course I'd love to see you. But it's hard to go back. I've been here a long time."

"It's only a visit."

"I haven't been back since I last saw you."

"What—you're afraid if you come back, you won't want to go back to L.A.?"

"There's a reason I've spent a decade here, Mona. New York is difficult to think about, sometimes. You know that quote, I mean it was a title of a book. I'm thinking of it. *You can't go home again.*"

"Thomas Wolfe. I'm just asking you to come to a party."

"You're asking a great deal."

"To get on a flight? I'll pay for your ticket."

"I can afford a plane ticket. I can afford many plane tickets."

"Come out."

"I have to think about it."

"You're afraid of New York."

"The longer you're away, the more it looms inside of you."

"You're afraid of me."

"You know how to intimidate."

"Liv misses you too."

"She's rich now, right?"

"Her boyfriend is."

"Exactly. The last I had spoken with her, she was head over heels in love. Grayson Moegenborg owns a gallery here in L.A. I bet you didn't know that."

"Al, she wants to see you."

"I want to see her too. I want to see you. I like hearing from you, your voice—it's wonderful and painful, all at the same time. A tumult, they'd say. I'm sick of artists. You're an artist, Mona, but you're not. I always loved you for that. You don't have the sick compulsion to create. I did. I may have said this, once or twice, that it would've been easier if I was a Jew. Crazy, right? Who'd want to be so hated? But you and Liv, you Jews, how you could *float* sometimes, maybe because you knew the world was going to throw so much shit at you anyway. Born with a target on your back so what was there to lose? If I had a Jewish father, he'd want me to paint. Work in his tailor shop, sure, but paint too. Just go to college, paint, that's enough. My fucking wop father. You were a fairy if you didn't want to wake up at 7 a.m. to play baseball at the Parade Ground. *Don't be a fucking fairy,* he'd say. I think of him, I think of Brooklyn. The whole place can burn."

"Brooklyn isn't just Al Falcone Sr. And we won't be in Brooklyn. Windows on the World. Top of the Trade Center. You have a drink and you go home."

"How is Saul?"

"Saul is Saul."

"How is your son?"

"The best thing that ever happened to me."

"You don't have to pretend, for me, the second best thing to happen to you was Saul."

"I'm not pretending anything. I want to see you for my birthday party. After this, that's the end of birthdays. Liv can celebrate mine without me."

"I'll try."

"I know that tone. If you were going to try, you would make it. If you come out, bring some artwork, okay? I'd like to see it. Maybe I'd buy something."

"I'd like to see you. Maybe I'll watch you play tennis. Are you still ruining egos out there?"

"Mine is intact."

"Then you are. Good. Well, I have to get going. I need to eat something. Terrence needs a walk. Terrence is my chihuahua. I bet you didn't think I'd become a dog person?"

"I still don't like dogs."

"Jews don't trust dogs," he said, beginning to laugh.

"I don't blame our people for that."

"Well, Mona Glass, you got me to think. Let me get back to you in a day. Here's my advice. Enjoy being forty-nine. Fifty is a bitch."

Whenever large social events after Emmanuel's birth came up, Mona had a decision to make about who should be there. There were friends, usually from tennis, who only knew vaguely of Saul. Many of her tennis friends probably assumed she was a single mom, though she never said as much. Saul could be a better partner, lover, and de facto husband than most men who actually married their lovers. Still, explaining her situation to those who didn't know it natively, like Liv, could be exhausting. This was true of work friends too. The *News* staffers and photogs she met on the beat were aware she had a son and didn't know much else. She believed, fully, in the idea of a private self and a public self, of separating a life into spheres. Her parents had done it. She would too.

It was a month until her fiftieth birthday when Saul brought Emmanuel home early from the game. She saw the terror in his eyes. Having never met Felicia and having heard so little of her from Saul, she could almost forget, for moments in the day, he was still married. That he had never abandoned the existence she first encountered three decades ago, when he was a newly-married man falling for an unmarried college student. Other men left their wives, remarried, started anew. Yet Saul never could. On the tennis court, she had trained herself to chase away negativity, the proverbial entering of a "zone," and over the years she would apply the best practices of competitive tennis elsewhere, since she always furtively hoped athletic triumph could be transferable. With Saul, she mostly succeeded in this version of the zone, their daily joy, raising the greatest son in the world together. If Emmanuel resembled her with his curly hair and milky skin, he had absorbed all of his mannerisms: the way he crossed his legs on the couch, trundled after balls, squared his shoulders, and pressed his little fist to his chin when he was deep in thought. It would be easy, and not always true, for a stranger to say simply that Emmanuel was his mother's son.

Other women, foisted into similar situations, could have pried their men away. Divorces happened all the time. Half of her tennis friends were divorced. Did she have some fundamental defect that prevented her from having the entirety of Saul? That couldn't get him to live in Brooklyn? It was true she had never beseeched him, that she had been cool, for decades, to the idea of a traditional marriage, especially after they faked one for her parents. It was true he had been the one who wanted, at one time, to move in together. Lately, though, the topic had died between them. Saul was comfortable shuttling between Long Island and Brooklyn, scooping up Emmanuel from school, watching afternoon cartoons with him, and getting dinner ready, usually premade meals from Key Food. At 7 or 8 p.m. he was gone and she slept alone. With his nightly absences and the presence of a son in the daytime, sex was slowly, unceremoniously, fading from her life. She could admit to herself there had been a certain thrill in hearing Al's voice again. She hadn't seen him in a decade but he sounded just the same, with that streetwise edge, and if the voice was unchanged, she could imagine the youthful ideal striding through the doors. For an hour, even, it would be worth it, she decided. She would find a way to get Al to New York.

She went inside and saw Emmanuel sitting in his room with his little lamp flicked on, a *Sports Illustrated* splayed on his lap.

"Mom, I have a question," he said when she walked in.

"What's up, honey?"

"Where did dad go?"

"Oh, dad . . . well, he had work to do."

"He has a hard night job."

"He does."

"I don't want to work nights when I'm older."

"You won't have to. You can do anything you want."

"Well, I guess I would work nights if I play for the Yankees."

"That's right."

He was staring straight into his bookshelf, seemingly swimming in his thoughts.

"You better go to sleep. It's late. And no snacking. It's very unhealthy to eat after 8 p.m."

"I know, mom."

"I love you, okay?" She took his forehead and kissed it.

"I love you too, mom."

After Saul brought Emmanuel home from school the next day, he asked Mona to come outside to go for a quick walk. He hoped, at least, it would be quick.

"God damn, I need a cigarette," Saul said when they had begun to talk.

To her surprise, he had pulled out a pack.

"You're smoking again?" Mona asked. "I didn't smell it on you."

"You know, I just bought it this morning on the way to work. I had this urge. It was like the past reaching out to grab me. God almighty."

"It's horrible for you."

"just needed it. Last night—I don't even want to talk about it."

"How is she?"

"Smashed up. Bad. She's a careful driver. It looks like the guy who hit her was very drunk. She was barely conscious last night. I stayed there until the early morning."

And then you went home to the bed you share with her.

"What's the recovery going to look like?"

"Well that's the scary thing. It's very uncertain. Mentally, she seems okay. No brain damage or anything like that. It's an open question how well she will walk again."

"Christ almighty."

"It was all so quick. I'm at the ballgame with Emmanuel and then this happens. I still can't quite believe it. I've been in a haze all day."

Mona watched the expression on his face change, from concern to something else she couldn't quite describe. Some blend of embarrassment and disgust, a subtle curdling. She reminded him of his reality. In that sense, Saul had hardly changed in thirty years. When he was with her, he liked to pretend his other life existed only as inconvenient white noise. Mona was his love, his life. His wife was a distant idea. Though he could be explaining Felicia to her, he was still able to do it in a way that kept his wife at a remove, like a friend he occasionally saw for coffee. For him to worry about his wife in front of Mona was a confirmation of what he hoped to forget: that for all the ways he had chosen Mona, he had really not chosen her.

"I just feel sick," Saul said quietly.

They continued walking, up a hill. To their right, past the trees and the humming Belt Parkway, was the strip of water separating Brooklyn from Staten Island. She had always conceived of it as a river feeding into New York Bay but it was technically a tidal strait called the Narrows. She would try, every day, to either jog or bike along the promenade. There was a perpetual validation in physical activity she could appreciate, metrics achieved, proof produced in her sweat-drenched body. There, she could continuously win. There was no backsliding, no muddling of what she had really done, no questions assaulting her memory. She didn't want to walk with Saul anymore, not right now. She didn't want to hear about Felicia. She wanted her sneakers to smack the promenade, the familiar one-two rhythm, sunlight on her face.

"You'll be out there all week then."

"It won't affect picking up Emmanuel from school."

"Of course."

"You and Emmanuel are my priority. Always."

"She's your wife, Saul."

"Yes, technically."

"No, *fully*."

"You didn't want to get married."

"You didn't want to leave her."

"I love you more than anything, Mona."

"You have someone else to worry about right now. Go worry about her. I'm not the one on a hospital bed."

"Felicia is—it's difficult for me to explain. It's not love, it's loyalty. I always felt a need to protect her."

"You don't need to explain her to me."

He stopped. He was jiggling the pack of cigarettes in his hands, his eyes wandering to a point beyond both of them.

"No, I think I do. I think I need to."

"I don't need to hear about it."

"I thought about leaving her so many times."

"But you didn't do it."

"I didn't know if you wanted me to do it! You're so independent, Mona. You've always been that way. You've always spurned convention and that's why I was drawn to you, why I kept coming back, why I stayed. We had a *pretend* marriage. I thought a real one would cripple you in some way, that it would make you less yourself. You won't be the Mona Glass I knew if you were a married woman. But I wanted to marry you! God damn it, here I am, in the middle of a street here, telling you, shouting, I wanted to marry you! I still do!

Every day!"

"Calm down, Saul, please."

"I couldn't tell Felicia I had a son with you and I was leaving her. She had lost a son essentially. I was going to tell her she was losing a husband. I imagined her dying from the knowledge. Her heart stopping. I imagined her dead from it."

"She wasn't going to die."

"A person couldn't go on like that."

His hand was shaking around a cigarette that he had lit, against the wind.

"Mona, I would've done things so differently. So many things. I would've started by meeting you first."

"Let's just talk about something else."

"I wish to God I met you first."

They walked on in silence. She wasn't sure she actually believed what she told him but she had nothing else to say, nothing of value. None of it deserved to be remembered. Of course, we go on. Time is an arrow pointing one way. Every day, she got older. But so what? She wouldn't be the first or last human to identify time for what it was, a relentless ghoul. She wanted to be a better tennis player at fifty than thirty and could believe, in the heat of the rally, she was one, that she would only get stronger as she aged until she died a superhuman. *All we can do* . . . no, we could do more. We could rage against fate. She was sorry too that he had met Felicia first, that she couldn't beam herself back to the '60s and send history on the course it deserved. But she was here and she had Emmanuel. She was here with Saul.

8

Mona remembered the construction, the endless web of cranes and scaffolding, the monstrous digs and capsuled explosions and a steel skeleton surging into the clouds. For older people, like her father, these Twin Towers were a violent intrusion. They ruined Radio Row, he used to cry out. I bought all my transistors there. The Towers had come from the future. No one wanted what was coming.

A restaurant, at least, was New York. A multinational corporation would rent a floor, perhaps, with the promise of access to a multi-floor restaurant and catering hall, the power breakfasts, lunches, and dinners always on tap. And those not bound, so directly, to capitalism's onward slog would spring for a night so high in the air, cocktails making their heads light, the ocean of dark sky pressed against the long, thick glass.

The people came. By the time Liv had booked Mona's fiftieth birthday party, Windows on the World was the world's highest-grossing restaurant, bringing in nearly $40 million a year. By most metrics, it was a wild success. Over the decades, there were restaurant critics who disparaged the food and drink, who pronounced its offerings passé, who vowed to never dine there again and urged others to do the same. Like the New York Yankees, Windows on the World had become a city institution with the lucre and heft to be regularly resented by those who believed they knew better. But the experience could not be argued with—there was majesty in being on top of the world.

The World Trade Center had a daily population of 130,000 people: the tenants, the businesspeople, the tourists. It was a city unto itself, like a science fiction dream made real just in time for fiscal calamity. In 1975, New York City was hours from bankruptcy. Mona still shuddered at the memory of her city on the brink. Each day seemed to herald a new disaster. None of it mattered to the Towers: 192,000 tons of structural steel, 3,000 miles of electrical wiring, 43,600 windows, 4,000 doors, 198 elevators, and 50,000 telephones. It was an accumulation of sums, a testament to the vast reaches of engineering.

These numbers could sustain a mediocre restaurant. Windows on the World was far from that.

Every day, it pulsed with bodies.

Liv told her stories. Boozy finance parties that ended with fucking on the carpet. Coke snorted on dining tables, in full view of the waitstaff. One chef cut a hole in the wall to have Heinekens delivered to him at a rapid clip. Cooks would throw curried kumquats at each other as hard as they could. There was a sense of glorious dislocation, she said, of knowing you were transacting business at heights unknown for the entirety of human history. "We live and work on a dream scale," Liv would say. She commuted to the clouds. Most of the time, the restaurant was elegant, sedate even, the host of so many hushed lunches among colleagues who didn't want their bosses to hear them or bosses who didn't want their underlings hearing them. It was a Manhattan restaurant. But it could be, at the turn of a moment, so much more.

Liv had been there the night of the blackout in 1977. "I watched the city turn off," she told Mona. Section by section, the city disappeared into darkness. Windows on the World lost light too, the diners in a panic. Backup generators restored power. All those ensconced on top were momentarily exceptional, the sky gods in light. They didn't know what they had, exactly, those last hours in an electric glow before they were cast off below. Liv understood. In the kitchen, she listened to a battery-powered transistor radio, scrounging up news.

"We thought we could die there that night."

Grayson Moegenborg told her he was there that night too. He was dining at the smaller restaurant in the complex, Wild Blue, with a banking executive. They were smoking Newports. Liv would not meet him for many years but she wondered, if in fact, she had come across him puffing away as the lights went out. While the night of the blackout was a terror for Mona, huddling in her apartment alone by candlelight, Liv had the magic of Windows on the World. Even later, wading out of the Towers and into the darkened streets, she could wander Lower Manhattan without fear. The Towers, so reviled once upon a time, had talismanic powers to protect those who worked there, she said with a smile. Mona couldn't tell if she was joking.

By the time Mona's party was booked, Windows on the World had long graduated from local curiosity to high-powered kitsch. It was where you had a party to celebrate a half century on Earth. Each time Mona asked about some party detail—the drinks, the finger food, how large the guest list should be—Liv said she'd take care of it, and she did. All Mona had to do was approve Liv's curated guest list. They knew almost all the same people. It was Mona's job to add and subtract as she saw fit. She made sure to include old friends of Saul's, like Izzy Locker and Sonny Cannon, and a decent mix of work and tennis friends. Everyone should have someone to talk to. Liv pushed the guest list to fifty, stretching the far limits of people she considered good friends, but told her not to worry, she was getting the steep insider discount. Grayson padded the list with a few Port Authority acquaintances. Four of Emmanuel's friends were on the list too. None of them, to her disappointment, were from Bridge Prep.

Saul was supposed to come into Brooklyn to drive Emmanuel back to Manhattan for the party. In the afternoon, he called to tell her his car wouldn't start. "Fucking alternator, probably," he said, sounding deeply aggrieved. His car was in the federal building's garage. A tow truck would take him out. "I'm sorry, it will probably be a few hours." Mona at least had taken the afternoon off. The *News* wanted her for a housing rally in Queens, a few quick shots for the Queens bureau, but they sent a stringer to fill in when she said she wasn't feeling well. Her editor was a full decade younger than her and had only a vague memory of Vengeance and the glory of her youth. This meant he paid less deference to her, to whatever memory there was of a prized photograph of a now forgotten vigilante. In truth, it didn't bother her too much. It was a job to her and she couldn't lose herself in the self-important mythos that sprung up around newspaper people, how their work was essential for democracy and not just ego-gratification. She had no illusions: a millionaire real estate baron paid her salary and she took photos for him. The newspaper business was mercurial as all hell—the *Post* had been on its deathbed in the early '90s and she knew people who had been purged during various sprees of cost-cutting—and she had survived this long, and could claim a livelihood. At some point, sooner rather than later, she'd like to retire or try something else but she hadn't given deep thought to what the something else would be.

Mona drove up to Bridge Prep's oval to wait in the line of cars for Emmanuel. Though yellow school buses ferried most of the kids home, there was a contingent that was picked up either by parents or hired drivers. The daughters of the Academy Award-winning actress and the local civil rights icon would disappear into black cars with tinted windows. Those who came to personally pick up their kids were, by definition, the poorest at the school. Mona was certain she had the lowest net worth of any parent, excluding those who had children come through a special program that funneled high-achieving children from low-income neighborhoods to prep schools.

She learned this from the fundraisers she had photographed, the few times spent among Grayson, and her observations of Bridge

Prep's parent class. The rich could not be alone. They could not abide without bodies. The idea of a chef or a butler or a driver bothered her because it meant her privacy was no longer sacred, no matter how much discretion they were paid to have. Human beings hear, think, observe. They bear memories. This brought her no comfort. Yet the rich only embedded more people in their lives as they accumulated wealth. Gardeners, tutors, nannies, strength coaches. Was it simply about trust? Forcing them all to sign non-disclosure agreements? There was a loneliness to wealth, she figured, an awareness of how singular it was to exist with so much. Bodies armored you against that loneliness. When you called, they answered.

It was still strange to her that Emmanuel was now going here. For a long time, the idea had seemed either distasteful or unreal. Public school had been enough for her, Melinda, and Vic. Saul went to public schools. So did Liv and Al. If you didn't go to public school, you went to Catholic school and she never entirely trusted them. The kids from her neighborhood who went there seemed to have an edge, a disquieting aloofness. They paid to go to school. This seemed, on its face, absurd, when the city was giving you school for free.

Why did she do it? Melinda's words, she could see now, had nibbled at her for years. Emmanuel's success was all that mattered. She would prepare him for a life without uncertainty. He would marry, have children, make money, be good. For Emmanuel, no pretend weddings, no chasing vigilantes through the night. She imagined him in a house with a backyard, grilling on Sundays, the neighbors clinking lemonade glasses. A grand piano in the foyer.

As he aged, from baby to toddler to boy with an independent vision, the traits of young adulthood hardening, her ideal about the importance of a public education began to wilt against the reality of her longing for Emmanuel to be exceptional. By the fourth grade, as he was still getting report cards about his well-written essays, moderate math skills, and lack of participation in classes, she began to wonder if she was doing everything she could. He had friends, he was objectively good, he *enjoyed* school, but would that be enough? If she knew she could do better for him or find a way to increase his chances of entering an elite college and securing the kind of life that should be his, wouldn't she?

Finally, at last, she called Melinda. Melinda liked to talk, not listen. Vic, her brother, would ask questions, act curious, politely affirm whatever it was she wanted to say. He was a quiet, easy man, married and childless, living in a co-op off the Whitestone Expressway. With Melinda, there was bluster and rage, a fight always brewing just out of view. For the slightest transgressions—a party missed, a sentence interrupted—she could banish you for weeks at a time, ignoring phone calls and messages.

When Mona called about the idea of private school, though, Melinda was delighted.

"There are several great schools around us. You can send him to Dalton, Trinity, or Buckley. In the Bronx, Fieldston and Riverdale are lovely. Those are the campus schools. Very leafy, I love the ambiance."

"I don't want him traveling two hours to school every day."

"You want something in your neck of the woods, then."

"Yes."

"Harold's cousin went to Bridge Prep. That's right by you."

"I sent Emmanuel to their summer camp one year. It has that big clock tower."

"They have a real lovely campus there too. I hear they're very good about getting their kids into Ivies, though not on the level of a Fieldston. Still, I'd consider. How are Emmanuel's grades? What are his extracurriculars?"

"Uh, he plays baseball and tennis."

"So do a million other kids. If you want to get him in there and get him any kind of partial scholarship, you need him to stand out. Especially with all the affirmative action kids. Look, get him into an instrument. Does that Saul play?"

"He did in college, I think. The trumpet."

"Do clarinet. Less clarinetists out there. It's an instrument with some class. Arnie Shaw, Benny Goodman. You remember our father playing those Benny Goodman records. Now it's esoteric. Get him lessons."

"Lessons, okay."

"He doesn't need to be terribly proficient. It's important he has it on his CV, that's all. There's a lot going against him. For one, Bridge Prep doesn't need another *white male*."

It was the first time she had ever conceived of her son as a white male.

"Okay."

"He's a local too. You're in Bay Ridge. They recruit from all across the city. All of these admissions offices have quotas, soft and hard. They want racial diversity. Geographic diversity. Special boys and girls. There are slots reserved for the very rich. Mona, you're probably going to have to hit the *economic* diversity slot."

"I'm not poor."

"By the standards of the investor class, the celebrity class, the sort of people sending their children to Bridge, you are brutally poor. Even Harold's *hospital* salary would only get him so far. You will be one of the only parents without second and third homes, excluding the scholarship children from the ghetto. Emmanuel needs to stand out. Get him an instrument to start. He's a good writer, isn't he?"

"He's great for his age."

"He needs to be *greater*. You should get him a writing and essay coach. Jack of all trades, masters of none don't get anywhere. Clarinet and writing. Make him the best damn essay writer in the city. It's all about practice."

"I'll get him a tutor."

"Harold and I want the very best for Emmanuel."

Mona started Emmanuel in clarinet lessons and hired a local writing coach, a young Greek guy who ran a test prep service company out of an apartment building around the corner from her favorite bagel place. It turned out he was actually quite popular with Bridge Prep parents. He was charismatic, barely thirty, and had once had near perfect SAT and LSAT scores. Instead of practicing law, he paid off his loans as a one-man band in the neighborhood he had grown up in, pulling down a comfortable, undisclosed salary from a stable of thirty or so parents. The guy had Emmanuel in a group of seven students every Tuesday and Thursday. There were always packets to take home.

The idea of Bridge Prep amused Saul.

"Sonny Cannon went to Buckley and he came out mostly right."

"I hope this is the best for Emmanuel."

"These schools have some odd people. I remember from my political days, all the donors' kids went to schools like that. It creates some type of worldview. But Emmanuel—he'll be good there."

"I'm doing the right thing?"

"You always end up doing the right thing."

She didn't believe this was true but appreciated the sentiment. Clarinet lessons were available at a music store in the neighborhood. The instructor had a gray goatee and looked like someone she could have met at one of those Greenwich Village coffee houses that she .never bothered to hang out at in their heyday. He spoke in waves, a rising and falling in his voice that put her at ease. Music was life, he said, music makes a life go round.

"Why am I doing all this?" Emmanuel asked her one day.

"You're preparing for the Bridge Prep entrance exam, I told you honey."

"They're going to ask me to play clarinet?"

"They could. But really it's about having a lot of things you can do."

"I can't really play, mom."

"But you will. Practice hard, like you do at baseball."

Before Emmanuel's birth, she couldn't fathom not only motherhood but the mothers who seemed to subsume their lives in their children, either shrinking down their egos wholesale or inflating them through their offspring, a vicarious power play that always sickened her. After Emmanuel arrived, she understood it a little more. She would die for her son. That was easy. She would do anything, too, to ensure he experienced the greatest success that was possible for him. It was such different parenting than what had been imposed on Vic, Melinda, and herself. As a child, she could wander the streets for hours. The only requirement was that she had to be home by dinner, usually when the streetlights flickered on.

She was only a little surprised when Bridge Prep admitted him for the fall of 1999, the start of his fifth grade. Emmanuel was a smart boy. He would not only hold his own against these children of privilege; he would, in time, crush them. What surprised her, though, was the paucity of his scholarship offer. The tuition at Bridge was $12,000 a year, the equivalent of some colleges. Since she showed Bridge that she had a single-parent household—Saul's income was not included—they had been entitled to financial aid, but that only came out to $2,000 a year, which the admissions office assured her was quite generous. Ten thousand dollars, annually, would have to be accounted for. She could almost make the numbers work. In a few years, she would have the mortgage of her co-op made off. Then just maintenance costs for the rest of her life, $680 a month, manageable enough.

"Fuck, I thought I'd get more," she admitted to Melinda on the phone.

"The officer is right. $2,000 is a pretty formidable offer."

"No it's fucking not! Ten grand a year. This was all your idea. I should have him over at the public school. It's a significant chunk of my take home pay. I still have the mortgage . . ."

"Hadn't you thought of this before?"

"I believed, sincerely, Emmanuel would get more money."

"Harold can help you."

"I don't want Harold's money."

"You are being obstinate."

"I will be in your pocket forever."

"Oh Mona, don't be like—"

"It's true. You would lord it over me."

"I would *not*."

Saul asked if she wanted to take out a loan.

"No loans."

What she feared was losing her staff job. Every year, it seemed like the *News* would bleed more money. She did well with overtime but she wasn't one of the well-heeled columnists, making several hundred thousand a year. She didn't sit on the editorial board. Mike Lupica or Jimmy Breslin could afford to send ten kids to Bridge Prep. She was going to struggle to get one there. Truthfully, she was getting sick of the hustle. She had begun to envy what Saul had: a job behind a desk. Set hours. Water cooler talk. A civil service union.

"I'm going to look for new work soon," she told him.

"But you're great at what you do. And I love seeing your name in the paper."

"Twenty years of it, the glow wears off."

9

Mona changed, put on some make-up, and waited for Liv to get them both. Emmanuel wore a button-down dress shirt she had bought out of a catalog and dark blue slacks. Bereft of ideas, she wore a black blouse and dark jeans. It was her party and she'd dress how she wanted to.

On the drive into Manhattan, Emmanuel rode in the back and she took the shotgun seat in Liv's Hyundai. They whipped down the Belt Parkway and onto the Brooklyn-Queens Expressway, the route she had taken thousands of times, roadway she knew in her dreams. Liv was more excited than she was, her eyes popping, her coral lips fluttering. This was the ease of not having children, of not carrying the extra burden of a life. Only Grayson's mood could dog Liv and as far as Mona could tell, a man that wealthy could never fall into a bad mood for too long , since money or friends or a glitzy event were always coming to resolve it.

Mona glanced up in the mirror to catch a glimpse of him in the backseat. His head was turned toward the window, his eyes locked on a parade of four-story rowhouses and warehouse rooftops.

Emmanuel could always surprise her. From the time he was a toddler, he had a quiet about him that was almost monk-like, an ability to sit and absorb details of reality. He asked questions in his high-pitched, watery voice. Last summer, when she had left CNN droning in her bedroom and was folding laundry, he wandered past her door, on the way to the kitchen.

"Mom I have a question," he said.

"Yes?"

"What's oral sex?"

Her knuckles tightened around the fabric and she instinctively jumped to shut the TV off, the scroll of headlines on the screen a nonstop announcement of Bill Clinton's affair with Monica Lewinsky. It had been the story of the year and she was sick of it, equally revolted by Clinton and contemptuous of the Republicans trying to destroy him over an act that didn't violate the law. What the scandal had done was mainstream vocabulary she hoped her son wouldn't learn until he was far older, out of the house and among friends who could explain it to him. She could choose to ignore Jewish holidays; CNN was an unignorable hegemon.

"We're not talking about that," she said to Emmanuel, not looking at him. "You should clean your room."

"I just cleaned it yesterday."

"Clean it again."

The fucking TV. She finished her folding in the screen's blank gaze, her reflection warping in the gray glass. Every goddamn day, in the *New York Times* and CNN and both tabloids, Lewinsky and Clinton. They should have just rode off into the sunset together, dumped Hillary, lived on a farm and left them all alone. She couldn't even begin to fathom how she would have answered Emmanuel's question in an honest way. He was eight. There was no conception of sex at eight, unless he was learning in ways she wasn't aware of, consuming information in shadows she hadn't breached.

Oral sex. You needed to learn what sex was first and she was not going to enlighten him. Her parents certainly never explained anything to her. Children, when they were old enough and ready, answered those questions on their own. Or the school would give him a sex education course. Maybe in another eight years.

Monica Lewinsky was an unfortunate person. She had known

women like that, those who met more far powerful men who wanted to fuck them. You didn't need a body or even a penis to lure a woman like that; Clinton could've been a eunuch. He embodied the eternal, terrifying power of a nation-state, bomber airplanes and mass troop deployments and civilization-annihilating nuclear weapons all waiting on his signal. He embodied death. And it couldn't hurt that he was boyishly middle-aged, with a Southern drawl and snowy, coifed hair, a figurine man, a bubblegum cartoonist's conception of a president.

Now the nation was ready to sacrifice Monica Lewinsky. She was a reminder of an ancient power dynamic people would rather forget. Mona could imagine how it played out, the Oval Office itself the only true means to seduction, a room to fuck in that literally belonged to history. What was a White House intern supposed to do?

It wasn't her fault that Mona now had to ignore a question from her eight-year-old son about oral sex. Blame the commander-in-prick.

Manhattan, a valley of glass in fading orange sunlight, waited for her.

"I'm a little nervous," she said to Liv when they were in the tunnel, minutes away from the World Trade Center.

"For a party?"

"It's just, it's so much. And so many people. I don't know."

"Mona Glass, are you becoming a shrinking violet in your old age?"

"Birthday parties were always dinner with a bottle of wine or friends over at the apartment. They didn't take on the heft of an event, to be planned for and worried over."

"It's all planned and ready to go. You just show up."

"You did so much work."

"Nonsense, this is easy for me. This is play. This is like you hitting an overhead smash. When's the last time you missed an overhead? *Really* missed one?"

"I probably knocked a few into the net."

"When? In 1982?"

Mona's eyes fell on the band of sidewalk just beyond their window, the men in dark suits hurrying to their appointments.

"I do like hitting overheads."

"You love it. I used to be so terrified in the beginning, when you'd knock me into a corner and I'd flail after a shot and lob it up for you, trying to save myself. This was back when I still thought maybe I'd beat you once in a while. I'd see you set under that ball, body turned *right* toward me because you never followed the proper technique of going sideways, and think, oh my God, she's going to knock this ball straight into my guts. *She has no idea where it's going.* But you always did. Every time. Controlled fury."

"My control got better as time went on. You had a right to be afraid in the early years. I just smacked the hell out of the ball and tried to kill everyone."

"This is my little domain here. Like the tennis court is yours. Windows on the World. There's a real romance to it, going to work up there. I'll retire there, God willing."

"You will. They love you there."

"A restaurant is a hell of a thing."

Liv drove them to a parking garage just off the West Side Highway. Mona insisted on paying and Liv just laughed at her and took a ticket from the machine. Emmanuel was quiet, still staring out the window.

"What do you think, Emmanuel?" Liv asked. "Are you excited for tonight?"

"I like going up there."

"You've been to the top of the Towers?"

"My dad took me on the observation deck. He was afraid to go to the edge."

"Mona, you hate heights too, don't you? You ever been on that observation deck?"

"God no. You couldn't pay me to go up there. I can do Windows on the World as long as you don't press me against the glass. But up there, open air—I'll pass."

"It's pretty cool," Emmanuel said.

"You're a brave kid," Liv said. "Grayson, he *hates* the observation deck too. You're a lot braver than him."

"He works in the Twin Towers, doesn't he?"

"That's right, he does. Seventieth floor. South Tower."

"I'd like to work up there someday."

"Oh yeah?" Mona asked. "What would you like to do?"

"I'll work there after I play for the Yankees."

"You want to retire to the Twin Towers. That's the life," Liv said. "Ex-Yankee superstar Emmanuel Plotz with his own private suite in the sky. You'll do it.

"They're my favorite buildings now. It used to be the Empire State Building. I like them more, though."

"They're my favorite too."

"They grew on me," Mona said. "I used to find them, I don't know, dystopian."

"We all once did," Liv said. She was sliding the car into a space while checking her lipstick in the mirror. "We weren't ready for that kind of future. It felt like buildings would keep getting bigger. We would be a city of skyscrapers extending infinitely into the sky and the ground would be nothing but shadow, the skyscrapers taking the sky from us. It felt like there was no limit. But the Twin Towers would be it—we wouldn't exceed them. Then, once we really realized that, they became quite remarkable. They were a pinnacle, not a warning. They were what we had achieved."

They were walking now, beyond the garage and down one of the pinched, sloping streets that snaked between the hotels and department stores. A gust of wind pushed them momentarily backwards.

"You know, I still don't know about Al," Mona said.

"You spoke with him before. You said there was a possibility?"

"He never confirmed. I left a message. It was a long shot."

"We had fun, didn't we? There's something about trios, being young, the city lights. If it all seemed like it was going to collapse around us, the city with its garbage smells and angry cops, we believed we would be survivors. We'd inherit the new world. You two had a blast, certainly. Chasing the vigilante."

"We never found out who he was."

"Maybe he'll come to the party tonight. I'll check the guest list."

"He set me off, twenty years taking photos. Strange how time is. I never saw myself doing it and then I kept doing it. The years accumulated."

"You need to show him the ropes," Liv said, gesturing to Emmanuel.

"He likes to write more. But you like messing around with the camera too, right?"

"It always ends up blurry," Emmanuel said.

"That just makes it artistic," Liv said.

They approached the immense plaza between the two towers. High winds reached them now, blasting out from the north and west. Mona gripped Emmanuel's hand tight. It was often like this, entering the plaza. There was a wind effect, physics mutated, and this led to endless scenes of gray-suited businessmen and bureaucrats shielding their wrinkled eyes with their left hands, their rights desperately clinging to briefcases. It was like being at sea. They passed around the Sphere, the 25-foot high cast bronze sculpture, still huddled against wind. Mona was forging ahead, just beyond Liv. They were headed for the North Tower.

"Almost there," Liv said.

They were arriving later than Mona liked. The invitations said six o'clock and it was already after six. Lateness, Mona quietly believed, was a kind of personal failing. Liv did not operate from this philosophy. She had ascended into a world where lateness was a social currency. Grayson Moegenborg didn't have to show up on time and never did. Those with money and the power that came with it never had to ascribe any particular value to time. Everyone else waited for him. Mona, as a news photographer, was in the business of documenting reality as it happened and to be fashionably late to a five-alarm fire, City Hall press conference, or a protest march across the Brooklyn Bridge was to not document reality at all.

"These elevators go really fast," Emmanuel said.

The elevators were large and they did. Mona had forgotten about their power, the disorientating sensation of a body rocketed high into the sky. Liv, who was on these elevators every day, knew this too well to remark on it. Emmanuel, she could tell, was focusing intensely on the feeling. He had a budding fascination with space travel, outer space, and NASA, and supertall buildings were as close as he could come, in the Earthly realm, to the enigma of other planets. If she stared hard enough at the Towers from a distance, she could imagine they were about to take off.

"Are you sure we'll have people?" Mona suddenly asked.

"Oh honey, do you think I didn't collect RSVPs?"

Mona had an image of an enormous and empty restaurant. An apologetic waitstaff informing her no one had shown up and no one probably would at all.

"I just worry no one's coming. It's an old fear."

"I'll wake up from a bad dream that I've missed a whole year of English or history class, that I'm failing and I'm about to be kicked out of school. I'm disoriented. How did I really forget about going to class? I'm still dreaming of school and I'm fifty."

"Stop saying that. Fifty. I'm comfortable with forty-nine. People may not come to this party."

"Mona—I can't keep people *away* from you. You are the queen fucking bee."

Emmanuel looked up.

"Pardon my language! Bad word. Wash it from your memory.

And here we are."

It still struck her, in an almost cosmic sense, how high this restaurant really was, more than a thousand feet in the air. Together, they walked into the main dining room, which Liv had rented out for the party. Mona saw that her fears had been unfounded. There were already dozens of people hovering near the windows, silhouetted against glittering Manhattan sky. Waitstaff floated around with trays of wine glasses and hors d'oeuvres.

"There you are, Mona. I was worried you were dead," Sylvia said, coming forward with a glass of red wine.

"Dead?"

"You, Mona, haven't been late in twenty-five years. I told people when I got here, it's 6:05, Mona's been struck by lightning. She's left us at the tender age of forty-nine."

She was holding Emmanuel's hand and he was staring up at her, not speaking.

"Say hi to everyone, Emmanuel."

"I haven't seen him since he was slamming backhands last week. By the way, Mona, this is Gladys." Sylvia turned to Gladys. "As you can surmise, Mona is our girl of the hour. She's always the girl of the hour, anyway. Mona is a bit like me—she goes places and kicks people's asses."

"No one is like you, Sylvia."

Saul had broken away from Sonny and was approaching her. He placed his hand, demurely almost, on her shoulder.

"Happy thirtieth birthday!"

"Happy birthday to me," Mona said.

"She looks great for thirty."

"I can't even remember thirty," Sylvia said.

Liv had appeared with wine. "This is good stuff, drink."

Mona finished the glass quickly. Emmanuel had wandered off with one of his friends from his old public school. They were talking now at a table and Mona was grateful Emmanuel didn't have to endure the adult banter anymore. None of the words were for him. None offered him anything. She understood this pain of childhood, even now. So much of the world wasn't for you.

Liv was handing her a glass and she could already feel the familiar warmth fanning across her. It was her birthday and she'd drink. Whatever she wanted.

Friends and friends of friends came in waves. Since Liv presided over the guest list and Liv secured the discount, she could ensure the room was packed on both of their terms. This made Mona happy. There was a heedless rhythm to parties she had forgotten, that casual collision of bodies and words that was, for her, a dip back towards youth. On the tennis court, she still felt young. Off of it, in the everyday whirl, she knew she wasn't and would never be again. She was a mother. She was wrinkling. She dyed her hair to hide her gray strands. Tonight, they were celebrating a milestone of age and suddenly, with the wine holding her, she felt ludicrously young. The city is beyond the windows, she thought. My city.

"And that's how Mona kicked the ass of the man on the tennis court who challenged her," Liv concluded, recounting a story from the 1970s.

Mona hadn't followed the thread and only perked up when her name was uttered with joyous conviction. That was the era when men could refuse to play her, the brute underside of gender politics. She never considered herself more political than anyone else but she supposed she was, looking back on it, asserting herself in such a way against men who had grown up with a cartoon conception of the opposite sex. Soft. Servile. Unworthy.

"When I saw her play tennis, I couldn't look away," Saul said.

"Melinda, did she ever teach you the game?" Liv asked her sister, who was standing nearby with her husband, nibbling on shrimp cocktails.

"Me?" Melinda seemed stricken.

"Yes, *you*, Melinda Glass."

Mona knew Liv was drunk because she had called Melinda by her maiden name. The name she hoped no one would know she ever had.

"I never wanted to play tennis."

"I played a bit in my youth," Dr. Harry Hyman said. "With my old wooden racket. My friend once took me to the U.S. Open, back when it was at Forest Hills."

"Mona, why didn't you teach Melinda?"

"You heard—she didn't want to play."

"She never wanted to be fun," Liv said.

"We can't all be *fun*," Melinda said.

"Everyone can be fun. Fun is innate. Fun has pulsed through humanity since the dawn of time."

"I'm more of a Hobbesian," Dr. Harry Hyman said.

"And why is that?" Grayson Moegenborg asked.

People kept appearing. Mona couldn't quite track them all. They kept sliding offstage and on.

"Why I'm more a Hobbesian?"

"Yes. That sounds dreadful."

"I would like *not* to be. But life can be nasty, brutish, and short."

"It doesn't have to be so nasty and brutish."

"But that's how it is, no, uh—"

"Grayson."

"Yes, Grayson. That's just my sense of things."

"I sense we're at the end of a century that saw tremendous progress and bloodshed, and in the next century, progress will overtake bloodshed."

"I hope you are right."

"The boys are boring," Liv said.

"Well I find it all rather interesting," Melinda said.

"You should go to more parties."

Having Liv as a friend could feel like a mild superpower. As the younger sister, Mona had no ability to put down or rebuke Melinda in any serious way. She always would have the advantage of age and time and, through her husband, wealth. Liv was unfettered; Melinda was merely another older woman to her, an ordinary Manhattan elitist lacking a sense of proportion. Liv understood the weakness, the fear of not having enough, the means by which Melinda strained to imitate the life she wanted to lead. She was not, Liv once clucked, *even* a millionaire. And she knew wealth before she dated Grayson. Windows on the World hosted, daily, the global masters of capital. She had planned receptions for cable TV executives, hedge fund managers, and the titans of real estate empires. They all wanted a piece of the sky.

In this context, Melinda's snobbery was, at best, pedestrian. Liv had argued against Mona sending Emmanuel to Bridge Prep. "It's a concession to your bitch sister," she said.

"I want him to have a good education too," Mona had replied quietly.

More guests arrived. Izzy Locker gave Saul a firm, hearty handshake. Hank Lefkowitz, who had officiated her fake wedding to Saul, was explaining his therapy practice to Heed Ezekiel, her old *Raider* editor, now nearing seventy, his round, bald head aglow. She decided this was the conversation she would wander into next. It was a collision of two parts of her life that suddenly, in a cinematic way, seemed amusing.

"The birthday girl herself," Hank said, reaching for a hug. He brought her in, maintaining control of a glass of brownish liquor in his right hand.

"Hank, it's been too long."

"And what about me?" Ezekiel asked.

"It's been just the right amount of time."

"Always a kidder. I remember I got you off the scrapheap and here you are. Shining every day. Your pictures pop, full color blast. Newsprint sickens me these days but I grab it and look for your name. Pretty easy to find. You're in the *News* daily."

"Hank, this is Heed Ezekiel. He ran the best, strangest, most fucked up newspaper in America."

"He was telling me a little bit about it."

"The city was the underworld and we were fallen angels. We brought what light we could to a fallen world."

"Or we made shit up."

"Oh yeah?" Hank was smiling.

"Fifty-fifty. Right, Heed?"

"Truth, like justice, is an illusion."

"Some top shelf liquor here," Hank said.

"Liv only provides the best."

"We needed a savior. We cried out for one. Here is Rudy Giuliani, now lifting up the maggot carcass of a city, saying we must resuscitate this body. But should it be saved?"

"The economy is great," Hank said.

"Rudy is a prick," Mona said.

"I see less squeegee men."

"Unhinged but necessary man," Ezekiel said.

"Unhinged is right."

"To this day," Ezekiel said, taking a firm drink of his own wine glass, "I wonder if Vengeance is stalking the streets, as an ordinary man."

"What are you up to these days, anyway? Are you still in the newspaper business?" Mona asked.

"Oh, absolutely not. Corporate communications."

"Heed Ezekiel, corporate communications. I think I've seen it all."

"A defense contractor. I tell younger men how to massage wars into palatable inevitabilities."

"That's unsettling."

"That, Mona my dear, is how our century ends."

She continued to drift, more drinks appearing in her hand, more disappearing. The city was dark and titanic and twinkling beyond the windows, like an undersea kingdom, and she wanted to press her body to the glass and lose herself in its vastness. It had been so long since she felt like this. Vic was talking to her and she was nodding along but not listening. He was a nice brother, Vic. Always less trouble than Melinda. Always willing to listen. Where was his wife? Oh, over at the sandwich platters. Right—Liv had made arrangements for all necessary foodstuffs.

Liv, the fairy godmother of her life. All lives.

Saul was laughing at something Sonny said and then sauntering her way. He took her elbow and whispered into her ear.

"You look beautiful tonight."

"You aren't so bad yourself."

It was true. He was sheathed in a midnight blue jacket and checked silk tie, his cufflinks glinting. Typically, post-work, he would come with his rolled up sleeves and a cheaper, wider tie, his slacks the same navy blue or gray he bought at a discount at Men's Warehouse. She had no issue with how he presented himself; compared to men of younger generations, his decision to never wear sneakers nor shorts was revelatory. But he had taken special care tonight. With the wine hot inside of her, she could dance.

"Sonny is talking my fucking ear off."

"How is he doing?"

"Making millions off foreign governments. You know he lives in that McMansion in Bethesda. His firm is doing absurd business."

"Like?"

"Foreign energy. Men who kill people without second thoughts. Small autocracies that need their hands held around the Capitol Building. Now he's on the host committee for a Bush fundraiser. He wants that dumb Texan in the White House."

"I don't really trust him."

"Bush?"

"Sonny."

"Sonny, fundamentally, is a person driven by moments. Like

most people. He's going back to church, you know. He's trying to find God again."

"Really?"

"It's the evangelical shit. That's Bush's shtick. Born-again. Recovering good-old boy. Some sinners are worthy of redemption, some aren't. Sonny thinks it's important he appear, in certain circles, like more of a Christian, or at least understand what the pulsebeat for the nation is. That's how he put it to me. *Pulsebeat.*"

"New York will always be the kingdom of the Jews."

Mona tilted her head, squinting at Sonny. "You have more hair than he does."

"I do."

"Sixty now," and she ran her hand through his hair, "and hardly a strand lost."

A man was playing the piano. Liv, without telling her, had paid for live music. Or Grayson had. She listened intently. Over the years, she had mused about learning an instrument, taking lessons like Emmanuel had done for the clarinet. Knowing an instrument had always seemed like an entrée into another type of life or a superpower to be acquired. Like a new language, it was proof of your American ability to amass, to increase and fortify privilege. She wanted to play the piano.

"Saul, I've always wanted to play the piano."

"You have? Since when?"

"It's been a little thought in the back of my head."

"You can take lessons, I'm sure. There are a few places in Brooklyn I know."

"Let's listen to the music."

Over in one corner, leaning on a table alone, was a familiar face she shouldn't quite believe. He wore a suede jacket and tight-fitting jeans, his eyes falling to the enormous window. Liv was talking to Grayson and two of her friends from the tennis court, laughing and distracted, her gaze tossed momentarily upward. Liv did not see him either.

"Oh my God. Oh my God."

"What is it, Mona?"

"Al is here."

He never said he was coming. He never confirmed. She had assumed he had no serious interest in flying across the country to see her. And why would he? They had spoken so little over the decade. She had the barest conception of his life in a city she had never bothered to visit. Easier to fly to another country than California.

"Al Falcone? Where?"

"Over there."

Al, from the way he looked up at her, had clearly seen her first, before she realized he was leaning against the table. A glass of red wine was in his right hand. He looked both inarguably older and unchanged. In his fifty-year-old face, she saw the kid of twenty, pushing through the wrinkles and the deep sunburn. He was thin, stubbled, gray spotting his dark brown beard, which had grown at some point between when she last saw him and now. She was moving toward him slowly, Saul in tow, unsure what exactly she was going to say to him.

"I got a flight," were the first words from his mouth. It occurred to her, in that moment, Emmanuel had not met Al since he learned to speak complete sentences.

"You came."

"This is the big birthday. You'll be even more depressed for every other milestone."

"I stopped celebrating birthdays at twenty," Saul said.

"How are you, Saul?"

They shook hands, solidly and grimly, as men did on television.

"I'm upright. When you get to my age, you're excited just to not be dead."

"You got a long way to go."

"I hope we all do."

Saul glanced off to his side.

"I'll give you two time to catch up. I'm going to get another drink."

"Saul," Mona said quietly.

"Yeah? Where's Liv?" Saul asked. "She needs to know Al is here."

"Liv!" Mona cried out.

Liv, deep in conversation, spun around.

"Oh my God, Al. Al!"

Liv ran to Al and gave him the kind of hug Mona could never offer anyone.

"I'm here from L.A."

"It's like you're back from the dead."

"The old band, back together."

"Jesus, Al, you can call once in a while."

"Time gets away from you."

"They don't have phones in L.A.," Mona said.

"That's right," Al replied. "We communicate by smoke signal."

"Please Al, tell us, what is it you've been doing over there? We need to catch up."

"Liv Gottlieb is dating a Moegenborg. I know that even in L.A."

"Not *a* Moegenborg. *The* Moegenborg. The rest are horrid. I need to bring Grayson over here. He's enmeshed in some dreary conversation with Port Authority buddies. I made room on the list—with Mona's consent, of course—for a few of his friends so he wouldn't be a bored, sad puppy, and instead of inviting one of his far more interesting downtown painter or writer buddies he brings a few of his lunch pals from work. Which is dandy. But what about the conversations? Grayson used to go to boxing matches with Norman Mailer. That oaf would've been fun to have here. It is what it is."

"I sadly don't have a wife to stab," Al said.

"But you must have a girlfriend," Mona said.

"I've got a studio out near Sunset Boulevard. The women in L.A. aren't the women in New York. But that's not so vital. It's good to be here. It's good to see both of you. I'm still a bit thrown off with the time change and I have this warm, irrepressible urge to get drunk. Seeing you both, I become twenty-five."

"Tell me at least about your paintings, Al."

"I sold a few to galleries. I worked galleries. Now I'm between galleries. There are some obstinate assholes out there."

Liv leaned in closer. She smelled, to Mona, like the inside of a martini glass.

"What kind of assholes?"

"Assholes with lip injections. And those without. I'd rather not get into it, but it's been a rough year."

"I'm really sorry to hear that. There's always a place for you here."

"A line cook at Windows on the World?"

"Well, I could use another line cook but no, you fool, in New York. The city is really roaring back. The old fear over your shoulder is gone. I won't say this in front of Mona—"

"Mona is right here," Mona said.

"—but Giuliani the fascist really cleaned the city up. You don't think about getting mugged. It's a city with its pizzazz back. You go outside and you're light on your feet."

"Unless a cop is coming to bash your skull in."

"I'm not sure if L.A. or New York suits me," Al said.

"Then where would you like to be?"

"I haven't figured it out. I wouldn't call it a midlife crisis because I'm definitely beyond the midpoint now. My dad died at seventy-five. It's a terminal crisis. I came here to see you and Mona and I came here because I have no idea what it's all amounting to."

"What do you mean?" Mona asked.

"A life. This life. What does it amount to? What have I done?"

"You've done a lot, Al."

"You have no idea. None of you know. I used to think of it as a ledger, a bourgeois accounting—either you chose to do it the American way or another way, the artists' way, whatever that was, and

I made the decision some time ago, maybe when we were all still young, to liberate myself from that accumulation sprint. I wasn't going to litter my life with American signposts. I told myself I would live with open eyes and a beating heart, painting and fucking my way to wherever it was I was supposed to go. Fame? Instead your checking account empties and there's nothing else. You're another poor fuck."

Al was speaking flatly, with less emotion than Mona expected for such a denunciation of a life lived. His gaze was steady, his fingers folded lightly around his wine glass. From afar, with his beard and tanned skin, he could resemble a travel author or a medical professional, his station assured until death. She had never known Al to doubt himself like this but how much did she know him anymore? How could she know anyone? She knew Saul. She knew her son. She knew Liv. Al had drifted from her. It began with the rejection, all those years ago. In his eyes, she could see it, the pain he had submerged with his art on another coast.

"Al, c'mon, we love you," Liv said. "Don't say that."

"It's the truth."

"You've been very successful. I'm sure you've done some incredible pieces. Art is a slow burn. You've got time, there's always opportunity—"

"You have no idea what you're talking about."

For the first time, Liv was quiet. The piano was still playing, the conversations across the restaurant floor blending. Voices, like raised spikes, could be discerned, and she thought she heard Saul's friend Izzy Locker laughing deeply. The three of them stood together without talking, perhaps the only people in the room at a loss for what to say.

"I'm sorry," Al said quietly. "I didn't come here to say that. It's good to see everyone."

She would have married Al to give him a better life but this was also not a reason not marry anyone. She was not with Saul so Saul could be his best self. She was with him, simply, because she loved him deeply, and his marriage to Felicia could not alter the bare fact of that love. There were times, when she was angry at him—angry, more importantly, at the choices he had made—that she would try, without knowing it, to will this love away, to make it evaporate like steam. If there was no love, she wouldn't care that he still retreated to a wife every night. *I don't love her like I love you. I don't love her at all.* He had said this so many times. Now she understood she would continue to hear him say this for the rest of his life. Felicia was in the hospital. There were questions about whether she would walk again. Saul would never abandon her, not when she was broken. He was a good Jewish boy. He would cling like moss to her.

"Al, how long are you staying in New York?" Liv asked.

"A day or two."

"Why don't you stay longer?"

"New York has a certain scent."

"You don't want to spring for a hotel for a few more days?"

"I don't have the Moegenborg coin."

"Ha. Stay with me then. Grayson and I don't live together. I have a second bedroom I don't use."

"You aren't serious."

"She is," Mona said. "Stay with her. Sometimes it's good to get out of the place you've been. Sometimes the psychic energy drags you down."

"It'd be a break. Stay with me. Stay as long as you like."

"I didn't pack enough clothes. It's this and one other pair of paints."

"We'll go shopping."

"I don't know," Al said.

"You know. You'll do it."

"I really don't know."

"It'd be nice to see you more, Al," Mona said.

"You all make it sound so easy."

"Stay a week. Stay a month. You pick," Liv said.

"People don't just *uproot* themselves."

"You aren't people. You're Al."

"A hall of fame high school center fielder," Mona said.

"Please do not remind me. You talk baseball and I hear my father screaming at me from beyond the gates of hell. Where he undoubtedly is."

"Your father was a trip."

"That's the old-world shit I fled in the first place. But I enjoy being here. I do. Let me think. It's a lot. I don't quite know who I am anymore."

"No one knows who they are."

"Mona does."

"I'm still figuring it out."

"That's a lie," Al said. "You figured it out at twenty."

The party floated on, drinks arriving in her hand, the alcohol slowly lightening Al so that, somewhere close to midnight, she was in a group of three or four tennis friends and Al and Liv laughing at a man they all remembered from the park who used to threaten to send his fellow Soviet opponents "back to the old country" if they kept calling his balls out. Mona swung her arms wildly to mimic his strokes. At some point, Saul kissed her goodbye and told her he had to drive back, that this was a fabulous birthday party and happy birthday and he'd see them all tomorrow. It was then she remembered she had kept her son out until almost midnight, this was inexcusable—even on a non-school night—and they had to go home now.

"I'll drive you, I'll drive you," Liv said. "Don't look so stricken."

Emmanuel's friends had gone home. She took his hand, apologizing until she felt herself running out of breath. It's okay, mom, he kept saying, his voice trailing off as they rode down the tower.

Felicia had not died. She was in a wheelchair, wheelchair-*bound* as he said repeatedly until he was told, at an agency holiday party, that term was considered offensive. There are people, the HUD staff explained, who use wheelchairs but are not bound to them. But my wife *is* bound, he said quietly. There was no hope she would walk again. She took the news, when it was delivered, more stoically than he would have imagined. She did not scream or cry. Her hair completely gone gray during the grueling physical rehab, she looked like a nun who had pledged her life to a higher power, her mind locked on tribulations that superseded the terrestrial realm.

For her sake, he couldn't stay out late anymore. He left Brooklyn at six to make it to Long Island, through the snarl of traffic, no later than seven-thirty. Other days, he departed Brooklyn sooner. Weekends were not a possibility. Instead of spending Saturdays and Sundays with Mona and Emmanuel at baseball games, the beach, or a trip to the boy's new favorite destination, the Liberty Science Center in New Jersey, he would stay with Felicia at their Roslyn house. With time, it seemed to him an even more lugubrious dwelling, gloom-ridden like a miniature castle, the photographs on walls the markers of all he didn't have any longer. Tad didn't call or write either of them. Lenore, despite her promises, rarely visited. He knew Felicia's suffering, in this context, was unrivaled, her spine smashed and her legs atrophied, the remainder of her life a maze of infuriating contingencies. He was suddenly aware of all the single-family houses, apartment buildings, restaurants, and storefronts that had been rendered utterly inaccessible or torturous for her, the jagged steps small and large, ramps and elevators never conceived by the people who were gifted with legs to propel them forward and back. Pity or annoyance greeted her wherever she went. She was no longer a first-class citizen.

At first, she insisted on a manual wheelchair to maintain her strength but as the year wore on and she tired of the struggle, she switched to electric. She was still, as always, attending civic meetings, but she could no longer rouse herself in the same way at the monthly gatherings. Her voice was softer, her head listing, her indignation more rote. There were New York disability advocates with pulverizing force, their charisma beaming through the nightly news, and he hoped, for her sake, she would transform into one of them. He quietly urged her to join a few organizations. There were people in the city fighting for more elevators at subway stations. "But I don't take the subway. I never have," she replied, ending the conversation there.

He tried not to pity himself when his wife was the one who needed help going to the bathroom. He tried to smile for her and keep as much of this existence from Mona as possible. Because Mona didn't want to hear about Felicia. In Brooklyn, with Mona and Emmanuel, he lived days of liberation.

In 2001, another year that once seemed like pretend, Mona was talking to him about switching careers.

"It's wearing on me," she told him in the spring, during a lunch at a small diner downtown. Light rain was pattering the window and her face was half in light, half in shadow.

"What do you want to do?"

"I'm going to give it until the end of the year. I'm sick of newspapers, I think. I'm sick of the lifestyle, the hustle, the time expected of you. I don't trust images anymore, either."

"You don't trust them?"

"I know how to create a photo, how to frame it, how to seize reality on whatever terms I decide are fit. I understand it all too well. I see photographs other people take in newspapers and magazines and I question them."

"All media, in some sense, is mediated."

"I can't keep getting called by a thirty-two year-old editor to get to the scene of a shooting. I can't keep elbowing my way through scrums. I can't keep pointing and shooting and pointing and shooting. I can't keep turning down these fucking afterwork drink hangouts and feeling bad about it. I need to move on."

"It's outlived its purpose."

"I was having lunch with Al not long ago. He was downtown. He's trying to jumpstart another project, this installation with shattered glass and acrylic. It may go somewhere. It may not. Watching him struggle does two things to me."

"What are the two?"

"I hate it. I don't want to see it. It's not ameliorating. And then—there's inspiration there. He has the time to do it. He has an emptiness in the day he can fill on his own terms."

"He's got that rent-free set-up with Liv."

"He does. I've got the co-op mostly paid off. Soon, I'll just have to deal with the maintenance, which isn't much. I need to earn money in another way. I envy you, Saul, in that office up in the sky. I envy the view. I envy sitting."

"Some days are pretty slow."

"I need slowness. I need a day that ends promptly at five. I need to make more in eight hours than I would in fifteen. The *News* will slash me eventually, anyway. Every few years, they seem to go through a contraction. Minor, major, minor, major. The business muddles along. I think this will be it. I'm giving it to the end of the year."

"Then you hang up your spurs."

"I look for something new."

"Do you want to work in government?"

"I would do what you do. I'm ready for ambiguity and the ease of afternoons. Long lunch breaks. Idle chatter. That little doze that comes on around three o'clock. The slump. I can't have jobs that follow me out the door anymore."

"I'll check in. We'll have slots. There was a little turnover with Bush so GSA is hunting for a few bodies. We could work together, same office."

"It can be an agency in that building. I'd like to disappear into that building."

"GSA is a big beast. I'll sniff around. I also end up getting coffee a lot with the HUD and SSA guys. It's funny. I've been getting restless there. Yet here you are, wanting to jump in these staid waters. I'm probably retiring in a few years."

"Staid. That word attracts me. I've photographed so many bloodied, broken people. I've chased so many corrupt politicians, celebrities, actors. I've ran through every inch of this city. It was Vengeance, you know. He set me on this path."

"You regret it now?"

"No. For a long time, it was life-affirming. I don't regret. I've done and seen so much."

"But there was no Emmanuel then."

"Right. He changed me in so many ways. I couldn't imagine being a mother and then I was a mother. I need to spend time with him. Especially now."

"I get that."

"He needs people in his life."

"What do you mean?"

He unsteadily sipped at his coffee, knowing exactly what was coming next. Thirty years of conversation meant she could rarely surprise him. He assumed, for her, the same was true.

"All I mean is we need to be involved. We need to be there for him."

"You don't think I'm there enough."

"I understand you have a lot going on."

"I love Emmanuel."

"I'm not questioning that. I never have."

"But the implication."

"It's just a fact. You are prevented from being around all of the time so I need to be present more. That's why I need to transition into a different job."

"I can make more time."

"Felicia needs you."

He never wanted to hear his wife's name in Mona's mouth. It was a reminder of what he wanted to forget: he was married to this woman and would continue to be.

"We're arranging for her home health aide to be around more. We're looking to make her live-in, convert Lenore's old bedroom into a living quarters."

Mona was right in that he could not alter, in any meaningful way, what he had made of his life, as a sixty-year-old man with a federal job and a paid off Long Island house and a wife who was badly injured in a car crash. Living this long was about understanding just how much of your existence was calcified by decisions made decades ago, when you were, in some sense, an entirely different human being, with competing wants and desires that had no relevancy for today. He wondered what he would have done had he been a decade or two younger. Perhaps he would not have accepted the conditions of a society so readily. Perhaps acceptance would have not been a consideration at all.

10

In the early spring, Saul relocated. A satellite office was opened at 4 World Trade Center, a nine-story low-rise building near the South Tower. His pay increased slightly and the office itself was larger, with floor-to-ceiling windows and a formidable oak desk he could sit behind with some authority. He lined the walls with his various certificates and photographs, pictures with Richard Nixon, George H.W. Bush, and Mikail Gorbachev, whom he had met once at a peculiar, rumpled restaurant two blocks from the United Nations. An office could remind you of a career. He felt equally powerful and dislocated.

It was a torpid spring, giving way to a torpid summer. The humidity, for the first time he could remember, profoundly bothered him. In July, his breath was short and he panicked, fearing a heart palpitation or a full-on attack, and a doctor told him to relax and watch his cholesterol. *You aren't dying, Mr. Plotz.* The shortness of breath continued. With Felicia, they sat in air-conditioned semi-dark, the hum of the machine the only noise passing between them. He felt lucky when she slept. Like a boy, he methodically read the box scores and transactions in the newspapers each day, trying to lose himself in the agate. Now, whenever he could, he tried to forget the self he left behind with Felicia and be the father for Emmanuel and the companion for Mona that Mona deserved, proposing dinners and even a vacation, one week in Washington D.C. and Charlottesville, Virginia, a tour of America's heritage. For Felicia, his explanation was simple: a one-week business trip to D.C.

"That's a long trip," she said, not looking at him.

He said that her nurse Sonya would be staying for the week in Lenore's old room. He had arranged it.

"You're very good at arranging, Saul."

"I want to plan ahead and make sure everything goes well. I feel bad about going."

"You don't feel bad."

She was facing the front window of their house. Their kitten Chester, a recent addition, curled near her feet. With the way sunlight rested on her face, she was almost beatific, a relic of a gentler time. He imagined a Medieval washerwoman peering out at her children frolicking on the village green, church bells clanging, overfed cows wandering in the mud.

He was bracing himself. Anticipating Felicia was always a greater challenge than Mona.

"Of course I do, dear."

"Wherever you're really going, I hope you have fun."

"I'm going on a business trip. I'll probably get lunch with Sonny Cannon. That will be my fun."

"I'm old enough, Saul, in that I don't need you to paper it over. I don't need excuses. Just go and come back. Disappear and reappear. Enjoy yourself."

"I don't understand."

"I was close, many times, to divorcing you. Many times."

"Damn it, what are you implying?"

"Is she new, this one? How many have there been?"

How many. He knew exactly how he could answer that question and he wasn't sure that the truth, for Felicia, would make it any better.

"There aren't any new ones. Or old ones."

"If you say so."

"I do say so. It's a business trip. There's a lot of reorganization going on with the Bush administration. New sheriff in town."

Felicia kept looking out the window, refusing to meet his eyes.

"Did you ever love me?"

"We love each other."

"Just don't become the aggrieved one here, Saul. I know you like that. This isn't one of those times."

"I don't even know what you mean."

Felicia began to smile. He hadn't seen her like this in a long time and he was unnerved. He longed for a cigarette, like old times.

"Do whatever it is that you have to do. What you want to do. I hope whoever it is you're going to see is nice and makes you feel like the man you believe yourself to be."

"I told you, I'm going on—"

"You were never a good liar, Saul. Lawyers don't have to lie as well as politicians. Politicians need to believe in their lies so whole-heartedly they become truth. I've seen so many good liars come before our civic. Republicans and Democrats. They believe with the zeal of the converted. With you, I can tell you don't believe in this business trip."

"I'm going to Washington."

"How many have there been, Saul? Three? Four? Ten?"

"I'm not having this conversation anymore."

"Twenty?"

"I'm going outside for a smoke."

"I'm too old to be as angry as I should be. The playacting of the aggrieved. I think I'll go have wine at Herb Weiner's house later."

"You can do whatever you want."

On the vacation, he wondered when Felicia first figured it out. Six months ago? Six years ago? Longer? She did not easily express herself. Her affection and rage could seem, to him, equally calibrated, with the same amount of forethought. She had also been reared by parents who told her to *suffer silently, to go play lose me, to take a long walk off a short pier.* Over time, he had shed some of the armaments forced upon him, the midcentury check on emotions large and small. He even cried, once, in front of Mona. He realized he would never know when Felicia first suspected he wasn't a faithful husband. Felicia still didn't know of Mona, of his devotion and his family. He wasn't sure what kind of rupture he would cause inside of her. She could shrug off an affair or three. She knew nothing of a child. And not just a child—Emmanuel Plotz, now eleven years old, attending a Brooklyn private school.

Saul spent the entire trip wishing it wouldn't end. They shot to the top of the Washington Monument, took pictures outside the White House, drove by the old RFK Stadium where the Washington Senators used to play. They were a family, the three of them, and several times, in passing, he had referred to Mona as his wife. He never wanted to return to Long Island. Maybe, finally, he could go through with it—file for divorce and start anew.

It was late summer, almost September, and he felt a fresh, deep sadness kissing Mona and Emmanuel goodbye in Brooklyn, the vacation done. It was 5 p.m. and he was due back by seven. He had told Felicia he would drive her to a civic association meeting.

"We had a lot of fun," Mona told him as he climbed into his car.

"I've never had more fun. Never."

11

In the new century, Tad came back. Enough time had passed in the shadowed rib of the strange country.

What he wanted to do, really, was change his name, and if his life was lived by the laws of cinema or novel-making, he would have done it immediately. But there were ordinary bureaucratic impediments he didn't want meet head-on or encounter at all. Paperwork to submit, documents to verify, slow-building confrontations in dimly-lit offices.

He would remain Tad Plotz. He could always say his name like a curse word.

In the new year, he got a job delivering Chinese food, riding a bicycle through the deranged street grid of Queens. His mother and father didn't know he had come back to New York. They didn't know much of anything.

He had last sent a letter to his sister at the end of 1999, wishing her a happy millennium. That was over a year ago now. Maybe he would send another. Maybe he would finally change his name.

He took a two-room walk-up in Jackson Heights, confronting the elevated train. For years, he had retreated from noise, seeking out the desolate towns along interstates, wading through weed-strewn lots to get his groceries. He had enclosed himself in rural Michigan, stared down death along the lake. He had systematically made the attempt to excise his past so he was merely a free-floating being of the present day, without memory and beyond time, but he would, despite his painful efforts, crumble inward, into himself.

Past thirty now, he needed to figure out what to do.

New York City was inevitable. It was the nightmare at the edge of his consciousness, its logic brute and unrelenting. A city was easier to disappear into than a forest. He delivered on the late shift, reporting to Wilbur Chiu, who owned the restaurant, Blue Star. Chiu was a serious man and he seemed to understand the New York nightmare very well. He spoke to Tad, at first, in clipped, single sentences, his eyes dark and shimmering behind rimless frames. Chiu usually worked the cash register, dismissing his subordinates to the kitchen, where they could cook or watch others cook. He seemed to welcome the unspoken collisions of the every day, the stoners hunting glass-eyed for spring rolls, the working mothers scrounging up pork fried rice for their children, the cab drivers guzzling cans of Coke between shifts. When he crossed his arms and stared, his eyes and lips would freeze as if he were receding in time, taking on the glory of a Romanesque icon. He was sure that Chiu, who hardly spoke to anyone and seemed to dwell alone, had once lived in ways that were unfathomable.

"Don't fuck this up," Chiu told him.

It had been years since Tad rode a bicycle but he took to it easily. He knew how to pedal and pedaled. Soon, he was good enough to slash his way between trucks and taxi cabs, challenging motor vehicles for his parallel seam of asphalt. Every few minutes he heard the machine pulse of the overhead subway and tried to hear the people inside, the thousands in communion with their work. He could pedal for Chiu forever, he decided. There were soldiers who died for generals. They collapsed in their own blood for ideas bigger than themselves.

When he wasn't working, he had time. Less than he used to when he lived in the cabin in Michigan's outer reach, but enough to create a certain pressure to fill it. That was the city. He was reacclimating himself. What he knew was that he had lost weight, too much, and his hair was long, too long, and he made a concession to vanity by going to the barber and buying dumbbells at the local sporting goods store. He would be a better version of himself for no one.

His apartment was spare, bereft of paintings, photographs, bookshelves, and dishes. He bought paper plates, plastic silverware, and positioned a single table in the middle of an empty living room with a pair of windows aimed at the elevated train tracks. When he walked the wooden floorboards, he heard a creaking that seemed too loud for his body, as if someone from below were threatening to break through. The walls were plaster, thin to the touch, and he sometimes dreamed at night the apartment would crumble, burying him in paint chips and ash. Next door, a husband and wife shouted about a baby. Their fights, peaking at five p.m., took on a rhythm he began to anticipate, and without a TV, a radio, or a computer, he found these intermittent clashes worth the struggle of staying awake. At seven, he began delivering for Chiu, finishing in the early morning. There were times Chiu was awake to greet him when he returned, his thick arms folded in front of the cash register.

One Saturday in the spring, when the ice had thawed and the back of his neck was warm with sunlight, he pedaled to the Central Queens Library in Jamaica. He would never buy a book but he could read them for free. Chiu had him delivering six days a week, which he preferred, and he decided to use some of the free hours to discover what his brain could still process. In his hoodie and dark jeans, he almost looked like everyone else, another man dimly on the move.

He read books about crime. Studies on murder rates and recidivism, how prisons were built, the unionization of police. In this section, the world was a series of cages to escape into or from, all nations evolving together in an effort to contain the worst impulses of the human species. The only crime he had committed, as far as he knew, was using drugs. All behavior, in the right circumstance, could be a crime, with the proper confluence of power and paranoia. He sat on a small wooden bench and read for hours, shadows creeping over him.

He ate more. His bones no longer announced themselves on his veined skin. He had flesh, light muscle and fat, and his skin took on new color, a tan from walking and biking in the sun, a blood flow to make himself less pallid. He had always been drawn to routines and now he had another: Saturdays would be for the library.

He passed whole weeks speaking to no one but Chiu. Even when he delivered the food, he nodded politely and extended the brown paper bag, the heat of the meat warming his palms.

There were times he considered his family. He had no friends anymore. But there was no way of undoing the reality of having been a child born to two parents, having been the older brother to a younger sister. They were all still out there somewhere, his own existence an offshoot of their own. He could almost rent a car and drive to Roslyn and sit outside and watch them, elderly mother and father, go to the supermarket, take out the trash, stroll hand-in-hand, if they did such a thing, around the cul-de-sacs.

The last he knew, Lenore was still living in Washington. She had always acclimated well to whatever was asked of her, the demands of modernity. He only had what she had told him in old letters, job promotions and vacation sites visited and concerns for his health. Several times, she asked to speak on a telephone.

I don't need voices, he wrote.

Delivering food at night meant seeing a city few wanted to see. If in daylight the city seethed, at night it seemed to exhale, like a sibilating beast bringing itself to heel. He passed vacant blocks lit only by neon, hookers roaming the pavement, lone men in caps smoking against brick walls. The homeless came in small, roving groups, pushing shopping carts, huddling in swollen jackets of professional football teams, staring Sphinx-like from their chosen street corners.

Twice, he was mugged. The first time was typical but almost deadly, a man with bloodshot eyes and a bent knife thrust straight out, an announcement of rage. He was older, a thick beard curling off his cheeks.

Gimme everything you have, he said. Gimme everything you have.

Tad complied. The cash amounted to forty-six dollars and twelve cents. He was in the middle of a delivery and the man demanded the food too. *Gimme everything.* This bothered him more. The large order of sweet and sour chicken with pork dumplings and fried rice (free can of Coke) was not his. Whomever he was delivering it to was hungering, in the early morning, for a meal and now it would not come. Chiu wouldn't be pleased. It was his reputation on the line.

Gimme all of it.

The man with the bent knife took the plastic bag of Chinese food and dashed in the opposite direction, determined to disappear. Tad would never see him again.

The second time, three months later, the mugger was younger, eighteen at best, and he held a gun straight at Tad's temple.

"C'mon," Tad begged. It was two o'clock in the morning.

"Turn it over, now."

This time, the mugger got fifty-one dollars and fifty-eight cents. To Tad's surprise, the barrel of the gun touched his skull. It was only brief, a fleeting moment of connection, and the fear he felt was deeper and stranger than any he had known. He could have died from it alone. He could tell the mugger didn't want to shoot, that he regarded the gun as a prop. But his lack of intention made Tad fear that dark luck would dispatch the bullet from the chamber anyway and bury it thoroughly in his brain. He was a kid who seemed to make mistakes. As Tad watched him scrutinize the dollar bills in his small hands, he saw how slight he was, nearly shaking.

"Leave the food, at least," Tad said.

"I don't want your fucking stinky ass Chinese food."

Even the way he spoke wasn't entirely convincing. The robbery was for someone else. He could almost feel sorry for the kid because the kid wasn't going to take a real cut from it. The cash would be divided and redistributed up the food chain, away from him. He was a prole mugger, performing grunt work for another. Somewhere, in a house with central air-conditioning, someone would count the money the kid rightfully stole. It was true: Chinese food meant nothing in this marketplace. Even Chiu's.

The kid, for good measure, pointed the gun one more time. The cash had been safely stashed in a side pocket. He held the gun for another moment, backpedaling into the darkness.

"See you later," Tad said when he was gone.

He resolved never to die on these streets, delivering for Chiu. When he returned to Blue Star, Chiu was hunched over the counter, reading one of the Chinese papers printed out of Flushing.

"No delivery?" Chiu asked. "Robbed again?"

"A kid with a gun got me."

"It was worse ten years ago. He would have killed you."

"What made ten years ago so special?"

"With more killing, more could be killed. It meant less to lose an individual."

"I'm going to go out with a knife next time."

"It will be a matter of luck. It won't matter if you have the knife or not."

"He let me keep the food. I made the delivery."

On a Saturday in May, Tad discovered the newspapers. There was an archive of local and regional papers. The *Queens Tribune*, the *Queens Chronicle*, the *Queens Courier*, the *Jamaica Times*. And the citywide dailies too. They were all on microfilm. He read them because he was interested, at first, in the language, the blend of economy and excitement, the grammar of the streets. He passed through decades. He heard the cries of community board members, city councilmen, civic association presidents, men and women outside constructions sites and school board meetings and ribbon cuttings, life lived in newsprint. He wondered how many of them lived today.

How many of them had died. What had become of Thomas Munsch of Bayside? Evelyn Weinberg of Flushing? Jerome Richardson of South Jamaica? Had they all joined the future?

Saturdays were for reading. Sundays through Fridays, for Wilbur Chiu. It was the barest of routines and he could feel, slowly, his anxiety slipping away. He continued to lift weights, keep his hair short, strengthen his legs through pedaling up hills, over curbs, between swerving trucks. There was a band of energy winding through him that had been unrecognizable. He didn't need the rush of coke. It was spring, it was summer. Chiu told him he could start delivering during the day.

"Sleep at night now."

"I don't mind the overnights."

"You'll start at noon."

"Okay, Mr. Chiu."

He learned the heat of afternoons, the frenzy beneath the train tracks and curbside on schooldays, the tidal roar of children freed from locked windows and mounting instruction. He saw the massing outside the bodegas, firecrackers in the gutter, fingers dangling through chain-link fences as basketballs popped off speckled pavement. Queens, New York City. His hatred ebbed. He wasn't home—nothing, he was sure, could be that—but he had come to a place where he could remain. The urge to leave was vanishing. All he required was a bicycle and Chiu's money.

Tad had a habit of arriving early, twenty minutes or so before his shift, and the late morning was a slow time, Chinese food a rarer choice for breakfast. After flipping through his newspaper, Chiu would look up and rub his temples. Occasionally, when the mood struck, he would smoke a cigarette, a Marlboro red. The cloud hung over his eyes.

"Do you know what you're after?" he asked Tad.

"I don't."

"Every human has a moment of consciousness raising. A moment when they understand what it is they want."

"I don't understand it."

"You're here."

"Yes."

"This city takes more than it gives. Like this country. But you cling to what it is you have. You take it, screaming, into the grave. That, to me, is one dream."

"I like biking the afternoons. I'm glad you switched me."

"I knew you would."

"It's a new energy."

"You walk a city, you bike a city, especially an unfamiliar one, and you can feel the city rising to you. You feel the past, like a snake, wrapping around you. A city is an opportunity to meet more ghosts."

"I spent a lot of time in the country."

"Across America?"

"Rural towns. I lived in a cabin in a forest. I left it all behind."

"I came to America as a boy. I came here, to New York. New York was enough. New York was a threat and New York was an answer. I said I would make my money here and I did."

"I'm from New York. I left. Now I returned."

"America is many countries. That is what always worried me. That I would pass out of New York and into another land more foreign than any I had known, its customs alien, its demands deranged."

"When I lived in the cabin, I could feel myself flaking away. I would see my limbs fall off, my skin, my eyes. I would see myself as an invisible, hovering presence, without sight or mind. In the cabin I would dream."

"My wife, before she died, would say things like that too. She believed she was leaving herself behind."

"I never thought I was dying. I just felt this diminishing. Time and language, out of reach."

"She didn't think she was dying either."

Wilbur Chiu was the only person he spoke to for any length of time. In the library, he was alone with his microfilm. On the street, he pedaled onward, his lips pressed together. At home, he either read a book he had borrowed or slept. The couple next door fought with more ferocity as the summer wore on. He heard clattering, crying, the breaking of wood. He was increasingly certain the husband was menacing the wife, that there was a near-daily eruption of physical violence.

In fear, he sat and waited for the sounds to go away.

On the first Saturday in June, he found the archive of a defunct newspaper he had never heard of. It had stopped publishing in 1985, or the archive only extended that far. It was a bellowing tabloid with tales of murders, sex, and political corruption. The name of the newspaper was the *Daily Raider* and the more he read of it, the more he began to understand it was unlike any newspaper. It was darker, odder, riven with conflict real and imagined, a newspaper operating on a more ferocious plane of engagement. Pigeons were slaughtered, for fun, at the gates of Prospect Park. A retired left-hander admitted to passing on his venereal disease to multiple women who weren't his wife. A neighborhood butcher believed he was the reincarnation of Adolf Hitler. Page after page, in blistering color, the headlines so bold that they seemed to punch at him through the microfilm. He began in the early 1970s and read as many editions as he could before the library closed.

"Do you remember the *Daily Raider*?" he asked Wilbur Chiu.

"It doesn't exist anymore."

"Yes. I found it in the library. I had no memory of it."

"It coursed through the city for a few years. It was a newspaper of blood and semen. That's how I thought of it. Everything that flows—the scum, the juice, the fluids that leak from meat. It was a newspaper for that part of existence. I make no value judgment. That's just what it was."

"I read these old newspapers. I don't know why."

"They are selective reflections of the past, the collective memory that will soon be carried online. My son is very engaged with computers. He purchased one for me recently. He believes this will be the entirety of the future."

"I've never been much for computers."

"Think of the terminology. You go *on*line. You exist, here, *off*line. Language, I do believe, defines who it is we are, what we do. It is a form of destiny. A civilization is led to believe this sort of flesh world is *off* and only there, on your screen, are you *on*. We move in a way that begins to reject all it is we have been. Thousands of years turned to ash. Again, no value judgment. You will learn, Tad, I don't do that."

It was on his second Saturday among the microfilm of the *Daily Raider* that he discovered their obsession with an entity named Vengeance. For long stretches of time, he was merely described. There were no photographs. Eyewitnesses said he wore a mask with two eye-slits. He preferred trench coats. Where were the photos? An article in 1974 stated that no newspaper, the *Raider* included, had photographed Vengeance. He liked to scrawl his name on walls and announce himself. The police were concerned because only the police could combat crime. "Vigilantism," said one police chief, "will not be tolerated in this city."

Vengeance started with broken up robberies. He beat, nearly lifeless, a gun-toting mugger. In time, he graduated to bigger game— and then, finally, the beheading of an alleged serial rapist, rolling the skull out on 42nd Street, leaving it there for hungry and terrified and perplexed eyes. On the forehead of Marius Shantz, in his bright, slashing red paint: THIS IS VENGEANCE. Handwriting experts were called in to confirm it matched the graffiti. He was, Tad could tell, an anti-hero of near-classic vintage, stalking the night, hunting crime and snuffing it out. It seemed his conception was entirely informed by an earlier pop cultural moment. The urban backstreet brawlers. Here was one, come to life. The culture could do this. Though he had spent a decade disconnecting from it, shunning TV and cinema and comic books and radio, he had internalized enough from his first two decades of life to have a sense of how American ambition might manifest itself. We all wanted to be superheroes. His own father had explained once that he spent his postwar childhood idolizing Captain Marvel, a rival to Superman, an orphan boy who could summon greatness from a lighting bolt in the sky. All he had to do was look upward and cry "shazam!" In an eyeblink, he would be transformed into a god. There was no bug bite, no mutation, no accident of genetics. He had merely become a better person.

Vengeance was not Captain Marvel. He was just a man with time on his hands. Tad understood. Every few days, Vengeance would be mentioned again in the newspaper. The NYPD had initiated a manhunt, dispatched officers across the city to catch this man who dared to wear a mask and do their job for them. "We believe he is psychotic," said a police captain in Manhattan. "We don't know what he's capable of. He does a good deed today, okay. What about tomorrow?" On one day, the *Raider* was calling for Vengeance to be dragged in front of a court of law for daring "to do crimefighting outside the bounds of law." Other times, the editorial board would rally fully behind Vengeance's project. "The NYPD is clearly not up to the task. We demand safety and sanity in these dire times. If Vengeance can restore order, let him restore order."

Each story about Vengeance emphasized that he had never been photographed. There was a desperation to the coverage, an indignity that he had to be simply described, again and again, with insufficient language. The newspaper wanted to bring Vengeance to heel by photographing him. They wanted his reality on their front page. It was at a time when the image, at last, had achieved primacy over the written word, with TV ascendant and photographs in full color, their sophistication enough to render imagination irrelevant. Yet Vengeance was thriving, Tad saw, in this gap between imagination and reality. The more days passed without a photograph, the more powerful he became.

"Do you remember Vengeance?" he asked Chiu the following Friday.

"The vigilante."

"Yes."

"I remember there was a time when it felt like only mystical beings from the shadows could save us. I will tell you that I've been in America since I was a boy. But it is Americans who can grow most alienated from their country. Immigrants have a devotion to the ideal. The myth will always carry meaning. They came here, therefore they cannot be disappointed. To reject America is to reject yourself—the decisions you made, what your essence became."

"I'm trying to understand."

"Vengeance arrived at a very specific point in history and many, silently, cheered him on. I was well into my thirties, my financial station secure. We tasted anarchy and saw him as an agent against it."

"One man against anarchy, huh? I'm not sure I buy it."

"Vengeance was a fundamentally conservative figure. He was here for restoration. Here was here to bring us what we believed we had before, but never had."

The following Saturday, Tad found the newspaper he was waiting for. On the front page of the *Daily Raider*, there was nothing else. THIS IS VENGEANCE. The photograph was close, in greater detail and resolution, if that was the right word, than he imagined it would be. The cloth mask and the two slits for eyes were clear enough to him to gaze into, to strain, through two decades, to understand. Half of the newspaper was dedicated to Vengeance, celebrating, in part, the *Raider*'s coup, with retrospectives assembled in haste, as if he had died. The myriad "exclusives" indicated they had defeated the competition. He sensed, knowing little of the newspaper's trajectory, this was the apex of the *Raider*. There would never be glory again like this and this made him unhappy, that life had been set in such a way.

He saw who took the photo. The name, in small print, Mona Glass. A Jew, he thought, like me.

According to the newspaper, the photographer had taken the image of Vengeance as he attacked her, trying to reach through the window of a car. He remembered his father telling him when he was young that most of life was luck and timing. It was a phrase his father often repeated, to almost musical effect. *Luck and timing.* For a long time, he thought he understood what it meant. The best and worst is due to chance: when you show up, what happens when you do. He had felt neither in his own life. Comprehension was theoretical. Only now, delivering for Chiu and sifting through newspapers in the library, did he begin to approach his father's words with any kind of permanent understanding.

Certain people believe they migrate through life under a lucky star and he had never been one of those people. He never had a reason to be. Now, for the first time, he could believe there was meaning in his return. His timing, once off, was now on. He continued to read.

The photographer interviewed Vengeance on the telephone. He would not reveal his identity. It was unlike anything he had ever read.

There are layers of hell and I am below them, between them.

This city is failing. You can feel it. I can feel it. We all believe in it, still, we collectively will it to life, each and every day. But for how long? How long can we dream? How long will you dream? Ultimately, I am for order over chaos, matter over anti-matter, creation over negation. The New York Police Department, which I know intimately, is a failed state. It is the Ottoman Empire on the eve of the Great War. It has exhausted itself. I step into the breach.

London Bridge is falling down. Falling down, falling down. London Bridge is falling down, my fair lady.

Carrying the words with him, he couldn't help but share them with Chiu before his next shift. When he entered the takeout restaurant, Chiu was scrubbing the countertop, whistling an unidentifiable tune.

"I read an interview with Vengeance," Tad said.

"I remember it."

"What he said?"

"How I felt about it."

"They are words unlike any I've read."

"It was unlike any time I had lived through."

"He sang a song."

"London Bridge."

"You remember."

Chiu lit a cigarette, settling into a thin folding chair behind the counter. He sat like an old-world monarch in repose, his fist balanced beneath his chin, his eyes drifting to a corner of light only he could see. He exhaled, the smoke traveling slowly from his mouth.

"His identity was never found out. The police couldn't find him. Neither could any newspaper."

"The song was a clue."

"Yes."

"How could no one find him?"

"Those who don't want to be found don't get found. I believe this. There is no better place to hide than New York City."

"He changed his name?"

"From old to new."

"How do you know?"

"Everyone who wanted to know could know. For all the fulminating of the police, the newspapers, I am not sure they wanted to know. There is more interest in potentiality. There is a chase afoot. No one really wants to know what they are chasing. Once Vengeance falls into custody, the story ends. If he disappears, he can still be out there. Enough times passes and he becomes unreal. He retreats into myth. The New York Police Department can be forgiven for never apprehending a myth."

"I imagine he is still out there."

"You are thinking of him now."

"I imagine he is close to us, Mr. Chiu. I imagine he is past fifty, gray at the temples, beginning to slump. He has a small apartment in Bayside, among the retiring Jews. He goes to the deli for a turkey on rye. He has packed his past away."

"Or he embraces it."

"Maybe he remembers all of it. Maybe he writes his name in his own blood. The apartment is wrecked, mutilated, beyond recognition. It has the odor of wartime. He still sings 'London Bridge.'"

Vengeance slowly disappeared from the *Raider*. There were more stories about eyewitnesses and police leads, crimes foiled. No one else, as far as Tad could tell, photographed him. Mona Glass was the lone person to take the image. As the 1970s wore on, there were other creatures of the night to occupy the newspaper. Marauding homeless. Hijacked subway cars. Son of Sam. It was as Chiu said. He had retreated.

It was a noble idea. A single person to stand against disorder. Put on a mask and drop into the night. Vengeance, for a moment, permitted the culture of fantasy to meet the brutality of every day.

Chiu seemed to understand.

The summer was long and hot. His legs and forearms were browned and muscled, his shirt tight against his back, the sweat staining and drying and staining again. He was careening through Queens midday, straining to beat his own times. Twelve minutes to 77th Street, six minutes to 30th Avenue, fourteen to the BQE. He saved all of his money but what he put toward rent and electricity and occasional grocery trips. His cash tips were filed in the drawer of a desk he had found on the sidewalk and carried upstairs. He had worked, on and off, since he was sixteen, and this was the first time the money mattered to him. It was labor vital, somehow, to who he was.

At the end of August, he biked from Queens through Brooklyn, streaking south. He would make the beach. At Coney Island, he collapsed in a small cloud, his lips dry. He was laughing. He lay his bike in the sand. Seagulls circled overhead. He had not eaten all day. A sand-caked canteen was drained. He could see the parachute jump in the corner of his eye, enormous and flowering. Boomboxes thudded with music he never learned. A volleyball arced over his outstretched body. Up above, the sky was streaked with white clouds, a passenger jet threading in and out of sight.

He hadn't come here since he was a child, on a day trip with his father, mother, and Lenore. That day had been quietly acrimonious, his mother and father debating where to put the blanket, how much water was enough, if they were sitting too close to the wrong kind of people. He remembered his mother referring to Coney Island as a slum.

The memory trickled out of him. He closed his eyes, allowing his mind to void itself. He tried not to think at all. The surf pulled in and out, the salty foam hissing. He felt the sun deep in his skin. He understood why people came here. He unbuttoned his shirt and lay in the hot sand in his shorts, letting his body gather heat.

In early September, having reached the end of his *Daily Raider* newspapers, he decided to skip his trip to the library. Instead, he wandered into Blue Star, where Chiu was smoking a cigarette and painting the walls. He had settled on a dark red, almost maroon. The paint had a distinct and dizzying smell.

"You decided to repaint."

"Have you ever made a decision without knowing why it was made for you?"

"Yes."

"There is a liberating aspect. Body and mind are not in their arranged marriage. That is a trick of Eastern and Western civilization, that both should be together. That they deserve to be joined."

"A mind free of a body. And a body free of a mind."

"A body that moves, unimpeded, undertakes the purest form of action. Unclouded by thought. Unclouded by societal rot. Action for the sake of action."

"That could lead to violence."

"Violence as purification."

"Did Vengeance believe in that?"

"Vengeance believed that he alone could deliver a society free of sin. He was an idealist. Under the strain, he disappeared."

"I want to find him."

Chiu stopped painting. He looked up toward the ceiling.

"Vengeance couldn't accept he would be born into the world that he would die in," Chiu said.

Tad delivered on all seven days at the start of September. On the eighth day, he delivered again. On the ninth, he decided he would go out once more.

"I don't need a day off," he told Chiu.

Chiu grunted at him.

The tenth, Tad decided, would be the last before his break. It was a Monday. He would work Monday and sleep deeply on Tuesday. He informed Chiu of his plan.

"When you sleep on Tuesday, let yourself dream."

He did.

12

In the first week of September, Saul received a call in his office from Grayson Moegenborg, the executive director of the Port Authority. He had friends at the Port Authority and had met Grayson a handful of times at parties he attended with Mona, since he was dating Mona's best friend. They hadn't talked in some time. Before Grayson began dating Liv, Saul had run into him, over the years, at Republican functions. He knew him to be a scion who was mostly called upon to fundraise for vaguely moderate or socially liberal candidates and bat away rumors that someday he would run for office himself. If he cared enough, he would have been a natural fit for the Silk Stocking District, where he kept a penthouse.

"Grayson, how are you?"

"Still upright. Good enough. How are things over there in the new office they upgraded you to?"

"I like the view. You're way up in the South Tower, aren't you?

"Seventieth floor. I'd say I like the view too. But I was never keen for heights. I'm here though, spinning my wheels up in the sky."

"You're closer to Windows on the World, though. Great coffee."

"Indeed. So Saul, the reason I called was to pick your brain about something. You enjoy working for the feds, right?"

"They've treated me well."

"That's good. I wanted to know, if you were looking for anything else, my deputy is leaving next month for a job in the private sector.

This is a good job, a lot of action, a lot of balls in the air. To be honest, I don't know how long I'll be hanging on as executive director. I'm getting a hankering to take things slower, spend more time with Liv, take up golf, do old fella things. If you wanted this—if this is something you'd be interested in—you'd have the inside track. On my recommendation, Pataki would appoint you."

"That is certainly something I could be interested in."

"Well, good. Let's meet in my office on, let's say, Tuesday? Then we'll ride up to Windows on the World for breakfast. I'm free around nine. Does that work for you? We can chat a bit more and see if this is a fit."

"That does sound good. I'll be there."

"Great. I'll see you on Tuesday."

Saul sat back in his chair, reflecting on what just had happened. Grayson, in essence, had dangled the possibility of a serious promotion: to move from being a respected, anonymous bureaucrat to the front-facing leader of a massive bistate authority. The Port Authority oversaw much of the regional transportation infrastructure—multiple major airports, bridges, a train network, and one of America's largest ports. The Port Authority leased out the World Trade Center. He had to wonder why Grayson was considering him. Well, he had to remember his own breadth of experience, his service with the federal government and Rockefeller and the law work he did, forty years in the rearview mirror now. He liked the idea of seeing his name in the *New York Times* again. He didn't know how much Grayson knew about Emmanuel, what Liv had told him, how closely they confided. The less, the better. He could look forward to Tuesday, a trip up to Grayson's office, and maybe he'd walk out with another job and a shot at a bigger prize. Pataki was up for re-election next year but he'd probably win. Saul could run the Port Authority for Pataki's whole third term if he played his cards right.

It was only later, on his drive from Brooklyn to Long Island, that he remembered he'd have to cancel with Grayson. He had a fucking dentist appointment that day. How could he forget? Probably had blocked it out because that Dr. Lippman wanted to pull a tooth. He could reschedule the appointment. That would be the easiest thing to do.

The next day, Saul called the doctor's office.

"Saul Plotz here, I'd like to reschedule my appointment for Tuesday."

"Oh really? What happened?" asked the receptionist.

"Something came up."

"Let me see here . . ." Saul could hear the shuffling of papers and the faint typing of keys. The receptionist sounded like she was twenty. "The next time we could get you in is October 15th."

"The 15th! What? Why can't we do, I don't know, September 15th?"

"The schedule is very packed, Mr. Plotz. I am so sorry. And your surgery is particular so Dr. Lipmann only wants to schedule it at certain availabilities. He will also be away the week of the 17th at a conference as well."

"Ah, I see."

"His conference trips means we've really had to juggle around the schedule. I'm so sorry. We can get you in for October 15th, then."

"No, you know what, let's keep it. I don't want to wait that long."

"So you'll be here the 11th then? We can keep you for nine in the morning?"

"Yup, September 11th. Thanks."

The mayoral primary was Tuesday, which meant the *News* was sending Mona running across the city to shoot the candidates. After the bus came to take Emmanuel to Bridge Prep—he was now, improbably, a seventh grader—she hopped in her car to drive to the Bronx to catch Fernando Ferrer, one of the Democrats, voting. Afterwards, the desk wanted her on Governor George Pataki, who was doing a quick photo-op at a hospital. Then she was tasked with following

Mark Green, the front-runner, through Brooklyn. Election night, as of now, was Green as well. It was going to be one of those times when she wouldn't be home until midnight but at least she would be paid overtime. Saul was picking Emmanuel up after school and then the babysitter would be there around 6:30 when he had to leave. Part of her could still be excited for the chaos of election day, the adrenaline rush of an unexpected outcome, a bit like the anticipation before a big tennis match. The obvious difference was that she was playing spectator with her camera. She was not the competition. She didn't even worry about photogs at rival newspapers getting photos. As she told Saul, she was ready for a different way to spend her days.

"Who's gonna be mayor?" Emmanuel asked her as she drove him around the block to his bus stop. He had been watching the nightly news with her lately and had started to grow more curious about what was happening around him.

"Well, today it's the primary. The Democrats are fighting it out. A lot of people think it's going to be Mark Green. He is the most well-known Democrat."

"He hates Giuliani, right?"

"Yes."

"And Giuliani isn't running again?"

"No, he is term-limited. There's a Republican running, a rich man named Michael Bloomberg. He is probably going to face the Democrat. It looks like it could be Green against Bloomberg, and then Green will probably win."

"The Democrat will beat the Republican then?"

"Yes. It's a Democratic city now and we're all a bit sick of Rudy's act."

Minutes after she dropped Emmanuel at his bus stop, her phone rang. It was the news desk. She sighed, flicked off the radio, and picked up her phone at a red light.

"Yeah?"

"Mona, hey, can you go downtown for us first?"

"What's up?"

"So we screwed up and Dembo is going to be up in the Bronx shooting Ferrer. Can you start downtown? They want you to grab a few people voting near City Hall, out of Tweed. A stringer will meet you to get the quotes. Take some photos of people voting for the spread and then head over to—who's next for you?"

"Pataki."

"Right. Go to Pataki next it."

She drove from the Belt onto the BQE, heading toward Manhattan. It was 7:20, a typical crawl, trucks flanking her on both sides. When she got downtown, she could stash her car in a lot and expense it to the *News*. As a longtime staffer, this was one of her few perks—leniency with charging gas, food, and parking expenses to the newspaper. With each new generation of staff, the perks diminished.

A few weeks ago, she went out to dinner with Al and Liv. Al was usually tied up managing the gallery in Williamsburg, which had become a haven for artists, to Mona's surprise. It was a neighborhood she had hardly considered for most of her life, a working class outpost for Irish, Polish, and Puerto Ricans, and now she was hearing more about, from Al and others, how this place was the new SoHo. It was good to have Al back. He had been living in New York since 1999, moving in with Liv for three months before renting an apartment near Grand Army Plaza. He was done, he said, with L.A. He was even talking to some members of his family again. As time passed, it was almost as if Al had never been gone at all. How had he lived so far away from her and Liv? He was painting again too and seemed to be making sales.

Like LeRoy Neiman, he was now focusing on expressionistic paintings of athletic contests. Last night, she had talked on the phone with Liv about Al, how it felt like they had all come together again, with life resembling an actual cycle for once and not merely a meander towards death.

"I never knew if he'd come back," Mona said.

"Come back from L.A.? Of course he would."

"You always knew?"

"You don't go to a place like that to die. You go there to stew. He stewed and came home."

"Now we just need to find him a girlfriend."

"I talked to him about that. I told him New York is full of eligible rich women desperate for men. You just have to show up. When a man hits fifty and he's not bald, fat, or dead, he's like one of those hot free agents the Yankees give fifty million dollars to. Al's got that dark Sicilian thing about him. Swarthy, mysterious. I tell him to go play the field."

"I should try to set him up with someone."

"He gets touchy. But at least he found his painting."

"You found your restaurant."

"And you, Mona, the big city photographer."

"This is the last year. This mayoral race will be the last big thing."

"You're going to miss the hustle."

"I won't miss the deadlines, four boroughs in one day, getting home at midnight. I need a life that runs on schedule."

"You must still get a kick out of seeing your photos in the newspaper."

"I do, sometimes. You know, it is a part of yourself there and it's rare, I suppose, to have part of you in a place where others can see. That did used to excite me. I remember the first time it happened, in the *Daily Raider*."

"I remember that well. You were the star of the city."

"Nothing is better than the first time you do anything like that."

Mona stretched out on her couch, the phone warm against her ear.

"What are you doing this Friday?" Liv asked.

"Friday evening? I don't know. Not much."

"Windows on the World?"

"Dinner? I could do it."

"Al too."

"Not a bad idea. Let's see if he's around."

"I'll try to bring a friend along. For Al. He's fifty-two and he ain't dying alone. I'll consider myself a failure if that happens."

"Fifty-two, shit. What an ugly number. I'll be that soon."

"I'm already there, honey, and it's not so bad."

Mona laughed lightly into the phone.

"I was fine dealing with the roundness of fifty."

"Well, wait until we're sixty."

Mona's car rumbled up the Gowanus Expressway and into the Brooklyn-Battery Tunnel, where traffic finally eased. The news cut out and she drove deeper into the tunnel. Primary day used to be like a holiday. Get out in the sun, photograph the candidates, hop from one set piece to another. When she was thirty or even forty, there was a veneer of excitement to days like these, something akin to adventure. She could rove the city, unencumbered. What she knew now was that she was done roving.

It was a little before 8:00 when she entered Lower Manhattan, veering off toward Church Street. Whenever she drove down this congested artery, past the World Trade Center, she thought of Saul and their semi-furtive lunches, walking side-by-side through the building crowds. Sometimes they would hold hands. Felicia, Saul once said with a smile, traveled to Manhattan once every decade.

She parked her car in a lot on Park Place and walked toward the Tweed Courthouse behind City Hall. When she escaped the gloom of the street, she gazed upward, toward a blue sky absent of clouds. Still summer, she thought. I'll take more days like this one. She had all of her equipment, multiple lenses and two DSLR bodies, a flash modifier. It was a little like going off to war, preparing for every contingency. As she crossed Broadway and walked to Tweed, she could see voters filing in and out. Her press credential hung around her neck. Her plan was to duck in, take a few photos of people walking into voting booths, catch a few scenes from outside, and head uptown to photograph Pataki before tailing Mark Green, the smarmy front-runner.

In the rush to get Emmanuel to the bus stop and drive into the city, she had forgotten her coffee. Usually, she stopped at a neighborhood coffee shop. There wouldn't be time to go into a Manhattan place and wait in line. She spotted a breakfast cart across the street, stocked with coffee, bagels, and muffins.

Resisting the urge to dart between cars against the red light like she used to do in her twenties, she waited dutifully with the tourists and crossed the street. She checked her watch. It was almost 8:40. The light changed and she ran, testing her legs on the pockmarked concrete. At the coffee cart, she stood behind one man in a Yankees t-shirt, Williams 51. It was navy, like the kind Emmanuel liked to wear. The man paid and took his two blueberry muffins, allowing her to step up and order her black coffee. She yawned, unintentionally, after completing her order. The man behind the counter, smiling wearily, disappeared to get the cup for her.

Coffee in hand, she caught the light and sprinted back across the street. She had to down the coffee quickly and get going, especially with the Pataki event due to start in less than an hour. She spotted the young kid who the *News* had assigned as the stringer. Fresh out of college, he was nervously approaching voters who were not eager to talk to him. Finally, to her relief, an elderly woman paused and let the stringer, who was named either Alex or Alan, ask her who she voted for and why.

"Mark Green is my candidate," she said softly. "I liked the work he did with consumer affairs and I remember him from his other races."

The stringer nodded slowly, his notepad jutted out. Mona approached from behind.

"And how do you spell your name?"

"It's Elda Dean. E-L-D-A . . ."

The sound was unlike any she had ever heard, a booming across the empty blue sky. Above Elda Dean's right shoulder was a wild explosion. Mona saw it before the stringer, who had bowed his head to sketch Elda's name in faded pen, the script whipping across his lined page. People began to cluster, pointing and staring, whispering among themselves. On instinct, Mona pointed her camera at the Twin Towers. The tower with the antenna was on fire now, a black cloud leaking from a wide gash near the very top. A cop at the corner whistled and spit near his toes.

"I saw a fucking plane just come in and hit it. Like a dream."

She knew she had to get closer. The *News* would want photos and she was closest. It was probably an accident, a small plane flying too low. As she hurried down Chambers Street and back to Church, where she could cut towards the Towers, she saw the dark cloud had gained strength, smoke of cosmic proportion trailing against the sky. She heard sirens, the police cars and fire engines and ambulances beginning their rush toward the accident. She was running and then jogging, stopping hard to take a shot before continuing onward, as close as she could go.

Windows on the World, she finally remembered, was in the North Tower. The one that was now on fire.

She couldn't tell, from her vantage point, if the fire and smoke were swallowing up all the ways out. Normally, Liv would be there now, managing the breakfast rush. But maybe she wasn't. Saul was supposed to get breakfast with Grayson Moegenborg today to discuss a possible job and then he had to cancel to get his tooth pulled. Liv could be arriving at work later. She remembered sometimes Liv started in the afternoon and worked late into the night. Today could be one of those days. If Saul had canceled on Grayson, Grayson was probably not taking a breakfast meeting. They both, right now, could be on Broadway, staring at the fire in the sky.

With her press pass, she moved past a police line that had been erected quickly on Church. Police officers were milling in the street, staring upward. The September 11th accident, she thought. On primary day, of all days. Her phone buzzed. It was her desk editor.

"Mona, where are you?"

"Next to the World Trade Center, getting shots of this—what is it, a plane crash?"

"Looks that way. Hey, just stay there. Dembo can follow up with Pataki. This may be the story now. Big plane crash on election day. Who knows, maybe one of the Democrats did it!" The desk editor was laughing to himself. "Wild times. It's never boring in New York, right?"

"Never boring, nope."

"Well, stay down there and watch out."

She continued to shoot, capturing the smoke cloud and flame from as many angles as she could manage from her position. The city, massing in the shadows of the Towers, seemed to be drawing its breath. It reminded her of when the tightrope walker traveled between the Towers, the unforeseen spectacle in the clouds, mouths agape. The fire continued to burn and she hoped the fire department could find a way to put it all out pretty soon.

She put her camera down and called Liv's number.

After five rings, it went to voicemail.

"Hi, Liv, it's me. I'm right near the Trade Center. It looks like there's a fire up there. I hope you're well. Come say hi when you're down or, if you're down here already, I'm on Church near the hotel. Okay, talk to you soon."

She decided, not knowing what to do exactly, to call Al. Saul would have been next but she knew he was at the dentist. Besides, he didn't answer his cellphone very much.

"Al, I'm downtown near the Trade Center."

"I'm watching on TV now. Jesus Christ."

"Where are you?"

"I'm at home. I had planned to go down to the gallery and then this came on the TV. I told them I'd be late. Crazy a plane would just fly into it, right?"

"Must have gotten really mixed up."

"Mixed up badly. Too badly. I hope to God it's an accident."

"Well, of course it's an accident. Planes don't *try* to hit buildings."

"They don't usually."

Mona took a breath. She knew he was thinking what she was thinking.

"I called Liv just now," she said.

"How is she?"

"It rang and went to voicemail."

"That's not a huge deal. She's probably tied up with Grayson. You know how they are. She's probably not into work yet."

"Yeah. Tuesdays may be her late day."

"Probably is, yeah."

They said goodbye and she continued to shoot the burning tower, unsure when exactly she should stop. It was possible, she supposed, it could smolder all day, and the *News* would want to leave her here. She heard a news report playing loudly from the radio of a stalling taxi, the female voice talking about the fire at the Twin Towers. She heard *small plane* and *survivors* and shuddered at the thought of likely death. Those poor people in the offices who were rammed on impact. Such an unexpected, absurd way to die. She imagined peering out from the soaring rectangle of glass, watching as the nose of an airplane erased city and sky.

The stringer, Alex or Alan, was making his way toward her, nervously peering skyward. She put down her camera and tilted her head to the side. He seemed only a few years older than her son.

"Get any good quotes?"

"I guess I'm a bit confused, because I was on primary day coverage and now it's the plane crash or whatever it is that caused that explosion."

"Listen, that's how news works. You always need to adjust. Events change. Especially in this city. I remember the Trade Center bombing back in '93. That was nuts."

"You think this is like that?"

"I don't think so. Tragically, it was probably an accident. You have all this barely regulated air travel, little airplanes and helicopters. An amateur lost his way and smacked the building."

"On such a clear day?"

"Up there, anything is possible."

She started taking photos of the streets, the heads dipped backward, eyes open as if waiting for rain. Terror mingling with wonder. She floated up and down Church, heading nearer to the plaza where men in crisp suits appeared to be shuffling from the tower that wasn't hit. Others were still drifting inside.

Car alarms, one after another, rang out.

She decided, once more, to call Liv. The phone went straight to voicemail.

Another cop, younger this time, sidled up next to her.

"You should watch out, ma'am, for falling debris."

"I'm doing fine. I need to get my shots."

"Right, yeah. You from the *Post*?"

"*News*."

"Eh, a bit liberal for me, but fine. You watch out though, like I said. We could be getting debris coming down here."

"Have you heard anything else about it?"

"Definitely a plane. Flew right in. My buddy saw it come across. But who the fuck knows, right? Some jerkoff who shouldn't be near a plane decides he knows how to fly it."

"I hope it was an accident."

"We all do."

Shortly after the cop left, her phone buzzed again. It was a Manhattan number. She didn't recognize it.

"Hello?"

"Mona! It's me. I'm sorry, my phone, it hasn't been getting reception. I grabbed a landline here in the kitchen."

"Liv, Jesus. It's good to hear from you. Where are you?"

"Windows on the World. There's some smoke coming up here. Something happened, there was an explosion, a crash—"

"A plane hit the building."

"That's what people are saying. It's getting a bit hard to breathe. We put in calls to the Fire Department and the Port Authority. I just wanted to say I'm okay and they'll probably be up here, sooner rather than later. We're trying to get everyone into a place away from the smoke."

"Is there a room or somewhere you can go?"

"We're figuring it out. Just tons of smoke. Stairwells filled. Grayson is here too. He's having a little coughing fit."

"Oh my God."

"We'll get through it, Mona. I just wanted to let you know I'm up here. I'll give you a ring in a bit. Maybe they can get us helicoptered out of here, who knows."

"Wow, I've never been on one of those."

"They're wild. Noisy. Well, I gotta go. Mona, be safe, okay? I'll talk to you soon."

"You be safe. You get your ass down here. I'll guilt-trip Al into getting dinner later. We'll need to get the smoke out of your hair."

"Yes, for sure. Well, I'll talk to you soon. I love you."

"Goodbye, Liv. Love you."

They didn't usually speak like this. It was a word that never came naturally to Mona, except in the context of speaking to her son and, occasionally, Saul. She wasn't sure why, only that her parents rarely said it. Perhaps they believed overuse would cheapen it. Either way, getting off the phone with Liv, she felt fresh unease. She wanted Liv to not be in the tower at all. She wanted her to be safe in bed with Grayson.

When Mona looked up again she couldn't be sure she was still here, in the reality she had been born into, or if she had slipped into a fissure in space-time, deposited into a realm of hellish underside, fire as plentiful as oxygen. For a moment, she could only stare, not scream. The explosion was louder this time. The attack had duplicated itself. Since she was a child cowering from Cuban missiles, she had always feared, vaguely, a new war would come to claim her, one with greater civilizational implications than she could imagine.

A plane had flown straight through the second tower. The memory, second's old, confirmed she was here, it was real.

The Twin Towers, on fire.

"Holy shit!" she heard behind her.

The movement in the street was unhinged. People were running, tripping on cement, rolling over the hoods of cars. Police sirens were filling the gaps of sound. She continued to shoot, backing away, the Towers flaking steel and cement and glass. Her phone was buzzing again and she grabbed it, hoping it was Liv.

"Mona, you still down there?"

"Yes I'm down there."

"Good. Dembo is on his way. We're sending more photogs and reporters. This is big shit. I don't know. They're saying on CNN, some people, that they think it's intentional. Could be. Who fucking knows. Are we at war? Maybe we're at war."

She wanted to slit the throat of the desk editor so he would stop talking.

"I'm shooting."

"Keep it up. Stay down there. That's the story now. We'll worry about Mark Green and Freddie Ferrer later."

Emmanuel. She had to run. If she wasn't with him, he wasn't safe. There could be more airplanes falling from the sky. Then bombs. She immediately thought of the bridges crossing the river, all of them bathed in fire. Manhattan was the worst place to be. She had to get the hell to her car.

She looked backward and took a few more shots.

The crowd moved with her but she was ahead, cutting between bodies, her elbows pumping. Black clouds drank blue sky. She needed to get out of Manhattan. Nothing else mattered.

If the desk asked, she'd say she stayed. She didn't care. The job could go fuck itself.

She was surprised by how vacant the parking garage seemed. People should be rushing for their cars, preparing to flee. She waved to the attendant, who nodded sheepishly and ducked down the ramp to get her car. It took less than five minutes but felt far longer, time slowing in opposition to her pulse. More buildings would be next. The Empire State Building, the Chrysler Building. Yankee Stadium. Nazis bombed London to the ground. The Americans obliterated two cities with atomic bombs. All of this had happened before. History was always curled right behind you, ready to strike.

She tipped the attendant extra and fell behind the wheel, gunning her car out onto Broadway.

Traffic was clear. She could hear the sirens, patrol cars and fire trucks speeding on the Brooklyn Bridge. She was done with the city. Liv had to get out and she would. The firefighters would get her. It was smoke. You could hide from smoke. The restaurant was huge. Liv and Grayson were tucked away, waiting out the fire. It was stressful, shitty, but they could laugh about it later. *Remember the time Windows on the World caught fire.* She almost smiled, her car rushing off the ramp and into the street, over to the entrance for the Brooklyn-Queens Expressway.

From the BQE she caught the holy hell of it, the way smoke was streaming from burning steel. It was cinema, bad fiction, a plot point dreamed up as too ridiculous for art and discarded somewhere else. She drove on thinking that soon this would all dissolve and she'd be back home, in bed, maybe with Saul at her side. Emmanuel sleeping in the next room, under his Yankee posters. Her phone would ring and it would be Liv. *Remember that time—*

The radio was beginning to use the word terrorism. It was a distant concept to her, men in foreign lands with submachine guns and hidden bombs, an explosion in a European square. The anchor didn't seem to be reading the news. He was talking extemporaneously, hunting for adequate adjectives. No one had information. A plane hit the towers, a plane hit the towers. Smoke in the sky, fire, police on the way, state of emergency. The more she heard the phraseology, the less it meant. The machinery of the automobile was an extension of her body, bearing her to her son. Once she was there, she would think again.

Bridge Prep had a clock tower that could be seen on the approach and when it pierced the horizon line, she began to breathe deeply. She was surprised no bombs had landed on the roadway to kill her. What she was increasingly certain of was that the Twin Towers were only the beginning, stage one of a cataclysm, like the assassination of an archduke. War was here. She never kept a gun in her apartment and she wished she had. Saul would be getting out of his appointment soon, which was in downtown Brooklyn.

When would the shooting start? If the bombs didn't fall immediately, they'd be parachuting out of the sky. Men in black marching downwind, guns pointing straight ahead. She always knew she'd have to run. It was why, more often than not, she wore sneakers. The better to escape crowds, the deadly conglomeration of bodies, death in the crushing heat. The sky was still blue when she parked in Bridge Prep's visitor lot and sprinted into the building.

It wasn't as if she would just find Emmanuel, that he'd present himself to her. The school was more a complex, a collection of wings and donor-funded extravagances, a theater and a fitness center and an Olympic-sized swimming pool and glass-boxed computer labs. Though her son had been going to the school for two years now she hardly knew her way around, hoping this carpeted hallway would take her where she needed to be.

When she saw a woman in the hallway who looked like she may know where students were, she stopped her.

"Excuse me, I'm looking for a student, a seventh grader, Emmanuel Plotz. I'm his mother—"

"Oh you should really check at the front desk."

"The front desk, okay."

"I'd wait until after chapel. All the students are there now. The headmaster is talking about the situation with the planes hitting the Twin Towers. It sounds very bad."

Before the woman was done, Mona was running faster than she had in twenty-five years, knocking through the double-doors that split up the long hallway. She knew where they had chapel. It was in the expansive theater, renovated just a few years ago thanks to the donation of a Tony Award-winning producer who had attended Bridge Prep in the '50s. Up a flight of stairs, a right, then a left, out past the balcony and the indoor swimming pool, chlorine gumming up her nostrils. Another right, a wobbling stairwell, then daylight, a procession of large windows looking out onto a flourishing garden, rosebushes and azaleas. Beyond the garden was the outdoor pool, where Emmanuel had taken summer camp swim lessons when he was younger.

To her left, closed double-doors. Catching her breath, she yanked them open and rushed into the air-conditioned darkness. Hundreds of students were sitting in the theater as the head of the middle school was addressing them about the attacks.

"An airplane flew into the Eiffel Tower—I mean, the Twin Towers, it appears . . ."

Small laughter in the theater.

". . . we don't know much yet but we are arranging for a half-day, for school to let out at noon today."

A boy pointed straight at her.

"Hey Emmanuel, happy birthday! It's your mom."

She recognized the boy from Bridge Prep's summer camp, where she had sent Emmanuel when he was younger. What she couldn't see yet was her own son. She walked closer, a lone adult proceeding toward the aisles, theoretically unauthorized.

"Mom!"

Usually, she embarrassed him. Children wanted to exist independent of their parents, propagating a fiction that they were living, even at age eleven, self-sustaining lives. It had never been a conflict for her because her parents so rarely ventured out to her place of play. They saw her for breakfast and for supper and that was it. Her mother wasn't coming to watch her at the schoolyard. Her father was always working. Like other children of the '50s, she had internalized that whatever it was that her parents didn't do for her, she would do for her own children, that she would become his world as much as he was already her world. This time, Emmanuel sprung out of his seat and ran toward her, stopping just short of running into her arms. The head of the middle school, still speaking, hadn't seen her.

"Let's go home," she said.

At the front desk, she told security to communicate to the school that Emmanuel Plotz was leaving for the day. "I'm his mother," she said with finality, pressing his hand tight. In the car he didn't speak, staring straight ahead. They drove the short stretch home, the radio shut off.

"Mom, what exactly happened?"

"We don't know yet. The planes hit both towers. It could be an accident. They're still getting information."

"Were you down there?"

"I was."

She decided, against instinct, to turn on the TV when they were inside. Every news station showed a continuous shot of the burning towers, the angles varying only slightly, eyewitnesses calling in from cellphones to explain to the broadcasters what it looked like to watch two of the tallest buildings in the world burn. The eyewitnesses were interchangeable to her, their phones crackling, their voices fluty and distant, their stories hinging on the unexpected absurdity of a plane flying directly into an office building. When she had poured Emmanuel a glass of water, she walked into her bedroom and called Saul. She couldn't think of what else to do.

The call went straight to voicemail.

Saul wasn't up there. That she knew. Yet he could have been and that made her deeply, suddenly sick, like the planet beneath her had been wrenched at a radical degree previously unknown in human history. She was teetering, her knees weak.

She called Liv.

On the fourth ring, she heard a voice.

"Mona, hey."

"Liv, how are you, are you down?"

"We're—there's a lot of smoke. It's very hot here. We're trying to get, to get to a place where there isn't smoke. Grayson—"

"Where the fuck are the firefighters?"

"I don't know."

"God, I'm going to call the fire department."

"I'm sure they're on their way."

The phone cut off. She called again and Liv's voicemail came on. *Hi, this is Liv, please leave a message and I'll get back to you as soon as I can. Thanks!* She dialed a second time. *Hi, this is Liv, please leave a message and I'll get back to you as soon as I can. Thanks!* She dialed a third time. *Hi, this is Liv, please leave a message and I'll get back to you as soon as I can. Thanks!*

She slammed the phone down and sat down hard on her bed. Her eyes felt very hot.

"They're saying a plane hit the Pentagon," Emmanuel said quietly, pointing at the TV.

"The Pentagon?"

"Yeah."

They sat together on the couch, her arm around his shoulder. There was a split screen of the black smoke pouring from the Twin Towers and the fire at the Pentagon. She had no idea if this was what they should be doing now. All they were going to do was watch the same images of the buildings burning ad infinitum until someone figured out how to put the fires out. Helicopters would have to make rescues. She imagined one, a sturdy FDNY chopper, freeing Liv and Grayson from their smoke-clogged prison.

A broadcaster said the President had made a statement. Terrorism against this nation will not stand. We will hunt down those responsible.

Now there was a shot of another broadcaster outdoors, standing on top of a building somewhere north of the Twin Towers. Just over half his face was in shadow. Then there was a cutaway back to the Pentagon.

As a broadcaster explained the confusion at the Pentagon, the first broadcaster called out from off camera.

"Wow, I need you to stop, I need you to stop for a second. There has just been a huge explosion and you can see a billowing smoke rising and I can't—I can't see that second tower but there was a cascade of sparks and fire and it looks like, wow, it looks like a mushroom cloud explosion, this huge billowing smoke in this second tower, this was the second tower hit, and I cannot see behind that smoke. The first tower in front has not changed and we see this extraordinary and frightening scene of this second tower just encased in smoke. What's behind it I cannot tell you. That is about as frightening a scene as you will ever see."

She was gripping Emmanuel's hand. He was holding his glass of water, not drinking.

"He's an idiot," she said softly.

"What mom?"

"The building isn't *encased* in smoke. It's gone."

She couldn't cry because if she did, Emmanuel would. He would see her and sob. When she was twelve, ready to turn thirteen, Cuban missiles almost killed them all. But they never came. This was the unsaid assumption of American life in the twentieth century. Apocalypse could approach, threaten, menace. It could suck the lifeblood out of imaginations. What it could not do was arrive. This is what made the genre of fiction so tolerable, why someone like Al could tell her about a comic book in which a false alien attack kills three million New Yorkers to save the world and she could nod along, safely perplexed. This was not supposed to be the counter-world. Airplanes did not topple buildings.

The TV showed the tower collapsing again. It was the South Tower, the broadcaster said. This meant the North Tower was standing. Liv was there. She could get downstairs and get out.

"Emmanuel, honey, give me a second. I have to make a phone call."

Hi, this is Liv, please leave a message and I'll get back to you as soon as I can. Thanks!

She fought the sensation that she was listening to a ghost. Liv couldn't talk because the firefighters had her and they were racing down the stairs, dousing flames with their high-pressure nozzles. Or the helicopters had arrived. CNN wasn't saying anything about helicopter rescues yet.

The cloud, taller than the buildings around it, was filling downtown.

"Why is this happening?"

"I'm not sure. We're still figuring out."

"Why did they do it?"

His hazel eyes were wide, lightly bathed in the soft glow of the TV screen. He seemed beyond tears, in a state of shock and reckoning she couldn't quite describe. She didn't know why they were watching anymore. There was no purpose to this kind of observation. They were adding nothing, saving no one, offering merely their fear. They were two useless specks of an equally useless mass audience. For the span of her adult life, she had told herself that through actions taken or refused, she could alter the trajectory of her reality. She could hustle after the ball, smash the serve harder, make a new demand of her body—it was all possible, if only she tried hard enough. In a way, it was the most American thing about her. It was, she had come to understand, her private manifest destiny.

She felt weaker the more they watched. Time was like the crawl of blood from a flesh wound, a bright streak rolling to the ground. The broadcaster was outside again, on his midtown building, his face in shadow. He continued to describe the smoke and the fire as if he were delivering new revelations, his necktie crisp and power red. Every few seconds, he reused an adjective. *Extraordinary. Terrifying. Unprecedented.* He was advertising the uselessness of human language.

She buried her face in her hands and hoped somehow Emmanuel wouldn't notice. What she wouldn't do was cry, not one tear, not now. Later tonight, under the covers. New York City would have a single ruined tower, a monument to the most fucked up single day in anyone's lifetime. She imagined visiting it with Liv, the smoldering memorial, Windows on the World blackened in the sky. Liv would need to find a new job. An episode of *Seinfeld* briefly came to her, George struggling at the unemployment office.

"Mom."

In *Seinfeld*, the Twin Towers don't fall to the ground.

"Mom."

"I see it, Emmanuel."

"Both of them."

The second tower, like the first, collapsed into a colossal cloud of fire and dust. The broadcaster was no longer trying to understand what was happening. Instead, more adjectives: remarkable, catastrophic, horrifying. A coordinated act of terrorism. Mona reached over and turned the TV off.

"Let's not watch this anymore."

An indeterminate time later, her landline rang. She answered it without checking to see the number.

"Mona, are you okay?"

"Yes. I'm home with Emmanuel. How are you? Are you still at the dentist?"

"Feeling sore and like shit but the least of my problems. I'm heading your way now."

"When I saw the second plane hit, I fled."

"Thank God you got out. They're saying lower Manhattan is just covered in dust clouds. It's unbelievable. All of it. I thought I had seen it all, genuinely. JFK assassinated. King assassinated. I remember the end of World War II. Sixty years, and I thought I had seen enough."

"I don't know what this is."

"Terrorism is the only word. Every three seconds, on the radio. I'm trying to see what intel I can get. It probably won't be much. No one knows anything."

"It's a war, then."

"A war, yes. If this isn't a war, a war will come out of this. I'm near the exit now. I'll be there in a few minutes."

"Stay on the phone until you're here, Saul. Please."

"Okay, I will. How is Emmanuel doing?"

"He's shocked. I turned the TV off. We're just here. I'm figuring out what I should do, if I should bring him to a friend's house or keep him here."

"It might be better if he's with other people too. I don't know. I'll be there soon, though. We'll figure this out together."

He came into the apartment in his shirtsleeves and tie. They hugged tightly and he kissed her. Emmanuel came running to him, hugging him. In the corner of the living room, the TV was a dark mirror, their merging forms bent in the glass.

"Are the Yankees going to get to play tonight?" Emmanuel asked him. "I really want to watch."

"I think they may cancel baseball until they figure out what exactly happened."

"We saw what happened."

"I mean who did it. It's going to be a very confusing and scary time, Emmanuel, but your mom and I are here for you, okay? We're right here. We aren't going anywhere."

They went outside together for a walk. Holding hands, they moved gingerly, dazed in the sunlight. She felt like a mannequin come to life, her legs uncharacteristically stiff, Emmanuel shuffling between them. They walked down the long stone steps to the highway overpass, which would take them to the waterfront promenade. By now, Liv would have gotten out. There were people who ran down the stairs before the Towers fell. She would run ahead of Grayson, the older man huffing, smoke choking but failing to kill him. They would emerge covered in ash or just tired and pale, elegant still, marching out into a brigade of firefighters and police dispatched from the outer boroughs to save their lives. At some point, Liv would call. Her cellphone was likely dead. Before getting home, she would have to stop in to the hospital. Doctors would check her vitals, ask about smoke inhalation, feed her and dress wounds. The process could take all day.

A titanic funnel of smoke trailed above them. It had come impossibly far, from the crater in Manhattan. When Mona saw the smoke, free now from her television screen and dominating Brooklyn sky, she could understand that this was not merely a historic day. It would be a day that triggered a new timeline entirely, a divergence that would haunt them all until they died. She was living and breathing through a pivot point. Kennedy's death had been one. Then, she had been a befuddled ninth grader, looking on as her social studies teacher sobbed into a napkin. A man, though—even an American president—was not one of the tallest structures in the world. His death did not mean thousands of others could be dead too.

"My office is definitely gone," Saul said flatly as they stood together on the promenade, one group of many who had come, absent any ideas, to stare at the cloud over Manhattan.

"It's possible it stood up in the wreckage."

"No."

"I should call Liv again."

"Yes. Give her a ring. I'm sure she's with Grayson."

Mona listened to the voicemail again. Was it possible Saul believed with the utmost certainty that his office had been annihilated and Liv and Grayson were alive? Could both ideas be held together? She was seized with the notion that Saul's office must be preserved for the two of them to be living and if the collapsing towers had flattened Saul's new World Trade Center perch then it was possible she would have to confront a probability she was not yet ready for, that seemed less tragic than beyond the realm of belief altogether—Liv *not* being alive. She was running one of the most famous restaurants in the fucking world. She was dating one of New York's most eligible bachelors. Saul was going to meet him for a job at the Port Authority. The meeting was still on. They just couldn't do it at the Trade Center.

"Where do you think your meeting with Grayson will be? If you each don't have your offices?"

"You know, I have no idea. They'll probably set up a temporary office somewhere. I just don't know where. All of this is bewildering."

"I don't think we'll have school tomorrow," Emmanuel said quietly.

"You can stay home no matter what," Mona said.

Just a few hours ago, she was getting ready to photograph a primary. Saul was having a tooth pulled. Emmanuel was in school, another Tuesday. When did another Tuesday become *the* Tuesday? When was history wrenched? Who dared to insert themselves into the course of events? Who could? She was still waiting for the second wave. Military planes traced the sky. She was looking for bombs, the death from above. There was nowhere to be safe. Not out here, among the crowds leaning over the promenade railing, their necks outstretched toward the great cloud of smoke.

"Has the *News* been bothering you?" Saul asked.

"No. And if they do, I'll them to go fuck themselves. Particularly my desk editor."

"Yeah. Don't go back into the city. Not now. It doesn't look good."

"This still feels like a dream."

"I remember reading something about the samurai, how they said life was the dream and death its awakening. I almost understood. Today is one of those days where you see the logic."

"I don't feel awake. I don't at all."

Emmanuel, they saw, had begun to cry. He was nearly silent, straining to suck tears back into his body. He appeared smaller, curled inward, his head pitched toward the ground. He was hoping they wouldn't see him.

She put her arm around him, not saying anything. Saul rubbed his back. Until now, the words would always find their way to her, language unfurled when it needed to be and put to use in calming him. She believed in the brightness of the future. She believed she could protect him. This belief informed every interaction, every pep talk, the readings of history before bed. Through bloodshed, progress was always perceptible. The Nazis were defeated. The Civil Rights movement overcame Jim Crow. Women's liberation beat back sexism. At the end of the day, a lesson.

What struck her was how absent of lessons this day was. There was a crater of smoke and fire and death, unknown bodies charred and crushed.

She told Emmanuel it was okay to cry.

13

Watching a terrorist attack unfold in a dentist's office had not been Saul's vision of the future. As a child, he imagined his middle age would be spent on Mars or on one of Jupiter's moons, the old inadequacies of Earth-life excised for good. If the planets couldn't promise utopia, they offered advancement—existence formulated without the burden of history, laws and technology borne from computer-fired logic, not the sins of flesh-genocide. As an old man, that was where he believed he would be. There would be towering cities of glass.

Instead, he was watching the TV in the waxen waiting room, the *Times* sprawled on his lap.

It was the second plane that did it. He figured this was true for everyone. One was an accident, two was a war. In news, they said three makes a trend. In the world of flesh and ruin, it only took two. He watched with the rest of the office, a knobby older woman in a shawl and a bald, spheroid man who kept picking at the skin between his fingers. The receptionist, who chewed her gum loudly, strained over her desk to watch the screen, like a fan reaching for a ball down the right field line.

Saul had to piss. This was part of the indignity of aging, one he discovered for the first time in his late fifties. Every hour or so, he had to go to the bathroom. Time humbled and broke; time stole his bladder. It was a burning he couldn't fight away. In the tiny stall, he unleashed a torrent and sighed. In the moment, he was happy to only think of the relief of a bathroom visit. Terrorists couldn't get him there.

But he hadn't seen the second tower get hit on TV. By then, he had been called in, the comely dental hygienist spraying his mouth and making him rinse. As far as he knew, one plane had accidentally struck one tower. It was Dr. Lipmann, of all people, who emerged with the news. "It looks like a second plane hit. This looks like a doozy." He was a fellow Jew with a profusion of gray curls sprouting from his otherwise bald skull. He had grown up in Flatbush and now pulled for the Mets, like Saul. Dentists were Jewish car mechanics, Saul's father always said, and he was sure Dr. Lipmann would agree with this opinion too if he didn't find it so insulting to the profession. Saul wondered if they should proceed. If America was under attack, was now the time to lose a tooth?

"We'll forge on," Dr. Lipmann said, as if he reading his mind. "Nowhere safer than a dentist's office, right? They can't fly an airplane through a two-story medical office."

Later, Saul would find out he was the last patient of the day. The gravity of the situation had seemed to sink in for Dr. Lipmann when the procedure was through. America would not be a place for ordinary dental visits anymore. He apologized to the spheroid man and the shawled woman, as well as another younger man who was sitting in the waiting room and thumbing through a two-month-old *Sports Illustrated*. Dr. Lipmann clenched Saul's hand. "I'll be seeing you soon."

Saul rushed to his car to turn on the radio. The updates were ludicrous, dispatches from parallel dimensions. The Twin Towers had *collapsed*. Two of the tallest buildings humanity had ever known, erased from existence. It was like being told extraterrestrials had teleported away the Great Wall of China and Mount Rushmore. His motherfucking office. It took him a minute to comprehend the mass death. There was no way everyone survived. Two buildings tumble into downtown Manhattan. The buildings, he had been told, were burning before collapse. People were trapped inside. His first call was to Mona, his second to Felicia. Felicia was at home, watching all of it. She updated him with precision. The South Tower collapsed first, at 9:59. She had looked at the clock. The North Tower was second, at 10:28. Saul couldn't understand how it happened so quickly. Felicia said the buildings got hot, the steel melted, they crumbled. But *how*, Saul asked. Having not seen it, he couldn't fathom such a cataclysm with no frame of reference, no memory. This wasn't an assassination, a bomb going off on a plane, an ill-conceived military invasion of a foreign land.

Two megaliths, collapsed into dust.

He drove on, dizzy. After Mona and Felica, he called Izzy Locker, who worked in Harlem running his real estate company. Izzy had left his office. He tried him at home, in Westchester. The cleaning woman answered and said Mr. Locker would be on his way. He then tried Sonny Cannon in his Maryland suburb. He was surprised, for some reason, to hear Sonny's voice.

"This is war," Sonny told him.

"Against who?"

"They're fingering Al-Qaeda. We've known about them for years. We dropped our guard. Now we go get them back."

"What does that mean, get them back?"

"What do you think, Saul? It's the business of our world."

"It's a bad idea."

"It's a bad idea to suffer the worst terrorist attack in modern history on your own soil."

"We can't be rash."

"Don't confuse rashness with the instinct of empire. The sun has been setting on us for a long time. This is proof of our weakness, our decadence. Do you know, the minute the second plane hit, I turned to my wife and said, *these buildings will collapse.* I felt it on an atomic level. My body was telling me. You must have felt it too."

"I was getting my tooth pulled."

"I remember you told me you were going for an interview."

"Grayson Moegenborg's office, on the seventieth floor."

"You could have been there, then."

"He might be dead."

"If he didn't get out."

"He takes his breakfasts at Windows on the World. Mona's friend, his girlfriend, works there."

"The loss is staggering."

"That's one word."

"It's hard to contemplate. That's why retribution will be swift."

After he spent the day with Mona and Emmanuel, walking along the water and watching with a mixture of wonder, confusion, and horror at the smoke cloud downtown, he returned to Long Island, where Felicia was in her wheelchair, watching the cable TV coverage of what would be called, because of the random date, the September 11th attacks. It hadn't occurred to him it was September 11th. Dates held little significance. Had CNN told him it was September 9th or September 4th, he would have readily believed them. 9/11, like 9-1-1, the two 1's erect like the Towers felled. Perhaps it wasn't a coincidence at all. He knew Felicia had been watching the TV continuously since the early morning, having risen only to go to the bathroom and retrieve water and fruit from the refrigerator.

"What have you learned?" he asked her in the quasi-dark, the screen's pale flickering illuminating their skin. She had left on the air-conditioner and there was an unsettling hum in the walls that made him want to stand up and ferret out the source.

"They expect, with the airplanes, thousands dead."

"Jesus."

"There are calls for retaliation."

If people like Sonny were calling for war, there'd be war.

His sleep that night was blank. His eyelids closed like coffin lids. He never slept much these days and usually awoke when it was still dark. No dreams came for him. When it was September 12th, he almost expected the Twin Towers to be recomposed in the sky, along with his spacious office stuffed with tchotchkes of a career well-lived. He was awaiting Grayson's call. The official order was to stay home and wait but he wasn't going to do that. He would get in his car and drive and see what happened.

Felicia asked where he was going. He said, earnestly, he had no idea. He needed to clear his head.

"Herb wants to have us over for dinner later," she said.

He drove to Brooklyn. All public schools were closed. On the radio, the talk had turned to terror. It was the language of the wounded and the aggrieved, the dark turn he had feared. A call-in news show affirmed broad cries for blood. The idea was simple: whoever did this would learn the pain of what it was. In successive calls, the ordinary people were learning a new map. Iraq. Afghanistan. Saudi Arabia. For most, they had existed as distant smudges on unreadable charts, outposts of sand and despair, unworthy of contemplation. Now they would be staging grounds for retribution. One caller said his brother was a firefighter who was caught in the collapse. They hadn't found his body but he was sure he was dead. *I want the savages who did this choking on their own blood.* His voice was shaking. *My brother loved this country.* Old men spoke of wanting to sign up for the military. They would fight alongside their sons. This would be a collective sacrifice like none other. America was not just a simple place to be defended. It was an idea, ineffable and mystical, a life-force.

He sat with Emmanuel in Mona's living room, going over his baseball card collection. Here's Paul O'Neill with the Reds. Here's Tino Martinez with the Mariners. He had game-used bat and jersey cards. Juan Gonzalez. A Don Mattingly throwback. They were like talismans of a lost age, when airplanes weren't hijacked and flown into office buildings. When war was safely buried in a newspaper.

"I think we're going to be at war," Emmanuel said.

"I don't know. It's a very complicated, strange time. Like nothing I can remember. But I don't want you to be scared."

"Are they coming back?"

"Who?"

"The people who flew the planes into the Twin Towers."

"I think we will be okay. There's a lot of security now."

"But there wasn't before?"

"Not enough, no."

As he bent over to watch his son slide cards in and out of plastic, he remembered when Tad was the same age, a slender, darker-haired version of Emmanuel, his smile fleeting. Tad did not talk to him or anyone. He carried on conversations in his own head—at least, this was what Saul imagined for his son, a rich and inaccessible interior life. He could be anywhere in the country. He could be dying, or dead. A small panic seized him: he would have no idea if Tad dropped dead tomorrow. The local police would not know of any relatives to contact. Tad wasn't talking to Lenore either. They would throw his body in an unmarked grave. Every victim of a terrorist attack would be memorialized and canonized; there would be newspaper obituaries and ceremonies and museums and maybe a made-for-TV movie. Tad Plotz would have none of that. He would pass from the planet as if he had never been here in the first place. And when Saul died, so too would go Tad's memory. All traces of Tad only existed in his head and in the photographs left behind in the Roslyn house. That house, at some point, would be sold off and another family would arrive to impose their own memories on the walls and then Tad would not even be a phantom because the implication of a phantom is the act of haunting and what would Tad, the exile, haunt?

Emmanuel decided to watch cartoons and Mona said she wanted to take a walk.

"I'm going to be with mom a few minutes, is that okay?"

"Sure, dad."

They circled the block, passing the legion of co-ops. Mona turned to him, a light tremor in her voice.

"I still haven't heard from Liv."

"It's possible she's still—"

"I've been calling hospitals."

"Everyone is pretty deluged. She may be in one of them, information gets mixed up."

"That's the thing. The hospitals aren't full at all. There aren't any *survivors*, Saul. You're either like us, here and alive, or you're dead."

"A lot of people are missing. They haven't declared a lot of people dead."

She had turned from him, her bottom lip tight, as if she were suppressing a small explosion in her throat. He wanted to hold her but knew that wasn't what one did with Mona, hug her and rock her and coddle her. She was not that kind of person. His hands dangled limply at his sides and he shoved them in his pockets, unsure of what else he could do.

"We'll see."

When his parents had died, he knew immediately. With Liv and Grayson, if the worst were true, they would never have bodies. There would never be a definitively understood moment of death. He didn't know what to do with this, how to forge onward without this finality. He also didn't know how to tell Mona he agreed with her. It was a formality. In lower Manhattan, missing persons posters had begun to appear near what they were calling Ground Zero. People were begging for information, for hope, the photographs staring out blankly from fluttering paper. It was as if it could be possible for hundreds of dazed, dust-covered people to be wandering the narrow crooks of city streets, begging to be found. Still, he felt the impulse to make a poster himself. One could confer the possibility of survival. Liv and Grayson, buried in rubble, broken breaths in a shattered darkness. Liv and Grayson, anything but dead.

He was told to report to 26 Federal Plaza, where his old office used to be. His particular division would be working across the street out of the federal courthouse on most days, from spare office space there. The directives came with certainty no one could possess. Over cups of coffee in conference rooms of sickly light, they contemplated their fates, when the next attack would be, whether the city would survive into 2002. People talked about living in bunkers. Threats were made to retire, move out of the city altogether, buy a condo in Miami where terrorists would never go. Nobody would bomb a beach, was one consensus. Another was that a second landmark was next, Empire State Building or Yankee Stadium. Anywhere with crowds, lives to ruin. Though it was generally understood you were supposed to go to the stairwell if you wanted to smoke, the men were all smoking, lighting cigarettes with impunity. He eventually joined in, slurping black coffee and puffing from a pack of Marlboros he bought from one of the corner stands that had opened up against all logic.

He tried to spend as much time with Mona and Emmanuel as possible. This meant, in turn, spending as little time with Felicia as possible. There was no way to resolve this paradox and he wasn't sure, if he had been granted the extra-dimensional powers to do it, he would. Felicia didn't seem to have any great desire for his presence anyway, as far as he could tell. She either watched TV or called for the paratransit service to take her to one of her friends' houses nearby, where she played mahjong, as their mothers all did, and watched more TV. There were times he wanted to earnestly tell her where he was, what he was doing. *I have a family with another woman. I have a son.* He felt more of a catch in his throat when trying to verbalize the existence of a son. It didn't seem fair, still, he had gotten the second chance. Both Tad and the dead didn't answer letters or phone calls. At least a dead child had a gravesite.

Unlike Felicia, he had been given a second chance. It was a blessing for one of the gravest of transgressions. No bad deed goes unrewarded. If she knew, what would she do?

It was still beyond his imagination.

14

Emmanuel came to the tennis court every Saturday, looking forward to the time he could walk off the court and eat lunch.

Sundays were his mom's time for games with her friends but Saturdays, through an unspoken agreement that came shortly after the attacks, were for him. They started in September, when the smoke cloud still trailed across the sky.

"Stay on your toes," mom said, smacking forehands at his stomach. "Stay on the balls of your feet. Don't be flat-footed. Let's go."

They would play for one hour, drills followed by singles, her demands growing with each successive trip. She had invested lessons in him and wanted him to be good, to enjoy the game as much as she did. "You can play this for the rest of your life," she said. Tennis wasn't just a game. It was an entrée into another kind of existence, one of physical power and social grace. He had seen her trophies, all jammed into various shelves in her bedroom closet, tucked away as if she considered such dominance to be an embarrassment of her past. But his mom, he later realized, was proud—she just felt no particular need to prove herself through gleaming gold plastic. The proof of victory could be found each week on the tennis court, against the men and women who tried and failed to beat her at singles and doubles.

He wasn't sure how he felt about tennis. Thanks to the lessons his mom paid for, he was an adequate player for his age, with the ability to hit a hard serve and backhand. He was being signed up for tournaments. It seemed, when he played against his mom, her goal was to make him good enough to defeat her at full strength. Each week, he tried. Each week, through her canniness or raw strength, he failed.

When he didn't run after a ball—when he flagged, his breath short, sweat stinging his eyes—she yelled across the court. "Let's go, let's go! Pick it up or I'm going home!"

Yes, please, let's go home. But saying that would only set her off. His mom loved him, she had never hit him, but her temper was a real, tangible, burning thing. She wasn't to be challenged. He had seen her unleash a tidal blast of *fucks* at men who played on courts without the permits required of every parks player in the spring and summer, men who refused to leave when she presented her own permit. They were, she typically said with derision, *Russians* who preferred *anarchy*, with no respect for the American rule of law. If he didn't want to be a professional tennis player, she said, he could always be a lawyer like his father. *You don't have to practice. You can just have the degree. It's a very honorable thing.*

They talked about everything except what happened. Once he had made the mistake of asking about her friend Liv, whom he liked to see whenever she dropped by their apartment for coffee before heading off with his mom to the movies or dinner or somewhere only adult friends went. Liv didn't have children of her own and he thought of her as an aunt, an extension of his minuscule family unit. They had visited her at Windows on the World, where he could race to the windows and gaze out onto the vastness of the cityscape and forget who he was, where he had come from. Up there, he was a creature of the sky, without body and the wants that came with it, and he could feel closer to whatever it was that lay beyond the Earth, the limitless, pain-free depths of outer space. Liv had told him she liked staring out the window too.

"It's a marvelous view," she told him once. "I like to sit here and look and think about all the people who weren't lucky enough to get to see it."

"What do you mean?"

"For most of human history, we could never go so high in the sky. It was all left to imagination. We're in a place so many millions of people never got to go. These towers are probably going to stand a thousand years. Our descendants, Emmanuel, will be coming up here too."

Mom never told him Liv died. When he asked about her after the attacks, she said they were waiting to see what happened. *There's nothing else to discuss.* And then they stopped talking about her. In late September, he saw she had left the *New York Times* turned to the obituary page, and while she went to take a shower, he began to peruse it. He had grown more curious about the content of newspapers after the attacks, cognizant that whatever had been printed on the page had a profound bearing on the country he had been born into and would probably die in as well. No other news existed except the attacks. What had happened, who did it, who had died. President George W. Bush on the front page, his face pinched and grim. Headlines were bolded, blocked, shouting to him.

The obituary page was more muted.

Grayson Moegenborg, Executive Director of Bistate Authority and New York Socialite, 61.

He had remembered meeting a man named Grayson at his mom's birthday party, with thick graying hair and blue eyes. He resembled, more than George Bush, a president. As he read the obituary, he began to understand why the newspaper had been left open.

. . . died in the Sept. 11 collapse of the Twin Towers.

. . . Mr. Moegenborg's office had been on the 70th floor of 1 World Trade Center, which was the first tower to be hit by a hijacked airplane and the second to collapse. Mr. Moegenborg's exact location at the time of his death was not known . . .

. . . In addition to his partner, Olivia Gottlieb, who also died in the collapse of 1 World Trade Center, Mr. Moegenborg is survived by his mother, Abigail, of Manhattan; a brother, Warner, of Darien, C.T.; his

former wife, Ethel Richards Moegenborg of Manhattan; and two sons.

The newspaper was stating plainly what his mom had never said out loud—not to him, at least. He knew she spoke with his dad in hushed tones over the phone and when they went out on walks together. What he was beginning to understand was that his mom only wanted so much of the complexity of adulthood to penetrate his life, though it all, in one form or another, had. They watched the news together. He listened to his teachers. He heard students mutter about "killing ragheads" and "standing up for the flag" and the startling number who were vowing, at eighteen, to go overseas and kill whoever did it, to "rain holy hell" on them. He understood there had been a civilizational rupture and the ground beneath his feet could never be the same. Blood poured into the soil. The Ground Zero crater smoldered like a vast hearth, dark magic at the city's base. He walked to the water almost every night to watch it, his mom pumping ahead.

When she came out of the shower, he had stopped reading. Unthinking, he had closed the newspaper though this, more than anything, would confirm he had read it, taken an interest. He knew Gottlieb was Liv's last name because his mom would say it on the phone, occasionally, in jest. C'mon, Gottlieb. Let's go, Gottlieb. Though he knew this was the job of a newspaper—to be unbiased, objective, true—it unnerved him how dispassionately death could be laid out. They had both died in the most horrible way he could imagine. In fire, smoke, confusion, not knowing what was happening and why. He had lived to learn the facts, terrorists hijacking airplanes, but what did Liv and Grayson believe? That this was a terrible accident? Why there, why then? His dad, he heard, had planned to meet Grayson that day. So it was coincidence that one lived, one died. Luck and timing, as his dad liked to say. He said it with a smile, understanding the cruelty beneath it. We should all have the right to be lucky.

They played tennis. She told him to rush the net, to not be afraid, to stand up with his back straight and volley, volley, volley. She was not a serve and volley player any longer, not in her fifties, but she had been reared on the spectacle of men and women in white dashing across bright grass to stop a return blast at the net, the ball rolling dead and free. "Jimmy Connor's mother," she said, "used to make him stand at the net and she'd knock balls at his head. She did this until he learned how to volley. She didn't care if she knocked his teeth in. But I *do* care about your teeth."

Before he played, she told him to apply copious sunscreen. Drink plenty of water. No soda, no Gatorade, no sugar shit. She worried about where he was going, when he would be back, who he was hanging out with. At the end of the day, she wanted him to catalog the day dutifully, to account for the minutes and hours lived outside her presence. All of it mattered. On the tennis court, it was his time and her time; she could watch him, encourage him, sculpt him. When he flagged, she let him know. For her, he would play.

In the months after Liv's death, he could detect small changes in his mom. She was not one to ever outwardly despair or even acknowledge sadness. Her emotional register, as far as he could tell, offered only joy or rage, the wrath saved for the tennis court and whenever he ran afoul of her rules. But there were junctures, subtle at first, when wrath appeared to win out or, more strangely, despair did reveal itself. For others, it may have been akin to lethargy or a slight disinterest in what had occurred around her—more frequent naps, more resigned sighs, a delicate tremor in her voice. She was still a news photographer. But as he was finishing seventh grade, she talked openly of quitting. She was not someone who complained much. Neither was dad, who had once said, with a smile, his own mother had taught him to "suffer silently," explaining that the children of the Great Depression were taught that emotions could mark you for weakness. "They were so worried about the world falling apart" His mom, a decade younger, didn't have the same sensibility; rather, it was a militant optimism grounded in the idea that if you worked hard enough, opportunities would be forced to present themselves. She never wanted to hear him being negative, putting *himself* down. If the media had created archetypes of the self-questioning, self-defeating Jews, she was a living, breathing rebuttal. His mother questioned nothing.

Except now. Her job was shit, she said. It was time to move on, time to quit. She talked to herself out loud so he would be forced to respond. On the phone, at night, she would talk to her friend Al, who ran an art gallery in Williamsburg. "I need to get out, I need to get out." There was a low-running dread to the spring and summer, his mom's slow-building rage adding a new weight to her interactions with his dad and her friends on the phone and the people at work she had told, in no uncertain terms, to go to hell.

15

High school was still at Bridge Prep because Bridge Prep was a middle school and a high school and there was no reinventing yourself here, in a school with a bureaucracy of alliances and friendships that had been calcifying since the fifth grade.

In the library, as he read a laminated *Time* Magazine, Alan Dencher, who was six-foot-four and weighed, at most, one hundred and eighty pounds, flopped down in front of him and began smiling, one blade-like knee crossed in front of the other. Dencher was in his biology and English classes.

"Who are you taking to the dance, Plotz?" Dencher asked, flashing his teeth at him.

Emmanuel noticed another kid from his biology glass, Landon Saltzman, had sat down in a plush chair next to Dencher. Both were undoubtedly going to the ninth grade dance. Dencher because he had friends, including one who was going to pitch for the varsity baseball team as a freshman, and Saltzman because a girl would want to go with him. He was short and slight but tanned, with blonde highlights and a shockingly luminous smile. He resembled a former child actor now slumming it in a high school. Usually, he traveled in a pack of three or four. It was odd to see him here, in the library, taking a seat next Dencher.

"What?" Emmanuel asked, pretending not to hear, his eyes still on the magazine.

"I said, who are you taking to the dance?"

Emmanuel didn't answer. He stared at the print in an article about how the Democratic Party was trying to win the House back from Republicans. He stared until the text blurred, until the language seemed to disintegrate wholesale on the page, lost in a welter of ink.

"None of your business."

"You aren't taking anyone, I bet, because no one is going with you. Isn't that right?"

He waited for Landon to chime in. Though Dencher periodically targeted him, Landon never had, and he figured this was going to be his introduction to bullying Emmanuel Plotz.

Landon, however, was not speaking at all.

"I'm not going because it's stupid."

"Do you even *like* girls, Emmanuel?"

He continued to stare into the magazine. None of it was visible to him anymore.

"Girls don't like you anyway, so it doesn't really matter, does it? No girl would want to go to the dance with you."

Dencher began to snort, the heat of his laughter reaching Emmanuel's ear. He couldn't see at all. The paper had gone white with his rage and he was swinging his left arm out, clawing at the air until he found Dencher's tie and began tugging as hard as he possibly could. Pulling downward, he turned to face Dencher.

"You fucking loser, let go!"

Another hot surge came up Emmanuel's arm and he dragged Dencher's neck down, pulling until Dencher was able to ball his large hand into a fist and scrape at his jawline. He turned to see the librarian, a small woman with clipped gray hair, rush over and yell at them to break it up. They did, with Dencher snorting, and Emmanuel grabbed at the magazine, fighting back the tingling of tears.

"Both of you, out now."

Dencher brushed past Emmanuel, muttering *you have no friends* and shoving through the double-doors of the front of the library. It was an occurrence so ludicrous yet laden with import; an open declaration, in a library, that he was hated. He wished he could ask Dencher what his original sin had been. He only wanted to get through the month, the year, the life. Since history was his only subject of relative success, he had the vague inclination to study it someday, to write about it, but other than that he had no real ambitions—maybe, if God gave him the strength, to be a professional ballplayer, and have sex someday. He knew he was in a different situation than kids like Moe who were targeted just for being Arab or the Black kids bussed from neighborhoods his mom wouldn't let him visit. He knew he could either be a soldier dying in Iraq or an Iraqi getting killed by an American soldier. All of these ideas he could suspend in his head, almost cherish—aren't I a lucky boy—and still take little solace in, because there would be another Alan Dencher to tromp along and remind him of how, for reasons he couldn't quite understand, he had failed to achieve any kind of standing in the pocket universe that was his life. He was short, weak, and angry. In comic books, people like him were miraculously granted superpowers. Outside comic books, they remained short, weak, and angry.

At lunch, he would hover. He knew that any table he sat at, by definition, could not attract other students. Sitting down first was an invitation to sit alone. Over the course of his middle school years, he had mastered a strategy of waiting, suffering longer lines and less time to eat in exchange for the appearance of lunchtime camaraderie. If four or five kids in his grade grabbed a table, he could join them, sitting just off to the side, allowing room for their actual friends to arrive and create a larger group. He could sit on the periphery and even attempt to make conversation. To an outsider, it would look like he belonged to the group.

It was an unlikely life, he thought. His mom and dad so clearly belonged. Though she cursed it, his mom was a prestigious photographer with her name in the newspaper almost every day. She took photographs of the mayor, movie celebrities, and even once photographed the Pope when he came to New York. Before that, she had taken the first photograph of a famous vigilante named Vengeance. Dad had a high-ranking job in the government. He wasn't sure what exactly he did but he knew he had also met important people, including the former president, Richard Nixon. Dad had his friends, Sonny and Izzy and others from work, and mom still had Al, as well as the people she played tennis with. None of them needed to wait for others to sit down at a lunch table. People would sit by them. What, then, was wrong with him?

In another year, Landon Saltzman, smiling barely, approached Emmanuel after gym and told him he wanted to hang out. *Me*, Emmanuel wanted to blurt out. *What do you want with me?*

Landon would want a lot.

16

Tad was dreaming as the world burned. He was walking on a shrouded path, the sky calm and silent, certain there was someone right behind him.

When he woke, it was afternoon. Without a television or even a transistor radio, he had no sense of what the events were, and never needed one. The manufactured churn of a frail society meant little as long as Chiu paid him, as long as his bicycle functioned.

Outside, he understood there had been a change. People were clustered together on sidewalks, whispering to one another. In storefronts, televisions were tuned to the news in unison, hissing behind glass. He walked carefully, passing through and around conversations, their fear pressing upon him. He knew he had to find Chiu.

Inside Blue Star, a lone bearded man against the window ate from a bag of spare ribs. He wanted the man gone. Behind the cash register was an employee he didn't recognize. For certain roles, Chiu preferred near-constant turnover, a rush of faces to keep the days interesting and unstable. This was not true of his deliverymen.

"Tad," Wilbur Chiu said from behind the kitchen, unseen.

He approached the register. The cashier, who was no older than twenty-two, sighed and drew backward. He seemed to know Tad was not going to order anything. Chiu emerged, holding a can of Coke, a cigarette dangling from his lips. He face looked flushed, as if he had just been laughing.

"Mr. Chiu, what happened?"

Chiu approached and the young cashier slunk backward, acknowledging he had no more role to play here. The bearded man sucked on his bone, readying to gnaw on marrow. Duck sauce splashed on the loose paper below his plate.

"You just woke up," Chiu said.

"I did. I was dreaming all morning."

"The twenty-first century arrived today."

"I don't understand."

"In succession, commercial airliners flew into the Twin Towers. Each airliner was hijacked and each tower toppled. It was a remarkable thing. I am still grasping for words to render it to you."

"It's difficult to believe."

"Thousands are likely dead. The airplanes were Boeing 767's. The physics of it are difficult. The spectacle was greater than I imagined, though ultimately less severe."

"Less severe?"

"To what was inflicted before. America is an inflictor nation. I make no judgments. Were I native—a white man, Anglo-European, of sturdy Christian faith—I would likely demonstrate my might in a similar way. What else is there? How does a giant not trod upon the Earth? How can one ask a god to leave peacefully? Never has a nation been invested with such ability to terminate life. Two atomic bombs were dropped on two cities, Tad. This is not a grievance, I am not Japanese and I can't say I care for the people. I merely look at yesterday and today. In some sense, this new destruction isn't impressive enough."

"You see it as retribution for 1945?"

"History is not a trade—it is not sports, nor is it physics. We don't swap genocide for a player to be named later. We simply have events, a ceaseless procession of events. We have the context of said events. It is not about retribution. It is about what happened then, and now."

"As one continuous thread, no beginning or end? I'm still trying to understand, Mr. Chiu."

"What I can say is it brings no comfort to anyone today that more devastation has visited a modern civilization before. Memory is limiting. Pain and understanding is finite. I experienced horror too. I did not want see the Towers fall. There was a symmetry to their existence that I had come to define myself against. There is a comfort to that. I did not want mass death."

"Who did it?"

"Do you think it matters?"

"They will need to be punished, I think."

"I used to think that way too."

Tad's throat felt like a closed fist. He attempted language and then thought better of it. Chiu had more to say.

"Like you, I used to view history as a simple exchange: tit for tat, eye for an eye, action and reaction."

"Do they know who did it?"

"Self-described terrorists, sowing terror."

"Nation of origin?"

"Nationality is the most durable myth."

"If they destroyed both towers—"

"A hijacked airplane was flown into the Pentagon as well."

"There will need to be justice, then."

"A meting out of justice."

"Yes."

"You want the scene, don't you?"

"I don't understand."

"These men will be smoked out over deserts, in the crooks of mountains. They will be waiting, perhaps, in caverns. In the darkness, they will greet death. The plotting is done. The deed is done. The execution stage has passed. They will have nothing but time, among their rifles and machinery. In will come the Americans, night avengers. Rat-a-tat-tat. Bodies leaking blood."

"Rat-a-tat-tat. I like how you say that. It might have to happen, yes."

"You perceive the future like the past."

"It's my only frame of reference."

"Are you angry for the country?"

"Can I see the footage?"

"After each commercial break, if they still permit commercials. Follow me."

Chiu led him to the back room, his de facto office. A small television was perched on a desk, flickering with images. The room, poorly lit with a single lightbulb, had peeling walls, a single poster of the New York City subway system pasted just above the desk. Chiu, as far as he knew, drove everywhere and did not ride the subway.

There were two folding chairs. Tad took one, Chiu the other. The television was tuned to CNN. Tad couldn't remember the last time he watched a news broadcast. The conventions were familiar, like memories imprinted from birth. The scroll of text, the men and women adorned in make-up and starched clothing, their expressions ornamental. They were talking. And then he saw. One plane, then two. A quick cut from the burning to the collapse, time condensed for a viewer who had already entered the future. Billions of people experienced what he never would, a hope and a belief that the Twin Towers would simply crackle and burn in the sky, smoking indefinitely, a fire in the clouds waiting to be put out by rain. He tried to imagine what this was like.

"When they were first hit, did you believe they would collapse?" he asked Chiu.

"I believed nothing."

"You felt the events were independent of your longing."

"To an extent. I was a watcher, like everyone else. What I will guess is that your desire for retribution will not leave you."

"I still feel it."

"If you were told the terrorist organization responsible, what would change?"

"I would know what to do next."

"You would. You would have specificity. Your anger and fear, sharpened. But it's useless."

"Longing will always have use."

"You and millions of others believe this. I understand. Since this is an important day, a life-changing day, I want to show you something."

Chiu bent over and put his hand in his pocket. He pulled out a small brass key and inserted it slowly into a compartment of his desk. He opened it, pulling out a drawer with an array of objects and utilities: staples, rubber bands, pens, rolled paper, electric wires, and an oxidized crucifix. Chiu reached deeper, his hand in the back of the drawer, out of view. He pulled out what appeared to be a piece of faded white cloth and held it up to the light.

"What is this?"

Chiu took off his glasses. The cloth had two small holes that stretched as he pulled it over his head. It was, as far as Tad could tell, a mask of some kind.

Through the cloth, Chiu seemed to be smiling.

"You must know it now."

He did. He had seen the photo too many times not to know, the photo taken by Mona Glass of the *Daily Raider*. The mask was just as it was in the very first photo, the one that seized the attention of a city. What he was straining to remember were the contours of that face beneath the mask in the photograph.

"Shit."

Chiu stood up.

"You are the first person to see this mask in some time."

"Are you? Are you him?"

"Am I him, he asks."

"Wilbur Chiu, Vengeance."

"I had been him. No one is now."

"Why are you showing this to me?"

"I want to say you are deserving."

"On a day like this. I'm deserving it now."

"The day felt right. I've been waiting and it felt right."

Chiu sat back down. The mask remained on his face.

"I want to know what Vengeance would do."

"You want to know how Vengeance would function in the new age of terror?"

Tad suddenly felt weak, his head lolling to the side. The television was still playing. Each minute, he could relive the explosion and collapse anew. A rebirth in hell.

"I don't know, exactly, what I want to know. I suppose I'm confused."

"A Chinaman cannot be a masked crusader."

"No, it's not that."

"Of course. That was a joke." And then Chiu was laughing.

"You were him when you gave that interview to the *Raider*. You were him for the decapitation of Marius Shantz."

"I was him for all interviews and conquests."

"And then you disappeared. No one found you."

"They were close. They weren't close. Crimes do not get readily solved. We watch police procedurals and imagine they do. As we see today, the power of the industrialized state can be overstated. A century of hegemony could not save America from today—a century of technological advancement, impenetrable wealth, and occasional brilliance. So what would the New York Police Department do? I left clues. It was the honorable thing to do."

"The song."

"London Bridge is falling down."

"What did it mean?"

"It had to do with a name. It was a connection I was hoping they would make."

"It was never made."

"Most aren't."

Tad's eyes drifted to the television.

"You stopped at some point."

"It had served its purpose."

"You, well—you talk differently now."

"Have you paid attention to human language? English in particular. It's the most nimble, malleable thing, and defines so much of who we are to everyone else. And though the inner life is richer than the outer life, the inner life is only seen by one. There is but one inner language, one running monologue that shuts off at death. We can always talk differently. The rest cannot be altered so easily."

Chiu began to remove the mask. His flesh was brighter in the overhead bulb than Tad remembered, as if it had been buffed and shined beneath the mask while he spoke. He was like a man newly escaped, his eyes wide and alive, the cloth curled in his large, strange fingers. He held it out to Tad.

"Take it."

"And what?"

"It's yours."

"It can't be mine."

"It is."

"Tell me why you stopped."

"I stopped because it was time. I had fought crime and understood, in the process, how limiting it was."

"Some thought you were a hero."

"You are a hero when you deliver someone their steaming hot pork dumplings."

"I don't see why you limited yourself. Marius Shantz was an abomination. Judge, jury, police—they were useless. He would've raped and raped, if you hadn't gotten there first, if you hadn't realized what you were capable of first."

"Tad, it was limiting because I learned the lesson you have yet to learn. I was a police officer, first, you understand. The newspapers properly speculated on that, based on the interview I gave. I was police and then I was beyond the police. In each role, each evolution, I believed punishment was enough. Now I am gifting you this mask. Here is what I once believed: that I was necessary. That without my young body plunged into darkness, there wasn't a purpose for life. I was the coordinate at which all relevant forces met. Muggers irked me. In 1969, I was held at gunpoint. As I contemplated whether I was going to die, I considered if there would have been a way to save myself, had I known I would soon have a gun to my skull. I decided, being young, a mask would save me. There was a limitation to my identity. I was prepared, in that moment, to abandon myself and never return. Why this flesh sack? Why Chiu? *Hey yellow man,* they used to say in the schoolyard. *Why are you yellow.* I do not want to make this about race, necessarily, because I believe my decisions would have been made regardless. I do. But what race is a mask?"

"What race?"

"Yes."

"I don't know."

"That's an answer. Beneath it, we are anyone. When you are young, that is liberation. You are young enough, Tad. You can believe that. For some, the loss of identity is a terror. For others, it's everything."

"Were you ever afraid?"

"On the streets? Not then. I believed, wholly, in the project. And this belief sharpened my sense of self. Only others would experience terror. I would rise beyond it. I could even subsume it."

"I read all the newspaper articles about you. Every article."

"I was a figment of imaginations, a fraction of a myth. You can be that too. Put it on."

Tad held the mask. He raised it, hesitating just before his face. It had a smell like pavement after rainfall. Chiu was smiling at him and he decided all he could do was stretch the cloth and pull it over his skull, feeling its tightness, the way it constricted his skin. He had never, for all he had done, wore a mask. Not for Halloween, not for winter storms.

It was new skin.

"How do you feel?"

"I don't know."

"Think about it. It's yours."

He knew, already, something had been decided.

17

"What do I do?" Mona asked Saul one day. They were sitting on benches across the street from her apartment, gazing out onto the bay at sunset. Tree branches shivered in the wind. It was January, but warm enough. The day before, she had gotten the strangest call from the news desk. She hadn't told anyone yet. In another time, she would have told Liv.

"Do about what?"

"I was going to quit the paper this month. I had planned it out. End of January. Done. And then I get a phone call."

"I support quitting one hundred percent, whatever you want to do. What was the call about?"

Saul himself was planning, at the end of the year, to retire and take his pension. After Grayson's death, someone else got the Port Authority job and the opportunity was lost, though Saul never framed it that way. They both knew how lucky he was.

"I keep wanting to quit. And then I don't. Now, they have a new assignment for me. We got the oddest tip."

"What was it?"

"Vengeance is back."

"What?"

"Someone is posing as him anyway. There was a kid who was doing a carjacking in Forest Hills. Suddenly he gets clubbed over the head. It was almost midnight, near Austin Street apparently. A witness says a guy in a mask did it. Then, the next day, the graffiti. Just his name, all red, on the side of a building."

"Christ, this again."

"It would be very funny to quit now."

"You're the Vengeance whisperer, so they want you I bet."

"I told myself I would leave the job after Liv and then it didn't happen and now, just when they really need me, it would be good to tell them to fuck off for good."

"Whatever you do, it will be the right decision."

"Why?"

"Because you will have made it."

There were times she had conversations with Liv. They could start while she was jogging or rallying in tennis or just sitting in the car, waiting for Emmanuel at baseball practice. Liv would begin talking to her. Once, Emmanuel had caught her lips moving. "Mom, what's up?" She said it was nothing because it was not what could be explained to a child who didn't know what it was like to have a friend for thirty years. A child of fifteen who had only known death on a television screen. She didn't take him to the funeral. She didn't even tell him it happened. An assumption was made. Usually, if she spoke to Liv, it was to recount incidents and events, how a man had cheated her on the tennis court, the way Saul farted on the couch, the odd slang from one of the new photogs, a twenty-something right out of NYU. She spoke and Liv listened.

Once, she asked Al if he did it too.

"I still hear her laugh," he said.

What she stopped doing was imagining the final moments. For so long, the pit inside of her—the pit, she understood now, that would never close, that existed in stasis, large or small, perpetually there—would make demands, ask her how it was for Liv. Was it fire? Did she suffocate? Did she jump? Liv, who spoke to her on the phone from that beautiful restaurant, waiting for help. Mona believed it was coming. A firefighter, a helicopter. She believed, even after the building collapsed. She believed because she couldn't do anything else.

At the funeral in Garden City, she didn't cry. It was only in the car, driving on the Southern State Parkway, that she began to sob, the tears so gargantuan and strange and unyielding. Her chest heaved, her body rocked. WCBS murmured the traffic report.

By the time she got home, she was done. She took a shower, dried off, and stopped rubbing her eyes, allowing the redness to fade. Emmanuel, back from school, saw her as she had always been. A son couldn't know his mother's sadness.

On Thursday, she shot another Bloomberg press conference, a ribbon cutting for a park in the Bronx. On Friday, on the way to a rally against a planned school co-location, she got a call from the news desk.

"You need to come in. Everyone is getting called into the news-room. It's not good."

Mona drove to the building on West 33rd Street, next to Penn Station. These days, she tried to be there as little as possible. Since she was out on the beat so much, she spent relatively little time talking to *News* staffers, with the exception of Christmas parties and occasional staff meetings. It meant she was not privy to gossip, to rumors true or false. It meant she had really no idea that the all-hands-on-deck staff meeting, for 10 a.m., was to deliver dark news. Staff layoffs were imminent. Human resources would be informing those who would not have jobs.

She learned, an hour later, she would not be on the Vengeance beat because she would be unemployed for the first time since 1974. The *News* bled money. It was now bleeding her. She expected to be numb, vaguely indifferent, but she wasn't. She was angry, she wanted to ball her hand into a fist and hit things, hit them hard. On Monday, she would report nowhere. She was going to quit, yes. Any day, any week, any month. She was going to leave but it was supposed to be when she sure as hell wanted to leave.

"I can't fucking believe this," moaned a reporter from the Queens bureau who was scooping up papers, notebooks, and packages of pens, whirling them into cardboard box. She was sniffling, fighting back tears.

"I know," Mona said, feeling useless.

"Those bastards."

Everyone was a bastard. She wanted, badly, to smoke, to light up in newsrooms like they used to. She wanted to tell them it would be alright, everyone lands on their feet, life is life. When the going gets tough, the tough get going. Instead, she stood stiffly, nearly inanimate. The office seemed to convulse. The layoffs were wide, nearly indiscriminate, targeting young and old. The *Post* was apparently preparing to downsize too. Everyone was. Advertisements didn't show up in newspapers anymore. They went online. She had an AOL account but otherwise couldn't quite fathom the internet, how screen life could substitute for flesh, for the pulse in her body. This was the future, then: people throwing their shit into boxes.

The newspaper would be efficient and nimble for the twenty-first century.

Drinks were planned. Laid off staffers were preparing to commiserate. Meanwhile, a memo to remaining staff went out. Reporters from the *Times* and *Village Voice* had already called to get details. Her desk phone, hardly used, was ringing.

She wanted to call Saul and see her son.

And she wanted to tell Liv what happened.

"You gotta be kidding me," Saul said on the phone.

"Looks like fifty staffers are out."

"Jesus Christ, really."

"That's it."

"You gave them so many years."

"I was going to go, and then they kick me out."

She decided she would have to explain this to Emmanuel. He was fifteen. He had begun to stay out late, make friends—she sensed a transformation, though he was harder to approach, smiling and nodding, monosyllabic when he wanted to be. There was a friend, Landon, who lived in Manhattan. She looked him up in the directory and saw he was Landon Saltzman, son of Murray Saltzman (no mother listed), and he lived on the Upper East Side. A Manhattan boy with money.

"I'm no longer going to be working at the *Daily News*," she told Emmanuel on Saturday, just before she went out for tennis. The two of them hardly played together.

"What happened?"

"They are having some financial issues and I was one of those laid off, honey. But don't worry. We'll be okay. I've been saving. Nothing's going to change and I'll find a new job."

"Dad will help us, right?"

"Of course he will."

No other son of two parents who were happily together would ask such a thing, she believed. She didn't wear a wedding ring. For so long, she assumed this had been enough, to have Saul help raise him and have dinners and family vacations, to do all the work of the nuclear family in order to negate whatever other questions could arise. He had asked once where dad went at night but he hadn't asked since. As far as she could tell, he felt he belonged to an ordinary American family and that was all she could ever want, for him to feel loved. A boy like that would never wonder if his father was going to help the family out.

Her weekdays were inordinately long, as if time had been stretched to its outer limits. Ten a.m. dripped like syrup into eleven. Emmanuel was at school, Saul was at work, and Liv Gottlieb was still dead. At noon, she called Al, who was on a lunch break at the gallery. She was proud of his steady success, the buzz he had been able to generate, his passion for curation matching his desire to create. She was proud of the comfort he had found in his life. He even had a partner, a woman he could marry.

"You'll get something very soon, Mona," he said. "You have a way of making the universe do what you want."

Was this true? If she did, Liv would be with her, having lunch downtown. They would be reminiscing about the wedding she and Grayson finally had, maybe in East Hampton. Liv would be telling her the *News* didn't deserve her, it was a rag, a shitty newspaper that could not last without Mona Glass's photography.

But that wasn't true. The newspaper would churn on until it didn't.

She decided, after a week, she would have Saul look for a federal job for her. Though she knew there had been a tightening there too. His pending retirement conferred both stature and weakness, she sensed. Men twenty years younger than him felt no particular need to pay deference to his experience. At work, he hardly used a computer. He was from an era of smoke breaks and long afternoon telephone calls, a bottle of vodka tucked under the desk for safekeeping. It was good to have, though he didn't drink much.

Another week passed. Saul assured her something would turn up.

"It always does," he said.

Emmanuel always wanted to go out now. This was new. They performed a dance, mother and son, and she didn't like it. He wouldn't say exactly where he was going. She missed scooping him up and putting him on the back of her bicycle to grab chocolate ices and then head to the tennis court. She even missed the chubbier Bar Mitzvah boy. The more questions she asked of Emmanuel, the less he wanted to say.

Where are you going provoked a murderous stare.

Out, he said. To see Landon.

He didn't seem to have a girlfriend. While this would present a complication she wasn't quite prepared to handle and invite a talk she would rather not give, it was also to be expected he soon would. He was at that age. He was curious. He would experiment with his new body. At fifteen, she never told her parents where she was going. But this wasn't the 1960s. Terrorists had obliterated the tallest buildings in the history of New York City. He had a cellphone now and he was sure as hell expected to pick up when she called.

"You can invite Landon over sometime," she said.

"He's not coming to Bay Ridge. It's too far on the train."

Occasionally, she checked Emmanuel's backpack but never found anything, never uncovered evidence at all that he was smoking marijuana or doing something worse. He was happiest, she could tell, talking baseball with Saul. Landon, she hoped, was a baseball fan.

A month later, Saul called with news. It was the middle of the day and she had been batting tennis balls against the cement wall of the handball court. She had already jogged when she woke up and done forty minutes of stretching. Later, she would ride her bike ten or twenty miles, circling Coney Island. As much as she cherished exercise, how her body still hadn't betrayed her at fifty-five, there was a limit to how much of it she could do before she craved something else entirely. A job, a purpose. If she spent a decade resenting the *News*, she was still a person who always had an appointed place to be and she had decided, a month out of work, she wanted to continue being this type of person.

"I think I've got something," Saul said.

It was a job in the press shop of the Department of Housing and Urban Development, in the Federal Building at Foley Square where Saul was again working after losing his Trade Center office. She would work under the press secretary, writing press releases and taking photos on behalf of the federal government to be included in releases. The salary, comparable to her *News* income, would come with a far better health plan. It was too late to contribute significantly to the pension—Saul had built up forty years under a tier that no longer existed—but if she stayed at it until sixty-five, she would have something.

"They'll want you in next week," he said. "The guy you're replacing apparently just quit. Some kind of midlife crisis."

Only death could be a crisis. Otherwise, she surmised, people were weak. She had watched, in one form or another, her friend die live on television. A job wasn't going to crush her. The next day, she woke at 5 a.m. and jogged down an unlit street, her breath hanging in front of her. When she jogged, she sometimes felt like she was suspended above the earth, an ice crystal dangling in delicate air. There was no one behind her and no one in front of her.

18

Saul opened the door of his house to find Felicia at the kitchen table reading the *Wall Street Journal*. A light snow was falling outside. That week, he had started teaching as an adjunct at the New School, lecturing on history and political science. He was officially retired from the federal government and it was invigorating to be in a classroom again.

Other than having to piss all the time and constantly needing his reading glasses, his once perfect vision shot, he didn't feel too bad. Izzy Locker was having issues with his kidneys. Sonny, whom he called once every month, had stents put in his heart. The real difference between being in your sixties and fifties, he believed, was the diminishment of raw energy. He had sex with Mona far less than he used to. He could no longer stay up late. An afternoon at the ballpark with Emmanuel was tiring enough to require a nap. He could no longer rush up five flights of stairs. Memories from fifty years ago were rich and thick, preserved in his mind like microfilm. He knew the starting lineups of the 1951 New York Giants, New York Yankees, and Brooklyn Dodgers. Memories of last week were soupier, liable to drip away altogether.

Felicia sipped her tea and told him to sit down.

"How was your day?" he asked her.

"I have something to tell you, Saul. It's difficult and I need you to listen to me."

He was still wearing his trench coat, slick with melted snow. Rather than wait to stash it in the hallway, he listened to his wife and sat down. She wore a dark sweater and seemed, in the dim chandelier light, to be very slight, as if she could vanish between shadows. He swallowed uneasily, feeling the burn of acid reflux.

"Tell me what's going on."

"I told Lenore already. She supports me."

"That's good to hear. I'm glad she supports you in whatever it is you need supporting in."

"I'm leaving, Saul. I decided. Herb and I, we decided we're going to get married. His wife has been gone a year now. We're moving to Del Ray Beach. I can't deal with New York anymore. Ideally, I'd like to sell the house."

"This is a lot to hear."

"You can't be surprised, can you?"

"Herb fucking Weiner."

"He's a good man, Saul, and he cares. We're almost seventy. Don't we deserve happiness? I see how you look at me. I've always seen how you look at me."

"I do love you, Felicia."

"*I do.* You qualify language around me. You restrict, you hedge, you hold back. I remember, years ago, watching you at a holiday party. Your eyes were so lively. Just about anyone who talked to you—you were a light. You would give anything to the passing stranger. But then you'd turn to me. With those dull, dead eyes. Right now, I see them. You've looked at me that way for thirty years."

"That's not true."

"And your women, Saul. I know you go off. Time isn't accounted for. Who are they? Who is the current one? I used to wonder so much. What do they have to offer you? But I understood when I started seeing Herb. Perhaps you found someone who looks at you the way Herb looks me."

"Felicia, I—"

"We've been so damn miserable."

"This is just, it's sudden."

"Herb has a condo in Del Ray Beach. Someday you can visit us. As I said, ideally, I'd like to sell the house. We can do this amicably."

"We're going to have to get lawyers."

"Yes, there will be things that have to get worked out, especially if there's a house sell."

"It can be fifty-fifty," Saul said.

"We should have done this sooner. I know it and you know it. Why didn't we? I want to say we didn't communicate. Time passes. Time defeats you. A promise is made and then a decade buries it in sand. I thought about it many times. But I'd hear my parents' voices in my head. Divorcing was the ultimate defeat, the ultimate embarrassment. When we grew up, no one did it. Jews, Catholics, no one. You made a decision and you stuck with it. You must have considered it."

"Never, Felicia."

"I don't believe it. This should have happened sooner. I want to sell the house."

"Do you need the money? I can give you something."

"We'll fetch close to a million. I spoke to a realtor friend. I can't come home here anymore and you're not going to want to sit in it anyway. It's enough, this home. Isn't it?"

"It was our home."

"You're sentimental? Really? You were hardly here."

She took another sip of tea. He began to unbutton his coat, shaking it from his shoulder. The melting snow was cold on his pinstriped shirt.

"That's not—well, a lot would happen. Work."

"Wherever you were, Saul, all these years, I hope you were happy."

It had been almost a month since he spoke to Lenore. The last he heard from her, she had found out she was pregnant. He was going to be a grandfather.

"I have to think about where I'll go."

"Take what we get from the house and buy something in the city. You can probably get a condo somewhere. That's what we do now— we acknowledge the crushing emptiness and adjust. You're not going to live here alone. You didn't even like it with me. I'm looking forward to Herb's condo. He has one bedroom, a kitchen, and a balcony overlooking the lake. It's man-made, but so what? I don't need much. The development is new. I'll be there by the end of the month."

"End of the month."

"That's right. Maybe you can stay with one of your friends in the meantime, once the house is sold. Until then, come and go as you please. I'm not angry, Saul. I'm too old to be angry."

He almost wanted to tell her. How would she react? Sipping her tea, her hands folded on her newspaper, she had the disposition of a sage, dispensing wisdom from an occluded space. *My son is sixteen, Felicia. He looks a little like me but more like Mona Glass, a woman you've still never met.* He could lay it all out now. In 1989, he made a mistake. There wasn't supposed to be a pregnancy and he tried to stop it and then, finally, he understood it was the best thing to ever happen to him. His life with Mona was always, somehow, building to this baby. From the moment he saw her as a sophomore, hand under her chin, a little pencil with bite marks rolling off the desk.

He closed his mouth and let her read the newspaper. After a minute, he cleared his throat.

"I'll look up a lawyer," he said.

19

When Emmanuel reached the front of his apartment building, he noticed his dad's car parked across the street. This was odd because he usually didn't come on Saturday unannounced. Having dad on a weekend was a special occasion, for vacations and birthday parties and unique day trips. If it was a peculiar aspect of his parenting, Emmanuel didn't talk about it. He knew his mom didn't like referencing it either.

He wondered if his dad was going to take them all out to lunch or maybe to the museum. He liked going with his dad to history museums, dozing in the backseat as the car took them to Manhattan, sports talk radio the background beat to their conversations.

As he approached the front door, he heard a strange sound. It was yelling, but not his mom on the phone, telling off one of her tennis friends. He heard two voices and one of them, he immediately knew, was his dad's. His instinct was to grab the knob and pull the door open and ask what exactly was going on, why his mom and dad were yelling at each other on a Saturday morning. If he came in the apartment, he knew they would stop.

He pressed his ear to the door and listened.

"You have some nerve coming here like this."

"Some nerve? I can't believe I'm hearing this. Really, from you. This is supposed to be one of the happiest days of our lives."

"You expect me to drop everything now and rearrange my life

for you?"

"I don't understand why you're so angry, I really don't."

"You don't understand?"

"No, I really don't."

"You're so fucking thick sometimes."

"Me? Okay."

"You call me one day and expect me, on a dime, to change everything for you because now it's so convenient for you? Did you think about your son?"

"He wants to live with his father! Ask him!"

Ask me? Emmanuel thought.

"Where is all your stuff going to go? Thirty years of shit, huh?"

"Stuff? We'll figure it out!"

"It's so easy for you. It always is. You could have done this years ago and you chose not to. You never did it."

"So that's what this is about. That's it. Mona, c'mon. You know it was complicated. You can't throw that in my face. I'm here! That's what matters. I'm here."

"What if she wasn't leaving you?"

"What? I'm not going to do a counterfactual here. She's leaving and the house is being sold and I'm *free*, Mona, for us. We can do it. We can get married."

"Don't say that in this house."

"Don't say what we always wanted to do?"

"Maybe I wanted to marry you at forty. Maybe at fifty. Maybe we don't all exist on Saul Plotz's timelines, on his whims, maybe, maybe—fuck, maybe we aren't all supporting characters in his grand little life. I made peace, maybe, with what we are. Or . . . or . . ." And he heard his mother sputter in a way he never had before. ". . . I just see you, after all this time, for what you are. You're a coward. You *needed* Felicia to say no first. You had the comfort of two women and, for a long time, I accepted that. I did. But I—we, me and Emmanuel—*we* have a life here."

"Mona, I love you."

"You're only here because your wife left you, you fucking liar."

"Don't call me a liar!"

"If she didn't have the balls to cut you off, you'd still be there, every night, sleeping like a baby."

"I didn't want to be with her."

"But you were, Saul. And you know what? I accepted that. I made my peace. We arranged a life. Now, because it's convenient for you, you blow it up. It's always on your time, your way, so everything is convenient for you and fuck everyone else. It's not how I'm living."

"I don't know what's gotten into you. You're nuts, you know that? I drove here today so happy, so ready to begin—"

"You know what? Get the fuck out. I can't do this right now."

"I just got here, Mona."

"Get the fuck out of my house now!"

He heard what sounded like a crashing or throttling, an object being kicked. He recoiled, jumping off the door, leaning back against the wall. There were footsteps from behind the door. It opened slowly.

He stared at his dad, unable to speak.

"Emmanuel, I—I'll see you a little later on, okay? Your mother is a bit upset. I love you."

He squeezed Emmanuel's shoulder and walked on, down the hallway, his gait unsteady. He hadn't noticed before how shrunken he seemed.

"You're back early," his mom said, propping the door open. "Well, come in."

Al did not like going to Coney Island. Perhaps it was because he had grown up so close to there, getting dragged to family beach trips as a child. For Mona, who had lived near Prospect Park, Coney Island was a longer subway ride and therefore, in its own small way, an exotic locale, or as far as Manny and Esther ever wanted to go. If pressed about Coney Island, Al would snort and call it a cesspool.

But there they were, walking the emptied boardwalk at the beginning of February, hardened ice and stray snow beneath their feet. Seagulls circled them, landing on guardrails and rooftops, puffing their chests like spoiled children. Mona had told him she wanted to go for a walk and he obliged. Emmanuel was not far away, playing handball. She hoped he would find his way back to tennis.

"I always liked this place more in winter," Al said.

"Less people. It does have a ghostly, appealing quality. You stare at the Wonder Wheel and it feels like you've come to the end of something. Amusements are meant to have bodies."

"I remember my dad and my uncle taking me here, slapping me upside the head. They were always pissed. Half of the time, you could never tell why. Just sweating, angry people. That's how it was down here."

"People are bastards."

"They really are."

They walked toward Brighton, past the aquarium. Apartment buildings of sour red brick reared up. On the boardwalk benches, old men sat bundled up in coats, trying to disappear into themselves. One gloved hand dropped bread bits to the ground, where seagulls began to swirl.

"He surprised me, you know, with that call," Mona said, attempting the conversation she decided, at last, she needed to have with someone else. It had been running in her head for weeks, parried off invisible interlocutors and, when she could bear it, Liv. Her rage had slowly diminished. It had become what she knew it would be, with enough time: desire.

"I don't blame you," Al said. "But sometimes we have to deal in outcomes. I sound like I'm in the military, I know."

"Outcomes."

"He wants to live with you. He wants to marry you. I think he always did."

"Then why didn't he, you know? When I was young, I pushed

him away. But I was twenty-four! When you're that age, a man in his mid-thirties discussing marriage is something that's not quite fathomable. You understand it intellectually but not emotionally. I couldn't be bound to him. I really believed that to be defined that way, as a man's wife, was to be in some kind of late capitalist bondage. But then we had a baby. And he was so loving, such a *good* father, the best father, and we slipped into this new arrangement, compromising ourselves. Well, no—*I* compromised. That's why I got so fucking pissed! Where was *my* real husband? He got to leave me and play house with a woman he claims he barely cared about, really, but he kept playing. He kept going. Every night, laying his head down next to her, in another bed. Why?"

"He lacked courage. Sometimes it's as simple as that."

"He couldn't look this woman in the eye and tell her he loved someone else?"

"Honestly?" Al was looking away from her, his eyes pulled toward the beach. The sun, a watery orange, was beginning to creep below the horizon line. "You know what I think? He's a great guy and you can be great and be a coward. You can embody all of it at once. I didn't used to think that. I spent years in LA, sure that I had failed because I had not met some ill-defined ideal set into my head at twenty-five. Feeling sorry for myself, snorting coke, going to the wrong parties. I know what it's like to run away from the things you care about, from who you are, to evade yourself. Saul can be so certain and he can be so weak. He can be all of it. He was afraid of his wife, afraid of disappointing her, even if he didn't love her. They had their own arrangement, their own understandings. He should've broken it off years ago, I agree."

"She broke it off with him."

"In the end, she had the courage. Maybe we commend her. She stood up and said she had enough."

"Saul told me she was having an affair with their neighbor."

"When your husband is gone all those afternoons, staying out late, that's what happens. I'll say this. Saul gave far more to you. You are his life. That I can't argue with. I've seen you two together. He'd jump off buildings for you."

"But he wouldn't leave his wife. He then expects me, after all this time, these decades together, raising a son together—just let him move in like it's 1975. That's it. I just lost it and maybe I shouldn't have. Or no—I *should* have, but now I should do something else."

"You should talk to him."

"He's been trying to call me."

"In the end, you know, he wants to live with you and be with you and be that husband. It took him long enough. It took circumstances he couldn't control or didn't want to violate. He got a real kick in the ass from that soon-to-be ex-wife. But he's saying to you, *here I am.*"

She grew quiet again, shoving her hands into the pockets of her jacket. A cold wind cut in from the ocean. The boardwalk was almost up, a brick wall and a ramp meeting them. Al's shadow merged with her own, so they were sliding together in the haze of light like a single, strange being.

"Liv would be telling me to stand my ground," Mona said.

"Liv would be telling you to forgive the fucker."

"You know, I kicked a book at him."

"What?"

"It was this sports encyclopedia. I was so mad I had knocked it on the floor and then I kicked it at him. Like a fucking soccer ball. Emmanuel was standing outside the door, listening. I don't know how long he was there for."

"Knowing him, he heard a lot."

"Emmanuel listens. I don't really like discussing these things with him. He knows his parents are fighting."

"One parent is kicking a book."

"It's embarrassing, right? I was so blindingly mad. I hadn't been that mad in a long time. It's scary and, somehow, a little liberating."

They were walking back now, toward the Coney Island side and the resting amusements.

"Look, you really thought about all of it. What your relationship had meant, the compromises you made. He was choosing you, in part, because he was forced to. But you know? He may have done it anyway."

"That's why I still have this feeling in my stomach. I don't know if he would have. If Felicia said to him, *I'm with you for life.* I'm imagining attending her funeral with Saul, who is now the widowed husband. Or the two of them are attending my goddamn funeral, holding hands. It's the counterfactual that kills me."

"We can go crazy thinking of counterlives."

"Sometimes, Al, that's all I do. In one, you're here with me and Liv. In another, I just took Saul from Felicia thirty years ago. And in another, he's coming to me, telling me he's left his wife, sold his house, and he's ready to begin a life together. Nine months later, Emmanuel is born."

"In all of these, I hope we got those Vengeance pictures together."

Mona laughed quietly. "Yes. Somehow, that's the constant."

They were near the handball courts now, elevated above them on the boardwalk. Emmanuel was on a back court dusted with sand, playing a game of singles against a man in a thick beanie cap and rubber bands around his gloves.

Mona leaned against the railing, letting breath fall out of her. Al rested next to her.

"I suppose I'll have to call him."

"How many voicemails has he left?"

"Six? Seven? One every few days. I play them when Emmanuel is out."

"Play one more, listen to it, and call him. See what happens."

"There's this sick feeling in my stomach that won't go away."

"When you're ready, call."

Mona leaned deeper against the railing.

"How are things with Gwen, by the way? When am I getting my

wedding invite?"

"We're figuring out. She's a bit like you, you know? Nontraditional. I want to be that way but the Italian in me is saying marry her tomorrow."

"As long as you're happy."

"I am. I really am. It's almost strange to say. I really am."

She watched as Emmanuel raced to his left and swung his arm back, smacking the blue ball crosscourt. It landed just in, flecking the line, and the man in the beanie cap cursed loudly. Like the tennis stars of her youth, Emmanuel pumped his fist, raising it in the air. The man clapped his hands together. Quietly, they shook. Good game, they said.

The man walked off and Emmanuel stood on the court, bouncing the ball against the wall. It took him a minute, maybe more, to realize he was being watched. The realization broke slowly across his face, which was so much like her own, how she once was. He turned, his shoulder leading him, and squinted in the dying sunlight at the two figures in shadow on the boardwalk. He raised his arm. His thumb was up.

"Let's go home," she said, loud enough for everyone to hear.

20

Saul bundled up in his winter jacket, lined with fake fur, and carried the patio chair to the gradually expanding patch of sunlight. If he read in the sun, he could enjoy the air like it was spring. He started with the *Times* and then worked his way through the *Post*, an old habit from his days when it was a liberal paper. At his feet was a wrinkled paperback, *Sometimes a Great Notion* by Ken Kesey, a novel he had read in his twenties, when it was first published. In the house were two more books, a Chekhov short story collection and a history of Reconstruction. It had been enough, so far, to last him the two weeks, though he would have to go down to the little local bookstore or the library soon enough to tide him over.

Izzy Locker's house, of course, had books. But Saul felt odd about reading and sullying them. His library was contained in a wall of custom-built bookshelves off the vast dining room and the books were as pristine as the house itself, regularly dusted by a housekeeper. He walked among the empty rooms of the six-bedroom house like a ghost, trying to leave as little trace as he could.

On the phone, Izzy had told him not to worry. "You really need a place to stay, Saul? Go out to my place in Southampton. It's the winter. No one's there anyway."

Every summer he had come as a guest to one of Izzy's barbecues. They were held in his rambling backyard surrounded by thick hedgerows shaped, vaguely, like cresting waves. Friends from various white shoe law practices, lobbyists, and occasional politicos would drop by. Izzy, as the only wealthy Black man any of them knew, would be goaded, half-jokingly, into running for office. "A seat in Congress?" Izzy would ask, laughing. "And take the pay cut?" Grilling bratwurst, he would marvel at the scene, whispering in Saul's hear. "They should call me the Jackie Robinson of West Neck Lane. Except once he put on a uniform, no one confused Jackie with the help. Half the people in town think I'm here to trim their hedges until I pull out my Amex card."

Though Saul had, technically, until the end of January to move out, he knew he had to get going sooner. Felicia was intent on cleaning out the house and he was too disoriented to resist. His fight with Mona had only further unmoored him, convinced him he was chained to his own planet spinning violently out of orbit and into an unknowable abyss. He had never expected it, though maybe, on reflection, he should have. Instead of inhabiting her perspective, trying to understand what her anger meant, he resorted to a desperate defense, like an old trial lawyer. Now she wouldn't return his calls. His ambition to sleep in her bed and unfurl a new life in a Brooklyn apartment with his son was put on hold, perhaps forever. He was going to spring for a hotel. It was Izzy, on a phone call in which Saul slowly began to explain his situation, who suggested he head out east.

"Stay there, Saul, until you straighten your shit out."

There were worse fates. He preferred Southampton in the winter to the summer. The narrow roadways were free of most vehicles and the shops were emptied, open merely to the relieved locals. He drank in a coffee shop alone. It was the Long Island of his youth, the potato farmers and lobstermen, on a spit of overgrown land plunged into deep, oceanic silence. In the mornings, he went to town. He returned to read, when the weather permitted, outside, hunting for sunlight. Whole days passed talking to no one. It occurred to him he had not lived like this in many decades, if ever. In Roslyn, he and Felicia would sit in quiet too, but there was the tenseness of another body, the potential for conflict. He would hear her walking steadily on the stairs, one creak, two creaks, winding upward to their bedroom. He could close his eyes and imagine she was a boutique machine, designed for the purpose of generating noise in an empty home.

The weeks in Izzy's summer home would have been tolerable if they weren't interspersed with his calls to Mona. At first, they were once a day, in the evening when he guessed she'd be home. The voice-mail message like a knife thrust to the gut, every time. *Hi, this is Mona and Emmanuel, please leave a message and we'll get back to you as soon as we can, thank you!* It was cheery, un-Mona-like, and he stammered through the first few messages, making sure always to bookend them with apologies. After each one, it felt like bundling a scroll into a bottle and casting it off into the Atlantic Ocean. He didn't know if Mona listened to any of them, if she was deleting them once she heard his voice. The last time they fought like this, truly, was when he had suggested aborting Emmanuel. It was yet another example, he fumed to himself, of horribly misreading a situation, believing Mona was thinking one way when in fact she wanted to do the opposite. Did he really love her, if he got her so wrong? In Izzy's backyard, he had time to ponder all of it, a great rot at his center.

He listened to a lot of radio. Sports talk, news, occasional jazz. The voices of the sports talk hosts were the most comforting, loud mouths of the city, their wrath preserved for only the most irrelevant things. He could never be the person to call into the station, to voice an opinion. That was a bridge too far. Emmanuel asked him once, during the most popular show on WFAN, Mike and the Mad Dog, why he didn't call in to talk about the Mets. You know so much about the Mets, dad. He smiled and shook his head. It was never really my cup of tea. I like to listen, he said. And would he see Emmanuel again now?

Marriage! The fucking institution. He had approached it, as a very young man, with a kind of wonder, a certification of adulthood. It was like passing the road test. At twenty-four, twenty-five, this was how he saw Felicia, the necessary piece of his ascension into a middle class ring of honor, a wife and a law job, perhaps a future in politics. Their sex had been tentative from the start, never improving despite their growing familiarity. It wasn't a matter of him begging for it more and not getting it or her feeling dissatisfied. Neither of them, looking back on it, welcomed time alone, or knew much what to do with it. There was a television or a radio to swallow up the inevitable silence. Then children. Lenore, now on the verge of motherhood herself, and Tad, who could very well be dead. Lenore didn't call him much anymore and he assumed that's what happened to children who grew up, except he could never imagine *not* talking to Emmanuel every day, with their sprawling threads on baseball and politics and the oddities of life.

Mona had been so different. What he should have done, the minute he saw her in that college classroom, was blow up his life. He could have done it. What was he, thirty? But God damn it, he imagined himself so old, his choices so calcified, his destiny with Felicia the straitjacket he would never throw off. Mona had to be his furtive wonder. Invented work trips that were just aimless days in Brooklyn, ambling in the park, ordering Chinese take-out. Why did he think that was enough? Why was he driving back to Long Island all those other nights? Why didn't he slam his fist down on the table and declare, yes, I will get a divorce? Because once he did—once he showed real fucking initiative—Mona would have welcomed his choice. Eventually, she would have. He felt, slumped in Izzy's patio chair, like a man with his palms pressed against a plate glass window, deranged with anger, his words unheard as his past looped on the other side, stupidity playing after stupidity. He pounded on the glass, spittle rolling from his shaking lips. *Choose her. Choose her.* His fists were red, bruised and bloody. *Choose her now!*

Only darkness, and the changeover of radio shows, told him time had passed. He was never a big drinker and he decided to pick up vodka in town. Inviting a friend out seemed insane. It was bad enough explaining it all to Izzy. And he didn't party now, he slept at 9 p.m., a blanket pulled tightly up to his chin. When he woke, it was always with dread, blinking slowly in early morning light. Another day had come and he hadn't heard from Mona. It became easier to lose track of the day, the week.

In the afternoons, he started walking. The little roadways of the rich and famous were free of traffic and he had them mostly to himself. He passed from one fortress of hedgerows to another. Occasionally, a dog walker or a jogger would come by, waving politely, with a hint of confusion. They were used to the sanctity of their time, unused to this old, new man approaching gradually in their wake, so swaddled in his dark coat. He was sorry to disturb, sorry to offend, muttering in his head like the homeless men on the subway, dangling cups of change. He walked one day until the sun set. On another, he was too tired to get back to Izzy's and had to rest against the tree, his back sagging off the trunk. At dusk, he shuffled back.

One week, two weeks. He drove once a week into the city to teach his class. Wednesday nights. It was the only time during the week he heard his voice. Then back, past Roslyn, over the Suffolk County line, and out to the Hamptons, the little southern fork. End of the Earth. He read his books and drowned in his thoughts. He wondered, once or twice, what it would be like to drive his car into the sea.

He lost the energy for leaving her voicemails. Each had dutifully included Izzy's house number and no one had called since he arrived. He began to hope one of Izzy's friends would accidentally call so he could have a conversation.

January turned to February. A snowstorm battered the east end and he hid in the house for two days, with enough canned goods in the pantry to carry him on. He finished his books but had no way to get to the library until the roads were plowed. It wasn't New York City; the town would take days, street-by-street, to make itself livable again. Through the window, the snow and ice had an uneasy permanence, as if, like glass, it had hardened over the landscape for good.

He didn't get the newspapers delivered so he couldn't read the *Times* or the *Post*. This would be his life, he decided. A man in an enormous house, alone, until Izzy eventually kicked him out. In the spring, he would find an apartment and settle into the silence, becoming one of those old men who left newspapers piled high on their kitchen table and stove. He could learn to feed pigeons. He could store stale bags of popcorn in the unused oven.

He watched the Super Bowl with a bowl of nuts and a glass of Diet Coke. The Steelers, whom he had disliked since the '60s, defeated the Seahawks, a team he hardly thought about at all. He couldn't spend every Super Bowl with Mona and Emmanuel—in a few instances, Herb Weiner had thrown parties they were obligated to attend—but when he did, he ordered Kentucky Fried Chicken, which Mona bemoaned for health reasons and then ate, and mashed potatoes and gravy for Emmanuel.

By the end of the game, he was asleep. He had stayed up later than he had in weeks and his body, sunk deep into the couch, had gave out. After days of blankness, images came to him. It was an old dream, one almost forgotten: an mammoth black wave appearing at the horizon line, taller than any known buildings. The wave rose steadily, holding against the sky like a mountain. He was the lone person to witness it all. Everyone had fled or disappeared. He was standing on a beach, his feet sunk in wet sand, the tide rapidly receding, bearing the ravaged ocean floor. He could do nothing more. The wave was coming to crush him and drown him, high enough to block out the sun. There was a small, dying voice in his head begging him to run. But run where? The wave was everywhere and everything; it was a continent of water in the sky, collapsing on him alone. He was terrified at last, the wave so close. He was going to die.

He heard a ringing. Once, then twice. Why was a wave ringing? He blinked and gradually opened his eyes. It was, he dimly saw, morning, pale light on the curtains. The ringing, though, had not stopped. His hand flailed toward the nightstand. The phone was ringing.

"Hello?" he asked cautiously. He wasn't ready to tell another voice he didn't want to refinance his mortgage or buy new car insurance.

"Did I wake you?"

He sat up, sweat breaking out across his forehead, his heart punching at his chest. Heat crackled through the pipes of the house.

"Mona."

"I decided to call."

"How are you? How's everything? It's good to hear from you."

"It's fine. You know, about to head to work. Emmanuel is off to school already. Big math test. I want him to at least get a B."

"It's a busy, important year."

"Did you see the newspaper? Another Vengeance sighting."

"I've been snowed in out here. The city seems to be okay, from what I heard on the radio. I haven't seen a newspaper in a few days. The road here isn't plowed."

"How is the place? Izzy's house?"

"Oh, big. In the summer, it really lights up. Now, it's me with my books and my bowl of peanuts."

"Do you like it out there?"

He exhaled into the phone, his gaze rolling toward the lace curtains.

"It's just me. After a while, there's only so much to like."

"I'm going to be honest with you, Saul. I don't know exactly what to do. I still feel strange about this. You coming to me, telling me Felicia was leaving you, moving in, marriage—it was a lot. We've been through a lot. I've been thinking hard about it."

"I understand if you don't want to see me."

"But I do. There is no one else I want to see. I resent that too, if that makes sense. *Wanting* you, like a kept woman, waiting dutifully on your own time to make a decision you maybe should have made years ago."

"I can stay out here for a long time. I'll get an apartment in the city, sometime this spring, maybe."

"Don't do that. Move in with me."

He didn't know what to say at first. Full sentences had caught in his throat. He was standing, phone in hand, the cord dangling outward.

"I would like that."

"Do it for Emmanuel, not me. He wants to see you. He asks about you. I know he's hurting. We'll figure it out. Pack up your shit out there."

"When should I come?"

"This afternoon is fine."

"This afternoon—that works, yes. I'll pack up."

"I forgot. You said your road isn't plowed? Wait until that happens."

"I'd bust through the ice."

"Okay, hot shot. Get the Town of Southampton to get you moved out. Maybe Izzy can make the call. They probably assume no one is living there right now anyway. You're in a section with summertime billionaires. They're all hunkered down in the city."

"I'll call Izzy then. As soon as they get me out, I'll drive to Brooklyn."

"We'll see where this goes. You and me, together all the time. I don't know. You snore. You can't get piss on the toilet seat. You're on trash duty, too. And no, I don't need a financial contribution. I can handle the maintenance and utility bills on my own. I got a garage space now, too. Number came up on the list. If you need to smoke—I know you like sneaking those old Parliaments—you do it outside. You don't smoke indoors. I'd like you to load the dishwasher too, when you can. That will be one of your tasks."

"I'll do it all, Mona. I'll dust every day."

"Cleaning woman comes once every other week. Nice Polish girl. Stay out of her way."

"I'll keep getting Emmanuel every day after school again."

"He'll like seeing you every day. You know, he's been going out more. He hangs out with this friend Landon. I don't entirely trust him."

"Emmanuel is a great kid. He wouldn't do anything wrong."

"But I don't know about Landon. We'll see. When you're here, we'll figure it out."

"Yes. Together."

"I gotta run, I need to get to work. I've got two releases to draft this morning. Don't slip on the ice out there, okay? I'll see you soon."

"Goodbye, Mona. I love you."

"Goodbye."

It was, he figured then, the greatest phone call he had ever had.

21

Emmanuel stood on the corner of East 88th, waiting. Every ten or fifteen seconds he checked his cellphone. There was no sound, no vibration, but he would imagine a text into existence and jump, his heart pounding. He looked up. Cloudy skies, rain approaching. There was sunlight at least. Just a few days before, the clocks had been moved forward. Spring, fitfully, was coming.

How long had it been? Twenty minutes? Landon was due on the corner twenty minutes ago exactly. East 88th and York. He checked his phone again just to be sure. Liberation day, he thought. Finally.

I'm done, I'm done.

In two months, he was graduating high school. Unlike most of his classmates at Bridge Prep, he was not heading to an expensive liberal arts school or an Ivy. He was one of the rare students going off to a public school in-state, by definition a failure. After the round of college tours, the family vacations to lush suburbs and exurbs, his mom had quietly told him she was sending him in-state for a lot less money. *The financial aid wasn't quite what we hoped.* She didn't say anything more. When he mentioned to one of his teammates on the tennis team that he had decided to go to the SUNY on Long Island, his coach, Marty DiMarco, leaned over and sneered.

"*There?* I thought you were one of the smart kids."

He didn't say anything to DiMarco, a portly, furiously tanned man who was only seen in track suits and a black ear piece, phone conversations consuming most of his time with the team. His daughter had played tennis at Yale. He didn't coach so much as sit, legs crossed, barking orders from a canvas chair. Emmanuel wished him great harm short of death.

Now he was out. It was almost done. His prom, like proms across America, was operating on a James Bond 007 theme for the year, 2007. He had no intention of going. The only girl he wanted to ask was dating Landon Saltzman, on and off, and he needed to disentangle as quickly as possible. Aurora was his crush and there would be no way now, or in the future, to pursue her. It wasn't so much he feared Landon himself, who he had learned only had so much sway in the market. It was the fear that, facing retaliation in some way, he would be sucked deeper into a situation he needed to escape.

That was what this evening was about. Giving his goods to Landon and going home.

His jacket pocket bulged with ten milligram and twenty-five milligram doses, both extended release and immediate release. It was, by his count, at least $700 worth, maybe more. Soon, it would all be gone. Landon would take it and give it to someone else and get his cut. Simple, easy, done.

If his mom or dad knew what he was doing or where he was, they would be enraged in a way he never wanted to see. They would see him for what he knew he was: a failure, a deviant, a kid who could not grow up quite right. Other boys weren't lonely. Other boys made friends, dated, formed ever-expanding cliques and went on adventures to the beach or the movies, sharing beers and smoking weed.

One of the only gratifying moments he could recall of the last year was his dad moving in. It was sudden and unexplained. One night, he said he was staying. The next morning, he was hanging over the pan, making scrambled eggs in an old Utah Jazz sweatshirt he had bought on sale years ago. It was unlike either of them to make declarative statements about the occurrence of profound personal changes in their lives. You were expected to observe and absorb. He did, because having his dad home every day was enough. At night, they flipped between the Mets and the Yankees games, and when the tragedy of the off-season came, transitioned to documentaries on the History channel, Nets or Knicks games, or the occasional Monday Night Football. His dad liked to make popcorn. When Landon didn't call him out for evenings, this was how he wanted to spend his nights.

He thought about the money. Working for Landon hadn't been about that, not at the outset. It had been enough to have a person much cooler than him take an interest, especially after Dencher, that piece of shit, tried to cut him down.

"Dencher is a real loser and he knows he's gonna grow up to be some middle management bitch," Landon told him the first time they really talked, out near the football field at the end of lunch.

"He's always going after me."

"Because people are after him. It's a food chain, a totem pole. He'll never be one of the football guys or the kids getting scholarships to the Ivies. He has no cache here, nothing to offer. I don't even think his dad is that rich. Runs a small furniture company or something."

Emmanuel wanted to tell Landon that he just as easily was describing his own station in the school, which suffered from this same rootlessness. There was simply nothing exceptional about him. Landon, on the other hand, could get by on the wealth of his parents and his conventional good looks. His hair was meticulously sculpted and gelled.

"Yeah. I mean, fuck him."

"What're you up to these days, anyway?"

"Up to?"

It was not exactly an answerable question. He could be up to going to the bathroom or masturbating or watching cartoons or heading to the batting cage. Again, he had no anecdotes to share that would make up an exceptional life. Unlike most of his classmates, he had never even traveled to a foreign nation beyond a road trip to Montreal when he was ten.

Landon moved closer to him, with the ease of someone who wasn't normally reminded of any physical or psychic boundaries. He clicked his tongue and checked his watch.

"I think you're a good guy, Emmanuel, despite what everyone says."

"What do they say?"

Landon shook his head. "Well, not very much. It was more a turn of phrase. I haven't heard much *good*. But I couldn't call you polarizing either. Because of that, you get left behind. I generally think that's bullshit. I see you as someone with potential."

"I don't know what I have."

"My father's from a banking family. It's a firm that goes back to Germany or something. We were the Jews rich enough to get out of Germany before the Nazis killed everyone else. He expects me, at some point, to go into the business, and maybe I will. That's why I'm here. But you know what I think? A lot of it is useless. Sad men pushing around meaningless money. Deep down, you must feel it too."

"I guess I feel useless."

"You want to strike out on your own, make your own adventure, your own identity. I can feel it. That's why I'm here. Most of the fucking kids here, they're little copies of mom and dad. You aren't a clone of anyone. Neither am I."

That's how it began. Landon invited him to his father's condominium on the Upper East Side. It was a three-bedroom in a building with a doorman, a gym, and a roof garden. The view was startling, of the East River in its unexpected majesty. Due east, he could see the United Nations building. Landon lived alone with his father. His parents had divorced when he was young; his mother was a soap opera actress who didn't want custody. His father worked the kind of hours that implied custody wasn't much of an interest either. Landon lived in a way utterly alien to Emmanuel, absent any kind of parental accountability. His father had even left him with a credit card, to be charged to his heart's content. At most, Landon spoke to his father a handful of times a week. Both liked staying out late.

Landon's crew were the Manhattan kids, those who rode Bridge Prep buses from the Upper East and West Sides each morning. They all, to a boy and girl, smoked weed, and many dabbled in medications they didn't have prescriptions for. Landon's girlfriend, Aurora, had snorted coke. After school, they got back on the buses and chose one friend's apartment to go to for the rest of the night, until they had to eventually sleep in their own beds. The choice was usually predicated on which parents were not home and Landon inevitably won out.

The first few hangouts, Emmanuel had no idea why he was there. These classmates had never spoken to him during the school day. They didn't care about varsity athletics or academics. With money and looks, they had enough to subsist on, and the validation they felt with their preternatural knowledge, by the standards of their grade, of chic restaurants and night clubs. Emmanuel began to perceive them as a collective consciousness, their identities melded in Landon's wake. Only Landon existed apart, in some unidentifiable way. Emmanuel sat on the sofa in Landon's living room and watched the friends talk to each other, among each other, the voices enfolding on themselves. Often, he had little idea what exactly was going on.

Finally, a few weeks in, he began to understand.

"I want to show you something," Landon said one day, after the others had filed out.

In a small closet in Landon's room was a black safe. Landon unlocked it quickly and reached in, pulling out clear baggies filled with multicolored pills. He waved them in Emmanuel's face.

"Do you want to make money?"

It hadn't been a question he ever considered. Every week or so, his dad would pass him a $20 bill. Since he went out so little and never felt a need to eat food that wasn't cooked at home, he rarely spent the cash he was given. Over time, he had saved hundreds of dollars, stuffed into an old Velcro Yankee wallet in his desk. Money was the sort of thing you needed only if you had friends or someone to spend it on.

"I haven't thought about it."

"You'll think about it more when you understand what's going on here."

He explained the trade. Emmanuel dimly knew some students at Bridge Prep took Adderall and Ritalin. Landon laughed loudly and more deeply than Emmanuel had ever known when he said he assumed ten or fifteen percent of the school was on it and they were all prescribed.

"Dude," Landon said. "They're all on it except you."

The students with prescriptions were the original suppliers, but there weren't enough of them at Bridge to make it worthwhile. More could be found in the city, at other prep schools, and Landon was well-wired with Dalton, Trinity, and Dwight. *Originals*, as Landon called them, could only take you so far. Doctors and compliant pharmacies were required to spread to supply at scale. *Pill mills* was another term Emmanuel learned for the first time.

"There are doctors who will do that?"

Landon laughed again. "It's harder to find those that won't."

The network was vast and the more Emmanuel observed it, the more he understood Landon was not so much a kingpin as a vassal, invested with clout and terrain but far removed from those who controlled the flow of money and information. Landon's investment was Bridge Prep. For a long time, he had dealt the pills himself, around school or off-campus, meeting buyers at 7-11 or the bagel place.

"The headmaster's people are on to me, though," he said.

Emmanuel recognized why he had been welcomed into the fold of a crew he knew little of and had no conceivable ties to, on any kind of level of interests or income.

"You want me to deal pills."

"Ideally, yes."

"And what if I get caught?"

"You won't. We do this safely. I've never been caught. I'm worried, that's all, because they know me. They could suspect me. They will not suspect Emmanuel Plotz."

"Because I'm nobody from nowhere."

"No, you're somebody. The right kind of somebody. Truthfully, you may end up doing more than any of us."

"Let me think about it."

He didn't need the money and he didn't need the threat of getting arrested. He could continue on as he was, quietly counting down the days until he could leave Bridge Prep. It was enough. If he was lonely at school, he was loved at home, and this gave him enough confidence to wake up in the morning. Turning Landon down would have been easy. As a child, he didn't even like climbing the monkey bars. He didn't particularly like risk.

What he did was walk. In the late evening, after his parents were asleep, he ducked outside, circling the block and continuing on, going the length of the neighborhood. It was an insane idea, to sell pills for Landon Saltzman. To put his reputation and future on the line. For what? Money? Landon's tenuous approval? The sly nods of the Manhattan hive mind? He was going to say no. That was it. Landon could find someone else.

In the morning, he decided to walk to school. He did it infrequently, though it only took him twenty minutes. Outside the parking lot, Alan Dencher was standing with his thumbs hooked in his pockets, talking to Taylor Beltz, a member of the lacrosse team. He knew there was no way to approach the school and get to homeroom without being seen. Dencher unhooked one thumb and pointed at him, shaping his hand like a gun.

"There he is," Dencher said. "How you doing, buddy?"

He ignored Dencher, chugging toward the building, faster now, sweat leaking between his thighs.

"Emmanuel, baby, don't walk away so fast. It's not like you have anywhere else to be. It's not like you have any friends to see."

He heard Beltz laughing. As he came to closer to the door, there were hard footsteps behind him.

"You heard that?" Dencher asked him, breathing into his ear. "You heard me?"

He began to run, shoving through the door and up a flight of stairs, elbowing past students on the way to class. Dencher's laughter echoed out of the stairwell.

What it came down to, he thought as he texted Landon and told him he'd meet him after school behind the field house, was that if he sold pills to students, he could not be laughed at anymore. He would ascend from nonentity to entity; an outward identity would be formed. This would have to be enough. His life under Landon would be pulled from one defined endpoint to another, goal to goal, and he would gain, through it all, purpose. An impalpable but true enough energy would pulse through him.

The illegality was besides the point. He would be selling what people wanted, what people—in a more sane world, perhaps—would have access to without fear of reprisal. Don't we all deserve to be our best selves? What if it came in a pill? Indeed, he said to himself. For many students, this is happiness. This is all they will get.

He shook Landon's hand. He would be able to take what he was told was a large cut, ten percent. A pill went for as much as $25. He could move dozens, hundreds.

"It's a school filled with students desperate to achieve things," Landon said. "They are the offspring of people who achieved things. It's all they know. They are like pigs swallowing their own shit."

This became high school. Emmanuel still skipped school dances, still hid in fear and shame from most girls. But they slowly began to notice him. Aurora, even, laughed at his small jokes, her light green eyes flashing his way. Landon said, offhand once, she was a good fuck, and he wondered truly what that meant, if it was just good for him or good for them both or they agreed, after the fact, to decree that it was good.

Most sales were made behind the fieldhouse. He also met students, when necessary, outside the old Blockbuster that was being turned into a Honda dealership. What he relished most was their gratefulness, how their faces trembled with weakness when he was near, their tongues rolling behind their lips with anticipation. He understood the power of the healer, how shamans could be revered across the centuries for their hidden wisdom. He began to consciously alter his gait, dropping his voice a half octave, his gaze cutting low and away. Lack of eye contact meant they had to hunt for his own and he could decide when to grant the privilege. Sometimes, he intentionally dragged his hand through the wrong pocket. He made them wait.

Landon was satisfied because he wasn't caught. Sophomore, junior, senior year, a blend of spring tennis, summer baseball, and dealing. Aurora was still the only girl he talked to. She said he had a "literary" personality and would do well somewhere else, far away from here.

"Bridge is the worst," she told him. "Everyone has found themselves. The problem is, the selves are so rotten they shouldn't have been found at all."

She wanted to act on Broadway. Or be a documentary filmmaker. Or be a full-time busker, sitting outside nondescript shopping malls, strumming a guitar for loose change.

"I just need enough to afford a motel room."

"It sounds like a grim life," he said.

"It's a life accountable to no one."

Aurora's mother was an heir to a snack food company fortune, passively drawing income for a co-op on Central Park West. Her father, a private equity executive, had left her family long ago. It was a mirror of Landon's life and that was maybe what drew them together in the first place, East and West Side, missing mother and missing father. They both drank aggressively, mixing rum and vodka and beer, and could shout at each other over the emptiest of topics: the color of an ash tray, where in Capri they had eaten lunch, why the Strokes seemed to have lost their edge.

As the ace dealer of Bridge Prep, Emmanuel was privy to all of it.

"How did you two meet?" he asked Aurora one day when Landon had, angrily, wandered out of the East Side apartment.

"Strokes show," she said.

Aurora and Landon met as freshmen. They both believed *Is This It* was the greatest album ever made. Landon began grinding on her. That was it. This little boy with blonde highlights, his pelvis swimming around her own.

"He seemed so in control of himself, you know? I'd never met a boy like that. He seemed to know everything. He was like one of the members of the band. Rich, tough, with that hint of enigma."

She was smoking one of Landon's father's cigars.

"Who says cigars are for men, right? What is that shit? I can like that taste too. These are real Cubans, you know. Landon's dad gets around the embargo. That's what money does. It gets to write its own rules for you."

For all the risk he took, knowing one campus security officer could ruin his life, he began to believe it was worth it, just to sit at Aurora's feet and listen to her talk. He couldn't know if his presence made a difference or not. He suspected it didn't, that Aurora was practiced at monologues and only needed a human prompt to answer questions from and any boy at any prep school would do. He had never attended at Strokes show. He still avoided alcohol, weed, and other drugs. He hadn't even tried the pills he was selling. To Landon at least, he was intentionally handicapping himself for no real purpose, for no plaudits or even a moral high ground.

"You want to go to a good college, right? It all starts here."

"So you take it for every test?"

"I stopped because I don't really give a shit either way but I know deep down you do. My dad is just going to send me to GW because he has a bunch of friends in D.C. and knows the admissions officer. Most expensive school in America, funnily enough."

If he wasn't at home with his parents or playing a sport of some kind, he was probably in Landon's apartment. The Manhattan crew slowly flaked away. There seemed to be new cliques forming, away from Landon. New faces arrived, those more closely tied to the trade. There were kids from Riverdale and Horace Mann who were now dealing coke. Landon mused about how he'd get heroin, the real good stuff, into Bridge Prep, how he could "turn the whole fucking school into a Lou Reed song."

"I think I can guess which one, you trite asshole," Aurora said, smirking at him.

"*Hey, white boy, what you doin' uptown? Hey, white boy, you chasin' our women around?*"

"Those are the lyrics you remember? God."

His only excuse to his mom was that he was hanging out with Landon. He decided to invent that Landon was a baseball fan and they were attending Yankee games.

"I can pick you up after the game."

"No mom, I can take the subway."

"I don't want you on the train that late. Take car service."

"I don't think I have to."

"I want you to, Emmanuel. You are not getting on the train that late."

"It's *packed* with people."

"It's dangerous riding at that hour and I don't want you to."

He wasn't sure why he argued so aggressively if he wasn't even going to the game in the first place. He supposed it was a principle. Usually these conversations happened outside Landon's apartment but one day he had to take a phone call from his mom in front of Landon and Aurora. When he was done, he returned to them in mild shame, fearing they would see just how cowed by his own mother he really was.

"Mom upset?" Landon asked.

"It's just how she is."

"That's cool. If I had a mom like that, I'd be doing something else right now. And if Aurora had a dad like that, she'd be doing something too."

"I do a lot, speak for yourself, " Aurora said.

"Sure. All I'm saying is what you have is rarer than you think, Emmanuel. Enjoy it. As weird as that sounds."

As a senior, he found he was already known to the freshmen who had just arrived at Bridge Prep. He existed in their consciousnesses, not so different than the star football players and academic award winners. He was only a conduit; no one, rightfully, regarded him as any more than a skulking presence who could deliver them their drugs, but he was still the presence. His relevancy could not be argued with and this mattered enough.

Dencher even came to buy from him. He never smiled or laughed at him anymore. He quietly handed over crumpled twenties and took what he needed. There was no acknowledgment of their past. It was as if it never happened at all.

He watched Landon and Aurora drop acid. Their pathbreaking metaphysical journeys were, to him, two people sprawled on the couch, rolling to the floor and cowering on the shag carpet. He finally put on the television, watching *SportsCenter* until Landon, sweating and panicking, told him to turn it off.

"The signals, man. I hate the signals."

No matter how much time he spent in the three-bedroom overlooking the East River, he could never be like Landon and Aurora because to be like them was to exist in a state of ultimate fantasy. Money was an abstract concept to them both. It appeared, it disappeared, and more would always arrive when it was needed. Landon was not enmeshed in a miniature drug empire for money, not when his father gave him a credit card he could charge whenever he wanted. He was not in it, as far as he could tell, to achieve a higher station among classmates when his looks and his father's wealth were sufficient. Was it the action? The challenge? Landon was in a position—rich, white, attractive—to create his own obstacles. Aurora could as well. And what were Emmanuel's obstacles when he was loved at home? He wouldn't be the first or last kid to feel isolated in school, to be picked on, to be too afraid to ask anyone to prom. He was not getting shot by police. He was not in Iraq.

In December, an unease began to build. Landon appeared less and less and when he did, to resupply Emmanuel, he was twitchy and red-eyed, his sentences erratic and slightly broken, like a tape had been skipping inside of him. He seemed tired and afraid. Over winter break, Emmanuel texted Aurora to ask her if she had noticed anything different in Landon.

"Landon hasn't talked to me in two weeks," she told him when they met, killing time at Union Square.

"What?"

"Something has gone really wrong. He won't answer texts. I think he should stop dealing. He's way over his head now. From what I can tell, he's been skimming off where he shouldn't be and I told him this once, that he couldn't get cute with his percentages. He's in the big leagues. The people who control this trade aren't high school kids with Daddy's black Amex cards. They're the kind of people with their own money and real problems and don't hesitate to fuck up people who fuck their shit up."

"I hope he's not in trouble."

"I want him to be alive and healthy. Beyond that, I don't know. Four years with him. Isn't someone supposed to say I love you after that?"

"I don't know, really. I mean, he's not ready to get married or anything."

"You think the words are about marriage? You're a little traditionalist Brooklyn boy, aren't you?"

"I don't think that. I don't know."

"He's gone too deep."

"Can we pull him out?"

"He'll have to pull himself out. There's so much he doesn't tell me. Or tell you. If I were you, I'd really get out soon. You're going to college. You're not going to be dealing the rest of your life."

"I know that."

"I don't know if you do, Emmanuel. I watch you. You're acclimating to this life. And you shouldn't be. You can do so much more. You're worth a lot more."

"Well, you are too."

"But I know that! I want you to know it for yourself. You're getting closer to making a mistake. Don't make one."

At the end of January, Landon texted him to meet him on York Avenue, near his apartment. He said he wanted to make sure Emmanuel was adequately supplied. In truth, he was, since he had slowed down his pace since the end of winter break, intending to wind down and eventually tell Landon he was done. He didn't want a resupply. But he did want to see Landon and ask him how he was.

Landon showed up, his skin sallow and sunken, his eyes further bloodshot. He nodded at Emmanuel and gestured north. "Let's get pizza," he said.

They sat in a pizza parlor, the temperature dropping outside. Landon hunched his shoulders over two pepperoni slices. Emmanuel, hoping to lose weight, opted for one. They ate in silence as fuzzy surfer rock played from wall-mounted speakers.

"How is everything?" Emmanuel asked.

"Everything?" A string of runny cheese was hanging off his chin. He flicked it away. "Not so stupendous, Emmanuel."

"Tell me what's up."

"I'm being followed."

"What?"

"Someone is following me. I think I might know who it is."

Emmanuel decided to get right at what he wanted to say.

"Maybe it's time to do something else, you know? I was thinking about it too. We made what we made. It was fine. Now we go."

"Easier for you. You should. Not me."

"Who is following you?"

Landon leaned in, close enough that Emmanuel could smell a curious scent, like a commingling of cigarettes and mouthwash. Landon's skin was no longer so clear; there were faint cuts and scars, dim pimples riding up his cheeks. His hair had grown long enough that now it dangled over his eyes when he spoke. Every five or ten seconds, he would brush it away.

"*Vengeance.*"

"The vigilante from the news?"

"It's him. I'm always seeing him out of the corner of my eye. He watches me."

"Are you sure?"

"I am fucking sure, Emmanuel."

Forty years ago, his mom had photographed Vengeance. He had heard the story often, the hysteria of it all, how getting an image of him had been enough. Then, as now, the police never caught him. She didn't like talking about it. Whenever he read articles, it was theorized Vengeance was many people, New Yorkers playing copycat, assuming the role for their own ends. Maybe that was true. Maybe one of the copycats was trailing Landon.

Landon could be hallucinating too.

"If you see him, I don't know, you could call the police."

Landon smiled at him, leaning back in his chair and shaking his head.

"I love you, man. Funny guy. Call the police. Yeah, I'll do that. We can both be prosecuted as adults in the State of New York. Good luck."

Out of sympathy for Landon, he took the resupply. He decided he would barely sell for a month and then return it. He wasn't sure if Landon could handle him dropping out. When he told Aurora about this, at the end of January, she was furious.

"Give him the goddamn pills back and get out. It's getting worse."

"I want to."

"You better fucking do it."

He texted Landon to meet up. This was the only way to reach him because he had stopped coming to school. No one had seen him. Aurora texted him that Landon still wasn't answering her either. He had seemingly dropped off the planet. Week after week, he hoped Landon would reemerge. Senior year, for the rest of the school, occurred in an alternate universe, with classmates planning for spring break and prom and summer road trips or jaunts to Europe before the beginning of college. He felt like he was watching a TV show, passively sprawled on his couch at home. No one bullied him anymore because he was the kid dealing pills but no one had much else to do with him either. The only person who answered him, other than his parents, was Aurora. No matter what, she returned his texts.

An odd occurrence: he won the senior class history award, the Mayflower. History was the only subject he could master. It was fact and narrative and he understood both, how to accumulate and arrange information. He wrote coherently and cleanly, with occasional adjectival flash, and he was rewarded with As. His AP European history teacher had apparently nominated him without telling him.

Bridge Prep did not mete out GPAs. Because it was a private school, it had chosen its own path of evaluation, letter grades and numbers, and he was going to graduate with an 84 average, which seemed about right. He was an 84 kind of person. The '90s would always float above him, out of reach.

In March, Landon reappeared. Emmanuel saw him in the hallway and ran to him. Landon glanced away, as if not recognizing Emmanuel would have been enough to make him vanish altogether.

They were between classes. Emmanuel had to get to Earth Science.

"Where have you been?"

"I can't talk here, man."

"Then where? I need to talk to you."

"You don't need to. You're good. Everyone's good."

"I'm not good. I'm done. Okay? I'm gonna flush it all down the toilet."

"Better not. People will not like it."

"Then take it from me."

"You want out? Too hot to handle?"

"Too hot. If you don't take it, it goes down the toilet in ten minutes."

"Don't do that. Here's a better deal. Let's meet uptown and I'll take it off you. We can't do it here. Too many eyes now. A lot of movement against us."

"Against you, you mean."

"No, my man. *Us.*"

Landon walked off and Emmanuel didn't hear from him for the rest of the day. He seemed to vanish again. The next day, a text message appeared. Landon told him to meet uptown, on East 88th and York. *You can give it all to me,* he said. Immediately, Emmanuel texted Aurora and told her he was going to meet Landon.

I'm getting rid of all the stuff.

Excellent.

That's what brought him to the moment with his jacket teeming with pills, standing on a street corner on the Upper East Side. It had been twenty-five minutes now. Landon was blowing him off. Should he have been surprised? He would have to dispose of the pills. What concerned him were the depths of the operation he still did not understand, what missing merchandise could do to a supply chain and what people would appear to try to balance the ledger. They were the sort of people who had made Landon into what he was.

He turned, on instinct, toward East 88th, staring down the block that led to Gracie Mansion. At first, he saw nothing unusual, merely the flow of pedestrians up a mottled sidewalk half-filled with sacks of trash. Behind a woman pushing a stroller came a figure, the face shrouded in a hood. Emmanuel squinted to see who it might be and as the figure gradually drew closer, limping and holding his side, he realized it was Landon. Landon was hiding his face. Landon was hurt. Closer now, he could hear his broken breaths.

"Your face."

Landon looked up at him, through streaks of blood.

"He got me, man."

"Who got you?"

"He did. He thought I had the stuff. But I didn't."

"What are you talking about?"

"I think, actually, I think—he was looking for you."

"Who, God damn it? Speak to me."

Landon smiled up at him, his lips cut and swollen. His eye had been blackened. His head began to rattle and he coughed deeply into his balled fist. Drops of blood dappled the pavement.

"I think I see him," Landon said quietly.

A man approached them from behind. Emmanuel turned first, away from Landon's haunted eyes. Emmanuel knew, when he saw him, what this was, that Landon had not been lying to him at all. He had not known fear like this, how deep and sudden it was, the way matter seemed to be collapsing on itself toward the single, darkest point imaginable.

He stared at the man's eyes through the mask. In daylight, broad and real, Vengeance was standing in front of them both.

"Emmanuel Plotz," he said.

Emmanuel couldn't speak. He could only stand and watch. Landon was hunched over, holding his ribs. They appeared, from his positioning, to be cracked.

"Emmanuel Plotz, you will get to see."

As his fingers reached for his mask, which covered his entire skull, police sirens broke open the quiet. One squad car, then two, then three. They screeched to the curb with theatric aggression. Their red and blue lights danced in his eyes.

"I didn't call them," Landon said. He was smiling now.

"I didn't either," Emmanuel replied.

Vengeance didn't move as the cops broke from their vehicles, guns drawn, and pointed them at his body. He gradually raised his arms upward. They circled him and pulled forward, grabbing from all sides, handcuffing him without any resistance. Through the mask, Vengeance seemed to be laughing.

Landon and Aurora were not like him. They were comfortable in moments like these, of disruption that would render only so much consequence for those who could always protect themselves, blasting off to another apartment or day job or hustle. The police told him they would need to ask him a few questions. What they were not going to do, he realized, was search him. They had not been told to come bust up a couple of pill dealers. They did not know who Landon Saltzman was or, if they did, they did not care. They had come for the masked man who still managed to find his way into newspapers and nightly TV broadcasts, the vigilante of the new millennium, the successor of an idea that meant much more in another time, when the existence of the city itself was called into question.

Vengeance knew him. And this had to mean, somehow or someway, he knew Vengeance.

When the police were done with him—he had so little for them, beyond that Vengeance had spoken to him—he walked off silently, away from Landon, crossing the street. He only knew he had to get back. He needed to ride the subway to Brooklyn.

His mom and dad were home, waiting for him.

V

Echo

1

Tad never figured out what Wilbur Chiu did with Marius Shantz's headless body. Wilbur Chiu was never going to tell him.

Tad only had the mask and the ultimate inability, despite his best efforts—his best faith—to kill. In that way, he was like every Saturday morning hero of old, swaggering yet impotent, unable to do anything more than forestall darkness. There would always be another episode.

The 2000s, the 2010s—these science fiction decades, neighborhoods encased in glass, screens glinting like blades in the sun, wealth supplanting violence. The murder rate tumbled, yet he had enough to do. He kept to the subway, idling on platforms and staircases, waiting for the inevitable. He kept to the streets he knew caused trouble.

Before his arrest—before his entry into the vertiginous 2010s, long before the virus—Tad was able to do so much. Emmanuel was almost an accident. He never, in the beginning, intended to get that close. But then he did. He felt the pull and kept coming.

The boy was the son his father had always wanted. Tad only wanted to see.

"You're growing," Chiu told him one day, not long before the police swarmed on East 88th.

"Growing how? I've got a bit more muscle, I guess."

"No, nothing like that. Your fear is abstract now. You see nighttime the way you see daytime. The people notice."

"It's tiring. But I like being tired."

He began to relish existing as an idea. His thoughts grew lusher, more fluid; he was, in age, more radiant. It was the mask. He had spent more time as Vengeance than Chiu. He had persisted in the substratum; no, he had transcended it, up to the camera-eye, and when the mask had to come off, the crackle inside of him did not abate.

The world met Vengeance. The world met Tad.

Suddenly, he was talking. In jail. Outside of jail. To the newspapers, the strange blogs, the television reporters, the streamers. By then, Chiu had sold Blue Star, sold the building—he owned it all, quintupling his investment from the 1980s—and retreated upstate. He shared some of the proceeds with Tad. It was enough, this sliver of the windfall, to buoy him. He moved into a one-bedroom apartment in Astoria, into a building with a laundry room. All of the walls were freshly painted.

He was fine, too, when attention quieted. The culture only ever held anyone for so long. He was intrigued, for a sizzling period, by the black swan election, the man who became president unlike any man who had ever been president before.

The president, once young, had met his father in an office in Queens, Tad's Queens now, this teeming borough. The president, now old, embodied the enormity and absurdity of his country, and Tad couldn't look away.

That's when the call came from the radio station. In a few months, they'd all be sick.

2

Mona rode down the avenue, faster as she approached where the people used to be.

Storefront after storefront gated and barricaded, apologetic paper signs taped in the windows. She was in the heart of it—the Italian place, the Peruvian place, the Indian place, the Turkish place, the ice cream shop, the taco bar, the Irish pub, the Greek pastry shop, bodega upon bodega—and it was at this time, with the sun high in the sky, that bodies would be thronging sidewalks, in the motion of the day. In another hour, schools would be letting out, children elbowing at the bus stops, bouncing basketballs, straining for the brightest hours before nightfall, the hours they were most free. In another time, the men would be sitting out in folding chairs, playing cards in the shade, scarves whirled around their weather-beaten necks.

Her bike swerved into the middle of the street, down the double yellow line. Other than police cars and ambulances, she had the asphalt to herself.

The neighborhood, like all neighborhoods now, was silenced. It was like, she imagined, the days after a bomb, when the survivors struggled back to life in the blankness they were left. But that wasn't quite right. A single bomb came with the promise of a discernible, linear narrative, no matter how catastrophic: a beginning and an end, explosion and recovery. This did not end. It persisted, with unfathomable carnage every day. It was not like one bomb but many, with more always in reserve. It all didn't seem possible until it was.

Her little neighborhood, in the southwest pocket of Brooklyn, in the shadow of the Verrazzano Bridge—it was still intact, still here, every physical structure. A bomb would have unsettled her less, she thought, pumping harder, her balaclava beginning to slip off her nose. The sweat building, she nudged it back up, her bike rolling downhill. A bomb would have announced itself. Burning wreckage, smoke in the sky, charred metals and shattered glass and dust scattered on the sidewalks, blood drying beneath it.

When she biked, she tried not to think about what really had happened.

Spring had come to mock her. She should be playing tennis, singles on Saturday, doubles on Sunday. She was into her seventies and played like she was forty. She should be waking up for coffee and a whole wheat bagel, eating it at the café across the street from Foodtown. All of her life, seventy years, and she couldn't believe how much of it she had taken for granted, the pleasure of a handshake, a kiss on the cheek, a winding line at the health food store, waiting for her fresh hummus and tabbouleh. It was all so *full*, the sounds and smells of a society clicking to life, the swell of conversation, honking horns and tumbling crates and the screeching of sneakers courtside.

Hundreds were dying every day.

Yesterday, Sylvia's brother had called her. She was being intubated. Sylvia, the great tennis champ, the bull who taught her son how to hit a forehand. The doctors were doing what they could.

"It's in God's hands now," he said.

"God," she wondered. "Where is He?"

"On vacation."

She counted the deaths closely until they surpassed the number killed on 9/11. That was April 7th. And then the count continued to climb. Twenty people in her co-op, at least, were infected. In the hallways, when she went out with her bicycle, she could hear them coughing through their doors.

Like Saul did before the ambulance had to take him, his body teeming with the new virus.

Talking to Sylvia's brother was a chance to think about something else, not Saul in an ICU. Not Saul, shriveled and pale, trying to laugh into the phone the last time she spoke to him.

"The food is not bad here, you know."

"Don't hit on any cute nurses."

"They're hitting on me!"

It began with the tickle in his throat. He couldn't get it out. "Dry cough," he said, rustling his newspaper.

Friday nights at the Greek restaurant, gone until when?

She had to keep biking. In the apartment, alone, it was what she had—the anticipation before the ride, the ride itself, the satisfaction of sweat drying on her body—and she needed to keep moving, up and down the neighborhood, to the promenade along the bay, the waters that had calmed her so much when she first moved here. Emmanuel was a baby, strapped to the backseat, going wherever she went. He was happy just to be carried in, for the sun to fall on his face and the birds to turn overhead.

Her rides started at ten and ended a little after noontime. Two hours, at this age, was what her body could handle. Then she would go home to read and watch television, in bed by eight, sleeping by nine. Al would call, and they would talk for twenty minutes or so. He was staying in the Hudson Valley with an artist friend, cooped up in a back bedroom, watching black bears gnaw at compost. At least, that happened once.

"You can come here," he said. "They'll find room for you."

"I'm okay. I need to be here, anyway, when Saul gets out. Who is going to pick him up?"

"Yeah."

Since she had followed the news since the end of January, early February, she was extremely well-supplied by the standards of her neighbors. She still hadn't run out of Lysol wipes. She had two large bottles of hand sanitizer, six boxes of alcohol swabs, two boxes of latex gloves, and a package of surgical masks. The masks were ordered before the rush on masks began, when people were still shamed for wearing them. She told Saul she didn't doubt it was going to get here, to jump from China and Europe and make it to New York City.

"Only the paranoid survive," she said.

"Maybe you should wear goggles and a snorkel."

The dry cough was harder, louder, unlike any she had heard. It was like he was breathing glass.

"A chest cold, Mona, that's it. Don't be so crazy."

"We need to get you in for a check-up."

"What are they gonna do? Stick a thermometer in me and tell me I have a cold? C'mon. I'll get through it."

It was harder for him to take walks. He told her he wasn't up to it, that he hadn't slept well. His chest was still bothering him.

"This cold, you know? It's still the season."

"You won't stop coughing Saul."

He slept on the couch. She stopped kissing him, started swabbing the doorknob three times a day. The kitchen counter was cleaned hourly. She went to the supermarket the moment it opened, battling for cleaning supplies. The shelves were progressively emptied out. Hand soap survived and she began scrubbing surfaces with that, scented lilac and raspberry.

At night, she listened to him. The coughs rattled from the living room, followed by the sucking of his breath. He kept a small transistor radio near him, listening to men with New York accents talk about the sports that weren't being played anymore.

"Saul, I'm worried," she said in the morning.

"Nothing to worry about."

"You aren't breathing well."

"I'm just—I'm tired, okay? You got me on this couch. I like that couch but, you know."

"I'll sleep out there then. You have the bed."

"I don't need the bed. Let me nap for a bit. I'll get my pizazz back."

In the afternoon, he was running a fever. She didn't need a thermometer. She felt his head and knew. He was still coughing, phlegm in his throat, spittle rolling down his flushed, weathered knuckles.

"Antibiotics will kick it," he said.

"You've been taking those."

"Well I know what you're thinking. I've hardly been out! How am I getting the virus?"

"Saul, it's everywhere. Anyone can get it. It's in this fucking building."

"Coranadovirus or whatever." He laughed. "I'll be fine in one day, two days. You'll see."

He moved like he was underwater, an unseen resistance building against his heavy limbs. At the kitchen, he wheezed in front of the refrigerator. If he wasn't napping or eating, he was coughing and gasping for breath.

"Is it cold in here? I have this deep chill I just can't shake. Maybe these antibiotics aren't too good."

"I'll see if they can send up heat."

It was quick. One moment, she was in the kitchen boiling water for pasta, Saul in the living room watching the five o'clock news. She lowered the burner on the stove and went to wash her hands.

"How much cheese do you want on it when it's done?" she asked from the kitchen. She was sliding out dry linguini, getting ready to crack it into pieces to throw into the boiling water. "You can have a little more because I bought the healthy cheese."

She didn't get an answer. This was rare for him, to not respond all. In the fourteen years he had lived here, he had never not replied unless he truly didn't hear her.

"I said, I got the healthy cheese!"

She knew before she saw him slumped, barely breathing, on the couch, his head turned sickly inward like all the blood had been rapidly drained from him. She was calling for an ambulance, sputtering on the phone, hanging up and waiting for the sirens that she always feared would come for this apartment. He was deadly sick and should have been at a hospital days ago, where he could fight it out. As the ambulance pulled up outside the front of the building, she began to understand why Saul wanted to be here. They both watched the news every day. People were going to the hospitals to die. Ventilators were death sentences. If he was going to suffer, he didn't want to suffer alone. She was ready to tell the ambulance to go away, that she'd figure it out here, when the paramedics knocked on her door and rushed in with a stretcher, masks swallowing their faces, and took Saul away.

"I'm sure he's positive," she said.

There was no riding along in the ambulance. He was taken to the closest hospital, NYU Langone, and told to wait for updates. Once the ambulance pulled away, she called her son.

"Your father is going to the hospital," she said.

"What happened?"

"He was fine and then he wasn't so fine. But he will fight through it. It seems to be a mild case. They want to take precautions."

"We can't visit him, can we?"

"No. Not right now."

She could never entirely tell her son the truth. Maybe it was that way with all mothers and sons, since they had witnessed the entirety of their creation, observed them closely at their most fragile and helpless. If her son was now thirty, he was also sixteen and five and a newborn, all these lives existing simultaneously, forever inching forward into a world of infinite brightness and peril. She couldn't tell the baby strapped to the backseat of her bicycle that his father might be dying. Emmanuel had been by just a week ago, for a Friday night family dinner, and Saul had only started to talk about the tickle in his throat.

Emmanuel didn't need to know everything, not with his own recent struggles. A few weeks earlier, the media company that employed him had laid him off, after only six months. He was writing on the criminal justice system, serious pieces for a news website that had lost much of its revenue when all their live events for the foreseeable future had to be canceled. It was like that everywhere, jobs disappearing as cities and states shut down or attempted to, the stock market yo-yoing, Trump insisting nothing was happening at all, what virus? She was sick of the president, but so was everyone else. She just wanted Saul to make it through.

"Do you need help with the rent?" she had asked Emmanuel after he told her.

"My roommates and I are figuring it out. Not right now. Another guy may get laid off too. We're actually thinking of doing a strike."

"What?"

"A rent strike, you know."

"You can't do that. Just not pay rent."

"They can't evict us during a pandemic."

"Emmanuel, you can get in a lot of legal trouble. I don't know. I'd reconsider. I can help you, I'm not spending any money right now, just home here reading my history books, watching TV, riding my bike—"

"Mom, it will be okay, I promise. I'm more worried about dad."

"If you need anything, really . . ."

She called as many of Saul's friends as she could to tell them. Sonny Cannon, ill with a gallbladder infection but virus-free, at least for now. He was no longer spry enough to argue with Saul that Trump had been good for the country, that he had performed an economic miracle before the crash. Izzy Locker, holed up in his Southampton compound, still sounding robust over the phone, telling her he'd pray every night for Saul. There was another call she could make, except she didn't have the number. Saul had never given it to her.

She had still never spoken to her. There was a condo in Del Ray

Beach and that was all she knew. Felicia would have to care because she spent those years with him. But if she loved someone else and she was comfortable where she was, the news would matter only so much. That was human nature, the drift of time away from wherever you used to be.

What she could do, after all, was call the station. But she was never going to do that.

She was biking down by the water now, starting at the pier and heading south, toward the Verrazzano Bridge, once the very largest suspension bridge in the world. The bike path had begun to fill again as people realized that riding a bike with a mask wasn't more of a danger than walking with a mask. She had been the first one out here, when it was deserted and the assumption was the air itself was toxic, that anywhere beyond the four walls of your bedroom was inviting death. Ambulances raced down the parkway. They were the new city soundtrack.

She kept riding past the bridge, in the direction of Coney Island. Unlike the other people in the building, she didn't resent those who left. If you had a cottage in the Hudson Valley or the Berkshires, why not hide? What moral value could she assign to being here, riding a bike on a nearly empty promenade? She could get angry thinking of Saul in a hospital. How the state and federal governments failed her. If she had been quicker, done something differently, kept him from going to the supermarket or the hardware store or anywhere the virus bred unseen—if she had ultimately been *better*, she wouldn't be here, trying not to think of his body in a hospital bed. She failed him. She needed to protect him and she didn't.

Avoid downward spirals, she told herself on the tennis court. Always avoid downward spirals.

This fucking virus. She stopped her bike, getting off to breathe, to feel the sweat roll down her body. She needed to be healthy for when he came home.

After the bike ride, she made a late lunch, a peanut butter sandwich and a bowl of carrots, and tried to read. It was difficult to focus on the words, a JFK biography. She was trying to read about Lee Harvey Oswald. They shared a birthday. Born exactly ten years before her. A lonely man who wanted to insert himself into history and did, a man who shattered dreams, perched in the sky. But they all went to school the next day. They weren't afraid to go outside, crowd into stores, ride the train to the ballpark. Until now, there had been no such a thing as a society brought to a standstill.

She had not cried since Liv's death and she wasn't going to now, she promised herself. There was no one to be strong for, no child in her apartment, but she strove to do as she always did, to meet each day eye-to-eye. Oatmeal each morning with raisins, the morning shows going in the background. The two-hour bike ride. Lunch and the afternoon wind down. Her phone calls to friends, to Al and her tennis partners, to Melinda and Vic, to Sylvia's brother for updates. To the hospital, finally, to see if there was anything new, an improvement to carry her into the next day.

Saul had left his transistor radio in the kitchen. Out of an old habit, or maybe his own absorbed into her, she began to listen in at night.

The show came on at 9 p.m. She remembered, a few years ago, the cheeky announcement in the *New York Post*, how they secured the exclusive and elevated it to the front page. It was very unlikely, the media columnist wrote, considering he had vanished from view, shortly after it was revealed to the world who he was. Why come back? Why now? He offered no comment. The small New York station was trying to produce more original local programming and rely less on syndicated talk shows from Florida and California. They needed to make a splash, they needed a voice, someone of the people to speak for the people to the people, or something like that. If his fame had diminished, there was still intrigue, and the show had remained sporadically on the air, going on hiatus and returning at particular intervals, whenever it suited their host.

The show, when on, had accumulated the beginnings of a mass following.

At 7, she flicked the radio on and turned the dial to the AM. She heard a crackling of static.

"Hello out there," the voice said. "I am here and you are there. Welcome to another night on a planet one hour to midnight. How are we feeling? What are we doing, alone in our quarantines, spinning out in madness? How would we like to be?"

She decided she would turn it off, but not before hearing him introduce himself. It was important, after all these years, to hear the name over a radio frequency. Saul had only listened once, the very first time, and shut the radio off. It was a rare time he was at a loss for what to say.

The radio hissed. After the static, he seemed to be clearing his throat. She waited for his voice to cut across the darkness.

"Tonight you're with me. You're with Vengeance. If you play nice, you can call me Tad."

Saul tried to reach Tad after his arrest. For a moment, he seemed dazed enough to believe Tad had always been Vengeance, the same man she photographed all those years ago. Tad would have only been a small child then. There had been a first, an unknown first, and Tad claimed in a jailhouse interview he knew who it was and would never tell. Tad was simply the new Vengeance, carrying on into the future.

Saul went to the police station, alone, to see him.

The Manhattan District Attorney's office attempted to build a case against Tad, based on years of reported assaults during the reoccurrence of Vengeance. But the case was tenuous and the publicity was not necessarily on the side of the prosecution. In the end, Tad spent three months locked away and was free to resume an unmasked life elsewhere. Saul spoke to him one more time, just before his release. He asked him why he had been compelled to wear a mask and fight crime.

"It was something I could do," Tad said.

"You can do lots of things! I can help you get a job, if you want, you can stay with us, we can figure it out."

"Your systems and logic are not my systems and logic."

"I can help you."

"Focus on your son."

"You are—" He stopped himself, on the verge of shouting. He realized who Tad was talking about. "You're my son too."

Tad disappeared again. Emmanuel, as far as Mona knew, never spoke with him after their encounter on East 88th street, when the police were tipped off to the sighting. The Vengeance mask found a following. She saw it in costume stores. Tad was a part of the culture, whether he wanted to be or not. There were debates over his meaning, the need for vigilantes in an age of terror, why one person would attempt this, if it was art imitating life or life imitating art, if he was just a deranged superhero fanboy or emblematic of currents far deeper and darker in the nation. All of it was very strange and eventually Mona and Saul sought to ignore it all, to ensure their son made it through college and figured out exactly who he needed to be.

She took the radio to bed, her eyelids heavy as Tad continued to speak. His show was now being carried on stations across the country. The vigilante radio hour. There seemed to be a hunger for it. A voice of warning divorced from the weakness of flesh.

"This is death on a new scale," Tad said through the radio. "A virus is a daisy-chain of death. A virus is the ultimate terror. The terrorist is just a human, confined by flesh and blood and emotional intelligence. A terrorist cannot kill on his own—he needs the deadly toys of his civilization. But what does the virus require? No organization, no suicide vest, no national grievance. No tedious concoction of fact and myth. No narrative, no message."

"A virus only needs you."

This was Tad's role now, to be a voice in the night. A voice didn't require a father or a mother. Through the darkness, her eyes closed now, she heard him tremble.

"I believed, at one time, a person could wear a mask and become whatever he wanted to be. Like you, I wanted revenge. I was angry. I was ready. We've been tried again and again, haven't we? In this machine America. What we do when the machine fails? What do we do when disruption isn't enough?"

She was near sleep now. In a few minutes, Tad would start taking callers. Lonely men and women from Chicago and Detroit and Queens, calling from empty diner backrooms and motels seething with insects and vans hurdling down freeways. She wondered if she should call the station and tell him that his father might be dying.

3

Emmanuel had a persistent cough and it hurt him to jog. These facts repeated themselves in his head. It was early spring, it was cold season, and not every cold was the virus. He wanted to believe that.

Every symptom was his symptom. He couldn't tell his mom. Only Aurora, over the phone, his voice cracking.

"Just stay inside and it will go away. It seems less deadly in young people," she said.

"That's what I'm doing. Ryan and Cole are out every day."

He had the smallest of the three rooms, no window. In the winter it was ferociously cold and in the summer it was hot in a sinister way, enough to seize your dreams. Four days into his cough, he had just enough energy to stand and go to the bathroom. It was like some creature had landed on his back to drink his blood, his air, whatever bioelectricity was left. He wrapped himself in blankets and waited, sipping lukewarm soup and doing little else, sleeping until he could feel differently, regain who he was. His mom called every day. He said he had a sore throat and it hurt to talk.

"It's not *that*," he told his mom, straining to sound definitive.

His dad had gone to the hospital. The terror he felt was deep and disorienting. He was thirty, he had the statistics on his side. He read updates daily, especially after he lost his job, which was devastating until it wasn't—until his body was his problem. He could forget about how he had spent less than a year at the news organization, a start-up dedicated to criminal justice reform that was not, finally, paying him a poverty wage to write about bail laws, the dangerousness of American prosecutors, and the prison-industrial complex. After bouncing around local newspapers that couldn't pay him $40,000 a year and then stringing for the *Post*, getting screamed at by assignment editors regularly, it was supposed to be the payoff. He was, in a new decade, working at a job he could be proud of, what he imagined when he graduated college almost a decade before. He was there and then he wasn't.

He had been lucky, in one sense. His mom never found out about the pill dealing and the cops never busted him. Lucky, lucky boy. They let him walk away, free to make new mistakes. Where had time gone? From the moment Tad Plotz revealed himself to now, collapsed on the bed, fighting for his breath and crushing his eyes shut and begging for it all to pass. The creature was done sucking at him and now had both claw-feet pressed on his chest, forcing the last breaths from him.

One night, two nights, three nights. He didn't come out of his room. All he could do was text Aurora. *I'm fine, I'm okay.* She sent him long paragraphs he couldn't muster the strength for, that he stared at longingly. He felt worse for her, even though they were in the same position now: without jobs. She had just been cast as the lead in a Sean O'Casey play at the Irish Repertory Theatre. For months, she had been rehearsing for April, when the play had its opening night. There would be no opening night, no performances at all. Every theater was shuttered. They had both been battling for unemployment benefits. Last week, she finally got hers, three weeks after she applied. He was still waiting. He knew he wasn't alone.

He was sure, one night, he was dying. He lay on his back, unable to move. If he rolled to his side, he coughed uncontrollably. When he closed his eyes, he saw a vast, burning lake, columns of fire shooting to a charcoal-colored sky. This was where he was headed. He swallowed chunks of mucus, spittle leaking over his lower lip. The lake waters rose to take him.

He saw his dad, his hand reaching from the flames. When his mouth moved, no sounds came out.

The ringing phone brought him a new voice and he sat up, shivering, sweat rolling down his back. He found the phone and lifted it up to his ear.

"Mom."

"Honey, please learn to pick up your phone. I've been calling."

"I haven't felt too well. Though now, actually, I feel a little better."

His strength returned. For the first time in days, he spoke to Ryan and Cole, who were on the couch together, playing video games. Cole worked IT for a pharmaceutical company and could do everything remotely. He wasn't sure what Ryan did; he assumed his parents just gave him money. They were gathered together in the basement of a three-story house in Williamsburg, all of it owned by ancient Polish immigrants. Their rent was paid in cash discreetly folded into envelopes. Once outside his room, he nodded to Cole and Ryan and said he was going for a walk.

"Get some air, man, get some air," Cole said, his eyes locked on the screen, pixelated soldiers exploding in their own blood.

Emmanuel staggered around the block. He had more strength than yesterday but pathetically little relative to what he possessed a week ago. He felt decades older, fast approaching death. He could feel spit flecks in the underside of the bandana wrapped around his face. At the corner, he sagged against the wall, waiting for a burst of energy to return to him.

Before all this, he had been talking to Aurora about moving in together. Her lease in Manhattan was almost up. They had been seeing each other for almost a year, which would have been unfathomable to his seventeen-year-old self, sitting on the edge of Landon's couch, watching the two of them drop acid. He remained Facebook friends with her in college and they occasionally hung out. She kept him apprised of Landon's trips to rehab, ordered by his father. Eventually, Landon and his father moved to Miami for his work, she said. Through social media, he knew she was in a long-term relationship for much of her twenties with a banker named Mark. A few months after they broke up, he started hanging out with her. Other than a brief relationship in college and another one with a fellow *Post* journalist several years later, he hadn't been with anyone in a serious way. Sex with someone you didn't care about was mildly revolting, he decided. He found himself, until Aurora, having sex very little.

Being with her had felt like an arrival. She was stunning, still, and wanted to spend time with him. They played video games at the Coney Island arcade, toured museums in the city, and she even suffered through a Yankee game. She wasn't talking to her mother anymore and this meant no trust, no inheritance. She was scraping out a life in Off-Broadway productions. It was, he sensed, how she always wanted it.

The discordant note was Tad. Aurora, like everyone, was astounded to learn the man wearing a mask and calling himself Vengeance was directly related to him. She couldn't quite believe he didn't know that he had a half-brother at all.

He preferred, above all, not asking about it, cutting off his dad's attempts to explain. Eventually, on a drive to the beach, his dad said that he always loved his mom and that was the truth, that he wished, often, he had met his mom first, before he was already with someone else.

"The most frustrating thing, Emmanuel, is you realize you only get one life. It's the most obvious truth, right? One life, one death. But when you're young and you're making decisions, you don't think of it that way. You imagine life not as one extended existence but a near-infinite number of chances to reinvent and reimagine yourself, to do things differently, and then you make the first major decision, the big one, and you slowly realize it wasn't the right one. What do you do?"

"It's a good question."

"I'm asking you. I don't know. No one knows. It's a decision to define everything else that comes next and you made it. When I met your mother, I understood the gravity of the mistake. Your mother was the person for me, the only one, and that was how it was."

"You had a child."

"Two. Lenore, who has children of her own now. Maybe some-day you can meet her."

"You didn't know Tad was Vengeance."

"No one knew. Your mother photographed the first one in the '70s. That was nuts. He almost killed her! Why did Tad do it all, fol-low in the footsteps of that? He never says. He went years without talking to anyone. I think he was a dislocated boy, and I didn't know what to do."

"Tad wanted to find me."

"He must have figured it out, somehow."

"That I existed?"

"Yes."

As college wore on, fewer people cared that Emmanuel was related to the vigilante in New York City and he liked it that way. He wondered what exactly had happened to him. His mom and dad didn't know. It was like before, his dad explained. Tad didn't like to be found. He would emerge on his own time.

When Emmanuel was a stringer at the *Post*, he—along with just about every city journalist—received a curious press release. A well-known, eccentric billionaire who owned a chain of supermarkets in Manhattan and made most of his money, these days, in oil refineries had bought one of the local radio stations. The billionaire had polit-ical aspirations; some, briefly, talked about him running for mayor. He was self-made, a Lithuanian immigrant who still wore rumpled suits and couldn't be bothered to comb his hair. His first move, when buying the radio station, was to stock it with talent. Fox had swal-lowed up all the A-listers he wanted. There were B-listers abound, but he wasn't going to spend all his time cultivating unknown talent.

His radio station was not going to be a farm system. If you weren't quasi-famous already, he had no use for you.

The man who used to be Vengeance would have his own show, every Tuesday and Thursday evening. It was a coup, the billionaire insisted in the press release. A vigilante would be talking to the nighttime masses of New York about whatever he chose. The press release said the man formerly known as Vengeance, Tad Plotz, had an interest in politics.

When the virus came, he decided to listen, to hear what his own flesh and blood had to say on the radio.

That night, the first night he began to feel better, he heard his brother.

"We always knew it was coming, didn't we? We always felt it, somehow. That something was breeding in the shadows. That it was coming for us. A pandemic. How inevitable—how ordinary, if you think about it that way. A globalized order shares an invisible disease. It was all building here. Our destiny was sickness—"

He turned it off. He had nothing else to learn. He decided he needed to pick up his phone and dial.

"Mom, are you still awake?"

She sounded tired, but she was up, and her voice took on strength as she spoke.

"Yes, yes. Emmanuel, how are you? How are you feeling?"

"I'm better. I'll be better. I don't know, I just wanted to call, I guess I'm just confused and scared right now, a little bit, if I had to be honest."

"We're going to get through this all, okay? You, me, and your father. We're going to pull through. You're a tough, strong kid, and I'm here for you. Right here. I'm not going anywhere. Neither is your father. He'll be out of the hospital. They just want to keep a watch on him, that's all."

"I hope so, mom."

"Are you feeling a little better, generally? How's your chest? Your breathing?"

"A little bit better, definitely getting there. How's dad?"

"Let's see if we can talk to him tomorrow. We can do that."

"I want to hear him."

"We'll talk to him. Your father is a strong man. He doesn't quit. He never has."

They paused. He could hear his mom breathing softly into the phone. He suddenly felt a burning in his throat.

"I don't understand this, why this has to happen, why now? This kind of hell. You want to understand it and you can't. It just shouldn't have happened. I feel terrified and I feel furious and I don't know what to do, I really don't, mom, I'm just here and all I could think was to call you but I know you don't know any more than I do, we don't know anything, we're alone in the dark, just dying."

"When Liv died, there was a moment when I believed I wouldn't go on."

"You never told me."

"I didn't talk about it. The moment came and the moment passed. I got up. It was the worst time of my life and now I feel this dread again. But I believe it will get better, and it will. We keep going, Emmanuel. That's it. I'm going to be at your side and then you'll be there for your children. I love you, okay?"

"I love you too. I'll let you get to sleep. I am starting to feel better."

"We will call your father tomorrow."

He stood up and felt the stirrings of an appetite. He had been losing his sense of smell and taste. In the mini fridge was a cup of yogurt and he would attempt it, he decided. He first walked out of his room and into the bathroom, where he was going to wash his hands. He washed his hands several times every hour now, when he had the strength. It was, in the flurry of impotent advice, what always seemed most useful to him.

The apartment was quiet. He stood in the bathroom and ran

the tap.

He watched the warm water as he counted in his head, one two three four five six seven, the flow spilling over his hands, the pressure flushing, flashing, and he thought of the ocean waves hitting the beach that would have been there without Moses building a parkway, all the times his mother took him out, his torso strapped to the bicycle seat and his head tucked in a helmet, and though he had no water view or windows, he saw the lights of the Verrazzano grow elongated in the waves.